CAROLINA CURRENT

BOOK ONE

Beyond the Stroke

ERIN HAWKINS

author's note

Please be advised Beyond the Stroke is a spicy romantic comedy with **open-door** romance, and **on-page** sexual content and profanity. Mature readers only.

While Beyond the Stroke is ultimately a story about healing, connection, and falling in love, it does include themes of emotional manipulation (in a past relationship), estranged parental relationships, and a break-in that disrupts a character's safe space. Your well-being always comes first. Please read with care.

Sending love and gratitude for spending time with these characters.

XO,
Erin

For anyone learning to let themselves be seen.
And for the ones who see us clearly—and help us shine

one

. . .

RORY

"You have to wonder if this is the end of the road for Rory Shields."

The voice cuts through the quiet afternoon like a slap. I glance at the screen. With gray hair and a smug grin, Roger Selby's face fills the frame. The words **Retirement for Rory?** are plastered under his name in bold.

I press the ice bag tighter to my knee.

"He's thirty-four, coming off a tough injury, and the competition is only getting faster. You look at guys like Xio Valdez stepping onto the scene, and Connor Fisk who's in his prime, and you have to ask—does Shields still have what it takes to compete at the highest level?" Roger Selby, Swim-Span's lead swimming correspondent, remarks before turning to one of his co-hosts. "What are your thoughts, Jim?"

Jim Koster, a legendary swim analyst, nods, considering Roger's point before speaking.

"I wouldn't count him out just yet. We are talking about a guy who has been at the top of this sport for over a decade. He knows how to push through adversity. But, I'll admit, the timeline is tight. If he's not at full strength soon, his chances for another medal run could slip away."

"What do you think, Jan?" Roger asks, motioning to Jan Stevens, an Olympic gold medal swimmer and former training teammate of mine at the Carolina Current. "Does Shields have a chance?"

Jan hesitates, the way a friend does before saying something that hurts. "Only if he wants it. But even then, comebacks at this age aren't just physical. They're brutal mentally. And someone younger might need that roster spot more."

"Let's not sugar coat it. He's not getting any younger, and swimmers don't have the longest shelf life. Even if he does make it back, is he still a medal contender, or is he just swimming to prove a point?" Roger remarks.

"You're no spring chicken either, Roger," I mutter at his visibly white hair on screen.

"So, you think Shields should retire?" Jim asks Roger.

"Definitely. I think with the MCL injury he sustained after nationals last year; he doesn't have enough time to rehab to full strength and get what is ultimately seen as an older body in the world of swimming into the shape he'll need to be in to compete with guys half his age."

I remove the ice bag from my knee and drop my leg from where it had been resting on my coffee table to the ground. While full body ice baths have been a weekly routine for years to keep inflammation down, icing my rehabilitated knee has become part of my everyday routine.

It'd be easy to drown out the noise of naysayers like these guys, but even my parents think I'm done.

The television goes dark, and I swivel my head to find my best friend, Eli Mitchell, standing behind my couch with the remote in his hand.

"That's all bullshit and you know it."

"Do I?" I thought I had. After the surgery, rehab went exceptionally well and once I was back in the pool, I felt like my old self again, but since I made the decision to return to Coral Cove, the training home of the Carolina Current, I've been bombarded with negative news media. It's not how I imagined my homecoming and return to training with my team would go.

Eli sets the remote on the coffee table, then drops into the chair adjacent to the couch. "These guys are idiots."

"What about Jan?" I ask, lifting my brows.

"You know my rule about calling women names."

I nod. Eli has a rigid exterior, and I don't mean his toned physique that has made him the world's fastest back stroker. But within that quiet, contemplative body is a heart of gold. He's by far the gentleman of the team. Cool under pressure and laser focused. The only time I've seen him get frazzled is when someone mentions his ex-girlfriend, Blair. He completely shuts down, so we've learned to keep her name out of our mouths.

"When athletes are injured, people speculate they can't come back, let alone stronger than they were before. You'll show them what's possible." He nods, affirming his motivational words.

"Thanks, man."

The front door slams shut, no knock preceding it.

Voices fill the hallway. I know it's not a home invasion, because outside of the aquatics center, my beach house is team headquarters. It's how it's always been.

Charlie Wallace strolls in with all the confidence of the reigning world record holder in both the one-hundred-meter and two-hundred-meter freestyle, wearing a backwards hat and a neon yellow t-shirt that says *Cool Vibes*, and carrying a cardboard box.

Behind him, Logan Wilson, four-time national champion, and international gold medalist in the one-hundred-meter and two-hundred-meter butterfly, follows carrying a bucket of chicken.

"If you wanted some, you should have ordered some for yourself," Logan tells Charlie.

Charlie motions to the bucket of grilled chicken pieces. "When you ordered a ten-piece bucket, I figured I could snag a piece."

Logan shakes his head in disappointment. "It's like you don't even know me, man."

"Yeah, you're like a toddler when it comes to sharing food." Charlie huffs.

Everyone knows Logan doesn't share food. We burn a shit ton of calories every day in the pool and while most of us can handle going a few hours without eating, Logan is known to get hangry if he doesn't keep his blood sugar up.

"Oh good, you're not watching it," Charlie says, motioning to the blank television.

"He was," Eli pipes up from where he's now checking his phone. "I turned it off."

"How'd you know about it?" I ask Charlie.

"Swim-Span reached out to me for a comment. I told them you're the GOAT and they can go fuck themselves."

I groan. "Seriously?" The last thing I want is to add fuel to the fire with this feature.

"Nah. Vivi told me not to respond."

I laugh because Vivi is the team's publicist and brand

manager. She's also Charlie's best friend. They've known each other since high school. She represents most of the swimmers on the team that require PR management. When Vivi told me about the feature, she'd advised me to not watch it, but I couldn't resist. Now, I'm torn between letting their words make me question my decision not to retire, and using them to push myself even harder.

"Fuck that noise," Logan grumbles around a chicken thigh. "They have no clue what they're talking about."

I chuckle at his grumpy demeanor, which Logan is known for being anything but.

It feels good to be home and surrounded by my teammates, my best friends. The guys that have been training with me for over a decade.

Eli, Logan, and I swam together at UC-Berkeley. They'd been high school teammates who signed with the Golden Bears when I was a junior there. We had two stellar years before I graduated, then when they finished school, they followed me to the Carolina Current. Charlie came from Stanford, a UC-Berkeley rival, which once we got to know him, we forgave him for.

While we know there's always new talent in younger swimmers and the relay team can change up until the starter goes off, the four of us have battled together the last twelve years. Holding off the French by a fingertip-touch to clinch the gold in Sydney, then a world record performance in Paris that cemented all of us in the record books. I've won plenty of races on my own, but it's this team right here that has made it difficult to imagine retiring from the sport.

"How's the knee?" Charlie asks, setting down the box on the coffee table before nodding to where I've set the ice bag next to me on the couch.

"Stronger than it's been in months."

"That's fantastic." He grins.

"Yeah, it feels good."

My statement is true, but there's still the possibility of injury hovering in the back of my mind. After an MCL tear last spring, I've rehabbed and strength trained to get back to where I was. I lost precious training time, going backwards instead of forwards and now I've got to make up for that. My priority is swimming and staying healthy for the upcoming team trials.

While my body has healed, there's still the mental piece of having been injured that takes time to reconcile. The psychological effects of returning after an injury, managing expectations, and making sure that while I want to get back to where I was before, I need to build up to it, not overdo it and chance the possibility of reinjury.

Swimming is as much a mental sport, if not more, as it is physical. With the long stretch between the summer games, you have to be internally motivated to keep showing up every day and working hard to shave what could be only a fraction of a millisecond off a split.

Outside of the games, most meets, even nationals, aren't televised. Unlike football and basketball and hockey, we don't get the chance to compete weekly and most people don't know who we are until the summer games come around every four years. Even though we train year-round and there are important international meets, it's the summer games that everyone is shooting for.

Yeah, I do need to think about how my injury has impacted my body, but more than that, it's the loss of support from family that has been frustrating. My parents have supported me throughout my career, but since I injured my MCL, they've been pushing me to retire. They think I'm done with swimming and want me to pursue other things. A broadcasting gig I was offered, which isn't the worst thing in the world, but also reconnecting with my ex-girlfriend, Daphne, and settling down. I'm not ready for that commitment and even if I were, I don't want to rekindle things with my ex.

As if she can read my mind from fifty feet away, my phone buzzes.

MOM

DAPHNE SAYS YOU HAVEN'T BEEN
RETURNING HER CALLS!

I'm not sure if her all caps use was intentional, but I wouldn't put it past her to be shouting via text message. I love my mom, but she is not known for being easy to get along with.

I've been back in Coral Cove for twelve hours and I've been inundated with messages from Daphne, and now my mom. It's clear they've formed a reconciliation task force.

Tossing my phone onto the couch next to me, I don't reply only to keep up the appearance that it's not just Daphne I'm not responding to.

My phone buzzes again, this time continuously as a call comes in.

Beside me, Logan glances at the screen.

"Oh, shit. Daphne is calling you. Did you get back with her?"

Charlie chokes on the protein shake he found in my refrigerator. "What? Please no. She's terrifying."

"She's sweet, but if you get on her bad side, then she's terrifying," Logan confirms.

"Yeah," Charlie concurs, "and when Rory broke up with her last year, we were on her bad side by default."

"What's that animal that looks all cute and sweet, but

will rip your limbs off and beat you over the head with them?" Logan asks.

"A honey badger?" Eli offers.

"Yeah," Charlie nods, "that's exactly how Daphne is."

"I'm not back with Daphne," I confirm.

We fizzled out a long time ago when she complained I was prioritizing swimming over her, which I was, because I'd always put swimming first, and I made that clear to her when we started dating. It was over a year ago when I finally called things quits. I'd hoped that the breakup would allow her to move on and find the things she wants in a relationship, things I wasn't ready to give her then and have no intention of giving her now or when I do finally retire from competition.

Daphne's father and mine are business partners at Atlantic Freight & Logistics, a logistics company specializing in transporting goods through North Carolina's ports and managing supply chains for major companies. Our families see a marriage between me and Daphne as a way to turn AFL into a family business.

Logan lets out a breath. "Thank fuck."

"So, we're all single, then?" Charlie asks, before directing his attention to Logan. "Logan?"

Logan grabs another chicken wing out of the bucket and waves it around. "Is that a serious question?"

While all of us have had girlfriends before, Logan is the king of no commitment. He says it's because he doesn't want to be tied down, but I have a different theory that involves a certain team trainer.

"Eli?" Charlie asks.

Eli doesn't respond but instead points to the box on the coffee table. "What's in the box?"

A smile splits across Charlie's face. "Team shirts."

He opens the box and tosses each of us a shirt. They're in Carolina Current blue with our last names on the back. I turn mine over and read the front.

"In hard, out wet." I read the white print.

"That's this season's theme." Charlie smirks. "I came up with it myself."

"Did Owens approve these?" Eli asks, referring to the head coach of the Carolina Current, Bob Owens.

"More like, did you get permission from Vivi?" Logan snickers.

The color drains from Charlie's face. Eli and Logan are messing with him, but it's clear that the thought of disappointing Vivi messes with his typically unflappable demeanor. They're lighthearted shirts that are meant to be funny.

"Don't let them give you shit." I stand to clap Charlie on the shoulder. "The shirts are great."

"If we can't give each other shit, what is the point?" Logan laughs.

"Where are you going?" Eli asks.

"Haven't been in yet." I nod to the beach where the Atlantic Ocean is lapping gently at the shoreline. "Going to head out there now."

"Rory?" Eli calls as I turn toward the hallway.

"Yeah?"

"You know I'm not blowing smoke up your ass. I meant everything I said."

He extends his right hand out to me in a fist.

"Yeah. I know."

My knuckles meet his, then I leave him there in the living room with Charlie and Logan, who's still eating his bucket of chicken, to change for a swim.

My phone buzzes in my shorts pocket. I don't even have to look to know who it's from.

While the guys are good at drowning out the noise of the media, short of changing my phone number, I know it's going to be a hell of a lot harder to avoid Daphne and my parents.

two

. . .

SUMMER

The leash tangles around my ankle just as Scarlett's voice crackles through my ear buds.

"Tell me you're not still dodging that guy from the dog park."

"I'm not dodging him. I'm strategically re-routing."

Scarlett sighs.

"Summer...it is time," Scarlett says dramatically. Her emphasis on each word reminding me of the beloved movie from my childhood.

"All right, Rafiki, cool your jets."

I hop twice, trying not to face-plant as Chef, an enthusiastic black labrador, lunges for a rogue leaf with the fervor of a dog who thinks he's saving the world.

"Speaking of the circle of life, you need to get back out there."

"Out where? I'm already living at the beach, having a fulfilling life with Edgar."

"I'm talking about your art."

"I know, I'm working on it," I mutter, adjusting my backpack against my shoulder. It's full of dog treats, biodegradable poop bags, and my sketchpad.

"Working on it isn't the same as doing it," Scarlett presses. "You've got talent pouring out of you, Sum. You just need a little confidence. A little flirting. A little...whatever the opposite of dog hair in your coffee is."

"Is this a pep talk or a roast?" I scoff.

"Both," Scarlett confirms with a laugh. "But seriously, it's time to start dating again and make new memories."

"I thought we were talking about my art."

"We are, but also I hate to think you might be lonely."

"I've got Edgar and my dog crew."

"People, Summer. Human beings. Maybe even a cute guy."

I maneuver the leashes back under control and glance around Coral Cove's sleepy streets. Sunlight filters through the mossy oaks, while the ocean breeze, salty and familiar, lifts the ends of my hair.

I consider Scarlett's goading.

"Cal and I sit next to each other on the bench while he's fishing."

"He's eighty and wears Velcro sandals."

"Well, not everyone is looking for a happily ever after."

"I didn't say you had to marry anyone, just enjoy yourself."

Enjoying myself wasn't just off the agenda with my ex, Tripp, it was forbidden. He'd taken every flicker of enthusiasm and told me it was childish, silly, too much. I learned to quiet myself, to shrink. Four years later, some part of me still forgets I'm allowed to want more.

And sex? It's a distant memory, which is okay seeing that the last time I had it, my ex told me I was bad at it.

"You think you're living life all free and on your own terms, but the reality is Tripp and your parents still have a hold on you. They're still dictating your life, whether they're in it or not."

With that statement, Scarlett strikes a nerve. To think that I left my suffocating life almost four years ago and I'm still not free from the past. It's not what I want to hear.

But she might be right.

God, I hate when she's right.

"Oh, look at the time."

"Don't give me that."

"No, seriously. I have to go. I'm playing a mermaid at a kid's birthday party in thirty minutes. I've got to take the dogs home and get ready."

"I'm dead. Send me a picture."

"There will be no photo evidence. Love you, Scar."

"Love you, Sum!"

I end the call and guide the dogs back toward their homes so I'm not late for the party.

"Mermaids don't wear glasses." That's the first thing out of Tenneil Lancaster's mouth as I approach.

She's referring to the clear plastic-rimmed glasses on the bridge of my nose that are my only source of sight after my last set of contact lenses shriveled up in their case last night. After a double shift at The Salty Pirate Café, I'd forgotten to put the solution in. Now, I'm wishing I'd just left them in my eyes. It seems Tenneil would prefer a mermaid with dry, bloodshot eyes over one with glasses from the way her nose wrinkles at the sight of mine.

But riding a skateboard is challenging enough on this boardwalk, it would be doubly so for the visually impaired, so it was glasses or risk the chance of running over a fellow beach goer.

"You know that's what Lasik is for," she says before taking a sip of the rose-colored spritz from the champagne flute in her hand. Her scalloped-edge white sheath dress and designer heels are an odd choice for a beach party.

Corrective eye surgery would be convenient, but unlike Tenneil, I like my glasses. Also, that type of surgery is a luxury and money is barely stretching to pay for necessities like my asthma medication. That's the only reason I'm subjecting myself to Tenneil's judgmental gaze as she peruses my seashell bikini top, biker shorts and long auburn wig.

It's her daughter's fourth birthday and she's obsessed with mermaids, the daughter, not Tenneil, so naturally she's hired a professional—err, me—to dress up as a mermaid to surprise her. It's what any waspy, yacht owning, nautical inspired clothing wearing woman would do for their preschooler.

"Totally." I force a beaming smile which feels like wearing a face full of plaster. I hate being fake, telling people what they want to hear instead of how I really feel, but a girl's got to do what a girl's got to do.

Her eyes narrow at me.

"You've got a tail, right?" she asks.

"You bet." Feigning enthusiasm, I pull the mermaid tail I rented from Coral Cove's costume shop, The Nautical Nook, from my backpack. The purple-pink ombre tail shimmers with iridescent scales and weighs at least fifteen pounds. It's a legit mermaid tail. I know this because in addition to the fifty-dollar rental fee, I had to put down a one-hundred-dollar damage deposit in case something happens to it. Which now that I'm feeling how heavy it is, I have a serious concern it might be impossible to move in. But Cardamom, the shop owner, assured me it was her most realistic piece of mermaid pageantry.

"Is this our mermaid?" A man in his forties, dressed in a pale-yellow polo with a gray sweater draped over his shoulders and cognac boat shoes, appears next to Tenneil.

"Supposedly." Tenneil eyes me again.

If she thinks I'm an imposter, she'd be right. I'd taken the gig from Darcy, a fellow waitress at the café who knows I'm in need of extra cash.

"Rich Lancaster." He extends his hand to shake mine. "I like what you've got going on." He points to the conch shell necklace around my neck that's set off by the pound of body shimmer coating my chest and arms.

"Ugh." Tenneil rolls her eyes. "Stop flirting with the mermaid."

He clears his throat and adjusts his belt. "I'm not."

"You are, too. And you're doing it right in front of me," she whines.

I suck in a breath. They remind me of my parents, and I'd rather this mermaid tail sink me straight to the bottom of the ocean than listen to them argue. The irony that Scarlett mentioned I should start dating again, while Rich and Tenneil here are the poster couple for anti-marriage.

"Why don't you have Jacinda refresh your drink?" Rich asks.

"She's with the girls. They're playing some game in the

pool." She waves toward the beach club behind the iron gate just off the boardwalk.

"Then get your own drink?" he proposes.

Tenneil fumes in outrage at the suggestion but ultimately decides it's a better option than staying here on the beach with us. We watch her walk angrily down the boardwalk in her four-inch heels before she disappears behind the gate.

With Tenneil gone, Rich turns back to me, giving me a half-hearted smile.

"All right, let me show you where I need you."

Under Rich's direction, I follow him to the end of the boardwalk and down the sandy beach until we reach the rocky bank of one of Coral Cove's famous inlets.

At the edge of the water, he holds his hands up, his thumbs pointing toward each other to frame the scene like he's a director showing me his vision. And Rich has a vision.

"You'll be sitting on that rock, then when I give the signal, you swim toward the beach and wave to the girls."

His instructions send an upsurge of uncertainty through me matching that of the water crashing against the rocks around us.

I love the ocean. I love to spend mornings on the beach with Edgar and the other dogs I walk. I love to paint it. It's vast and beautiful and complex and never looks the same. The lighting, the waves, the people on the beach. It changes on any given day. Water has always been fascinating to me.

But I hadn't planned for vigorous activity today.

My eyes fall to the inside of my backpack where my inhaler is.

The ocean probably isn't the best place to test out the aerobic capacity needed for paddling around in a mermaid tail. In my defense, when I took this gig, I thought I'd sit on the beach and take pictures with the birthday girl and her friends before pulling an Ariel and trading out my tail for human legs.

"What about the pool at the beach club?" I motion back toward the Beach & Racquet Club's white gates where Tenneil disappeared. "Wouldn't it be easier for the girls to see me?"

"Mermaids don't swim in pools; they swim in the ocean. It's more realistic this way."

To Rich's point, mermaids aren't real, so I should be able to take liberties with a species that doesn't exist, but he wants an authentic ocean mermaid experience and with his next words, he hammers that point home.

"It's what I'm paying you for." His thick brows arch in question. *You want to get paid, don't you?*

I nod, but my fingers tighten around the strap of my backpack. The water laps at the shore behind me, cold and endless. I used to dream of being a mermaid when I was a kid. Now, the idea of dragging this tail into the ocean just feels like drowning in someone else's fantasy.

I have to make a choice. Either I find a way to get through the next hour as a visually-impaired, asthmatic mermaid whose swimming skills are questionable and collect the much-needed money, or I'm out the fifty bucks for this costume rental.

And I'm wearing body glitter for god's sake. At this point, there's no other option but to get my ass out to that rock and muster up some mermaid magic.

"Right. Okay." I nod with false confidence, removing my glasses and carefully setting them inside their case in my backpack.

Rich waves me toward the water, looking on as I use the fin of the mermaid tail as a flotation device and start kicking my way out to the rock. As I make my way, I'm certain the choppy water lapping at my face is going to wash off the boatload of glitter. If sharks could sniff out body glitter like they could blood, I'd be in serious trouble. The only thing I have going for me is the buoyancy from the salt water. Its assistance in flotation is a tradeoff for the sting it's causing my eyes.

Getting out to the rocky land mass isn't as challenging as I thought it would be. By the time I climb up onto the rock, I'm feeling more confident about this whole thing. I just have to make it back to shore.

On the rock, I take in a slow, deep breath to assess my body. I'm all too familiar with the triggers of my asthma—cold water, salty air, and physical strain. And this scenario is the trifecta.

You can do this, I tell myself, hoping to will my desire into being. It hasn't helped my financial stress yet, but if I can make it to shore with no issues and collect this money, then things are going to be better. For now.

I pull on the tail, settling it above my hips, then fix my wig, and wait for Rich's signal.

Except, I can't see shit without my glasses. I squint, hoping to locate Rich on the beach, but now there are multiple people and from this distance it's hard to tell which one he is.

But then I see a flurry of activity by the gates of the beach club. *That must be the girls coming out to watch.*

I throw up my arm to wave. It's been eight years since I gave a pageant wave but muscle memory in my arm and hand pull it off seamlessly.

When all the activity on the beach settles, I decide it's time to make my entrance. Slowly, I shimmy down the rock, but the plastic fin at the end of my tail is slick and provides no grip. I'm close to clearing the rock, but right before I plunge into the water, I slip and scrape my arm on the rugged surface.

The sharp sting of the salt water against the scrape has me wincing.

You know what's harder than swimming with two legs for this mediocre swimmer? Swimming with a nylon mermaid tail wrapped around those unskilled legs. Mermaids are supposed to be good swimmers, you know, because of their tail and fin. But this fin isn't functional. It's a sparkly purple and pink bedazzled fin that catches the afternoon's sun rays perfectly but offers no aid in actual swimming.

Also, I don't know how water works. Not in the ocean wave kind of sense. One minute, I'm making headway, the next I'm back where I started. At this pace, it'll be dusk before I make it to shore. Oh, and that whole waving and looking graceful thing Rich mentioned? That's not happening at all. I can barely keep my head above water, let alone manage an elegant wave at the same time.

It's hard to focus on swimming when there are so many thoughts swirling in my head.

I'm risking my life for three hundred dollars.

If this tail is ruined the costume shop isn't going to give me my deposit back.

Once I sink to the depths of the Atlantic, who will look after Edgar?

Breathe, Summer.

But it's the reminder to do the one thing that my body sometimes just can't do properly in this type of situation that has me panicking.

My chest tightens, making it impossible to get a full breath.

My breaths become shallow, making it impossible for my lungs to deliver the much-needed oxygen that my muscles are begging for. With heavy limbs, I tilt my head up toward the sky, gasping for air that refuses to enter my body.

I'm sinking and there's nothing I can do. Even the octopus wrangling a tentacle around me knows I'm done for.

But it doesn't yank me under; instead, it lifts me up.

That's when I realize it's not an octopus, it's a solid, human arm wrapped around my chest. And suddenly my head is higher above the water.

"I've got you. You're going to be okay," the deep, soothing voice assures me. It's so kind and unassuming, I want to wrap myself inside it and take a nap. It's the type of gentle, calming voice that could lull you to sleep on one of those meditation sleep apps. Or at the very least make you feel safe during a bad storm.

I'm no longer drowning, but I'm still fighting to breathe.

All I can do is sputter and attempt to calm my breathing as the man pulls me along. He's making far better progress and it's not long before I feel the sandy beach beneath my back.

On shore, the coughing begins. It's my body's desperate attempt to reset my airflow. I'm gasping for the tiniest breath.

I want to move to my hands and knees but this damn tail won't let me.

There's commotion around me. Movement and voices, yet I can't focus on any of it.

I squeeze my eyes tightly, trying to expel the remaining water before slowly blinking it away. Finally, my eyes open to reveal the source of peace. The man kneeling in front of me.

Oh, *wow*.

My near-sighted vision reveals that this guy is gorgeous.

Strong jaw, piercing blue eyes and the fullest lips I've ever seen on a man. They look like pillows that would be soft and plush, yet unyieldingly firm if necessary.

Even with his hair wet, I can see it's sandy in color with some natural highlights from the sun.

He's shirtless, as one might be while swimming in the ocean, with beads of water dripping down his golden skin. He smiles at me, a devastating smile that combined with his five o'clock shadow has me panting.

Maybe I did drown out in the water after all because my body feels all light and tingly, like I'm floating outside myself.

It's a startling feeling that I'm not used to.

If I were into fairy tales and Disney princesses, then this would be the moment when the birds sing and the audience sighs *how romantic*. Scarlett would eat this up.

But not me. Because at the same time I'm realizing the man who pulled me out of the ocean is gorgeous, I'm acutely aware that this mermaid portrayal has gone off the rails. That the job I was hired for was not carried out and now I'm a beached mermaid whose auburn wig is floating somewhere in the Atlantic along with my dignity.

Oh, and every breath I attempt to take is like sucking through a straw.

Breathe, Summer.

I can't.

The man is moving his lips, saying something my oxygen-deprived brain doesn't register.

I close my eyes to help me narrow the focus on my breathing. Every part of me needs to focus on that.

But it's not working.

With every breath that feels impossible to take, my anxiety rises. The panic feeds into my ability to breathe, and it becomes an endless loop of struggle.

Finally, I open my eyes to connect with the stranger's and manage to get out two words. "M-my in-inhaler."

three

· · ·

SUMMER

The man nods in recognition so I must have spoken clear enough for him to understand.

There's a flurry of movement, the man yelling out to the crowd and eventually he returns with my inhaler. He must have been guided to my backpack and found it there.

I ignore his worried stare and take a deep inhale of medication. Or as deep as I can for what little there is left inside. Then, I wait.

He waits, too. Kneeling in front of me, quiet and patient while my airway relaxes.

Within a few minutes, the medication starts to work and my breathing slowly returns to normal. He must notice because that dazzling smile of his reappears.

"That's better." He nods, brushing his thumb across my knuckles. "You had me worried."

I think he's just being nice, but when I meet his gaze, I see the sincerity there. And the worry.

I nod. "I'm okay now."

"Do you need to go to the hospital?" He scans my body. "It would make me feel better if you got checked out."

"Well, it wouldn't make me feel better to pay for an emergency room visit."

"I get it, but we need to make sure you're okay."

"We don't need to do anything. I'm fine now," I say, firmly.

The children, who had been instructed to stay back, have inched closer.

"It's Prince Eric!" Ten four-year-olds squeal in unison.

"He rescued the mermaid!" one girl shrieks excitedly.

"No, *she's* supposed to rescue *him*," comes a disapproving voice.

I'm wondering if they think my asthma attack is part of some skit. I wish it was. I wish I could stand up and laugh it off. But standing in this tail is impossible and laughing right now would cause further pain to my aching chest.

"Oh, my goodness! Is that Rory Shields?" a woman behind us calls.

His name hits like a rogue wave—Rory Shields. Of course. I've seen the sign at the edge of town. The golden boy of swimming. Coral Cove's hometown hero. And now, my accidental lifeguard.

There's a murmur throughout the group of bystanders. And now that I'm not dying, the crowd moves closer, many of them trying to draw the attention of the man who rescued me.

A shadowy figure looms over me and I squint up into the sun to find Rich shaking his head.

"That was not what I hired you for," he hisses. Tenneil stands behind him, with crossed arms and a pinched, sour face. As far as expressions go, she's a one trick pony, and disapproval is all she knows.

I swallow the lump in my throat. I've been around people like Rich my whole life. Up until a few years ago, I was on his side of this transaction so I know exactly what is going through his mind and I hate that I was ever associated with people like him.

My mouth opens, but nothing comes out.

"Are you out of your mind?" Rory barks as he returns his attention to me. To where Rich and Tenneil are towering over me. "You sent her into a red-flag surf for a stupid photo op?" He motions down the beach to the lifeguard stand where a red flag is waving in the breeze.

"O-oh," Rich stammers. "I didn't realize."

"She could have gotten pulled under, you idiot. You think a plastic mermaid tail is going to help her fight a rip current?"

Rick blinks. "I—I apologize." And Tenneil behind him is standing there with her mouth gaping open. It's clear no one has ever put her in her place before.

"If you ever put her, or anyone, in danger like that again, you'll be answering to more than an angry swimmer." Rory lowers his voice. "And if there weren't children present, I'd tell you how I really feel about you."

With that, Rory bends down to scoop me up.

"All right, Ariel, let's get out of here," he says loudly for everyone to hear.

"What are you doing?" I whisper as he starts walking toward the parking lot.

"Play along." He winks. "And then Prince Eric and the little mermaid lived happily ever after," he calls to the birthday party before adding to me, "Now smile and wave."

"Daddy, that's the best birthday surprise ever!" I hear the birthday girl call.

four

. . .

RORY

I'm fucking furious. Angry at Rich for being an oblivious asshole, but also annoyed that she didn't set boundaries when he asked her to do something that put her at risk.

Or maybe I'm projecting. I haven't exactly nailed the whole boundary thing myself, especially with my parents, who always have their own agenda.

I don't know Rich, but he strikes me as the kind of guy who sends a steak back three times and thinks his money entitles him to control people. I've seen it before. Coral Cove Beach & Golf Club has plenty like him.

Growing up, I swam laps at the fifty-meter pool, ate over-priced crab cakes, and listened to men like him talk over everyone. Not all of them were bad, but Rich reminds me of the worst kind.

After I lit him up, he walked off like a dog with his tail between his legs.

I wanted to say more. Get him tossed from the club, but

the squeal of the girls' laughter playing on the beach reminded me of the occasion. A birthday party for a four-year-old who didn't get to choose her dad.

Now, with the mermaid in my arms, I carry her toward the parking lot.

"Oh, I need my bag." She points at a tan backpack I'd grabbed earlier.

I shift her in my arms and hand it over.

"Thank you."

As I continue to walk, I notice how warm and soft she is against me. How her bare skin, slick with saltwater and sand, feels pressed to my chest. I steal a glance at her and notice the way sections of her blonde hair are still wet, clinging to her cheeks, while other parts are drying in wispy waves. She looks wild and beautiful.

Beneath wet lashes, she glances up to catch me staring.

When our eyes connect, something slams into me. Hard. Like a wave knocking the breath of out my chest.

I tear my gaze away. Focus. Just get her to safety.

At the edge of the lot, I spot a bench shaded by Loblolly pines. "There."

"You can put me down now, Baywatch. I'm not going to drown on the sand."

I huff out a laugh. She's snarky. I like it.

"You're still wearing a tail."

"It's fine. I'll manage."

The second I'm close enough to set her down she wiggles out of my arms, and I immediately mourn the loss of contact.

"I need to take this tail off and change." Unbuckling the backpack, she rummages around in it and pulls out a pair of shorts. "Do you mind?" She gives me a sharp look and circles her finger, indicating for me to turn around.

I get it. She's in a swimsuit, but still vulnerable, so I turn my back.

As I wait for her to change, I stand there, arms crossed, still angry with the situation she was put in.

"You shouldn't have been out there. It wasn't safe."

"Trust me, I didn't want to be out there. Rich requested it and I needed the job."

I nod slowly, but my jaw tightens.

There's no sound of movement behind me, just the harsh, raucous cries of the laughing gulls overhead.

"You okay back there?" I ask.

"Y-yeah, I'm good."

"First time cosplaying as a mermaid?" I ask.

"Yes, if you must know. A friend offered me the job and I said yes."

"Then why do it if you knew it might trigger an asthma attack?"

"I didn't know I'd have to swim." She groans. "And this thing is not easy to get off."

There's another minute of silent struggle.

"Damn it." Her breath comes out in a frustrated puff.

"You need help?" I ask, turning my head slightly, but still giving her the privacy she asked for.

She's quiet again, like she's contemplating her options.

Then, finally, "Yes." But I can hear the reluctance in her voice.

I get it. We're strangers and she's in a vulnerable position, but there's no way I'd take advantage.

With her request for help, I turn around to face her.

"I'm Rory."

"Yeah, I caught that back at the party."

"And you are?" I ask.

"Ariel," she says, smirking. "Don't you remember?"

"You're really not going to tell me your name?"

She squirms on the bench. "Maybe after you help me out of this tail."

"Okay." I nod, then kneel to examine the problem.

A quick tug of the material at her hips tells me this tail isn't going anywhere without a fight. After having made similar mistakes wearing gear into the ocean that was form fitting, I know exactly what the issue is.

"This material wasn't designed for salt water. The salt increased the friction when it dried, and created a suction effect."

"Are you an expert in this kind of thing?" she asks, her blue eyes challenging me.

"Hydrodynamics. It's kind of my specialty."

Her eyes widen. "What do I do?"

I give her a reassuring smile. "Don't worry. I've got you."

"Okay, so do it," she requests, motioning toward the tail.

I move in closer.

"Wait! Don't rip it. I have to return it."

"I won't rip it. But I need to break the suction."

"Break the suction? How are you going to do that?" she asks.

I lift my hands out in front of me.

"With your freakishly large hands?" Her eyes bulge. "How are you going to get those inside?" She motions toward her hips. "They're not going to fit. It's too tight."

At that exact moment, an older woman walking her dog appears along the path next to us. She looks taken aback at our conversation and hurriedly steers her dog down toward the beach.

"Oh my god. Did she think..."

I laugh. "Yep."

"Get your head out of the gutter!" she yells after the woman. "I'm a mermaid in distress!"

"All right," I say. "Let's get this done."

"So, you have to stick your hands," she points to the waistband of the tail, "here?"

"You okay with that?" I ask.

She presses her lips together, thinking, then slowly nods her head. "Yes."

"Hold onto the bench."

She grips the edge, and I attempt to wedge my hands between her skin and the stuck material.

It's not working. I frown.

"Flip over."

Her jaw drops. "Excuse me?"

"I need a better angle."

"You've got to be kidding me."

Gently, I guide her to her stomach. As she shifts, I catch sight of a delicate wildflower tattoo on her wrist.

"Okay, I'm ready."

I pull my attention away from the tattoo, and slide my fingers under the waistband. The fabric clings stubbornly, but it starts to give.

"I think you got it." She sighs with relief.

Not yet. The sides are loose, but we still need to clear her ass.

I hover over her, gripping her hips, while trying to ignore the feel of her beneath my hands.

"Almost," I mutter.

"It's so close. Please! Just get it off!" She groans.

With a final push, I slide my hands along the small of her back, breaking the suction. She lets out a relieved whimper.

"Ah, sweet relief," she groans, head resting on the bench.

I tug the tail the rest of the way off. "You're free."

She's still lying there when a voice cuts through the moment.

"That's them."

Both our heads lift in the direction of the voice. The woman who had walked by earlier with her dog is standing there pointing at us. Next to her, a security officer.

five

. . .

"You, arrested for public indecency. That would've been iconic," Darcy says with a wicked grin, snapping her gum as she punches in her table's order.

The Salty Pirate Café is filled with its lunch crowd. The small wood building painted in a tranquil sea-blue is located on the boardwalk just feet from Emerald Beach. It's a good five miles down the beach from the Coral Cove Beach & Golf Club, but word about what happened there yesterday with me and Rory has already made its way through the town. The good news is that no one knows it was me. No one except my co-worker, Darcy since I told her what happened.

"I didn't almost get arrested. We weren't doing anything wrong."

She moves aside so I can punch my orders in.

"Yeah, I know, but man, I wish I could have seen what that woman did. I mean there had to have been something that made her think you two were going at it on a bench in broad daylight."

I won't admit it to Darcy, but while most of me was relieved to get that damn tail off, Rory's hands on my hips, then my ass, sparked other feelings. Tingly ones that had no place in that moment. Because who gets turned on when a man is helping them out of a stressful situation?

The way his massive body had hovered over me, one knee on either side of the tail for leverage. The heat of his bare chest warming my back.

As I type, I catch her studying me. "What?"

"You're thinking about him, aren't you?" She wiggles her eyebrows suggestively at me.

"No," I lie. "And I'm sorry I told you."

"Okay, but seriously. If you weren't doing anything wrong, I don't understand why you left."

While Rory had been assuring the nosy woman and the club's security officer that nothing indecent was going on, I'd grabbed my backpack and the mermaid tail, and snuck away.

"I was tired of the entire situation. After nearly drowning, then not being able to get the mermaid tail off, I needed to get home to Edgar." I leave out the part where I had an asthma attack and only took a half of a puff because I've been rationing my medication.

"How is that adorable creature?" she coos, her pink ponytail bouncing as I follow her to the kitchen.

"He's doing great."

Edgar is recovering from a dental extraction for a tooth abscess he had. He was in so much pain, I'm relieved that he's feeling better. Even though it required me to use money that I had allocated for my asthma medication, I don't regret taking care of him first.

"Order up," Mick calls as he places two plates on the counter under the warming lamp. Robby, another server, swoops in to grab them. Mick pauses in front of me, holding up a ticket for table six. "Summer, no substitutions."

"It's not a substitution, it's an add-on. She doesn't want to waste the crab cake, so leave it off and give her the hush puppies instead," I explain.

Mick shakes his head and waves me off. "I can't stand around and argue with you all day."

Mick and Alice are the owners of The Salty Pirate Café, and while Alice is a cheerful, boisterous woman, who claims to be a direct descendant of an infamous pirate, Mick, her husband, and the cook, is more likely to pass for a surly swashbuckler.

Kale and Royce are the line cooks, assisting Mick with the lunch rush.

Kale grins at me. "Watching you two argue is one of the best parts of my day."

Royce laughs. "For real, man? I'd say getting a smile out of Summer is the best part of mine."

"Because they're practically impossible?" Kale laughs.

"Keep it up, guys, and I'm going to encourage all my tables to order the gator tail today."

Their groan, and Darcy's peal of laugher, reaches my ears as I pick up a water pitcher and head back out to the dining room to refill my tables' water glasses.

Three months ago, when I drove into town, I had zero waitressing experience. That's to be expected growing up in a house where I was instructed to ring a bell if I needed assistance with anything. And I mean *anything*.

My mom said success meant never having to lift a finger. If you could pay someone to do everything, you'd made it.

At five, I'd thought it was thrilling I could order the

housekeepers to clean up my messes instead of having to do it myself. By thirteen, I'd realized I was living in a golden birdcage.

It was the opposite of raising your child to leave the nest and become a contributing member of society.

I'd sneak into the kitchen with Bess, the lead housekeeper, and beg her to show me how to cook things. Francois, the actual chef, refused to let me help. He was too afraid his gig as our family's private chef would be at stake.

But that was another lifetime.

After refilling waters and checking my tables, I head back to the kitchen.

"Order up," Mick calls.

I wipe the moisture from my hands on the black cotton apron tied around my waist, then reach for the plates.

When I step out onto the patio, the cool breeze off the water touches my face, sending a few loose whisps of hair from the side of my ponytail across my cheekbone.

"Fish tacos and the grilled mahi mahi." I set the plates down in front of the young couple. "Do you two need anything else?"

"Would you take a photo of us?" the woman asks, reaching for her purse.

"Of course."

I accept her outstretched phone, then hold it up to take their picture, making sure I capture the backdrop of the ocean waves unfurling onto the sandy beach behind them. Most of the spring break tourists have left, but I'm learning that there's no down season in Coral Cove. The pristine beach, beautiful coastal homes, and adorably quirky shops and restaurants are an attraction year-round. The town itself is charming and cheerful. I fall a little bit in love with it every day.

"There you go." I hand the woman back her phone.

She glances at her phone screen to check my work. "Thank you," she says in approval before setting it back on the table.

I turn to leave their table, but the man summons me back with a lift of his hand.

"One more thing," he says. "Any idea how to find a Covey?"

I press my lips together, steeling my face to his question. I should be used to it by now. It's not the first time someone has asked me. But the anxiety that tourists probing about the anonymous paintings elicits hasn't eased at all.

The woman waves me off in jest. "He's kidding." She throws him a pinched look. "Obviously, we know they're totally random and one could pop up at any moment. That's the fun of it."

"It doesn't hurt to ask. We're only here a few days, so we need to stack the deck if you want to find one."

Still addressing her boyfriend, she points a finger toward me.

"It's not like she knows where one would be. If she did, she'd claim it for herself." Her attention turns to me. "Right?"

Before I can answer, her boyfriend starts talking again.

"Maybe she already has one and would help us out. She's a local after all. I'm sure she's got some good intel on where they typically pop up."

"I've already researched. When someone finds one, they post it on the social media page." She taps at her phone. "Three days ago, a woman and her kids from Michigan found one. See?"

While they're going back and forth, I rub my arm

absently, then freeze. A streak of yellow paint catches my eye. Damn. I thought I'd cleaned it all off.

The man turns away from her outstretched phone and settles his gaze back on me.

"Any information you might have would be appreciated."

"Last one was three days ago?" I ask, recalling the sunset beachscape of bright oranges and yellows giving way to a purplish-blue sky with lush green plants peeking out of a sandy beach.

"According to the Covey social media page. Unless someone found one and didn't report it."

"I'm sure one is likely to show up soon then," I offer encouragement, while keeping my face void of emotion.

He dips his head in my direction, eyes pleading. "Any hints on best places to look?"

"Jason, I can hear you." The woman covers her ears. "This feels like cheating."

His panicky eyes dart to his girlfriend, then back to me. "Please. She's driving me nuts with this. It's taking over our entire vacation."

I glance around the restaurant's wooden deck, then back to him.

But before I can open my mouth, Darcy edges up to the table.

"Ah, another Covey enthusiast," she comments, nodding toward the woman.

"You have no idea." The man sighs. "It's on her bucket list."

"Where do y'all live?" Darcy asks.

"Denver."

"I love Denver. I have a cousin who lives there. The Highlands neighborhood, I think?"

"We're near City Park, on the east side of town."

Jason opens a map of Coral Cove. On it, there are markings and dates.

"She's been tracking where and when Coveys have been found to try and guess the next likely location." He angles the screen toward me and Darcy.

"Wow." Darcy drops her head to study it. "That's pretty sophisticated."

I can't help it. A wave of pride rushes through me as I glance over the map on his screen.

"Okay, let me give you some advice," Darcy says.

"We'll take it." Jason nods eagerly.

"You don't find a Covey; a Covey finds you."

"That's your advice?" He sits back in his chair, clearly annoyed to have gained no information.

I point to the map. "Maybe near the library? One hasn't been found in that area yet."

Jason perks up. "Yeah? Okay. We'll check it out."

"Enjoy your meal," I say, before following Darcy back inside the restaurant.

"It's fun to mess with them," she says.

"Yeah, I know."

While Darcy heads toward the kitchen, I turn down the hallway to the restroom.

Inside, I fix my ponytail, then wash my hands, making sure to scrub off the paint on my arm, before I head back to work.

"Fish biting today, Cal?" I ask, kicking back on my skateboard to come to a stop in front of the elderly fisherman.

"No luck." He shakes his head, then repositions his beat-up green hat on his head. "My bait's dried out."

"Sorry about that." I reach in my backpack and pull out a brown bag. "Today's special is a shrimp po'boy with coleslaw and pickle chips. And I even threw in one of those blondies you like."

His eyes light up with appreciation. "You didn't have to do that."

"I know," I say, as Paulie, one of my afternoon dogs, noses at his elbow. "But I wanted to."

Cal gives Paulie a scratch behind the ears and her tongue lolls out the side of her mouth. Pearl and Mattie weave between my legs while Sunny sniffs at Cal's tackle box.

"You've got good company today."

"They put up with me for the snacks," I say with a shrug, as I reach for my backpack.

Cal chuckles, then adds. "Well, so do I."

I smile, untangling the dogs' leashes. "I'll see you tomorrow."

He gives me a wave, as I drop my skateboard onto the dock and pedal to get started.

"Summer," Deb, one of the town's security officers, calls, "no wheels on the dock."

"Come on, Deb. Make an exception for Cal's meals on wheels," I call as I fly by with the dogs running along beside me.

She gives me a stern look, but waves me on.

Once I've dropped the dogs at their homes, I turn left at Nude Food, Coral Cove's organic and waste-free market, and make my way down Ocean Breeze Avenue toward the library.

Before I pull the canvas out of my bag, I glance around to make sure no one is around, then unlatch the closure and slide it out before placing it on the window ledge of the library, under the water-resistant awning in case it rains.

Recalling the wave of panic that the couples' inquiry at the café today had brought on had me questioning everything.

The anonymous paintings had been a way for me to take back my art. To pour the passion I have for painting into something fun that didn't require me to be seen. But now that the paintings have become something, the notoriety of what the townspeople and visitors have dubbed Coveys, that old feeling is starting to emerge again. That I'll be found out and everything will be taken away.

I'm a grown woman now.

I am in control of my passions and joy.

No one can take that away.

I stand back and take in my work.

I'd passed the beach bungalow on Hanover Way a few days after I'd arrived in Coral Cove. I'd taken Edgar on a morning walk and I'd gotten lost when I'd stumbled upon the quaint gray bungalow with the yellow door. Although the beach house could use some love, and another artist might make adjustments to the reality of it, I'd captured it as it stood. Unruly grasses blocking part of the large front windows. Rugged wooden path in need of repair, and a picket fence with a missing section in front. It's one of my best pieces. As I reach to set it on the bench beneath the overhang, I hesitate, the ache in my chest making it difficult to part with it.

There will be others.

In three months since I moved to Coral Cove, I've left nearly twenty pieces around the small coastal town. Walking the dogs has gotten me familiar with the town and people's comings and goings. On our morning walks, I'll usually scope out a place I think would be good to leave the next painting, then later, after my shift at the café, when dusk has softened the shadows, I'll leave it for someone to find and hopefully bring joy to their space.

The aspect of sharing my art in this anonymous way has been thrilling. There's no pressure, no face behind the art, just joy, and that's all I want.

I take one more glance at the beach house painting, then hitch my canvas backpack over my shoulder and head for home.

six

. . .

RORY

My phone rings for the third time in a row. I pull it out of my pocket to silence it but this time it's not my ex, it's Vivian, the team's publicist.

"Hey, Viv," I answer.

"Don't 'hey, Viv' me."

It's immediately clear that she isn't just calling to catch up.

"It was an innocent situation taken out of context," I preface, knowing she's going to bring up what everyone else within a ten-mile radius of Coral Cove already has.

There was nothing salacious about the mermaid situation, but someone snapped a photo of me hovering over her on the bench and that image is making the rounds. You can't see her face, just me on top of her, hands down her pants. I mean, tail. It's fucking ridiculous.

While I was talking to the club's security officer and manager, she vanished without any explanation and without backing my account of the situation. The club manager apologized once he realized who I was and dismissed the security officer. Annoying, because I hadn't done anything wrong, and that should have been reason enough, not my local celebrity status.

"That, my friend, is eighty percent of my job," Vivi jokes.

"What's the damage?" I ask, knowing she's right. There's what happened and then there's what people, mostly the media, portray.

"You're the golden boy of swimming, a national hero, and while the media has always loved you, they can turn quickly." She sighs. "I can deal with the media, but unfortunately, I can't deal with your mom."

"She called you?" I groan, stopping in front of the library to take in the familiar brick building with its white and green striped canvas awnings. I've already heard from my parents regarding the mermaid incident, my mom leaving me several voice messages about it.

"Yes. And unlike you, I picked up."

"Hey. That was your choice."

"I'm a publicist, it's never a good look to avoid people."

"What did you tell her?" I ask, curious.

"That it was an act of heroism. A battle with wet Lycra that required your specific skill set. She wanted to know if there was anything going on between you and the woman."

"No. I don't even know her name. She disappeared before I got it."

"Seriously? The photos had me thinking you were on a first name basis."

"We were interrupted by the club's security officer."

"Yeah, I got that part." She laughs.

"Interrupted before I could get her *name*."

"So, the mermaid thing. Is this a fetish I need to be concerned about?"

"She was dressed up for a child's birthday party. I was helping her take off her mermaid tail."

"Hmm. It looked like you were helping her with more than that."

"I thought you called to help me navigate this."

"Okay, I'll stop teasing. I can put out a statement that you were lending a helpful hand, but that's the extent of the situation. Or, I can say no comment, which everyone knows means something is up."

"Is there a third option?" I ask.

"I know the situation with your parents and your ex has been a source of distraction for you, so why not create a counter distraction?"

"What do you mean?"

"Embrace the mermaid. Oh, and Hydra-Fuel reached out yesterday."

"Why didn't you lead with that?"

"I like to get the unpleasant stuff out of the way first. It makes the good stuff that much better. You know, work out first, then eat cake. That kind of thing."

"So, Hydra-Fuel, huh?"

Swimming isn't hockey or football. There are no multi-million-dollar contracts being signed. So, unless you're sponsored, you're paying out of pocket for coaching, gear, and travel.

When I thought my career was over last year, several of my sponsorships ended. A long-time contract with Aqua-Edge, a high-performance swim gear line, as well as endorsement deals with Visa and Colgate. Vivi's been working on a Hydra-Fuel endorsement and it sounds like things are getting finalized.

"They want to shoot in a few weeks. A montage of you swimming and working out in various ways. Should be an easy campaign."

"Sounds good." I temper my response, but the reality is it feels fucking amazing to still be wanted by major corporations. "I'll have my legal team review the contract. I'm sure they'll have some feedback."

"I'll forward it to everyone."

"Thanks, Viv." I hesitate for a second, then shift gears. "Unrelated, but how are your detective skills?"

"I'm a publicist, not a spy," she chides. "But I'm also a woman, so pretty damn good."

"The mermaid's name."

"I'll do some digging."

"Thanks."

I end the call with Vivi, then pocket my phone.

I rake a hand through my hair and roll out my shoulders.

That's when I notice something on the window ledge of the library.

Stepping through the landscaping of woodchips and shrubs, I reach the window and discover it's a painting.

At the same moment I reach for it, my phone buzzes in my pocket, this time reminding me of the appointment notification that Charlie had sent me yesterday.

With the painting in hand, I make my way down the block to Spruce, a medical spa and salon in Coral Cove.

Inside the waiting room I find Logan, Eli, and Charlie.

Logan nods to the painting I'm holding, taking it from my hand to examine it. He beams ear to ear. "You met a mermaid and you found a Covey? Fuck, man, you're a god damn good luck charm."

I ignore his comments about the mermaid. The guys

already gave me shit about the woman leaving me high and dry this morning at practice.

"What's a Covey?" I ask.

"A few months ago, these beach paintings started showing up randomly around town. Someone came up with the name Covey. It's a mash up of Coral Cove and Banksy, the British anonymous street artist. There's even a social media page for people to post when they find one." He hands it back to me. "Where'd you get it?"

"Near the library."

"Wait. Isn't that *your* beach house?" Charlie asks.

"Fuck. I didn't even notice that before." Logan moves in for a closer look. "It must be fate that you were the one to find it."

Eli groans. "Logan's into some woo woo shit lately. Auras and meditation. He dragged me to an aura cleansing workshop last week."

Logan smirks at Eli. "You liked it."

Eli lifts his chin toward Charlie. "This better not be another aura reading."

"Trust me. This is nothing like that," Charlie says, his cheeks turning a tinge of pink.

Just then, the receptionist greets us with forms to fill out and sign.

I scan the document.

"Why the hell is this form all about bleach?" I ask.

Eli drops the clipboard on the table and moves to stand. "Bro, I'm not bleaching my hair. We did that before Paris and I looked fucking terrible."

"Nah, man, you looked cool," Logan argues.

Eli shakes his head. "It washed me out and you know it."

The receptionist gives a wave of dismissal. "You can

disregard the bleach section, that isn't part of your services today."

While I'm happy bleach is off the table, I'm still wondering what we're doing.

I turn my attention to Charlie. "What exactly are we doing here?"

"As you know, we have a tradition. The tattoo before Sydney. The hair dye before Paris. We have to set the tone for the months of intense training before trials."

He's right. It's tradition. The previous medley teams I'd swam with in Singapore and Atlanta had done the same thing. Back then, I was the young, inexperienced swimmer looking up to the older leaders. I'd been seventeen and twenty-one, so they'd been tame. Before the games in Singapore, there was a towel we passed around, each of us drying off with it after every practice that week, never washing it, which is disgusting now that I think about it.

While Charlie talks, two words on the form hit me like a truck: anal waxing.

"What the fuck?" I hiss. "Anal waxing? Really, Charlie?"

Eli starts laughing which does not seem to be a normal reaction for his usually serious nature.

"What the hell is going on?" I ask.

Eli's eyes are alight with amusement. "Some girl told Charlie his ass was too hairy."

"I told you that in confidence," Charlie whispers.

"Yet, here we all are." Eli gestures to the waiting area.

Logan shakes his head. "First of all, can we all agree that anyone who is back there should be comfortable enough to handle what they find? Hair and all."

The pink tinge of Charlie's cheeks deepens. "I need the moral support and figured this was two birds with one stone. We're always eliminating body hair for drag purposes anyways."

Eli shakes his head. "You cannot convince me that waxing my asshole is going to shave time off my split."

"Now that it's out there, we might as well share. Anyone else have this issue?" Charlie asks.

Logan shakes his head. "I don't have any comment on this subject. I've never looked at my asshole and I really hadn't planned on it."

"Liar, you know you like ass play. You told me about one of the women you hooked up with was into it and you couldn't believe what you've been missing out on this whole time. It's why I suggested it to Marika and how she discovered I have a hairy asshole. So really this is all your fault."

"Your hairy asshole is my fault? It couldn't possibly be your Italian heritage?" Logan claps back.

Eli and I exchange a glance. Today is the weirdest fucking day.

"Are you scared?" Charlie goads Logan in a baby voice. "Do you need someone to hold your hand?"

"I'm not getting my asshole waxed and even if I was, I wouldn't need anyone to hold my hand while doing it."

"How are you shy about this? We see your dick in the shower every damn day," Charlie argues.

"Yeah, but I draw the line at showing you all my asshole," Logan growls.

"Fine. Be a baby. I didn't want to see your asshole anyway."

I shake my head at the ridiculousness of this conversation. I think we might be too close knit for our own good.

"It's Rory's decision," Eli announces, nodding toward me. His eyes filled with the respect representative of the twelve years we've been teammates and friends. Without directly saying it, this is likely my last international run and the last time we'll be doing something like this as a group.

Do I want to wax my asshole? Absolutely not. I haven't even read the fine print to know what the procedure and side effects are. I've never even seen my asshole to know if I'd be a good candidate. I know what's on my razor when I shave before a meet, though, so I'm guessing I've got something back there.

I glance over at Logan.

"No one has to do it," I say, shifting my gaze to Charlie, "but it'd be really fucking cool to support our teammate and have this experience together."

Charlie grins ear to ear.

Eli nods in confirmation.

Between me and Eli, Logan grumbles.

A female tech walks out pulling a pair of blue latex gloves on before she glances at us and grins. "Who's first?"

Logan's thumb jerks in my direction before he gives me a wicked smirk.

"You're up, Captain."

My ass cheeks have never touched each other the way they do now. It's unnerving. I'd thought a short run this morning would help loosen up my knee, but all it's done is draw attention to my freshly waxed asshole and taint.

I don't embarrass easily, but the pretzel pose I had to hold for the wax tech to get under my ball sack was humiliating. And when Logan's screams echoed down the hallway, I was glad I'd gone first.

After last night's shenanigans, I'd gone home to finish unpacking, placing my newly acquired artwork on the dresser in my bedroom. More than the fact that it was cool that someone had painted my beach house, the painting was stunning. I'm no expert, but even to the untrained eye, it's obvious that the artist is extremely talented.

After a three mile out and back run along Emerald Beach, I stop at the water's edge to let the cool water rush over my feet and soak in the beauty of my surroundings. While California had been successful in regards to rehabilitation for my knee, and spending time with my sister, Whitney, it's good to be home.

"Lulu! No!" I hear the woman call right before a small golden dog darts past me and into the water. Before the tide can pull the small dog out with it, I reach down and scoop it up.

The pup's eyes are filled with mischief, its mouth open like it's smiling, none the wiser that it could have been swept out to sea.

When I turn to see the woman chasing after the dog, I can't help the grin that spreads over my face.

It's *her*.

When she spots me with her dog, there's a moment of hesitancy on her part, like she's weighing her options. For a second, it seems like she's considering abandoning her dog rather than face me. But ultimately, she decides to come for the dog.

She reaches out and takes the dog from me, checking to make sure it's okay, before squinting up at me with a scowl on her pretty face. "Are you stalking me?"

My brows lift at her question that feels more like an accusation.

"This is the part where you thank me for rescuing your dog."

"Thank you," she grumbles. "And it's not my dog. I'm just her walker," she motions toward the boardwalk where three dogs with their leashes tied to a post are waiting patiently, tails wagging.

"So, you're a dog walker and a part-time mermaid?"

She blinks up at me from under her black, 'salty' baseball cap.

She's even more gorgeous than I remember. My eyes trail over the smooth, sun-kissed skin of her long legs. She's wearing denim shorts and a loose tank with a lacy layer beneath. Her long hair is pulled back into a ponytail looped through her hat.

I know boundaries and I respect them, but right now every part of me wants to find some excuse to make contact.

Yesterday she'd been friendlier, but today those turquoise gems of hers flash at me with enough fierceness to knock me back on my heels.

I watch her eyes explore my shirtless chest and torso. Her stoic face might have been able cover up her perusal but at the last second, her lips part to take in more air.

"To answer your question, I'm not stalking you. Stalking would require planning. This is just a happy coincidence."

"If you say so, Rory Shields." She's already turning to walk back up the beach toward the other dogs, so I follow. On the way, I grab my shoes and t-shirt that I'd left in a pile on the beach while I was running, then jog to catch up with her.

"If you tell me your name then these frequent encounters could be more friendly, wouldn't you say?"

She whips around, and that long, blonde ponytail

smacks me in the chest. When her face comes back into view, her pretty mouth is twisted into a frown.

"Who says I want them to be friendly?" she asks.

"I guess I should have taken the hint yesterday when you abandoned me during the interrogation about our bench activities."

Back on the boardwalk, she attaches Lulu's leash, then unties the other dogs from the wooden post. I slip on my shoes, then drop down to rub the head of a sweet looking Dachshund. The name on its tag says Cali.

"Hi, Cali. Nice to meet you."

"Cali doesn't like strangers."

When Cali plants her paws on my feet and leans into me, I glance up at Wildflower. It's the name I'd given her after replaying everything the past two days and wondering if I'd made her up.

She sighs. "I'm sorry I left. I had to get home to Edgar."

"Edgar?" I chuckle at the formal name. "Who's Edgar? Your boyfriend?"

She presses her lips together.

"Um…"

"I get it. Maybe this thing with Edgar is a situationship? Something you haven't put a label on yet?"

She rolls her shoulders back. "No, we're definitely together."

I nod and give her an easy smile, but beneath my ribcage, disappointment surges through me. It makes no sense. I'm not looking for a relationship right now, but seeing this woman again is doing funny things to my insides. And hearing her talk about the guy she's dating is strangely devastating.

"I've got to get going." With one hand holding the

leashes, she opens her backpack with the other to pull out a skateboard.

I'm not ready to let her go. I nod to the board. "You skateboard?"

"No, I just carry it around with me so I can ward off strange men that try to talk to me."

She's talking about me, of course, but I think she's kidding.

"Strange men, huh?" I look around. "I don't see any of those around, but I'll hang here so no one bothers you." I give her a wide grin.

The exasperated look on her face has me in a chokehold. It's like she doesn't understand why I'd want to be near her, and it's that expression that only makes me want to get closer. To know more about her.

"How long have you been shredding?" I ask.

"Long enough."

She's giving me nothing, yet I'm having the best time talking to her. Or at least trying to talk to her.

"Are you upset with me?" I ask.

"What?" She looks confused.

"Did I do something wrong? With the tail removal? During your asthma att—"

"No," she cuts me off sharply. "It's not you. It's me."

"Wow. Already getting the speech and I don't even know your name." I tap one of the wheels of her skateboard, sending it into motion. "You know, I've always wanted to learn."

Ignoring me, she guides the dogs down the boardwalk, and I fall into step beside her.

"Yeah, well, today's not the day, Flipper."

She turns to sidestep me.

"Flipper?" I beam at the nickname. It's not masculine or

sexy, but I'll take anything that has this woman's brain giving me a second thought. "I like it."

She laughs under her breath. "You would."

"Why's that?" I ask.

"Dolphins are the aquatic equivalent of a golden retriever."

I nod in understanding. "Golden retrievers are playful, trustworthy, and loyal. I'll take it."

I watch a hint of a smile pull at the corner of her lips. It's far better than the scowl she pinned me with earlier. I'm making progress with her, and I don't want to stop now.

"Come on, Wildflower. One try."

"Wildflower?" She scoffs.

"Yeah, like your tattoo." I point to the tattoo on her wrist.

Her nose wrinkles, but I swear there's an almost smile hidden beneath her exasperation. She stops suddenly and gives the command for the dogs to sit. One by one, she doles out treats and words of praise.

"What a good boy," she tells Chef, the black lab, in a sweet, yet husky tone before giving him a treat. Fuck, I just know I'm going to replay that later and pretend she's talking to me.

Be a good boy, Rory, and get on your knees for me.

Yeah, there's no way that's leaving my brain now.

Once the dogs are all attended to, she turns to me.

"You know the phrase, big tree, fall hard?" She scans a finger up the length of my body. "That's in reference to you. You're the big tree."

I chuckle. "You think I'm going to fall?"

"My board's too small for you. Gravity and center of mass will only assist in this disaster."

That wasn't a straight up no, so I must be wearing her down.

"I accept your challenge." I take the skateboard from under her arm and place it on the ground.

"It wasn't a challenge. I'm just saying this is probably going to end badly."

I'm easygoing by nature, but I didn't get where I am in swimming without a competitive streak. This isn't a real competition, but now that she's doubting me, I feel the need to prove her wrong.

I place one foot on the board, then the other to get a feel for it, before I toss her a sincere smile. "We need to work on your confidence in me."

"We need to work on your reliance on that charming smile to get you anything you want."

"So, you're saying I'm charming?" I tease, pinning her with another smile.

She sighs again and shakes her head. "Let the record show that I am against this and am not held liable for any injury you might obtain." She spreads her hands apart to indicate I'm free to give it a go.

"Any pointers?" I ask, stepping on to the board.

Even at an angle, my size fourteen running shoes hang off the edges of the board. I get what she meant about it being too small for me, but I'm not going to waste this opportunity to keep spending time with her.

In the back of my mind, I know I shouldn't be putting my body through unknown situations. My knee is fully healed, but doing something stupid, like trying to impress a woman with skills I don't have is asking for trouble. But when she extends her free hand to help me balance, guiding me down the boardwalk as the dogs follow, I know I'm stopping now.

I've never ridden a skateboard in my life, so I default to what I've seen on TV.

I start picking up speed. Wildflower jogs beside me, the dogs trotting obediently at her side. I catch the slight hitch in her breath and I wonder if this is pushing her asthma too far.

I didn't realize I could move this fast.

"Rory!" she rasps. "Slow down!"

I'd love to, but we never discussed how to stop. I drop a foot to the ground, trying to brake just as she and the dogs catch up.

She reaches for me with her free hand, but the dogs yank her backward, and all my momentum redirects... straight toward her.

I twist, trying not to crush the smallest dog directly underfoot. My reaction time off the blocks is second to none, but it doesn't serve me now. Not with the skateboard, the dogs, and Wildflower all colliding into one chaotic swirl.

And then, it's too late.

I hear a crunch. I brace for pain in my knee...elbow... wrist, but other than the shock of the fall, I feel nothing.

I glance down to assess the damage.

I'm not hurt.

Because Wildflower broke my fall.

Her left wrist is bent awkwardly and pinned under my shoulder.

Shit.

seven

. . .

My wrist is throbbing. And Rory Shields' hard, shirtless body is spread over me like avocado on toast.

"Shit. Are you okay?" he asks.

He'd asked the same question when he pulled me from the ocean, but now, as the cause of my peril, his handsome face crumbles with pain.

For how much of a dead weight he was a moment ago, he springs off me, releasing my wrist from where it was trapped between his shoulder and the ground.

"I'm fine." I start to roll my wrist out hoping the movement will ease the tightness, but the shooting pain causes me to wince.

"You're not fine." Rory's expression tightens, like my pain physically affects him. "We need to get your wrist checked out."

I pull my wrist away as gingerly as I can despite the thrum of annoyance running through my veins.

"What I meant to say is that I'll be fine," I grit out. "I'll ice it or something."

He pulls his shirt on and I'm thankful that I no longer have to stare at all those rippling muscles of his. Ignoring every word I just said, he collects the dogs' leashes, then takes my uninjured hand in his and starts leading us away from the beach.

"Come on. I'll drive you."

I'm in denial that anything is wrong with my wrist because that would only add to the growing list of shit things that have happened this past week. I'm starting to wonder if Coral Cove is where I'm meant to be. The other towns I've lived haven't required this much interaction with people. Most notable of all, there's been no man like Rory with his muscles and perfect smile and good heart.

"Rory, I can't go to the doctor," I say, pulling my hand from his. "I don't have insurance. I can't afford the ER."

If anyone knew who my parents were, my statements would be laughable but since they haven't been a part of my life for years, everything I'm saying is true. I've even had to ration my asthma medication to make it stretch.

My words settle between us. I know he heard them, but he's already gathered my skateboard and backpack, and is walking off with the dogs.

"My Jeep's this way."

"Rory," I call, but he keeps walking.

The only reason I follow is because I can't let him take the dogs. I need to get them back home.

"Did you hear what I said?" I rush after him.

He stops in front of a deep green Jeep Rubicon. The windows, top and doors are taken off. It's a rugged vehicle in a warm green that suits him, which is a weird thing to think about a guy I barely know.

He sets my stuff in the trunk, then loads the dogs into the backseat before turning in my direction.

"Medical services are on me. I'm the one who made you fall."

The pain etched on his handsome face makes my chest squeeze. I don't like it. Even though I'm the one hurt, I'd do anything for him to stop looking at me like that.

His large hand cradles my hurt wrist. Leaning closer, he brushes his lips delicately against my wrist bone.

"Please, Wildflower." This time when he says the nickname, my hackles don't rise. It's got to be the endorphins released from my injured wrist putting me in this woozy, punch-drunk state. "We need to get it looked at. At least an X-ray to rule out a fracture or broken bone."

"Is there any point in arguing with you?" I ask.

"No."

Still in a daze, his firm hands wrap around my waist to hoist me up into the passenger seat. He reaches across my body to buckle the seat belt and the scent of him, laundry soap, sea salt and masculine sweat, invades my space.

"I could have done that myself." It comes out as a faint whisper.

"I know. You're incredibly capable." He grins, as if he knows other people acknowledging that I'm competent is my jam.

Chef, Lulu, and Scout sit obediently on the floor, while Rory sets Cali on my lap, snuggling her beneath the seat belt to keep her safe.

"I'm taking you to see my team's athletic trainer. She'll examine your wrist."

I nod, the throbbing pain making me more agreeable than I would normally be. The pain makes me notice unusual things about Rory. Like how his long fingers wrap around the steering wheel, leaving his thumb to slide over the front of the smooth leather.

On the drive, I can't help but think about how hot he looks. His muscular thighs pressed against the confines of his board shorts. Big hands, long fingers.

He catches me staring and grins.

I inhale sharply. Maybe the pain is making me delirious.

We make four stops, dropping off each dog along the route, and Rory helps me get them inside and settled.

Finally, he pulls into the Coral Cove Aquatic Center parking lot and rushes to open my door.

Inside the aquatic center, the smell of chlorine hits my nose, clean and sharp.

"The athletic trainer's office is this way." Rory guides me through the lobby and down a hallway.

We enter a room, and inside Rory waves to a young woman with coppery blonde hair braided over her shoulder.

"Hey, Rory." She wraps him in a big hug, before pulling back, her brows drawing down with concern. "Please tell me your knee isn't bothering you."

"It's not me." His palm, warm and secure on my lower back, ushers me forward. "My friend fell. She hurt her wrist. *I* hurt her wrist, and I was hoping you'd look at it."

There's a clearing of a throat, and the woman at the front desk to our right shakes her head. "Rory, she's not a member of the swim club. She's not under our trainers' care."

"I need you to make an exception." Rory's usual friendly grin is replaced by a hard line. "Please, Winnie."

Winnie waves off the woman at the front desk. "I got this, Karen."

We follow Winnie to a room down the hall and she shuts the door behind us.

"I'm Elowyn Mitchell, the Carolina Current's athletic trainer. Everyone calls me Winnie."

"Nice to meet you." I shake her hand with my uninjured one.

She grabs a form and places it on a clipboard.

"Your name?"

My eyes flick to Rory's. I could run out of this room right now, drive my van to another location and pretend none of this ever happened, but my wrist is throbbing. It's like it has its very own pulse. So, I have to stay and see about this injury, and that involves sharing my name.

"Summer."

At my admission, Rory's smile finds its home again.

"Summer?" Winnie prods.

"Summer McKee," I relent, my lips threatening a smile at the sheer glee in Rory's eyes. If I didn't know better, I'd think he masterminded the whole thing just to learn my name.

"Are you happy now?" I ask once Winnie has gathered my information and stepped out of the room.

He shakes his head, that heartachingly pained look on his face again.

"Not until you're all fixed up."

Winnie returns a few minutes later and starts the exam.

"How'd this happen?" Winnie asks while gently rotating my wrist as part of the exam.

Rory presses his lips together and I can't help but think about our discussion earlier on the boardwalk. *Big tree, fall hard.*

"This giant man fell off a skateboard he had no business riding and crushed me in the process."

Winnie shakes her head. "Boys are idiots."

"Exactly."

"I'm right here," Rory says, waving his arms in mock exasperation.

"We're aware," Winnie replies, tossing a knowing grin in my direction.

After the X-ray, which was negative for a fracture or broken bone, Winnie fits me for a brace. "This should be worn day and night for one week. Take ibuprofen to help with pain and reduce swelling.

"Rory, don't you have practice now?" she asks, guiding my fingers into the brace before velcroing it closed below my wrist.

He glances at the clock on the wall. "Shit. Yeah, I do."

Running a hand through his wavy hair, he stands. "But I can wait a few more minutes."

That's what he says, but I can see a panic stealing over his features.

Winnie tsks. "If you're late, Owens is going to have your ass."

"You should go." I nudge.

"I hate leaving you like this."

Winnie sighs between us. "You two are adorable."

"We are nothing of the sort," I scoff, trying to gain some perspective. "And I'm fine. I probably don't even need this." I lift my arm with the brace and shake it around, but my wrist still protests.

"Yeah, you do," Winnie argues. "At least until the swelling goes down."

Rory turns to Winnie. "Can you make sure she gets home?"

"Of course."

"Thanks." Rory drops a quick kiss to her cheek, before turning for the door.

For a second, I watch him go, broad shoulders and

muscular back rippling against his t-shirt, but the fact that he kissed Winnie on the cheek and didn't even say goodbye has me quickly dropping my gaze, pretending the brace suddenly needs adjusting. I feel silly for wanting his attention and even more stupid for making myself feel bad that I didn't get it.

Nothing about this situation should matter because Rory and I are barely acquaintances, but my chest is doing that pinching thing again. It's bringing unwelcome awareness that despite my brain's attempt to override it, the content of my left ribcage is having a strong reaction to Rory.

A moment later, there's a squeak on the tile floor.

"Oh, and Summer?"

I look up to find Rory abruptly stopping at the door before turning and walking back toward me. I swear he looks like he's going to wrap me up in his arms and keep me forever.

"Yeah?" I say so casually, even I'm impressed by my cool indifference. He takes my sprained wrist in his hand, and kisses my fingers, the only thing exposed by the brace. Warm, soft lips tickle my fingertips.

"I'm sorry I hurt you."

It's annoyingly sweet. I want to melt into a puddle, then scream at him for making me weak. But there's no point in any of that because he's already rushing out the door.

After Winnie finishes up the paperwork for my visit, like she had assured Rory, she offers to drive me home.

Leaving the aquatic center with Winnie, we don't go out the main entrance I came in before, but instead, she navigates me down a long hallway past one of the indoor pools, then out a side door that opens to the largest outdoor pool I've ever seen.

The lanes are occupied by swimmers. The sound of water splashing is almost rhythmic.

It's impossible to pick out which swimmer is Rory. They all look the same in white swim caps and dark goggles, moving steadily down the lane, their strong, muscular arms angling out of the water. It's hypnotizing.

"There's Rory." Winnie points. "Lane four."

When my eyes land on him, I discover I was wrong. They don't all look alike. Now that I've got eyes on him, Rory stands out. He's a masterpiece. A human work of art as he slices through the water. When he turns his head to breathe, the corner of his mouth reaches upward, seeking out oxygen. It's like watching a machine operate. Every stroke is effortless.

"My brother, Eli, is next to him." Winnie keeps talking to me about the other swimmers in the water but it's impossible to take my eyes off Rory. I saw Rory's chest and abs on the beach, the strength and chiseled definition of them. It's clear every muscle has its task and is trained for peak performance.

I wish I had my sketchbook. I could spend all day sketching his movements. The human form in movement is something I've been working on. Beachscapes and still life come naturally to me, but capturing movement like this is where I want to improve in my art.

"—so that's how they became the Carolina Current swim club."

I realize Winnie has been talking to me the entire time I've been watching Rory swim.

"Cool." I shrug, trying to slip back into my mask of indifference, but it doesn't fit the way it did earlier. It feels too tight now, putting pressure against my temples.

"How long will they swim for?" I ask.

"This practice is typically two hours. And that's just time in the water. There's dryland, too. And their weight training program."

"What's dryland?" I ask.

"Mobility exercises, stretching, core work."

It makes sense that a swimmer would be building muscles with weight training and working on flexibility as well, but I'd never thought about a swimmer training by doing anything but swimming.

"My car's this way." She motions toward a gate on the far side and I follow her through it. "Where am I taking you?"

"The Salty Pirate Café."

She nods, backing the car out of the parking spot.

"God, their hush puppies are to die for."

"Yeah, they're pretty good." I play with the strap on the brace.

"You must be new to Coral Cove."

"I've been here a few months."

"Where do you live?" She asks.

"RV park. I have a camper van."

"That's cool. I've always wanted to travel more. I bet you love being able to pick up and move at a moment's notice."

"It's nice." When I'd fixed it up and left Tennessee, the freedom of it had been the only thing I wanted, but after a few years on the road, I'd been craving more consistency. That's when I found Coral Cove.

"Are you going to be staying in Coral Cove for long?"

"I don't know. Maybe."

After a short drive, Winnie pulls up to the lot at the back of the restaurant.

"Thanks for the ride." I start to get out of the car, but she calls me back.

"Summer, wait."

"Yeah?"

She pushes her sunglasses up to the top of her head. "Woman to woman, I have to warn you about Rory."

My chest constricts at her edgy tone. A rush of displeasure that Rory, who I don't know at all but can only see as being a good guy, might have a bad reputation.

On one hand, it doesn't matter what she has to say about Rory. I don't need anyone to warn me about the guy. My parents' toxic marriage and my ex-boyfriend, are all the warning I need to stay far away from relationships.

The other part of me is curious about what she has to say.

"Yeah?" I ask.

She sighs dramatically. "Rory Shields is a chronic over-helper. You drop something? He's picking it up before you even realize it's fallen. Struggling with a grocery bag? He's already carrying it. Feeling cold? Boom...he's wrapping you in his hoodie before you can protest. It's relentless."

I get it. Winnie wants me to know that Rory is just a nice guy. I'm not special and he's super helpful to everyone. That's fine.

"So, you're saying Rory bringing me to get my wrist checked out is totally normal and to not read into it because he'd do this for anyone?"

Her lips twitch before they split into a mischievous grin.

"Oh, no. He definitely likes you. And the way he looks at

you?" She fans herself. "I had to splash some cold water on my face after I did your X-ray."

I blink, thrown off by the shift in the conversation.

"We should hang out sometime." She glances at her watch. "I've got to get back, but I'll have Rory give you my number."

Before I can protest, Winnie pulls out of the lot and onto the street.

He definitely likes you.

What is this, fourth grade? Check yes or no?

Pfft.

I glance down at my wrist. *Wildflower, for your tattoo*, he'd said.

I shake the thought loose and walk into work.

eight

· · ·

RORY

I hated having to rush off to practice and leave Summer, but the second I finish my last set, I head for the locker room to quickly shower and change.

Summer.

Throughout practice, her name had been a chant in my head.

I like calling her Wildflower, but Summer suits her perfectly.

When I text Winnie to ask about Summer, she tells me she dropped her off at The Salty Pirate Café a few hours ago. It might be a long shot, but since I've got nothing else to go on, it's where I'm going to start.

That's how I find myself outside the blue wooden building that houses one of Coral Cove's most iconic restaurants. I pull open the door to find the dinner crowd already in full swing. The protein shake I grabbed on my way out of the aquatic center was enough to hold me over, but the smell of fresh fish is enticing and after Coach put us through a rigorous workout, I could stuff my face right now.

"Hey, Rory. You need a table?" Mae asks from the host stand upon my approach.

It's a small town, and there are perks to being known. Like getting a table at the most popular restaurant during the dinner rush.

"Hi, Mae. I'm looking for someone." I glance toward the dining area. "Blonde hair. Blue eyes. Freckle under her left eye and a small scar on her chin." Mae blinks at me, and I realize I should find less obsessive ways to describe Summer's face. "She looks like an angel, but is feisty as hell. I think she was here earlier so she might have already left."

Out of the corner of my eye, I catch a swish of a blonde ponytail.

Summer.

"Found her." I point in Summer's direction.

"Oh, Summer." She nods, then glances down at the map of tables. "She's working out on the patio this evening. Would you like to sit in her section?"

That's when I see the plates in her hands. The heavy ceramic pottery-style plates full of crab cakes, shrimp and grits, beef brisket, and my favorite, seafood pot pie.

The realization hits. Summer's a waitress here.

But her wrist is hurt and Winnie had told her to rest it.

My left knee would tell you I'm not always one for following my athletic trainer's orders but eventually injury catches up to you if you don't take care of yourself.

My stomach growls at the sight of that seafood pot pie. But I ignore the bottomless pit that is my stomach, pulling my attention from the delicious food back to Summer and her arms full of plates. She makes her way through the sea of tables, sidestepping to let a patron pass. A tight smile on her face, I can see her fingers gripping the plate tighter and the wince that follows.

I catch up with her just before she reaches the door to the patio.

"Summer," I call, "what are you doing?" Realizing as the question leaves my mouth that it's not the most intelligent. It's obvious what she's doing.

Her eyes narrow. "I'm working."

"Yeah, but you shouldn't be." I grab the two plates weighing down her injured wrist.

"What the hell?" she hisses, reaching for the plates. "Give me back the plates. I need to serve this table."

"So, lead the way." I motion with the plates in my hands for her to lead me to the table, but she doesn't move.

Her eyes flare with annoyance. I can see that she doesn't like my approach, but I can't sit back and watch her work in pain.

"Rory. Give me the plates."

"Nope. Winnie said rest and ice."

"And I can't afford to not work."

I glance around, beneath the glow of the hanging patio lights, the tables are filled with hungry patrons waiting for their food. The line out the door will keep Summer and the rest of the staff busy for hours. I can only imagine how her wrist will feel after a long shift of hauling these heavy plates. It won't be good. She needs to rest it so she can get better.

"I'll help you then."

Emotion flickers behind Summer's eyes but she pulls her gaze away and shakes her head.

"I don't need your help. Now, give me back those plates. The food is getting cold."

I step back, to keep them out of her reach.

"Then we should get going." Again, I motion for her to lead the way.

"Rory, seriously. People are staring."

She's right. Our little tiff in the middle of the dining room is drawing attention from the tables around us. But I'm used to being interviewed on national television dripping wet and only wearing a jammer so their stares don't bother me.

"So?"

"So, I don't need you making a scene. This is where I work. I don't need my boss thinking I can't do my job."

She's so pretty when she's annoyed with me. I'm beginning to realize she's gorgeous all the time but especially when those blue eyes flare with annoyance and her upper lip curls with exasperation.

Beneath the zipper of my chino shorts, my cock stirs. Is that a kink? I never realized a woman being thoroughly annoyed with me could be a turn on.

My ex, Daphne, had a tendency to be annoyed with me, but with Summer, it's different. It's playful.

Summer sighs, giving up the fight for the plates for a moment to massage her hurt wrist through the brace.

"When's the last time you took an ibuprofen?" I ask.

"I haven't taken anything since the trainer's office. Now can I—"

"Rory Shields, is that you?" I turn around to find Alice, one of the owners of The Salty Pirate Café, headed our way. "It is you. I heard you were back in town for training."

She wraps her thick arms around my waist and gives me a squeeze.

"Hey, Alice. It's good to see you." I throw her a friendly smile before awkwardly attempting to hug her back without dropping the plates I'm still holding. "Got back yesterday."

"And you're just now stopping by?" She pouts.

"I had to unpack and practice has kept me busy."

She waves me off. "I'm just kidding. But it's great to see you." She glances at the plates in my hands, then to Summer who's still holding her wrist.

"What happened to your wrist?" Alice asks, concern passing over her features.

"Skateboarding accident," Summer says.

Alice shakes her head in dismay. "How many times have I said that thing makes me nervous for you?"

Summer shoots me a glare. "Yeah, it is dangerous. People should really know what they're doing before they jump on one all willy nilly."

"Willy nilly?" I chuckle, delighting in the sound of the nonsensical phrase.

"You heard me."

Alice ignores our back and forth in favor of examining Summer's wrist.

"Oh, goodness. Well, are you able to finish your shift? If you need to rest, surely, we can cover you."

Even with Alice's offer to cover Summer's shift, I know that's not what Summer wants. She won't get paid if she goes home. After the mermaid cosplay debacle and now her insistence to work, it's obvious she needs the money.

"No. I'm fi—" Summer starts, but I quickly cut in.

"That's why I'm here. To help. If you and Summer will allow me."

I glance toward the patio where multiple people have their phones up, taking pictures, possibly even recording this moment. Alice follows my gaze.

"And how do you two know each other?" Alice asks, curiosity spilling over her features.

"We don't," Summer is quick to announce.

"Not exactly true." I give Summer my best charming smile. "We met the other night. And again, today."

Alice's eyes widen. "O-oh, I see," she stammers, her cheeks blushing a deep crimson.

Summer's eyes bulge like she's hoping her pupils will reach out and strangle me.

Did that sound like I was implying Summer and I hooked up?

"She was cosplaying as a mermaid at a children's birthday party. I helped her out of her mermaid tail."

I don't think that's any better. Oops.

"Uh-huh." Alice's conspiratorial smile makes me think she doesn't believe me. "Serving and busing only, Summer will still need to take orders."

Then, she walks off, fanning herself with an order pad.

I turn to Summer again to apologize, but she's already walking away, so I follow in her wake.

He's so hot.

Dude's stacked. I wonder how many calories he eats in a day.

I bet his swimmers are good swimmers, if you know what I mean.

Does he work here now?

Some not so quietly.

"Rory Shields, will you marry me?!" is shouted from a table of women in the corner enjoying what appears to be a ladies' dinner.

"You're already engaged," her friend announces loudly.

"I know but he's one of my hall passes. Warren wouldn't mind."

I offer a practiced smile as I pass. Being "on" in public is second nature. My parents drilled that into me early.

Smile. Be charming. Be perfect. But tonight, I don't want perfect. I just want to help Summer.

"I apologize for the wait," Summer says when she reaches the table whose food I've been holding hostage.

The table of three is a woman in her mid-forties and her two teenage sons. "I think this special delivery is worth the wait."

Summer directs the dishes in my hands to each person, then picks up the water carafe to fill up their water glasses. I'll have to add refilling water glasses to my list of duties.

"Can I get you anything else right now?" Summer asks.

"Do you mind terribly if we get a picture with you?" The woman directs her question to me, beaming flirtatiously, while her sons attempt to hide behind their phones.

"Not at all."

The woman hands Summer her phone, while I get into position in the middle of the group. Right when Summer snaps the photo, the woman drops her hand and squeezes my ass.

Summer hands the phone back and abruptly leaves the table.

"Enjoy your food. We'll check back soon," I offer before departing to follow Summer through the dining area, and through the kitchen doors.

"Who the hell—" the man behind the cook station starts to bellow, but he stops midsentence. "Rory." He claps me on the back. "What are you doing in my kitchen?"

"Hey, Mick. I'm helping Summer out."

"Just for today," Summer quickly chimes in. "And he's only carrying plates." She holds up her wrist.

"Did you fall off that skateboard?" Mick asks. "I keep telling her it's a dangerous form of transportation."

Summer holds my gaze, her brows lifting in question. *You going to tell him, or am I?*

But behind us a pink-haired waitress clears her throat,

shifting the group's attention, allowing me to dodge that question.

Summer turns in her direction. "Oh, yeah. Rory, this is Darcy. Darcy, Rory."

"I heard you saved our girl from a shark."

Summer groans. "There was no shark. How does this story keep getting twisted?"

"Because it sounds cooler with a shark." Darcy's pink ponytail swishes as she tilts her head to inspect me. "Nice to finally put a face to the name, Rory Shields."

"Has she been talking about me?" I wink in Summer's direction, catching a glimpse of the outrage on her face before returning to my conversation with Darcy.

"Nonstop. Can't get a word in."

"Order up!" Mick calls.

Darcy grabs the plates from the counter. "Gotta run."

When my eyes land back on Summer, she's glaring at me.

"I can't believe you showed up here."

"How else was I supposed to contact you? I don't have your phone number or address. Winnie wouldn't give it to me. You know, HIPAA laws and all that."

"Did you ever think there's a reason you don't have that information?"

"Because you didn't have a chance to give it to me?" I offer half-jokingly, knowing it's not the case when the woman wouldn't even tell me her name.

"You could carry plates tonight, but I know a thing or two about injuries and if you don't take care to rest them, they get worse or flare up when you don't have help. So, if you let me help you tonight, I won't bother you about it again."

She contemplates this for a moment, before relenting. "Fine."

Over the next few hours, Summer lets me be her shadow around the restaurant. Carrying plates, busing tables, and often, talking with the patrons.

"You're too nice to people." She comments.

"Says the woman whose job relies on customer service skills."

She sticks out her tongue at me.

"Next time someone takes too long to order, be sure to do that," I tease.

Later, when the restaurant is near closing time, I take a few minutes to talk with a group who is vacationing for a family reunion before busing their table.

"What was all that?" Summer points back in the direction of the patio where I just finished signing autographs and taking a few photos.

"What? I was helping you out. Giving the people what they wanted."

"This is a restaurant. Not a meet and greet with Rory Shields."

I shrug. "I thought it would help with tips. I've been charming all night. Not to mention the number of times women have stroked my arms and patted my chest. One even grabbed my ass. Please tell me those tips reflect the ass grabbing."

"Rory, seriously? Why didn't you say something? Nobody should be grabbing your ass."

"It's part of the gig."

A line forms between her brows. "Of being a waiter?"

"A public figure."

"That doesn't mean people are allowed to touch you inappropriately."

I like the way her nose twitches and her jaw pops. Like she's upset on my behalf. I've never seen anything like it. Daphne was always game for however my popularity could benefit her. She would have encouraged groping if it meant she made connections with the right people.

I drop into the seat beside her. "So how were tips tonight?"

"Good," she confirms, producing a large quantity of bills from her apron pocket.

"Good? Or great?" I wiggle my brows in jest as she counts the cash.

She shakes her head at my teasing, but once she's done, a small, satisfied smile pulls at her lips.

"Fine. You're right. Your charm and willingness to please every customer paid off."

"I knew it would."

"Here." She extends a wad of bills out to me.

"No." I wave her off. "That's all yours."

"You just worked six hours. It can't be for nothing."

Six hours? Being in Summer's orbit, the time had flown by.

"It wasn't for nothing, Wildflower. I did it for you."

Our gazes lock. For a moment, there's a flicker of vulnerability behind Summer's eyes, but as quickly as it appeared, it's gone.

"Because of my wrist."

Technically, she's right. But in this moment, I'm realizing her hurt wrist was my excuse to help her, not my only reason.

There's something about Summer that has me intrigued, wanting to know more. I've spent my life around many different types of people and have gotten pretty good at reading them. There's a difference between someone who genuinely wants distance and someone who is putting up walls to protect themselves. So, while Summer seems prickly and guarded, in our few interactions, I've seen glimpses of another side of her.

Like her interactions with customers. Though she's not bubbly or overly friendly, she does care about doing her job well. She appears casual, but holds herself with a certain elegance that is captivating.

I could walk out of this restaurant right now and she'd probably breathe a sigh of relief. With her asthma, that would be for the best.

Maybe I should leave her alone, but I *can't*.

That's the oddest part of this.

So, my body stays rooted here for reasons my brain doesn't yet know why.

Suddenly, I get an idea.

"Here." I pull my wallet out to hand her five one-hundred-dollar bills. "This is from Rich Lancaster. He forgot to give it to you the other day after all the commotion at the party."

She stares at the money extended out to her.

"That's not from Rich."

"Yeah, it is," I say confidently, even though the look she's giving me tells me she's already sniffed out my ploy.

She eyes the money, then me. "The job was going to pay three hundred dollars, not five hundred."

"Because of what happened, he wanted to give you a generous tip."

"That's interesting. Rich already sent me payment this morning and it was two hundred dollars. He said he couldn't pay me for the full time because I left early." Her lips quirk to the side. "Nice try."

Damn it.

Short of secretly putting the cash into her apron pocket when she's not looking, I have no recourse but to tuck it back in my wallet.

Summer shoves her tip money into her apron and stands. "You want to grab some food?"

I stand to join her. "Are you asking me out on a date?"

"No, I'm asking if you want to get food from the kitchen and eat it here at the same table as me. It's not a date."

She doesn't wait for me to answer, but starts walking back toward the kitchen, so I follow, because fuck yeah, I want to eat. I'm always hungry, but more than that, I want to keep hanging out with her. I'm drawn to her in a way I've never experienced. But then I remember her comments from earlier on the beach.

"Do you think your boyfriend would mind?" I ask.

"My who—" her brows draw down in confusion before suddenly lifting, "oh, Edgar. That's right."

"Yeah, Edgar." I stretch my neck from side to side like I'm warming up for a fight. "Is he a big guy?"

She shakes her head. "Edgar isn't the jealous type."

"Hmm. I'd be jealous if you were my girlfriend and eating dinner with another guy."

"Well, good thing I'm not." She motions to the kitchen again. "You want dinner or not?"

"Only if I can drive you home after."

"How is that a condition for dinner? I'm offering dinner, you can't pile on another request."

"Can't I?"

She shakes her head. "No. It's...demanding."

"I'd call it persistent."

"Call it what you want, it's still annoying."

"You don't look annoyed."

"Maybe I'm too tired to look annoyed. It's been a long day and I'm hungry and drained. Edgar would understand."

"It's a good thing you're dating Edgar and not me."

I fucking hate Edgar.

"Yeah, it is."

She hands me a plate that Mick has dished up. It's a sampler platter of all the café's best dishes.

When I hold it under my nose, my mouth salivates. "Mick, this looks phenomenal. Thank you."

"I know how much you guys can eat, so there's more where that came from."

Summer and I sit at a table across from one another. Besides the fish and hushpuppies, her plate is loaded with pickles.

"I see you like pickles," I comment on the three dill spears next to her hushpuppies.

"Summer loves pickles," Darcy offers, setting her plate down and sliding in next to Summer in the booth.

"What else does Summer love?" I ask.

"Dogs, the beach, art," Darcy grins, "oh, and Edgar."

"Yes, I've heard about Edgar." A tight smile forms on my lips. "He's a lucky guy."

Fuck Edgar.

nine

. . .

"Did you get enough to eat?" Rory asks, turning to glance at me from the driver's seat.

I allowed Rory to drive me home after he agreed he wouldn't show up at the café for my shift tomorrow. After some ibuprofen and a plate-free evening, my wrist feels rested, so I'm determined to work my shift tomorrow without any assistance. Without Rory Shields' charming smile and annoyingly attractive face popping up at every turn.

His question makes me smile. He polished off two helpings of the sampler platter and all the shared crab cakes. Mick even brought over another plate of food after. I'd been full, but Rory managed to put that away as well.

"You've asked me that three times already."

He shrugs, his expression turning thoughtful. "When you have an injury, you need to make sure you're eating well. To help your body heal."

"I'm good. All I need now is sleep."

I can't wait to crawl into bed. The wad of cash from my tips tonight is a bulge in my pocket. For all my complaining about Rory's help, he came through with his charisma and personality which boosted my earnings.

I'm conflicted. Rory's charming, sweet, and obnoxiously good looking, as well as a talented swimmer. No person should have that much going for them.

When he showed up at the café earlier, I'd been annoyed at his insistence to help me. As we worked, we slipped into easy conversation one moment, then playful banter the next. As the evening wore on, like a slow drip from a crack in a wall, I'd felt a trickle of relief. A temporary ease from the loneliness, and respite from the burden of being completely on my own.

I never ask people for help, and I've found that being distant and guarded has kept others away. But what has easily sent people running in the past, doesn't seem to work with Rory. He lets my sarcasm and irritability roll right off, then comes back for more. It's like he's got impermeable skin. Maybe that's why he's such a gifted swimmer.

And that is all the more reason to squash this budding friendship or whatever it is.

Besides, while he felt obligated to help me because of my wrist, there's no reason for us to hang out after tonight. He's got training and a million other professional athlete things to do.

So, after tonight, Rory and I will be going our separate ways.

The thought leaves me with a flicker of disappointment. For all the teasing and at times snarky banter between us, I'm not sure why the thought of not seeing him again bothers me. It shouldn't.

Before I realize it, we're pulling into the RV park.

"This is me." I point as we approach my camper van.

I expect him to simply drop me off, but he pulls parallel to my van and cuts the engine before rushing to the passenger side to offer me a hand. I pretend not to see it as I gather my things and hop to the ground. He shuts the door behind me and follows me toward my van.

This morning, my van had been nestled between two RVs but now there are empty campsites next to me. That's the beauty of a campsite, the people are always coming and going, some are nosier than others, but no one ever gets too attached. I like the anonymity of it.

With a long day behind me, the sight of my cozy camper van gives me comfort.

After I graduated college, I'd sold anything of value to purchase the camper and renovate it. I'd traded a closet of designer clothes, shoes, and handbags for the used van and spent several months remodeling it to fit my needs.

To me, it represents independence and the freedom to choose my own path, wherever it takes me.

"Okay, well...bye." I give a quick wave, ready to end this.

But Rory doesn't retreat.

"The color is perfect." He pats the side of the van, checking out the detailing even though it's hard to see in the dark. "It's very you."

"How is it me?" I scoff, because it's not like this guy knows anything about me. He knows I like pickles and dogs.

"It's the same color as your eyes."

I study the front of my van, wondering if he's right.

"Azure. Light and vivid, like air."

If that's a line, he's pulling it off with the sincerity of a Boy Scout. He holds my gaze and a rush of giddy anticipation swirls low in my belly, but I shut it down quickly. Nope.

No attachments. That's been my rule in every town. Coral Cove has captured my heart more than any other place I've been, but that doesn't change my desire to stay free from any entanglements.

I need to tell Rory to leave. No, not just leave, but leave me alone.

I'm turning to deliver my speech when I notice the side sliding door to my van is ajar.

"What the—" I step forward, tentatively reaching for the handle.

Rory is right behind me. "Hold on. Did you leave the door open?"

"No," I whisper. "I mean, it gets stuck sometimes and the deadbolt is rusted and won't lock into place. I think the salt water corroded it. I was in a rush this morning and forgot to double check it."

"Someone might still be in there." He puts a protective hand out, then steps in front of me.

Edgar.

I rush past him because nothing could be more terrifying than not knowing if Edgar is okay.

"Edgar!" I call into the dark van.

My stomach sinks with dread, wondering what we'll find. I pull the door the rest of the way open and my heart pinches. The small space, which I normally keep tidy, is a mess now.

Looking around, I strain to see any movement. Any sign that life is in here.

"Edgar's gone," I pant. My chest constricts, the severity of the situation threatening to kick off another attack.

Stay calm, Summer. Slow your breathing.

"Your boyfriend?" Rory asks behind me as I push past him.

"What?" I blink, then remember my lie about Edgar.

It doesn't matter now.

"Edgar!" I call as I make my way to the front of the van. "Ed—" I start again, but hear a rustling sound at my feet.

I drop to the ground. There, tucked under one of the van's back tires is Edgar. He peeks his head out, so I bend down and show him my hand. Relief rushes through me at the sight of his dark nose and big eyes shining in the moonlight. Slowly, he inches his way out toward me, and I scoop him up.

"This is Edgar?" Rory asks, a slow smile spreading across his face.

"Yeah." I cradle the flustered dog to my chest.

"You're dating a geriatric pug?" He smirks, knowing full well he's caught me in a lie. Rory extends his hand to dip his fingers under Edgar's chin.

At Rory's touch, Edgar melts in my arms. I'm certain it's because he finally realizes he's safe from whatever transpired here earlier. I hate that I put him in harm's way by not having my van properly secured. A security that I can't afford. Not with the bills that have been piling up.

The thought makes me nauseous.

Rory's face softens. "I'm happy your little guy is safe."

"Thanks."

With Edgar in my arms, I step inside the van to take further stock of the situation. Most of my books, which I keep on a built-in shelf above the dining nook, are knocked on the floor.

"I know this isn't how it usually looks, but this place is incredible." I turn to find Rory's large frame stretched to the top of the van, his wavy, sandy-blond hair brushing against the ceiling as he looks around my home with curious eyes.

Fortunately, I don't own much of value. It's a tight space,

so besides valuables like my laptop and phone which I bring with me to work, there isn't room for a lot of possessions. The things I do own—books, plants, art supplies and clothing—have been rummaged through but I'm not certain anything was taken.

That doesn't prevent me from feeling violated and vulnerable.

It might be a vehicle, but it's my *home*. Everything I care about is inside.

I remind myself to focus on my breathing. I can't afford to get worked up.

"Summer, you okay?"

"I'm fine."

To keep the tears at bay, I busy myself with tidying up the space. Setting the pillows back on the bed, tucking the books into the shelves above.

Besides items strewn about, at first glance, it doesn't appear they took anything. But then I see it. The bin I keep my painting supplies. The set of oil paints that Scarlett had sent me for my birthday aren't there. They'd looked so pretty and perfect in their case. And I'd been saving them, wanting to wait for the perfect occasion to use them.

And now they're gone.

"Is anything missing?" Rory asks.

I swallow; my throat tight with emotion as I squeeze Edgar. My lower lashes doing everything in their power to hold back the flood gates as it all comes crashing in. My wrist. Overdue bills. Medication I can't afford. And now this break-in. All I want to do is get Rory away from me so he won't see me lose it.

"No."

"Probably some kids messing around, but we should still report it to the police."

"No, it's fine."

Rory pulls out his phone and starts taking photos of the disarray.

"What are you doing?" I ask.

"Taking photos for evidence. For the police report."

"No, don't do that. I just want to put everything back." His photo taking suddenly feels more violating than the break-in.

He doesn't stop, though. I know he's only trying to help, but the more he documents this moment, turning my cluttered belongings into evidence, the more it sinks in that someone I don't know was in my space and the more anxious I become.

My hand wraps around his forearm. "Rory. Please. Stop."

Slowly, he drops his phone into his pocket, then holds his hands up.

"Okay. Sorry. I thought I was helping."

"Well, you're not." I clear my throat. "It's been a long day, you should go."

His warm eyes attempt to catch mine, but I can't look him in the eye or I'll break. "Summer, I'm not going anywhere. Your van was broken into. We don't know who did it or why and your door is still broken."

I bite my lip. I know he's right, but that doesn't stop me from hating the situation.

"Summer, please. What can I do to help?"

"You want to help?" I ask.

"Yes. I'll do anything you need me to."

"Go home."

He bites the inside of his cheek.

"Summer—"

"I'm tired. Please go." My tone is clipped, that's all I can manage at this point.

"I hate the thought of you staying here alone."

"I'll be fine. I have Edgar."

With a soft smile on his face, Rory scratches Edgar underneath his chin. "Nothing personal, buddy, but you're not exactly a guard dog."

I ignore his comment but I know Edgar won't scare anyone away. He already failed once.

"You could park your van in my garage for the night? I've got plenty of room."

I give him a withering look. Something about this man tells me he gets everything he wants. Gold medals. World records. And any woman in his bed.

He must read my mind with that last one.

"You and Edgar can have my bed. I'll sleep on the couch."

"We'll pass," I say, at the same moment Edgar whines in my arms.

Rory motions toward the door. "I can call a locksmith first thing in the morning."

"You don't have to. It's not your problem."

"It's not a problem. I know a guy—"

My sardonic laugh cuts him off. "Of course you do. You know everyone."

Rory Shields has a ton of friends, connections, and fans. He's got roots in Coral Cove which is just another reason to keep him at arm's length.

"It's really no trouble. I can make a quick call."

"Rory," I steel my voice before I continue, "I don't need your help. Please *go*."

I motion to the door before turning and setting Edgar down on his bed. Then I move toward the sink, putting my back to Rory to wash my hands.

"Sum—" he starts but I cut him off.

"Good night." I emphasize the two words to give them the finality I desperately need.

After what feels like a lifetime of his eyes burning into my back, he finally relents. "Okay. Goodnight."

Behind me the door opens, and a second later, it closes with a thud behind him.

I let out a caged breath, then tell myself to hold it together long enough to change into pajamas and brush my teeth. Knowing once I'm settled into my bed, I can let go.

I'm patting my face dry on a towel when there's a loud thump outside the van. The sound has me jumping a mile and banging my head on the cabinet above the sink. Edgar stirs in his bed but promptly lays his head back down.

Rory was right, Edgar is not a guard dog and after the night he's had, has no trouble sleeping through what could be a second break-in.

Anger is white hot in my veins. Not only from the bump forming on my head, but because I hate feeling vulnerable. And if the person who rummaged through my van earlier has dared to come back, they're going to be sorry.

With one hand rubbing the throbbing lump on my head, I reach into my closet for the single golf club I acquired from a golf course's clearance sale a few years ago. With the club raised above my head in preparation for swinging, I yank the door open.

But there's no intruder.

There, lying on the ground outside my van, is Rory.

I drop the club to my side.

"What the hell, Rory?"

He winces at my scowling face.

"Sorry. I was getting comfortable and I bumped my shoulder into the door."

"Why are you lying on the ground?"

He sits up, arms casually draped over his knees like him being here is the most natural thing in the world. "I'm sleeping here."

"What?" I can't believe what he's saying. "No, you're not. I said I'm fine."

"I know you did," he swallows, his comforting eyes drop to the golf club in my hand before meeting mine again, "but I won't be okay if I know you're sleeping here alone in a van that doesn't lock."

I press my lips together, slowly shaking my head.

"You need to go home, Rory."

He shakes his head. "I'm not going home, Summer."

My jaw tightens at his refusal.

Who does this guy think he is? Hasn't he done enough today? It's like he thinks his job is to make everything right with the world. I don't need him to fix anything for me. I know how to look after myself. I've been doing it for years.

I could call the camp site manager to have him removed but then that will bring up the issue of why he's here and I don't want to deal with the break-in right now. And, technically, he's not doing anything wrong unless you count being irritatingly concerned for my wellbeing a violation.

"Whatever." I slam the door on Rory's handsome face, then toss the golf club onto the dining nook bench.

Beneath the bench, Edgar jolts awake. He'd fallen asleep in the few minutes since I'd been in the bathroom. Must be nice.

"If he wants to sleep on the hard ground, let him," I tell Edgar. "I told him to go home so it's his fault that he's being stubborn." I rage chug a glass of water, then climb up into my loft bed.

I lie there waiting for my heart rate to slow and my

breathing to even out. Between the break-in and Rory refusing to leave, my body has been through a rollercoaster of emotion in the last half hour that is making it impossible to relax.

A few minutes of tossing and turning, and I can't stop thinking about Rory lying outside on the ground. I'm torn between annoyance that he's not listening to my wishes and gratitude for him not leaving. It's a tricky place to be. I don't know this man at all, yet there's something so utterly comforting about him. It's infuriating.

Finally, I throw back the covers and wielding the golf club again, I yank open the sliding door.

Rory is still on the ground, exactly where I left him.

"Fine. You can sleep on the floor in here," I announce.

Without a word, Rory dusts off the debris that's accumulated in his hair at the back of his head, then rises to his feet to follow me inside. For the second time tonight, I climb into my loft bed, but this time I toss Rory down a pillow and a blanket.

From my perch, I watch as he folds the blanket in half as a makeshift mattress, then fluffs the pillow once, twice, three times before he tucks it under his head.

A few minutes later, I'm settled back into bed, but sleep is nowhere near.

"Summer?" Rory calls out, interrupting the quiet between us.

"What?"

"I'm sorry today was rough."

I swallow thickly, Rory's words bringing up the emotion I'd been working hard to suppress.

"I'm here if you need me."

I suck in a silent, shuddering breath.

The tears I've been holding back are too heavy to keep at

bay any longer, so I bury my face into my pillow and let everything out.

"Hey." Rory's soothing voice floats over my side. He's standing at the side of the loft. "You can tell me to fuck off, but I can't lie down there and listen to you cry."

"Because it's too loud and you can't sleep?" I sniffle.

"No. Because it's breaking my heart."

"Oh." I bite my lip to stifle the emotion that his words bring.

"What do you need, Summer?"

It's a moment of weakness, which for the last four years I've been determined never to show.

What do I need?

A new lock on my van.

Health insurance.

Money to pay for my medication.

Safety and security.

But all those things come with a price. And if there's one thing I learned from my family, letting someone take care of you is a debt that you end up paying with your soul.

I can't need Rory for anything that will cost me my independence.

"A friend," I whisper.

"Okay," he replies, settling in beside me.

With Rory lying beside me, rubbing gentle circles against my back, I let all the stress and worry and disappointment flow from my eyes until there's nothing left. We don't speak again. The sound of his rhythmic breathing and his warm palm on my back finally lulls me to sleep.

ten

. . .

SUMMER

A noise outside startles me awake.

After years of living in my van, I'm careful to sit up slowly so I don't bang my head on the ceiling.

I slept so hard it takes me a moment for my brain to catch up. Then it all comes crashing back. The break in. Edgar missing. Rory was here.

Rory.

The space next to me is empty, but I know he was here. His scent still lingers on the pillow. I roll onto it, eyes fluttering closed as I breathe him in.

A man has never seen the inside of this van, let alone slept in it.

Last night, Rory saw a lot he wasn't supposed to. Like me crying, for example. A snotty, emotional mess. That is reason enough to keep my distance.

I mentally comb through my long to-do list.

Walk the dogs, take Edgar to his vet appointment, work

at the café...and figure out what to do about my van's broken lock. Also, it might be worth walking the area to look for my missing paints in case the intruders had dumped them somewhere.

Clank.

There's that sound again.

Tossing Rory's pillow aside, I climb down from the loft and throw on a sweatshirt before I look out the window to see a man sitting in a metal camping chair facing my van. There's no vehicle or sign of Rory, but it doesn't matter, I can handle this myself.

I glance around the van for Edgar but he's nowhere to be found. *Again.*

How does one tiny pug cause so much chaos?

"What are you doing?" I call.

The man shoots out of the chair, the sudden movement causing the creaky metal to fold in on itself and collapse, falling to the ground.

"Hi there, Miss. I'm Walter."

"Walter who?"

"Walter Mathis. I'm here to fix the lock on your van."

"Rory called you?" I ask, already knowing the answer.

"Yes, but he told me to let you sleep. Not to start working until you were up. And to keep watch in the meantime."

I sigh. Of course, Rory didn't leave me here sleeping without protection. He'd been adamant to not leave me last night and now, even in the light of day, he hired the locksmith to be my bodyguard. I want to be annoyed but that seems to be the issue I'm having with Rory...he's impossible to be mad at.

And I liked having him here last night. But I'm also aware I can't let it happen again.

Things are getting too comfortable, too fast.

Like how good it felt falling asleep in his arms.

It must be the lack of physical touch that's making me feel all sorts of strange things for this guy. A guy I barely know, yet feel completely at ease with.

The moment I see Rory pull up in his Jeep with Edgar in the passenger seat, I don't know whether to swoon or spit venom. Self-preservation has me choosing the latter.

"Where have you been?" I snap, marching over to the passenger seat to retrieve Edgar.

"Well, I had early morning dryland practice, then I came back here and you were still sleeping so I took Edgar with me to grab coffee."

"And you trusted this guy—"

"Walter's the name," Walter chimes in from where he's at my open van door, studying the lock.

"I had no idea where Edgar was. I woke up and thought he'd been kidnapped."

"Sorry about that. Based on how hard you were sleeping, I figured we'd be back before you woke up."

"You were out cold. I heard you snoring from out here." I turn to find Walter hiking up the waistband of his pants right before fastening his toolbelt around his midsection.

My jaw drops at Walter's accusation.

"What is he talking about? I don't snore."

I expect Rory to agree with me, but he just gives me a soothing look.

"Don't worry. It's nothing a nasal strip can't fix."

I don't want to be deeply offended by their casual conversation about my nighttime breathing habits, but part of me hates other people knowing such intimate details about me.

But I know a nasal strip won't fix the issue. It's more likely that I'm snoring because my airway is inflamed. If I were using the right dosage of medication, instead of rationing it, I'd be less likely to snore.

"I'm going to get started on the lock. Should only be about twenty minutes or so."

"Thanks, Walt. We'll be inside."

Rory lifts the coffees in his hands, motioning for us to step inside. I follow—for the coffee, I tell myself.

eleven

. . .

RORY

Inside the van, I hand Summer a coffee. It's a small space and Walter is working right behind us but as he hums along, I notice he's put ear buds in to listen to music.

I'd thought her van was incredible when I saw it last night, but seeing the space in the daylight intrigues me even more. In the small kitchen there are wooden countertops and white cabinets with antique glass knobs, along with a cast iron stove and a small refrigerator in a teal color that matches the exterior of the van.

A group of plants hang from macrame pots between the kitchen and living area. A plush, patterned rug runs along the length of the floor where the loft is located toward the front of the van. Wooden shelves are built above the sitting area for book storage, and of course the dining nook with Edgar's dog bed underneath.

Summer sets Edgar down in his bed and he immediately

props his chin on the corner of it, his big eyes shining up at us for a moment before his eyelids sink.

"Wasn't sure how you like it, so I left it black."

She studies it a moment before taking the cup and setting it on the wooden countertop.

"Thanks."

I watch as she reaches into the refrigerator, my eyes following the line of her long, bare legs extending from her tiny sleep shorts. Her blonde hair is tousled from sleep and her eyes are puffy from the crying she did last night. None of that changes the fact that she's the most beautiful woman I've ever laid eyes on.

Did I have a raging boner half the night?

Not while she was upset and crying, but later, in the middle of the night when her ass had nestled itself against my crotch and every nerve ending in my body sprang to life. I would have had to be dead for my body not to respond to the feel of Summer pressed up against me.

She pours some oat milk from the refrigerator into her coffee then reaches for a mug from the small cupboard above the sink and dumps the coffee mixture from the to-go cup into it.

She catches me staring and narrows her eyes. "What?"

"Not a fan of paper cups?" I ask.

She shrugs. "I like drinking from a real mug."

Summer's secretive nature makes catching a glimpse of something simple, like how she takes her coffee, feel like discovering buried treasure.

Even now when she's staring at me like I'm a problem to be dealt with, her attention on me ignites a ripple of heat that expands throughout my chest.

I remind myself that not only am I avoiding Daphne because I don't want to get back together with her, but I'm steering clear of any commitments outside of swimming. When I was younger, there was leeway for distractions without suffering the consequences, but injury and the miles on my body now require complete focus. Now, I need to be one hundred and fifty percent focused on my training program.

It's what I told myself when my watch alarm buzzed at four-thirty this morning interrupting a cramped, yet peaceful slumber. I'd done a few of my physical therapy stretches while I waited for Walter to arrive, then rushed home to grab my gear and was in the weight room by five-thirty.

It had been a leg day, which I used to love, but now I'm cautious about my knee. Even with a reduced weight program, my legs are killing me. I drop onto the bench that serves as a couch, picking up one of the pillows there to move it aside to make room for my sizable frame. That's when I notice it's in the shape of a pickle.

Beneath my fingers, it's pleasantly soft, so I give it a squeeze. Under my hands, the pillow's plush material shrinks down before expanding upon my release. "This is cute. I didn't realize the pickle thing extends to décor." I sniff the air. "Wait a minute. Does it smell—"

"Like a pickle? Yes." She takes it from my hands and sets it back in its place beside me on the cushioned bench. "My best friend, Scarlett, gave it to me."

It's the first piece of information that Summer has willingly offered about herself since I met her.

"And Scarlett is a childhood friend?" I prompt.

"We met in college our freshman year. Both reluctant legacy pledges for Delta Zeta at UT."

"Texas?" I inquire.

"Tennessee," she clarifies.

"You didn't want to be in a sorority?" I ask.

"Do I seem like someone who would fit into a sorority?"

I scan her from head to toe. With her bed head and clear-rimmed glasses, and those threadbare cotton sleep shorts exposing her long, tan legs, she's gorgeous and mysterious. Honestly, Summer doesn't seem like the sorority type, but only because she doesn't fit the mold people expect her to. She appears to be someone who refuses to be boxed in.

"Um—"

"Never mind. Don't answer that."

"So, you and Scarlett didn't pledge?"

"Oh, we pledged. It was that or break our mom's hearts. In my case, lose my spending stipend."

"Did you get in?"

She nods. "Yeah, unfortunately."

"I went to UC-Berkeley. No fraternity for me. Swimming was my life. Still is."

That's when I see the box of art supplies on the shelf above the window by her dining nook. It's tucked away, almost hidden, but the streaks of dried paint along the side make it more noticeable.

"Are you an artist?" I ask, reaching for the box to get a better look.

Not answering my question, Summer snatches the wooden box out of my hands and places it back on the shelf. "I think we're done with whatever this is."

"This is called getting to know each other."

"Really? Because it feels like you going through my stuff. Should I come to your house and rummage through your personal things?"

My lips twitch at her proposal. "I did extend the invitation last night."

"Hmm," she murmurs, as if she's not exactly sure how to respond.

While I'm an open book and wouldn't mind if she came to my house and looked through my stuff, Summer is not the same. She doesn't like talking about herself.

At that moment, Walter yanks the van door open, a shiny new set of keys dangling from his hand. "Miss Summer, you're all set."

Summer accepts the keys, and Walter packs up his tools then gives me a nod before he leaves. He'll send me the invoice later.

With Walter gone, Summer and I sit in silence for a moment. We both watch Edgar get up, take a drink from his bowl, then settle back in for another snooze.

"Thank you for calling the locksmith, and for everything last night."

"You're welcome."

Summer reaches in her purse and pulls a wad of cash out. Her tips from last night.

"How much was the lock?"

I shake my head. "I'm not taking your money."

"Rory, you have to."

"No," I stand, "I don't."

"Fine." She stuffs the money back in her wallet. "I'll call Walter and pay him directly."

I shake my head. "Not happening, Wildflower."

Her eyes flare, at my unwillingness to let her pay for the lock, or at the nickname, maybe both.

"You're so fucking stubborn."

She crosses her arms and juts out her chin, giving me the most cock-stirring look of defiance. The urge to push her up against the counter and explore that obstinate mouth of hers is strong.

I take a step closer.

"Look who's talking."

Her eyes narrow at me, but it's the way she sucks in a shuddering breath that tells me she's not used to anyone pushing back. To wanting to challenge her, break through this wall she's got up.

It also makes me wonder how often her asthma is triggered.

"How's your breathing been? Since the other day when you had the attack?"

"Good. Nothing to worry about. I'm fine."

Her response rolls off her tongue, her features never wavering.

My watch buzzes with a schedule notification. I don't have to check it to know what it says. My weekly schedule is engrained.

I've got a meeting with my nutritionist in twenty minutes, followed by race footage analysis, then practice, so I can't stand here and argue with her all day, no matter how much I want to.

"I have to go. I've got an appointment."

Her eyes fill with relief. She thinks she won. Goal achieved.

She has no idea how badly I want to prove her wrong right now.

But I can't, so I back up and reach for the door handle.

She scoops up Edgar and follows me out of the van.

"Fine. Pay for the lock. But let's not make this into something it isn't."

"Maybe Edgar wants to see me again."

"He just met you last night. He'll move on."

Summer holds Edgar tight to her chest, like she thinks I'm going to snatch him up.

"Oh, I forgot," I say, reaching for the bag sitting in the front seat of my Jeep. "I found these on the sidewalk down the street when I was walking Edgar this morning."

She peeks in the bag and gasps. "My paints."

"So, they are yours?"

She nods.

"You said nothing was missing."

"I guess I didn't notice."

"They looked brand new. Never used. I didn't even think they were yours until I saw your bin of painting supplies."

When I hand her the bag, her eyes light with exhilaration, then as she tends to do, she contains it, and casually takes the bag from me.

"Thank you."

"I'll see you later, Wildflower."

I hop in my Jeep and shut the door before she has time to argue with me.

twelve

. . .

SUMMER

Like he promised, Rory doesn't show up at the café for my evening shift.

It's a relief to know I'll be able to focus on my job without his smart quips or that charming smile.

There'll be no effort spent suppressing the smiles he somehow teases out of me. No reminders that he spent the night making sure I was safe, fixed my van lock, or found my stolen paints because I won't have to see him.

I replay the moment when he handed me the paints. How my heart had leapt at the discovery and how even though I'd told Rory nothing was missing, he'd somehow known.

But as the hours tick by, I become less annoyed with Rory and more annoyed at myself. I spend most of my shift regretting how I left things with him. Earlier, I was annoyed at him for not letting me pay for the new lock and for his insistence on getting to know each other.

Now I'm annoyed that I can't even be mad at him because he's too damn nice.

As Darcy and I exit the restaurant's back door with Kale on our heels, Darcy lets out a piercing squeal. My first thought is the raccoons are back trying to get into the trash bins, but then I look up to find Rory standing there in a pair of gray shorts and a blue Carolina Current t-shirt. He's got a backwards hat on and the large athletic watch he wears is peeking out from where his hands are tucked into his pockets.

The moment I see him, my heart lurches. The tiny weight in my chest lifts, traitorous and unwelcome. I shouldn't feel relieved. I shouldn't feel anything.

What is happening?

The giddy excitement at seeing him is followed by annoyance that he can elicit a rush of feeling from me. I love it and I hate it at the same time.

Darcy and Kale acknowledge Rory, then wave a quick goodbye before heading off in the opposite direction.

"Hey, Wildflower." He says it so casually, like we hadn't left things weird between us this morning.

"What are you doing here?" I ask.

"I came to walk you home."

"Rory—"

"I still don't have your phone number so I couldn't call you to see how your wrist is."

He nods to where the brace is still fastened around my wrist.

"It's better," I say, my hand tracing over the brace. "Less achy than yesterday."

"Good."

I'm confounded by his inability to feel the tension between us. The suffocating weight of whatever this thing is.

"Are we going to pretend like things weren't heated between us earlier?" I ask.

"Define heated." His smile is half smirk while his eyes do that thing where they comfort me while simultaneously make me question everything. "Come on, we can talk about it on the walk."

"I don't need you to walk me. I have my skateboard." I motion to my backpack where my pink board is peeking out the top.

"Winnie said no skateboarding until you're healed. You'd hurt yourself even worse if you fell now."

"I don't plan on falling. That was your fault, remember?"

His phone buzzes. When he pulls it out of his pocket to look, my eyes drop to the screen.

Whitney.

"Hey, Whit," he answers, but doesn't take his eyes off mine.

Not wanting to intrude on his conversation, I turn to start walking down the path, but a moment later Rory jogs to catch up.

"My sister, Whitney. She's in California. Just finished up school at UC-Berkeley. She's a swimmer, too."

I nod, refusing to give a second thought to the way my stomach eases with this information. I couldn't care less what Rory is doing in his personal life. A girlfriend would mean he wouldn't be here pestering me.

"Do you have any siblings?" he asks.

"No," I answer truthfully, but also with a firmness that I hope will shut down this conversation. "Listen—"

"I—"

We both start talking at the same time.

"You go." He nods for me to finish what I was saying.

"I'm sorry I snapped at you earlier, but you have to let

me pay for the lock." If I pay for the lock, then I'm free and clear. No debt owed, no favor hanging over my head. No more reason for Rory to be hanging around. Except, there is the small thing of him saving me in the ocean the other day.

He studies me a moment. "Only if I can get your phone number."

I scoff at his request. It's just like last night when he insisted he give me a ride home when I offered him dinner after we worked my shift. "I don't think you understand how this works. I want to pay you back; you can't take the payment *and* demand I give you my phone number."

"I didn't demand. I asked."

"And I said no."

For a moment, he looks at me like a fox sizing up a hen, then the corner of his lip curls up and a carefree smile breaks out across his face.

"Okay." He nods. "But has anyone ever told you, you catch more flies with honey than with vinegar?"

"Yes. Have you ever thought leaving honey out attracts flies and I don't want flies buzzing around?"

"Exactly. They get stuck. Then, they die a slow, sticky death."

"Thanks for the tip. And you're not walking me home. I'm walking home and you just happen to be here."

"Okay." He nods. "Whatever makes you happy."

"You know what would make me happy?" I ask, kicking a pebble on the sidewalk.

"Hmm?"

"If you went home and let me walk home by myself like a fully capable adult."

He chuckles. "Yeah, not happening."

I huff, stopping in my tracks. "You know what else would make me happy?"

Rory stops beside me and turns, his gaze steady. "What?"

"If you actually listened to me."

Rory steps closer. He's towering above me, his thighs nearly touching mine. "You know what would make me happy?"

I swallow, trying to not let his proximity affect me. "What?"

He leans in. "If you admitted that having me here doesn't bother you as much as you pretend it does." His voice is rough, with amusement and something else entirely.

That's when I feel the lump against my thigh. It's not as impressive as I'd imagined it would be. Not that I've imagined what Rory's hard cock would feel like, because I haven't. Obviously.

I take a step back and glance down at his shorts. "Is there something in your pocket?"

"Actually, yeah."

Rory laughs, then proceeds to pull a cellophane package out of his shorts pocket and starts to unwrap it.

I recognize it as a Little Sunshine Cakes choco swirl roll. I'd know those things anywhere.

"Do you want a bite?" he asks.

I stare at the log of chocolate cake and frosting he's offering me. "No."

We start walking again, and as he eats, he makes the most obscene noises. A deep, throaty moan with every bite. When we pass a couple on the street, I think about ducking behind a tree to avoid being seen with him.

"I would think choco swirl rolls wouldn't be in a swimmer's diet."

"It's Friday." He grins around another bite. "Cheat day."

"That's what you choose to eat for your cheat day?" I ask,

perplexed. "Out of all the possible choices you have to indulge?"

"Yeah, they're fucking awesome."

I stick out my tongue, making a disgusted face.

He devours the last bite. "Not a fan?"

If I wanted to get into it, I could tell Rory that my family owns Little Sunshine Cakes and the reason I can't stomach a choco swirl roll or a sweetie bun or a nutty bar or lemon tart cake is because I grew up eating them and now not only do I not like the way they taste but they remind me of my parents who were controlling and put their desires for wealth and status ahead of anything else.

I shake my head. "I ate too many of them when I was a kid."

Then, I look away because my stomach turns, not from the sugar, but from the memories.

"That's how I feel about bananas. Too many overripe bananas growing up. I can put them in protein shakes but alone their texture makes me gag."

Once his choco swirl roll is consumed, Rory fills the rest of the walk talking about his day, asking me about mine, and other nonsense.

"I have to make a stop along the way." I nod to the bag of food I'm carrying. "So, feel free to go home now."

"Who's that for?" Rory gives me a suspicious look.

"A friend."

He grins. "Aw, you shouldn't have."

"Not you."

"So, you're admitting we're friends?" He beams.

"No, it's not for you and we're not friends."

"That's not what you said last night," he calls behind me.

I ignore him and keep walking until I reach Cal's house which is on the corner next to the RV park.

When I arrive, I find Cal's waiting on the porch for me.

"Who's that?" He motions to Rory's shadowy figure standing on the sidewalk.

"Nobody."

Cal adjusts his glasses and squints. "That's Rory Shields."

"Hey, Rory." Cal waves his wrinkled hand. "Good to have you back."

"Traitor," I mutter.

"What's that?" Cal questions, moving his finger up to adjust his hearing aid.

"Nothing." I sigh. It's par for the course that Rory is known and loved by all. This is his town after all. I'm just temporarily living in it.

"Thanks, Cal." Rory waves back enthusiastically.

"Make sure Summer gets home safe."

"Will do," Rory says as I close the gate behind me.

All I can do is roll my eyes and keep walking.

"Cal's a great guy. It's nice of you to bring him food."

"It's on my way home, so it's not a big deal."

I hurriedly cross the street to the RV park entrance, but it's impossible to lose Rory. Those long legs of his make striding out easy.

"I'm sure it's a big deal to him," Rory points out.

"Do you have an incessant need to argue with every-thing I say?"

He presses his lips together, but can't hold back his grin. "No."

Rory's phone buzzes in his pocket again. When he pulls it out to look at the screen, he lets out a frustrated puff of air.

I tell myself not to look, but my eyes are disobedient.

Daphne.

"How many sisters do you have?" I ask.

"Daphne's not my sister, she's my ex."

My brows lift at how easily that information was offered up. When women's names showed up on Tripp's phone, he told me it was none of my business. I'd believed it for a while, too. Trusting him more than I trusted myself.

"An ex that's still calling?"

"Yeah, I ended it six months ago but now that I'm back in town, she's been calling me."

When I unlock my van, Edgar eagerly greets me at the door, but after a quick hello, he leaps into Rory's arms, licking his face and nuzzling into the crook of his neck.

"Hey, little guy. I missed you, too."

Watching them is like watching best friends reunite. It's sweet, but also annoying because Edgar is my dog, and he's known Rory for a day.

"Okay. Thanks for walking me home. Please don't do it again."

"You're welcome." He grins, giving Edgar a scratch behind his ear. "And I can't make that promise."

He doesn't leave, so I pretend not to notice and start unloading my backpack.

When I turn to find Edgar cradled in his arms, the two of them gazing lovingly into each other's eyes, I decide getting ready for bed will encourage him to hit the road. I grab my contact lens case next to the sink and take out my contacts. Luckily, I'd found an extra set tucked away in the bathroom yesterday which will last me another few weeks.

I reach for my glasses on the table beside him and slide them on, hoping maybe looking smarter will get him to take the hint.

"Have I told you I like your glasses?" he asks.

I turn to study Rory, whose body is now taking up the entirety of the bench in the dining nook of my van while he strokes Edgar's back and decide I need a new tactic. Maybe if Rory thinks I'm not opposed to him being here, then he'll leave. Reverse psychology and all that.

"Thanks." I reach above the sink for a mug to make hot tea. An evening routine since the warmth of the tea helps relax my airway. "I've needed corrective lenses since fourth grade. What about you?"

"Perfect vision."

"Yeah, that tracks."

"You're saying I'm perfect?" he teases.

"I didn't say that, but it's clearly what you heard."

I stretch and yawn, it might be exaggerated but it's necessary since Rory isn't taking the hint. "I'm exhausted. I would imagine you are, too."

"Yeah, I'm ready for bed." He sets Edgar down and a moment later the sweet pup is curled up in his bed, breathing noisily.

Rory stands, his tall, broad-shouldered frame filling up all the space that once was between us.

He starts to pull at the neck of his t-shirt.

"Whoa, whoa, whoa. What are you doing?" I stammer, my eyes immediately latching onto the sliver of smooth, bronzed skin that is exposed beneath his shirt hem.

"Getting comfortable. Last night I was warm with my t-shirt on."

My mouth gapes open in outrage. "My lock is fixed. There's no reason for you to stay."

"It's fixed, in theory. But the question is, has it been tested?" His brows raise in challenge.

"Tested?" I cross my arms over my chest. "No. I didn't ask anyone to try to break in while I was at work."

Rory does a sweep of the van. He looks in the bathroom, checks the front cab and doors, then glances up into the loft.

"Are you satisfied?" I ask.

"No. What if something else happens? Like, a tire blows or a tree falls on the van in the middle of the night?"

"A tree? Really? That's your concern?"

"Yeah, you can't predict nature. Or vandals. Or…rabid squirrels."

"Squirrels?" I laugh at the thought. "I'm not afraid of squirrels." My eyes narrow on Rory who is now refusing to look at me. "Are *you*?"

He scoffs but when our eyes meet, I can see the discomfort there.

"You mean the furry-tailed chaos machines that frolic like harmless critters one minute, then dive-bomb you from a tree the next?"

I press my lips together to stop myself from laughing. "Rory, have you been attacked by a squirrel before?"

"No, but there's always the potential."

"You are tall so maybe they get confused. Maybe they think you're another tree to jump onto."

"Very funny." He smirks and I'm wondering if this is all a setup. A reason for him to stay and play protector.

I blow on my hot tea before taking a sip. "I'm not usually funny, you must bring it out in me."

"I'll sleep on the floor and we'll pretend like I'm Edgar's bodyguard."

"You'll sleep in your own bed at home and we'll pretend this never happened."

We just resolved our earlier disagreement about me paying for the new lock, but somehow we've already found ourselves at another impasse.

"*Summer.*" His charming smile is replaced by a frustrated scowl.

"*Rory.*" I mock his frustration like a petulant teenager.

We're in a standoff between my tiny kitchen and dining nook.

"Just because the lock's fixed doesn't mean I'm okay with you sleeping here alone."

My hackles rise at his declaration.

"Guess what?" I fire back, stepping closer until my fuzzy slippers bump his feet. I'm ready to let him have it. "I—I—"

The words are lost on my tongue as the warmth of Rory's body floods my space. He's warm, but the skin of my arms prickle with goosebumps at our proximity. It's like I've stepped into some alternate space. A space where my powers to combat Rory's charm no longer work.

So now it's just me staring at Rory in his backwards hat. My eyes mesmerized by the way a few tufts of his thick, wavy hair peek out the front of it.

"You know what you bring out in me, Summer?"

"Frustration?" I guess, my eyes dropping to his lips.

He gives a quick shake of his head while his hands settle on the cabinet above.

"Protectiveness."

I feel that protection. The way his large, solid body covers me like a shield, keeping me safe. But it's nerve-racking, too. Something I'm not used to. Something unknown and intimidating.

"And what if I don't want to be protected?" I whisper because any other volume won't fit in the miniscule space between us.

Rory's lips are inches from mine.

Those firm, luscious lips that I've caught myself staring at more than I want to admit.

He drops a hand from its position above me, tucking a piece of hair behind my ear before his palm settles on my jaw. His eyes intently search mine.

"That's not an option." He dips his head and my legs wobble. It's taking every muscle fiber I have to not melt into a puddle right now.

Rory's lips are on a crash course with mine when Edgar barks—sharp, loud, and completely ruining it. We break apart instantly. Both our eyes are on Edgar as he stares toward the door, a low growling sound I've never heard coming from him before. It's like he's trying to play protector along with Rory.

"Do you think it's the rabid squirrels?" I tease, doing my best to recover from whatever just happened between us.

"Might be. I better stay the night, just in case." He winks. "You'd be devastated if they attacked me on my way home."

His cheeky smile has me all but convinced this thing with the squirrels is made up. I could call him on it and we could start another round, but I'm tired. And not ready to acknowledge whatever that moment was between us.

Rory creates his makeshift bed on the floor again, and I toss down his pillow. The one that smells like him from last night, the one I curled up with earlier today when I opened the back window of my van and sketched in my notebook.

This shouldn't feel normal.

I pull the sheet up over me and roll over.

But for the first time in a long time, I feel safe.

Protected.

thirteen

. . .

RORY

"You look like hell," Charlie announces right before he snaps me in the side, using his goggle strap as a sling shot.

"Jesus, Charlie." I flick him on the ear. I know he hates it so it's the only thing that I can do to get back at him.

We've just cleared the pool after practice and are headed to the locker room for showers.

"Late night?" Logan wiggles his eyebrows playfully.

It wasn't that late, but I spent another shitty night on the floor of Summer's van. I told myself it was for peace of mind. Either sleep in my bed worrying about her or stay close and know she's okay.

While Summer snored softly from the loft, I replayed the moment I almost kissed her.

Repeatedly.

It only added to my sleepless night.

I lean against my locker and take a deep breath. I could probably fall asleep right here, but then I'd miss my meeting with Vivi to create content for two of my sponsors, and the podcast appearance I have scheduled after that, then my appointment with Dr. Carpenter, the sports psychologist I've been working with after my injury.

"What's going on with you?" Eli asks, dropping on the bench next to me while the other guys hit the showers. "Is this about your parents?"

Eli's mention of them reminds me I haven't responded to my parents' request for dinner on Sunday night at the club. My mom didn't come out and say it but I know Daphne will be there.

My parents are hoping to get us back together. I don't know how to make it any clearer that I don't want to get back together with Daphne, and I need to focus on swimming. I don't have the emotional energy for any of it, so I've ignored it and hoped it would fade into the background, but it hasn't.

"I spent the night with Summer."

Eli's brows shoot up.

"On the floor of her camper van."

"Ouch." He chuckles quietly. "Nice to know the Rory Shields charm can be resisted."

"It's not like that with Summer."

"No?" he asks, surprised.

"I'm attracted to her." *Wildly attracted to her*, my brain corrects. "But there's more."

Eli shakes his head. "What happened to avoiding distractions?"

"That's the thing. I think I'm more distracted when she's not around. Like I need to know she's safe and everything is good with her so I can focus. And she's got the sweetest pug named Edgar."

"Edgar? As in Edgar Allen Pug?" Eli asks, cracking a

smile. "There's a pug that has his own social media account."

"Pretty sure it's just Edgar." I make a note to ask Summer when I see her later. Unlike yesterday morning, she didn't tell me to leave her alone. I think it's a sign we're becoming friends.

Eli nods. "So, what are you going to do about Summer? You can't spend every night on the floor of her van and expect your body to be in its best form."

"I know. I have to figure something else out."

A few minutes later, I let the shower's hot spray melt away the tension in my muscles.

I don't know what I want from Summer. With my training and travel schedule, I can't make a commitment, but I know I can't stay away.

Later when I knock on her van door, Summer opens it with resigned reluctance. She's not surprised to see me but she's also not as irritated as I thought she might be.

Maybe I'm growing on her.

Last night, I discovered that she loathes my favorite cheat day snack cakes, but I also discovered things that she does like so I picked them up at a local gift shop on my way over.

When she motions for me to enter, I hand her the reusable shopping bag.

"What's this?" she asks, peeking inside.

"Some herbal peach tea since I know you like tea before bed. A pack of fairy lights to give you some mood lighting but also to make it easier to see at night if you need to get up. And a mini first aid kit. Since you won't let me be your bodyguard, I'll at least be your medical supplier. Oh, and some gourmet pickles." I pull out the jar. "Marisella at the gift shop said these are the best."

"This is—"

"A peace offering," I interject before she tells me she can't accept it. "You've made it clear you don't want me intruding in your life, and if you want me to leave, I will."

I run a hand through my hair, exhaling, because I know what I'm about to say makes no sense.

"I know this sounds crazy, but ever since I met you, I can't stop wanting to be around you. Now that I know you exist, I can't just pretend you don't. I'm not trying to push you into anything, because I can't make any kind of commitment either. But I like being near you, and if you let me be here for you, I think you might like it, too."

Summer swallows hard and forces a smirk. "You sound ridiculous, you know that?" But her voice lacks its usual sharpness.

I offer her a grin. "Yeah. I know."

She turns to set the bag on the counter and pulls out the jar of pickles. A failed attempt to open it with her injured wrist has her holding the jar out to me.

"How's your wrist?" I ask, opening the jar easily before handing it back to her.

"Still sore, but getting better each day." She takes a pickle from the jar and bites into it, making a show of narrowing her eyes in scrutiny while she chews. Then, she swallows and a small smile pulls at her lips. "Okay, you can stay."

She makes two mugs of peach tea, then puts some

pickles on a plate and sets them on the small counter by the bench that serves as a desk and dining table.

"They'll be even better when they're cold."

"So why the pickle obsession?" I ask.

"The crunch. The sour tang of the brine." She eyes me. "What is it you love about Little Sunshine Cakes?"

"Where should I start?" I hold up the pickle she offered me and pretend it's a choco roll. "Perfect ratio of cake to filling. The chocolate's not too sweet, but still satisfies my sweet tooth. And it's a hit of nostalgia. They're something I enjoyed as a kid, and still holds up as an adult.

"They were a novelty that my parents would only buy if I did well at a swim meet." I laugh, recalling a memory. "I used to pick the chocolate coating off the sides and eat it first. It helped make them last longer."

Summer takes a long sip of her tea, while I bite into the spicy dill pickle.

"I preferred the old logo. The one with the smiling girl in pigtails." Summer's face is a hard blank. "You know what I'm talking about? Before they changed it to the sun a few years ago?"

"Yeah, I remember."

She doesn't respond, so I let it go.

We drink peach tea and eat spicy dill pickles. It's weird. The two things don't go together at all but Summer is enjoying herself and I'm just happy to be here.

When we're done with our snack, Summer clears the dishes and rinses them in the sink.

"You can't sleep on the floor again," she announces.

I sigh. "It's late. I don't want to fight about it. Just one more night. That will give me time to get the security cameras installed."

Her head swivels in my direction, her mouth gaping open in outrage. "You can't do that without telling me first."

"I am telling you. That's literally what this is."

"I'm already rethinking this whole thing," she says before disappearing into the tiny bathroom.

"It's too late, Wildflower," I call, standing to roll my tight shoulders back. "We consummated our friendship over tea and pickles. There's no turning back now."

While she's getting ready, I do some stretching. A few lunges in hopes that my muscles won't tighten too much while I'm sleeping on the hard floor again. Then, I brush my teeth at the sink with the travel toothbrush I tucked in my pocket earlier, before I start arranging the blankets on the floor.

Edgar is already in his bed, noisily snoring. I move my head close to his in hopes of understanding how such a tiny dog makes so much noise.

"I said you can't sleep on the floor," Summer says from behind me, where she just exited the bathroom.

"Where am I supposed to sleep?" I ask, looking around while also contemplating if lounging in the driver's seat would be more comfortable than the floor.

Summer crosses her arms and presses her lips together, her eyes looking up at the loft bed.

Oh.

"With *you*?" I ask to clarify.

"Never mind," she says, moving toward the ladder and climbing up. My surprised tone clearly has her rethinking the offer.

I scramble to pick up the blankets off the floor and follow her up the ladder, my back and shoulders relaxing at the sight of the comfortable sanctuary that is Summer's loft bed. I'd laid here for a while the first night, rubbing her back while she cried, but ultimately decided to give her space once she fell asleep. I know how comfortable the mattress is and don't want to deny my body the opportunity to get a good night's sleep.

"I want to. If you're okay with it?" I ask, hopeful.

"Fine," she says, pulling up the sheet to get settled.

Getting into the loft is the tricky part, I have to climb the ladder to get up but at the same time bend down so I don't hit my head.

Once I'm up, I carefully crawl into the space beside her.

After I'm situated, my entire body relaxes into the mattress. Sweet relief.

It's quiet between us. I'm thinking Summer has already fallen asleep, until she whispers, "This is weird."

"What's weird?" I ask, shifting my body so I can hear her better.

"Us. This. I've known you for like four days and now you're my bunk buddy?"

Those are her words, but she doesn't hesitate moving her pillow over to make more room for me. It's a snug space, but the comfort of the mattress, and my proximity to Summer, who smells fantastic, is all I need.

"Are these Egyptian cotton?" I ask, loving the feel of the soft cotton sheets on my skin.

"Threadbare."

"Is that a brand?" I tease.

"No."

Summer shifts and in the tight space, her hand brushes against my chest.

"Oh my god. Are you naked?!" she shrieks.

"I'm not naked. I just took my shirt off."

"That's naked."

"Not to me. I live most of my life shirtless." I stretch my

arms over my head before resting my hands over my chest. "I don't mind if you're shirtless."

I can practically hear her roll her eyes. "Nice try."

"What? There's no harm in a friendly, shirtless sleep-over. We are friends. You said so the other night."

"I said I needed a friend. Not that you were that person."

"Ouch." I rub my chest, over my heart where feelings for Summer are quickly taking up residence.

She shakes her head. "Trust me. I'm saving you from a lot of emotional baggage that being my friend would involve."

"Speaking of emotional baggage, shouldn't friends know more about each other?" I ask.

"We're not that type of friends. We're more like acquaintances."

I consider it for a moment. "How many types of friends are there?"

"Let's see. Friends you call in an emergency."

"I took you to the doctor," I point out.

"Because you injured me."

"Fair point. What other types?"

"Friends with benefits." She clears her throat. "We're definitely not that kind of friends."

"No? I think there are a ton of benefits to being my friend."

"You know what I'm talking about."

Yeah, I do. While I'm disappointed we're not friends with benefits, it's also cool because I don't think I could be Summer's friend with benefits. I'd want *more*.

The thought surprises me.

What more do I want? Or have time for?

Hadn't the end of my relationship with Daphne been because I needed space? I couldn't put the energy into the relationship that she needed. Couldn't take the next step she wanted; a proposal. But when I'm around Summer, she doesn't drain me. It's the exact opposite.

"Your ride-or-die friend," she continues.

"Scarlett," I say, reminding her she shared that bit of information. "She's your ride-or-die?"

"Yeah." She's quiet a moment. "What about you?"

"Eli's my best friend on the team. We've known each other for over a decade and are each other's biggest supporters. He's been keeping me sane and supported with my parents giving me so much pushback on my career decisions."

"Your parents aren't supporting your career?" Her tone reveals disbelief. "I would have thought they'd be super proud of you."

"They are, or they have been. But they've always been one step ahead, thinking about the future. They know my career will eventually come to an end, so they want me to start preparing for that moment. They want me to settle down."

"Settle down how? They want you to stop swimming?"

"They're pressuring me to get back with Daphne."

"Really?" Summer rolls toward me, tucking her hand under her pillow for support.

"They've been pushing me to give it another go with my ex because her dad and mine are in business together. For them, it would be nice and easy if we got married and kept the business in the family."

"Why'd you two break up?" she asks.

"I was injured and needed time to think about my next steps in my career. It wasn't fair to her to put her life on hold when I didn't know what I wanted. She wanted to get married, but I wasn't ready." I take a breath, and decide to be completely honest. "And I knew we weren't right together. That I was staying with her because of our parents' desires. I felt guilty about it for a while but I know I did the right thing by ending it with her."

"I can relate."

"You can?" I don't know anything about Summer's family or past experiences. She's a woman living out of a camper van who is determined to only rely on herself. So, it makes sense that there might have been something or someone in her life that made her feel like she needed to be on her own.

She nods, but doesn't elaborate. It's late and I don't want to push her. The fact that she let me stay the night is a huge step on its own.

If Summer can relate to my predicament, then maybe she'd be willing to help. In my head, a plan starts to take form.

"You know what would help me out?" I ask.

"No, but I'm sure you're going to tell me."

My lips twitch at her snarky tone, but I proceed anyway.

"If you came to my family dinner with me tomorrow night."

"As your human shield?" Her laugh is easy and light.

"As my date."

"To show your parents you've moved on?"

"Yeah, but also because I'm ninety-percent sure they've invited my ex to dinner."

"I could probably take this chick. Does she work out?"

"I don't need you to get into a fight, although that would be hot to see you fighting for me."

She waves her wrist. "You're right. I can't afford any more injuries."

"So will you come to dinner?" I prod.

She's quiet a moment, contemplating, and just when I think she might do it, she shakes her head. "Can't. I have to work."

"Sure. I get it."

My response comes quickly. I'm used to smiling my way through whatever expectations people throw at me. Easygoing and flexible.

If I don't hold my own against my parents, I'll end up married to Daphne out of guilt.

"Goodnight, Flipper," she says on a sigh. Under the dim glow of the fairy lights we hung earlier, I watch her eyelids softly close.

"Goodnight, Wildflower."

A stubborn weight settles in my chest, and I try to shake it loose.

I can't be mad that Summer said no. She doesn't owe me anything. I'm the one pushing for this friendship.

But just once, it would be nice if someone showed up for me.

fourteen

. . .

SUMMER

When Rory showed up last night, my instinct was to turn him away. I'd even rehearsed it in my head a dozen times, but when I'd seen him standing there, hopeful, and sincere, all my practiced words scattered. Because pushing Rory away is exhausting. He's got too much resolve.

So, I'm trying a new tactic: let Rory have his way so he thinks he doesn't have to try so hard. Maybe then this odd acquaintance of ours will quietly fizzle.

But damn those pickles he brought me were good. So good that I ate a couple with my breakfast burrito this morning.

Will you come to dinner with my parents?

In the moment, it had been an easy answer, so it's confusing to me while I've been stewing over it all day.

While I walked the dogs this morning.

As I painted alone on the beach with my paints from Scarlett that Rory had recovered after the break in.

Even when I helped Cal bring his fishing equipment to the bench where he sits on the boardwalk.

The situation with Rory's parents sounds eerily like the one I've experienced myself.

I recall the out-of-body experience of watching my parents and Tripp gathered around the dining table, talking about my life like I wasn't an active participant. My mom was practically planning our wedding. My dad all grins and hearty laughter as he and Tripp discussed Tripp's promotion in the company. My family's company. The one my grandfather started, but that had no place for me because Tripp was the man and he'd be taking care of me.

"Let Tripp take care of you. It's better that way. And then you can do your little paintings." My mom had smiled so unaffectedly, like what she was offering me was all I could ever hope and dream for.

Fuck that.

The memory has my heart pumping vigorously.

Is that what Rory's dinner with his parents will be like?

I wipe down the recently vacated table, my arm working in a quick motion as my mind vacillates between annoyance that Rory even asked me to go to dinner with his parents—because we're not that close, I've known him less than a week—and a niggling sense of something that feels a lot like protectiveness.

As another table turns over, the latter is becoming stronger, because if I don't show up for him, who will? And how has this man, this charming, affable man, managed to wriggle his way under my thick, reptilian skin so quickly?

Is it the fact that even though he paid to have my van door lock fixed, he still refuses to let me stay there alone? Or is it because I can't stop conjuring the vision of him shirtless on my van floor with Edgar cuddled under his arm? Or the memory of how my fingertips brushing ever so slightly against his bare chest last night had sent a jolt of electricity through my veins.

No. That's not important.

The real issue is Rory's kindhearted. Unselfish. The kind of guy who means it when he says he wants to help. And all he asked was that I come to dinner to be a buffer with his parents.

The weight of these thoughts has my resolve crumbling so fast that I rush over to where Darcy is resetting a table.

"Hey, Darce, can you close for me tonight?" I ask.

"Hot date?" She smirks, reorganizing the sauce caddy. She's been adamant something is going on between me and Coral Cove's golden boy, but I refuse to admit anything because that would be acknowledging Rory Shields has a way of making me think about him when he's not around. Like right now, I'm wondering if he's miserable. If they've guilted him into giving up his dreams. Or worse, if his ex is there already, smiling sweetly and stroking his arm like they're a couple again.

"I need to take care of something."

Rory, that's what.

But I keep that thought to myself because I don't even know what I'm supposed to do, what Rory needs from me, but the fact that he asked me to be there tonight, I know it's the right move.

"Go," she nods toward the exit, "I got you."

"Thanks."

In the back room, I untie my apron and toss it in the laundry bin.

"Where are you off to?" Mick asks.

"I have an appointment," I say, grabbing my things from my locker.

"A date?" He grins which looks odd on his usually stern face.

"It's not a date," I call as the back door slams shut behind me.

It's not a date.

"Miss?" The Matre'd gives me a once over. I didn't have time to change, so I'm still in my red Salty Pirate Café polo and black skort. I catch the way his nose wrinkles in disapproval. "May I help you?"

His tone is clear. *You don't belong here.*

Part of me is annoyed at his judgment, but another part of me is filled with satisfaction that I don't look like I belong here. It's what I've been working toward the past few years to distance myself from my old life.

And the way he's looking at me makes me think his version of helping would be to usher me out a side door, so I decide to bypass him altogether.

"No." I wave him off and move toward the dining room.

"Miss!" He's quick to call after me, but the appearance of two appropriately dressed guests suddenly has his attention pulled elsewhere.

In the dining room, a few heads swivel in my direction as I search for Rory and his parents.

I'm passing by a table when a woman lifts her wine glass in my direction.

"Another Chardonnay."

Her assumption that I'm part of the wait staff is clear.

I stop at her table and pluck the uncorked wine bottle out of the chiller resting there.

"Certainly," I say with a saccharine smile, refiling her a glass. Then I grab an unused glass and pour some wine in it —just a splash for me. "Cheers." I lift mine and walk away, ignoring her gasp.

Was that rude? Maybe. But so was her assumption that anyone not dressed in Vineyard Vines should be serving her.

Wine glass in hand, I scan the room again. I'm expecting to hear his warm, resounding chuckle or see a beacon of light guiding me to him, but I got nothing. No Rory.

But then, I spot him through the window at a table on the patio. Or at least I think I do.

The man's broad, athletic body is draped in a suit, but his shoulders are tense.

The shape of him is right, but the way he's holding himself is all wrong.

I didn't realize I knew that much about Rory's body and the way he carries himself until this moment. This man's posture is nothing like the Rory I know.

Pushing through the door, I slam back my wine before setting the empty glass on the server station as I pass by. Rory's back is to me, so it's his parents who see me approach first.

His mom is perfectly pressed in a cream linen dress, his dad's salt and pepper hair and tan skin stand out against his white and blue striped shirt and coordinated baby blue blazer. They look like they're fresh out of a *Southern Living* catalog.

I take a moment to observe their tight, strained faces before I proceed toward their table. As I'm walking over, both of his parents' mouth stretch with beaming smiles as their attention shifts to the brunette who has appeared on the other side of Rory.

"Daphne." Rory's mom's face lights. "What a wonderful surprise!"

Still positioned behind Rory, I see his back stiffen further before he woodenly reaches for his water glass. Daphne's already taken the seat next to Rory, and with her hand coquettishly draped over his arm, she leans in closer.

From what I know about the situation, Daphne's appearance isn't a surprise. It's the reason he invited me, to throw a wrench in their plans to reunite him and his ex. All he wants to do right now is focus on swimming, but his parents are making it difficult for him.

With all the stressors in my life, my van being broken into and the fact that I can barely keep myself above water with mounting bills and expenses, I wouldn't trade it for the situation I see Rory in right now. The freedom to make choices in my life and not be beholden to others is something I set as a standard for myself when I left my old life years ago.

And the way I don't even recognize this version of Rory is a fucking devastation. The protective instinct that urged me here tonight is now at an all-time high.

Having dealt with my own controlling parents and their manipulation, I hate seeing it happen to someone else. Most of all, I hate seeing it happen to this kind, generous man that from what I've seen always plays the peacemaker and does what he's told.

The good news is that I don't have that problem. I couldn't care less what Rory's parents think about me. That will make foiling their plans even sweeter.

Finally, my lingering presence is acknowledged with a

hard stare from Rory's mom. "Did you need something?" she asks, acid on her tongue.

"Oh, me?" I press my fingers into my sternum while batting my lashes innocently. "Yes. I'd like this woman to take her hands off…"

At that moment, my attention shifts to Rory, who has just turned in his chair. The moment he sees me, something shifts. The stiff line of his back eases, his shoulders drop, and that slow, familiar smile pulls across his face—real and grateful. The kind of smile that feels like it's just for me.

My body tingles at the sight of it.

With my hesitation, Daphne's face pinches with annoyance. I don't know if she's constipated or if that's her reaction to being challenged. Though judging by her irritated expression, I'm guessing that doesn't happen often. I want to smack it right off her. I also want to taze her hand that is latched onto Rory. Watch her silky blow out go all wiry from the electric shock.

I have no idea if that's actually what happens to someone when they're tasered but it brings me pleasure to imagine it anyways.

Rory had asked me to be his *date*, but from the tension at the table, I realize that's not going to cut it.

From what I know of Rory's mom, she's the type to plot against a girlfriend that she doesn't approve of. Even in her floral Magnolia & Rowe dress, I can tell Daphne is a woman that has no issue fighting for what she believes is rightfully hers. And from the look of her possessive arm cling, she believes that about Rory. I can't leave any room for opportunity. To truly get his parents and Daphne off his back, I need to crush all hopes of a reconciliation.

I need to go all in.

"...my husband." The words tumble from my lips with thrilling satisfaction.

At my announcement, three sets of eyes bulge.

"W—what?" his mom stammers.

"Rory, who is this woman?" his dad demands.

Rory's lips twitch, likely fighting the desire to break out into a huge, conspiratorial grin, except he had no way of knowing I was going to do this because up until ten seconds ago, neither did I. He stands and wraps an arm around my waist. One of those muscular forearms he possesses, and I do my best not to squirm with giddiness at the contact. It's a challenge. After all, my body is highly aware that we've never touched like this before, but we can't let them know. It would ruin the fun.

Rory clears his throat. "Mom, Dad. This is Summer." He beams down at me before turning the same proud smile back on his parents. "Summer Shields, my wife."

fifteen

. . .

RORY

My wife.

Those two words linger between the five of us.

I'm the one who said them, yet I'm as shocked as everyone else.

Next to me, Summer sways, but the arm I've got around her lower back tightens to steady her.

My parents and Daphne gape at us, but beside me, Summer is stunning in her red polo and black skirt. She must have come straight from work. In fact, based on the time, she left work early.

I'm so fucking happy she's here. I pull her in and press a kiss to her temple.

It's a simple gesture. Sweet. But one look at my mom's face, and you'd think I'd lifted Summer onto the table and put my head between her legs.

Another second of silence passes before my mom starts crying.

No, not crying. *Sobbing.*

"That's absurd," my mom wails. "How could you marry someone without telling us?"

"I—" I begin, but my mom cuts me off. Apparently, she's not interested in the answer.

"Why?!" She covers her face with her napkin, and rocks back and forth. "Why is this happening to me?"

"Is this some kind of a joke?" my dad barks. "Why would you marry someone like...someone like her?"

Summer stiffens beside me. "That's not very nice. You don't even know me."

I'd gotten caught up in the moment with Summer. I'd seen where she was going with her plan. Full commitment. Legally binding. That would be the only thing that could put a stop to my parents' insistence that me and Daphne were meant to be. But the fallout from that one thrilling moment isn't good. This is spiraling out of control quickly.

Daphne rushes to my mom's side. "Mary Ann, you just had a facial, the salt from your tears is going to dry you out."

"Oh, y-you're right." But it only makes her cry harder.

At the tables around us, people start to glance in our direction, whispering.

Once my mom realizes her audience and what kind of scene she's making with her sobs, she stands and rushes for the door. My father, who also hates a scene, but because they involve showing any kind of emotion at all, stands to follow her.

On his way out, he stops at my side.

"You've upset your mother. Now I have to deal with it," he hisses.

I'm used to doing what they need me to do. And tonight, my mom expected me to sit here and happily converse with my ex-girlfriend, with the plan of us getting back together.

So, having a woman they don't even know announce that we're married has thoroughly ruined her evening.

With my parents both gone, Daphne stands from where she was perched by my mom's chair. She gives me and Summer a tight smile.

"Rory, when you're done playing games, you know where to find me."

"It's not a game, sweetheart. We're in L-O-V-E, love," Summer announces loudly.

Daphne rolls her eyes before hitching her designer purse onto her shoulder and brushing past us. At one time, I cared for Daphne, but our relationship wasn't right. Something was missing. It's even more evident now we want different things.

With the entire dining room staring at us, I grab Summer's hand and guide her through the room. My mom's overdramatic cries echo down the hallway, so I pull us through a side exit near the pro shop, the opposite direction of where Daphne and my parents went.

"Well, that was wild," Summer says, a self-satisfied grin on her face.

"Says the woman who walked in and announced that we're *married*."

"I know." Summer's blue eyes light with glee. "Did you see their faces?"

We walk down the path on the edge of the golf course, then through a side gate that leads down to the beach.

I press my lips together to stifle a smile. I don't want to hurt my parents but knowing my mom's theatrics were based on the loss of her own desires for my life, not because she was truly worried I'd made a mistake is disheartening. "Yeah, I was there."

"God, what jerks. They didn't even say congratulations.

Your mom made it all about her. How would you getting married make them so upset?" She pauses; eyes locked on where I'm still holding her hand. "I mean besides the fact that you never mentioned you were dating anyone. Or that they'd never met me."

My jaw tightens as I process my parents' reaction. Summer is right.

For years, I thought I owed them. Early morning meets, club fees, travel expenses—they gave everything to support my swimming. They sacrificed things in the pursuit of my dreams and they never let me forget it. Guilt is my mom's favorite form of currency.

Over the last decade, I've used money from swimming to help with their businesses, I've done everything they've asked of me, but it's never enough. I've always felt like I owed them something. Like my life wasn't mine and I don't know at what point they would have been satisfied.

Summer drops my hand and turns toward the beach path. Her shoulders are tense, her pace brisk, like she's trying to outrun the conversation.

"Are you okay?" I ask, wondering if the chaos of what just happened is catching up to her.

"Just...give me...a minute." Her purse drops from her shoulder and onto the sand next to her.

At the sound of Summer's shaky breathing, my heart rate ticks up.

"Where's your inhaler?" I ask.

"I don't need it. I'll..." She sucks in a wheezing breath, "I'll be f-fine."

By the sound of her labored breathing, I'm not reassured. I pick up her purse and pull out the inhaler in there. But something is different about it. I'm no expert on inhalers, but it feels lighter now. Turning it in my hand, I notice a number on the bottom. It doesn't take an expert to know that zero means there's no medication left.

"It's empty."

Summer opens her eyes briefly to roll them at me. She takes another shallow breath before answering. "Yeah, I know. It's not a big deal."

Her cavalier attitude sends a jolt of frustration into my blood. "Not a big deal? You're literally wheezing."

"I'm not wheezing. I'm just...breathing with personality."

I can't believe she's joking about this. "Oh, so struggling to inhale is a cute little quirk now?"

"Some people bite their nails. I breathe like Darth Vader." She demonstrates to prove her point.

"Summer, this isn't cute. You're scaring me."

"It's not an attack." She pauses to inhale slowly, then exhale. "I'm getting it under control."

"If this *was* an attack, and your inhaler is empty, what was your plan?"

"I don't know...maybe breathe less?"

That snarky tone of hers is usually a huge turn on but in this situation, it's downright infuriating.

"Not funny."

"You're not funny," she says calmly, focusing on her breathing. "You're freaking out over n—nothing."

"I'm freaking out because you act like breathing is optional!" I'm sure my frustration with her isn't keeping with the calm environment she's trying to create but I can't fucking believe she doesn't see this as an issue.

"Give me a minute." She sucks in a deep, uneven breath before exhaling. "I'll calm down."

"No." I shake my head, refusing to wait and see if she can breathe properly. "We're getting this filled." I hold up her inhaler. *"Now."*

Picking up her purse, I motion for us to start walking in the direction of the club's parking lot. Thankfully, Summer lets me guide her in that direction.

I'll admit, her breathing isn't as strained as it was when I pulled her out of the ocean, but I'm also not waiting around for it to progress to that. I can't imagine how Summer feels. What it must feel like to struggle to get air into your lungs.

I've trained my body to go without oxygen for impossible stretches. Watching her now, I'd trade lungs with her if I could.

When I open the passenger door to my Jeep, she doesn't protest, likely because she doesn't have the spare air.

I pull out of the parking lot and head for the pharmacy.

"Rory, I can't," she says as we drive along. "A refill is nearly five hundred dollars to pay out of pocket." She sucks in an unstable breath. "And I don't have insurance."

She'd told me before when I hurt her wrist, but at the time I didn't think about the impact that would have on her ability to fill her inhaler prescription. I've always had health insurance, with my parents, and then through the team. As a professional athlete, I have the best coverage money can buy. It's always been necessary for health and injury prevention, and when I had my surgery last year, it assured me top medical care. I hate that Summer can't afford it.

I'd easily pay so much more so that Summer could breathe properly. But also, that's an insane amount of money for necessary medication.

"Why's it so expensive?"

"I can't use the generic brand. I'm one of the small percent of people that it causes side effects in."

"What are the side effects from the generic brand?" I ask.

"Heart palpitations."

"Jesus Christ."

With one hand on the steering wheel, I run my other hand through my hair in frustration.

"How long have you been rationing your medication?" I ask.

"I was doing okay. Then, I had some unexpected expenses that put me behind. Vet bills for Edgar, and my van needed maintenance. Things piled up and I had to skip a month."

"Your life-saving medication should be top priority." I turn to give her a pointed look to drive home my point. "We're getting you that medication now."

"Rory, I refuse to let you pay for it. It's an obscene amount of money."

Summer won't take something for nothing. It's endearing and annoying.

At the pharmacy, I pull into the lot and park my Jeep.

"I'm really...okay now."

I turn to Summer.

"What about next time? When it's a real attack and you can't calm your breathing?"

Her eyes fight to cover it up, but I see it there...fear. While she wants to project this calm exterior, she isn't fooling me. She's scared.

"The medication is cheaper with insurance?" I ask.

"Yeah, but I don't have it. And while I've researched it, my monthly premiums are too high for me to maintain."

I can't believe this is her reality. I'd pay ten times the cost if it meant she could breathe without fear. And then the thought hits me, so obvious I can't believe I didn't think of it before.

"Marry me."

"What?" She scoffs. Then when she realizes I'm dead serious, "*No.*"

"You proposed earlier."

"I didn't propose. I said we were already married."

"Which is a repercussion I'm going to have to deal with when my parents find out it's not true."

"But—"

"It's simple. We get married. You get access to my insurance, which is top notch, and I get my parents off my back. It's a win-win."

"Did you suck in too much pool water today? I'm not marrying you." She crosses her arms. "I'm not marrying anyone. *Ever.*" Her eyes flash like a hurt animal that's been cornered.

I study her carefully. "What do you have against marriage?"

"Everything." She closes her eyes and leans back into the seat. "Who voluntarily signs up for a lifetime of arguing, distrust, and unhappiness?"

"That seems like a harsh assessment of marriage."

"Well, it's the one that I have."

"Are your parents divorced?" I ask.

"No, that would have been better. There's nothing worse than a couple staying together that should be apart." She sighs. "And the expectations? The commitment, the 'til death do us part? How can a relationship thrive under that kind of pressure?"

I give her questions a thought. It was only a week ago I vowed to keep my life void of distractions. To focus solely on swimming so I wouldn't have any regrets with how my training and ultimately the outcome of my last run for gold turns out.

"So, ours won't be like that."

"I can't talk about this now."

She's wheezing again, and I realize my proposal along

with Summer's distaste for marriage might trigger an attack. Right now, I need to focus on getting her medication.

Leaving our discussion behind, I exit the car and move to the other side to open Summer's door. She's already got it open and while she attempts a sidestep, I grasp her hand to redirect her into the pharmacy.

As we approach, the woman behind the counter eyes Summer. "Miss, like I said—we don't do payment plans."

My chest clenches at her rebuff. She's just doing her job, but it's heartbreaking that Summer hasn't been able to refill her prescription that is a lifeline in an emergency, because she doesn't have the means to do so.

"Good. We're not asking for one." I hand the woman my credit card. "We'll take one month's supply, please."

The woman takes my credit card and looks up Summer's prescription.

"Give me a few minutes."

I nod and move away from the counter.

"Rory—" Summer starts after me, but I turn and guide her to the corner of the pharmacy.

"I'm not in the mood to argue," I say, more gruffly than I intend to. But while she's been treating this whole thing like it's normal, I've been going out of my mind with worry.

My hand cups her jaw.

"Damn it, Summer. You may be the one who can't breathe properly, but watching you struggle and feeling so fucking helpless is god damn torture for me."

With our eyes locked, she swallows thickly. Her hand reaches up and encircles my wrist.

"I get it. It's scary for me, too. I joke about it because if I don't, then I'll cry instead." She inhales deeply, and my eyes drop to watch her chest rise and fall, looking for any sign of distress. "Edgar needed surgery. He had a tooth abscess and was in a lot of pain. The surgery was expensive, something I hadn't planned on."

"You prioritized Edgar's surgery over your medication?" I know Edgar is important to her, but he's a dog. Summer is going without her medication because she spent the money on Edgar's health care instead of her own? I want to commend her on being a caring human being, while also throttling her for being reckless.

"Yeah."

I inhale sharply. Now I'm the one who has to control their breathing. "Do you know how careless that was?"

"He's all I have. I couldn't stand to see him in pain."

My eyes scan her face. I've known Summer less than a week, but she's already carved out a space inside me that I didn't know existed. Again, it's that feeling of not being able to stay away from her. Needing to protect her and make sure she's okay.

"Yeah, I get it."

"Summer McKee," the pharmacist assistant calls. Summer's inhaler is ready.

She hands Summer the paper bag with her medication in it. Then, she hands me back my insurance card.

"I ran your insurance card and with your plan the medication is thirty-eight dollars."

"For a month's refill?" I confirm.

"Yes."

My eyes find Summer's and even though she knows what I'm suggesting, she simply takes the bag and walks out.

sixteen

. . .

SUMMER

Rory proposed.

In the pharmacy parking lot.

Okay, it was more like a demand.

Breach of independence!

Walls up. Scowls loaded. Snark engaged.

But my body, noticed the way Rory's jaw clenched with protectiveness. How his cornflower blue eyes were filled with concern. And then, in the pharmacy when he'd stood there, broad shoulders squared, arms crossed like he was ready to fight the whole damn world for me, I'd felt safe. The same way I'd felt when he wouldn't let me sleep alone in my van after the break-in. Safe and cared for. Like for the first time in a long time, someone was on my side. And it had felt good. I'd found my shoulders lowering away from my ears as a trickle of calm had washed over me.

I liked the feeling, but it scared me, too.

I can't depend on a feeling. Those have steered me wrong in the past.

After we picked up my prescription at the pharmacy, and I'd taken a puff from my inhaler, Rory drove us to a local burger place near the beach for dinner since we hadn't had a chance to eat anything at the club.

I'm browsing the menu, contemplating dinner with a side of matrimony while Rory is using the restroom.

I'll admit, I did start this whole thing by telling his parents we were already married, so that's on me.

But getting married isn't an option. After everything I experienced with my parents and Tripp, it's something I vowed never to do.

We won't be like your parents.

That was Rory's argument when I told him about my parents' toxic marriage.

But how does he know that? He can't predict the future and there's no way I'm going to put myself in that position.

But getting married would keep his parents off his back, or at least from discovering our lie, and I could be on his health insurance to reduce the cost of my medication. We found out that with his insurance, my medication is thirty-eight dollars a month. *Thirty-eight fucking dollars!* I could stockpile it for years at that rate.

But I can't *marry* him, can I? Getting married would be like walking into a trap I've spent years making sure I stay free from.

My eyes lift from the plastic-covered menu to find him stopped at a table with two young boys and their parents. He's signing something and giving the boys high fives. His smile is genuine and unbothered as he waves goodbye. Then, he's turning and walking toward me.

It's annoying how sincere Rory is and how easy it is to

believe him. To trust him. My guardedness usually pushes people away, but not Rory. It's like he thrives in hostile environments. He's like the ocean waves slamming against the rocks. No matter how much resistance there is, he keeps showing up, eroding my defenses in a way that's natural and unstoppable.

Rory drops into the booth across from me.

"Fans of yours?" I ask.

"Isn't everyone?" He grins.

My lips twitch at his confident gaze. "Pretty sure of yourself for someone whose recent marriage proposal was rejected."

"About that—" Rory starts before the waitress appears with our drinks. She sets down a Dr. Pepper for me and a chocolate milk for Rory.

"Thank you," I say, pounding the straw against the table to remove the paper wrapper before inserting it into my soda.

"What can I get y'all to eat?" the waitress asks around the smacking sound of her gum. She reminds me of Darcy.

I order the classic cheeseburger with extra pickles while Rory orders the double bacon cheeseburger, no onion, and a basket of fries.

"Is that all?" I lift my brows, surprised he didn't order half the menu.

"Yeah, I'm not that hungry." He hands the waitress his menu.

My instinct is to analyze what I did wrong.

Is it because of my announcement to his parents? Or my wheezing on the beach?

I push those thoughts away. Rory's hunger level has nothing to do with me.

When the waitress leaves, Rory stands, then slides into

my side of the booth until our thighs are pressed against each other.

"Excuse me. What are you doing?" I jerk back.

"Showing you what it would be like if we were married."

"Um, no." I turn to scowl at him. "We wouldn't be a same side of the booth couple."

"Why not?"

"Because that's weird."

"I like being close." He props a muscular arm over the back of the booth behind me. "Physical touch is my love language."

"Of course, it is."

"What's yours?"

Scarlett made me do one of those quizzes senior year. All three versions said the same thing, physical touch. I won't be sharing that with Rory.

"Personal space."

He chuckles. "That's not a love language."

"It is if you want me to even consider your proposal."

Rory moves to the other side of the booth with a huge smile in place. "So, you're still considering it?"

I stare at his handsome face filled with optimism and warmth. He's a good guy. Why does he want to marry me?

Because it wouldn't be real. He needs a decoy wife. Maybe my standoffishness is appealing for an arrangement like this.

"How do you know this arrangement won't be miserable? We don't know anything about each other."

"That's not true. I know you like pickles and Dr. Pepper. And I know you like painting."

"What?" My heart rate ticks up a notch at his mention of me painting. "How?"

"The way your face lit up when I returned your paints." His smile is soft, like he's remembering the moment.

My heart pounds, but I swallow back the discomfort. "They were a gift from Scarlett. They meant a lot to me."

"And Scarlett is your best friend and would know what kind of gift would make you happy."

He lifts his brows. *Gotcha.*

"Fine. I paint. It's a hobby." I stir my straw around in my soda. "What about you?"

"Hobbies?" he asks.

I nod.

"Training and traveling for competitions take up most of my time, but I enjoy music. Going to concerts. When I'm in town, the Tunes & Tides concerts at the Emerald Beach band shell are a good time. Hanging out with the guys. Playing video games." He takes a sip of his water. "Snuggling on the couch with my wife."

"Ah, congratulations. Who's the lucky lady?" I say with mock-sincerity.

"You," he says, tossing me a wink.

My body responds by melting further into the cushioned booth.

"There wouldn't be any snuggling."

"Oh, come on. You know you get handsy when you're sleeping."

"I do not."

The waitress arrives with our burgers and I take a moment to dress mine. Putting the onion and lettuce to the side, I stack the tomato and pickles on the burger before squeezing mustard on top of everything, then cut the burger in half.

I take a bite. As the blend of savory meat, sweet cheddar cheese, tangy mustard, and sour pickles hit my tongue, I sigh. Maybe it's the chaos of the last few hours, but damn this is the best burger I've ever had.

I look up to find Rory's burger hovering halfway to his mouth as he stares at me.

My eyebrows lift. "What?"

He blinks, realizing he's caught. "Nothing."

I take a huge bite of my burger. "Doesn't look like nothing," I say around a mouthful.

Maybe I'll gross him out and he'll withdraw this silly marriage idea.

"Just thinking."

I tilt my head and finish chewing the bite of burger. "Dangerous."

That gets me a small smile, but it fades as his eyes stare intently at me.

"I was thinking..." He leans forward slightly, elbows on the table. "That you don't even realize when you let your guard down."

I stiffen at his words, my guarded personality taking offense to his observation.

"Just now, when you took that first bite of your burger? You did this little happy sigh, like it was the best thing you've had all day. And for a second, you weren't overthinking. You were just...you."

He's right. I felt it. The ease of just being here and eating. With *him*.

But other than Scarlett, I don't do that with people.

I set my burger down and stare back at him.

"That's why you were staring at me?"

"Yeah." He picks his burger up again. "It's a good look on you, Wildflower."

My body flushes at his words, but I cool it down with a drink of my soda.

For the rest of the meal, Rory doesn't mention us getting married. He tells me about the guys on his team, and his goal of returning to the Olympics for his final run. The way his face lights up when he talks about his teammates and how much he loves swimming, it makes my chest ache. It's how I feel about painting. Except, while I paint in the shadows, Rory is pursuing his passion publicly.

And I could help him.

My eyes snag on Rory's basket of fries. I opted for a side salad, but those fries look good. He must catch me eyeing them because he grabs a handful and puts them on my plate.

"There's more where those came from." He winks.

"Thanks." I give him a small smile, my stomach tingling with the sweet gesture.

"You two make a good-looking couple," the waitress says, laying the check on the table. Rory snatches it up before I even blink. He's got great reflexes.

"She makes me look good." Rory smiles at her, then when she walks off, he grins at me. "If that's not an endorsement, I don't know what is."

We finish our dinner, then Rory drives us to the RV park.

When we arrive at my van, I don't even question Rory coming in and making himself at home.

He pulls off his shirt and tosses it on the bench like it's an old habit now.

The water glass in my hand slowly lowers as my eyes slide down his naked torso. I watch as he picks up Edgar and cradles him between his chest and bulging bicep.

I cross my arms to hide the way my nipples pebble beneath my tank top, then move past Rory to climb up into the loft.

Now that I'm in my own space, I see why Rory's unhappiness under his parents' control hit me so hard. It's a mirror of my own childhood.

Behind me, Rory climbs up then settles in next to me. The scent of mint toothpaste mixed with his cologne, and the faintest tinge of chlorine, is a heady combination.

He sighs.

"What?"

"My mom texted me. She thinks we're lying."

"Because we are. We've known each other for a week. Who gets married that fast?"

"They don't know that." He shifts to his side to face me. "And people in love do crazy things."

"People in love." I laugh sardonically. I hadn't hesitated to tell Daphne that Rory and I were in love but that had been out of spite. But what is romantic love? An ambiguous measure of feelings you have for someone that ultimately leads to resentment and disappointment? Or a feeling that at first is so intoxicating, that one day you look up to see you've completely lost yourself in someone else?

"Have you ever been in love, Summer?" Rory asks.

My parents' relationship was constant fighting, hurtful barbs lobbed like grenades, all in the name of love. If that was love, I wanted no part of it. Then, I'd met Tripp, and for a while he made me think I was wrong about the whole love thing. Turns out, he made me think I was wrong about a lot of things.

My relationship with Tripp isn't one that I like to claim. It wasn't simply a young love that didn't work out. A relationship I can look back on and see all the ways the relationship helped me grow and discover who I was. It's the opposite. In my relationship with Tripp, I shrank into a version of myself I didn't recognize and instead of learning who I was, he dictated it.

"No." And then because Rory makes me so damn curious about everything, I ask, "Have you?"

His eyes lift to mine. He searches my face for a moment, as if the answer to his past love life is written there, then rolls onto his back, resting his hand next to mine.

"Yeah."

He must be talking about Daphne. I don't confirm because I don't want to talk about their relationship. I know Rory has a good heart and if he loved her, she must have redeeming qualities. Tonight, I didn't see any but they've got to be there.

I roll to my back, both of us now staring up at my Flaming Lips poster while the rustle of Edgar settling into his bed beneath us fills the dead air.

"I don't even know what a healthy relationship looks like."

Awareness creeps in as Rory's pinky finger edges closer to mine.

"But you know what you want. And what you don't. Isn't that what matters?"

It's quiet between us as I chew on my bottom lip and consider Rory's questions.

I know I don't want to be like my parents. Be complacent in my relationship. Unhappy and unwilling to change something that isn't working. Life is too short to be miserable.

And I know I'll never allow another man to treat me like Tripp did. Feeling small and unwanted in my relationship with him are still wounds I carry. Therapy at the university free clinic helped me see that, but I haven't challenged those beliefs in a new relationship, I've simply avoided them.

Now Rory wants me to make the marriage I fabricated tonight legit.

Because if his parents and Daphne were to find out our

marriage isn't real, he'll be miserable dealing with the fall out of my false declaration. And distracted from his training.

Ugh. This is such a mess.

Could I really marry Rory?

I never planned to get married. I'm not waiting on Prince Charming, and it's not like marrying him would be wasted. It would be practical. Responsible. For my health, and to help Rory.

"If we did get married, your parents would leave you alone, right?" I ask. As soon as the question leaves my lips, an erratic pounding beneath my rib cage begins. It's my body's unmistakable response to the idea of marriage. I focus on taking measured, even breaths, willing my heart rate to slow.

"If there's a ring on your finger, and a valid marriage certificate, there'd be no room for discussion."

"Then you could focus on swimming? And be the GOAT?" That's what one of the articles I read about Rory had called him. That with twenty-five medals, he's the most decorated swimmer of all time. And another run in Los Angeles would cement his status. As long as he stays focused and healthy to make it there.

He chuckles. "Yeah."

"What about logistics?" I ask. "If we did get married? Hypothetically speaking."

"You and Edgar would move into my house. You can park your van in the garage. It'd be safe there. And you'd have health insurance."

"Swoon." I roll my eyes playfully even though he can't see me.

I pretend to shift, letting my fingers move another centimeter until our pinkies are brushing against one another. The simple movement has a rush of electricity lighting my body up like a sparkler on the fourth of July. Everything tingles, everything *burns* inside me.

"I know it's the practical things that get you all hot and bothered."

Rory's voice is low and deep, right next to my ear, causing a rush of warmth between my thighs.

I wish I could control my body, continue to deny what being around Rory makes me feel.

Until now, I've done a decent job ignoring Rory's absurdly handsome face and unfairly chiseled body. But if we do this—if I move in with him—he'll be everywhere.

And shirtless, no doubt.

"You know nothing of the sort," I counter, hoping my attraction to him isn't obvious.

Health insurance would be a game changer. Cheaper medication would help me get my head above water with other expenses.

I quietly squeeze my legs together beneath the covers because access to Rory's insurance isn't the only thing that's getting me worked up.

This is transactional. Get your hormones under control.

I love living in my van, but a house would mean more space for Edgar. From below, his soft snoring filters up to the loft followed by a shaky snort.

I'd also have a place to store my paintings, and maybe slowly compile a collection for a gallery show. The idea has a ribbon of excitement twirling inside my belly. But a show would require putting myself out there. Putting my art on display for everyone to see and judge. I'm not ready for that. But I'll never be if I don't have the space for my art.

Why am I even considering this? Marriage is the miserable institution I watched my parents navigate. The blaming. The gaslighting. The insecurities and fighting. The tears and disappointment. Bickering that would build into an explosive fight, only to be swept under the rug and the cycle start over again.

There was no abuse, at least not physically, but I don't know how either of them wasn't emotionally scarred from the rollercoaster. I know I was. Still am. And yet, they're still together. Posing happily on *Business Today* magazine covers, no one the wiser that their advice for how to run a successful business while being happily married for twenty-five years is a complete sham.

I glance back at Rory, and that ache in my chest is back. The one that had spurred me into action earlier tonight when I'd marched across the dining room at Coral Cove Beach & Golf Club and declared that Daphne remove her hand from my *husband*. It's the same troublesome feeling that got me into this position.

I should pluck that feeling by the root and yank it out for good, but the origin is unknown.

So instead, I try to imagine Rory treating me the way my parents do each other. Him nitpicking my clothing deci-sions, while I nag him about how often he golfs. I don't even know if Rory golfs. There are so many unknowns between us.

Or the way Tripp had treated me. Acting like I was everything to him in public, but recoiling at my touch the moment we stepped out of view.

The only way to make sure I don't end up miserable like my parents, or hurt like I was with Tripp, is to keep my heart out of this. A marriage of convenience.

"Maybe," I turn my head toward him, "this could work."

My eyes have adjusted to the dark, making the spread of Rory's smile visible.

"Yeah?"

There's so much optimism and gratitude in that one word.

"If we do this, it would be a marriage in name only."

"Which means—"

I rush to answer his inevitable question.

"We're not involved romantically. No intimacy and no sex. I want to keep it simple between us. We're doing this to help each other out, and I'd rather not complicate things with any emotions. No pesky romantic feelings. You know?"

"What kind of feelings should we have?" he asks.

"Fondness."

Rory chuckles under his breath, but it sounds a little too warm. A little too hopeful.

"You make it sound like we're in the 1800s marrying for a dowry."

"No, we'd be marrying to keep your parents off your back so you can train with no distractions. So you can qualify for another summer games and shatter all the records."

His lips spring into a grin. "I like your confidence in me."

"Yeah, well," I smile back, "I think you've got potential, Flipper."

I move to tap him on the nose, but before my finger lands, he catches my wrist and presses his lips to my palm. "Thank you, Wildflower."

The sincerity in his voice makes my chest squeeze. It also reminds me we need to agree on the most important rule of all.

"Just so we're clear, you're not allowed to fall in love with me."

"Okay." He smirks. "That means you're not allowed to fall for me, either."

"Not a problem." I pull my hand back to break the connection between us.

It's silent for a minute, before I add, "Don't make me regret this."

"I won't." He stretches again, sighing with exhaustion. "I'm going to be the best fake husband."

I don't doubt that Rory would be a good husband, but something about the way he says it makes it feel like a threat. A vision of a life together flashes in my mind. Beach camping under the stars, nights cuddled on the couch, early morning walks with Edgar before Rory heads off to the pool for training.

We've done none of those things together, yet the image is so vivid.

None of that aligns with what I've witnessed marriage to be. What I've experienced in previous relationships.

What am I agreeing to?

With the quiet around me, my thoughts start to spiral.

A few minutes later, I open my mouth to take it all back, but Rory's already asleep.

seventeen

. . .

RORY

"What's this?" Logan holds up his phone from where he's standing in front of his locker. Naked.

"A wedding invitation," I say, pulling on my jammer.

"It's *your* wedding invitation," Logan replies, confused.

"I know."

I sent the text ten minutes ago, right before I walked into the aquatic center.

"What? I didn't see that." Charlie grabs his phone, brows wrinkling. Relief flashes across his face when he finds the invitation. But it vanishes just as fast. "It's for tomorrow."

"Yeah, I'm aware."

Most of the team is already on the pool deck warming up. After Summer agreed to marry me last night, I booked an appointment at the courthouse for tomorrow at eleven. I want to keep it low-key, but there was no way I wouldn't invite the guys.

"Have you seen this?" Charlie asks Eli, who's just walked over to his locker.

"Logan's dick?" Eli smirks. "Hasn't everyone?"

Logan's still standing there, one hand on his phone, the other clutching his chest in mock disbelief, his dick swinging in the breeze like he's got nowhere to be.

"Bro, put some clothes on." Charlie groans. "Your flaccid dick is way too close to me."

"Don't be insecure, man. Everyone's built different. It's not the size; it's how you use it."

Eli shakes his head. "You were that kid at the beach in a shirt and no pants, weren't you?"

"We spend so much time with our junk in wet Lycra, is it so wrong to want to air everything out?" Logan counters.

I tune out Logan's naked logic and turn to Eli.

"Where've you been?" I ask.

"I stopped by the physician's office to check on Winnie."

"What's going on?" Logan asks, suddenly serious. A rare shift from his usual absurdity.

"Last night I had dinner with Winnie and the guy she's dating."

"What guy?" Logan frowns. "I thought she was taking a break from dating after Brett, the narcissistic anesthesiologist?"

"They met online. He's a pilot."

"What's the verdict?" I ask.

Eli and I have bonded over being protective older brothers—trying not to meddle too much, but still wanting to keep our sisters safe. I've been lucky. Whitney's too focused on school and swimming to date anyone seriously.

Eli shakes his head. "I don't like him. Gives me weird vibes. But she says he's great so what am I supposed to do?"

"We could threaten him," Logan suggests, eyes lighting up. "Tell him he can never see her again."

I squeeze Eli's shoulder. "I think we let Winnie live her life, but monitor the situation."

Eli chuckles half-heartedly. "Says the lucky asshole whose sister never has boyfriend drama."

Charlie's palm finds Eli's other shoulder. "We all love Winnie like a sister, so we'll make sure he treats her right."

"I got it!" Logan says. "We put a tracker on his car. One misstep and he's swimming with the fishes."

"Thanks, guys." Eli strips off his shirt and tosses it in his locker. Then, he points to Logan. "You need to stop reading those mafia romances."

Logan's grin fades. "You'll have to pry them from my cold, dead hands."

"Now, can we please talk about the fact that Rory's getting married tomorrow?" Charlie says, pointing at me. "Do we even know this chick?"

"Watch it," I warn, my blood spiking at his tone. "Her name is Summer and she's going to be my wife."

"That's what I'm saying. You're marrying someone none of us know."

"I know her," Logan says, finally pulling on his jammer. "She's a waitress at The Salty Pirate."

"C'mon, Cap." Charlie urges. "There's more to this story."

He's not wrong. I was still on a high from the way Summer had shown up for me. The way she confidently claimed me as hers. I liked it because for once I knew it wasn't someone doing it for their own benefit. She had done it for me.

But when I woke up this morning, the relief of Summer saying yes had shifted into something else.

Disappointment.

Another thing I can't explain.

A convenient marriage is exactly what I need right now. I don't have time for anything else. My life is full, my training is all consuming, and I don't have the energy for something real.

Summer's doing me a favor. Taking the pressure off by agreeing to a fake marriage.

And yet, I can't shake this feeling.

Maybe it was the way she looked at me lying in bed last night, guarded and unreadable, like she's holding something back. Or maybe it's the way this arrangement boxes us in, closing off possibilities, that until Summer slammed the door on them, I didn't even realize I might want.

It shouldn't bother me, but it does.

Because if I wanted to kiss her, if I wanted to see where things might go, that's not on the table anymore. It's like being disqualified before you even get off the starting block.

Now, as the guys give me shit about it, I'm forced to put on a casual smile and tell them I know what I'm doing when that's the furthest thing from the truth.

No feelings. No intimacy. No *sex*.

The thought of Summer being around all the time, seeing her in my space, in my life, it makes me uneasy in the best way. I'd already admitted that I have this need to be around her. To know she's okay, to make sure she's safe. But I know at the root of that, it's something more.

For all the friend talk we've been passing back and forth, there's no denying I'm attracted to Summer.

Simply being in her presence turns me on. Our pinkies brushed last night and I got hard. How am I going to handle faking a marriage with her? She'd been adamant that there be no romantic feelings between us but does wanting to know what she tastes like and what kind of sounds she makes when she comes violate that rule? According to Summer, it does.

The more I think about it, the more I wonder if this is all going to blow up in my face.

"It's an arrangement," I say finally. "One that lets me focus on swimming."

"An arranged marriage?" Logan asks.

"If it were arranged, he'd be marrying Daphne," Eli mutters.

"So, you're marrying Summer so you don't have to marry Daphne?" Charlie asks.

"Yeah, kind of."

"Nice." Charlie nods. "I think I like her already."

My phone lights up with a text.

SUMMER

Winnie sent me a wedding day checklist.
Rings?

I'll stop by Rowley's Hardware and grab a couple from the toy vending machine.

SUMMER

Cool. I'll check that one off.

I start to text her that I'm kidding, but stop. If she thinks we're exchanging bendable rings from a vending machine she's more likely to go through with it.

I submitted the insurance form to add you to my coverage. Should be in effect as soon as we submit a copy of the marriage certificate.

thank you

I stare at my text. It feels like I should say something more, something less transactional, but I'm not sure Summer wants that, so I toss my phone in my locker and slam it shut.

"Are we going to gossip all afternoon or actually train?" Coach calls out as he walks by us.

We grab our gear and follow him out to the deck.

"This doesn't look so bad." Charlie nods to the white board where our blocks are written out.

Owens walks up and casually adds two extra sets to every block.

"Fuck," Charlie groans.

Owens smirks. "Figured I'd give you something to talk about later. When your limbs are too tired to move, your mouths won't be."

The rest of the guys drop in the water, but Owens motions me toward him.

"Shields."

"Hey, Coach."

"I received an interesting text from you earlier. Thought it was a joke. I expect that from Logan but not you."

"It's not a joke," I confirm.

"I pride myself in knowing what my swimmers are going through. Mentally, physically, emotionally. You getting married tomorrow? Can't say I saw that coming."

"It makes sense. Keeps my parents off my back. Keeps things simple."

Owens raises an eyebrow. "Marriage is simple now?"

I let out a dry chuckle. "Simpler than dealing with their matchmaking."

He folds his arms, nodding slowly. "I trust you to make the right call. You've always had a good head on your shoulders. But remember, this is your last run. You need to stay locked in. No distractions."

I nod, feeling the weight of his words settled against my shoulders.

"I'm focused, Coach. Nothing's changed."

"Good. Because once you're on that starting block, nothing else matters."

I nod, confirming his words.

As I hit the water and start my warmup, I ignore the feeling that something has already changed.

eighteen

. . .

I'd spent all day yesterday prepared to take back my agreement to marry Rory, but then he'd shown up with his teammates to the café to eat dinner after practice.

They all looked exhausted from their training session, and were ravenous. As I brought out plate after plate, Logan commented that the café needed an all you can eat option.

Even though he was visibly tired, Rory was the life of the group. Watching him with his teammates, it was easy to see why he's the team captain. The position is not just based on his age, but the fact that he's easy to approach and playful, while also a leader respected by everyone.

Rory needs this. He needs the freedom to focus on swimming. And even with my strong stance against marriage, it eased the anxiety knowing ours would have a purpose.

This morning, after another peaceful night with Rory by

my side, I woke up, walked the dogs, then grabbed breakfast for me and Cal.

"Hey, Cal." I drop onto the bench next to him. Edgar nuzzles into his leg, eager to greet the elderly man.

I unwrap the breakfast burrito and hand it to him. Maintaining his grip on the fishing pole, he takes the burrito with his free hand.

"Bless you, Summer."

I pull another burrito out of my bag and we eat in silence for a minute.

"Fish biting today?"

"Nah, but I like the ritual of it."

I nod. I get that.

"Plans later?" Cal asks.

"Um, yeah. I'm getting married."

Cal chokes on a bite of his burrito so I whack him on the back. It would figure that the news that I'm getting married would nearly kill him. Marriage is like a death sentence.

He eyes my unkempt hair and baggy t-shirt with utter confusion. He can't even see the remnants of eye makeup from last night that's hidden beneath my sunglasses.

"Like that?" he asks. "I'm not up on all the trends you kids are into but even I know that's not wedding attire."

"I don't subscribe to the patriarchal belief that I need to look my best on this day. The man who wants to marry me should accept me for me, no matter what I look like."

Or maybe it's because after years of putting so much effort into everything I did only to be met with indifference, the desire to try where a man is concerned has vanished.

That's why I'd laid out the rules for me and Rory's marriage: no feelings, no intimacy, no complications.

It's what I want, and Rory agreed without hesitation.

It should be a relief. It *is* a relief.

Yet, there's a flicker of something I didn't expect. Something sharp and unwelcome curling in my chest.

At one particularly insightful moment, I'd even labeled it.

Disappointment.

Disappointment that Rory didn't push back. That despite our constant reassurance that we're just friends, it was the proof in that moment that he didn't want me. The same way my ex hadn't.

It might seem ridiculous for me to compare Rory and my ex, they're not the same, but it was a reminder that I won't put myself in that situation again. A situation that made me feel like I wasn't enough. Constantly bending myself to fit into his version of who I should be to earn affection and prove my worth.

With Rory, I'm getting what I asked for, and I should be glad he didn't try to negotiate our arrangement. It would only make things messy.

So, I push the niggling feeling away.

"Who's the lucky guy?" he asks.

"Rory Shields."

Under the shade of his brimmed hat, Cal's smile spreads. "I had a feeling."

"What kind of feeling? Did it involve heart palpitations and shallow breathing?"

Cal ignores my comment. "Seeing you two together made me miss Mildred."

She passed away five years ago, and she was the light of Cal's life.

No one's ever been that important to me. Except Scarlett.

"You told Scarlett yet?" Cal asks, like he can read my mind.

I sigh. "Not really. She's going to have thoughts."

She's been my ride-or-die since we were nineteen, and if anyone knows how deep my marriage aversion runs, it's her.

So, I text her a quick "Getting married today. Don't freak out."

Three seconds later, my phone rings.

Of course it does.

I excuse myself from Cal's peaceful fishing excursion just in time to get an earful from Scarlett.

"Tell me you're joking," she says by way of greeting.

"I'm not. It's a courthouse wedding. No flowers. No fuss. Just paperwork."

She groans. "Summer...what are you doing?"

"I'm helping a friend. I need health insurance. He needs to get his parents off his back so he can train. It's not real."

"You're legally binding yourself to a man, and it's not real?"

"It's Rory," I say, like that explains everything.

Because it kind of does. He's becoming the one person I can't say no to. And Scarlett knows.

The silence that follows is long and heavy.

"You really think you can do this without catching feelings?"

"I already laid out the rules," I say. "No intimacy. No complications."

Scarlett doesn't laugh. Doesn't even scoff. Just lets the quiet sit for a moment too long.

"I hope you know what you're doing, Sum. Just...don't lie to yourself about how you feel."

Before I can respond, a shriek cuts through the air.

"Summer!"

It's Winnie.

"I gotta go," I say quickly.

Scarlett sighs. "Fine. But I want pictures. Not wedding photos. Proof of life."

I end the call and rejoin Cal just as Winnie comes racing down the dock toward us, waving her arms wildly.

She'd texted me earlier asking if she could help me get ready for today. I'd agreed only because I don't know what one should wear to a courthouse wedding for their marriage of convenience and Winnie seemed so excited to help.

But now I'm wondering if I can jump off the side of the dock without her seeing me.

"There you are," she pants, out of breath from the full-on sprint down the dock.

"She found me," I whisper to Cal, whose raspy chuckle warms my heart.

"We've got to get you ready!" Winnie exclaims.

Cal quirks an eyebrow, giving me a look that means *I told you so.*

I groan but let Winnie lead me away.

An hour later, with my hair blown out and a soft, natural makeup palette applied, I'm Winnie's vision of a blushing bride.

After finding me on the dock, Winnie brought me to Whimsy, a boutique clothing store, owned by her friend Cora. While Cora picked out a white lace mini dress with a sweetheart neckline and flared skirt, Winnie converted one of the fitting rooms into a hair and makeup station where she worked her magic on my appearance.

With Whimsy being only a block away from city hall, Winnie and I walk over after my transformation.

The crisp morning has softened into a balmy spring day while a breeze teases at the hem of my dress, making me hyperaware of how I look.

"Rory's not going to know what hit him," Winnie says with a wink.

Inside city hall, Winnie leads me down the tiled corridor to where the small courtroom is located.

"I'm going to use the restroom," I tell Winnie.

"Okay. I'll see you inside."

I nod, trying to keep the nerves at bay.

Outside the double wooden doors, several couples linger. By the way they're dressed, it's clear they're getting married today, too.

I watch a woman straighten her fiancé's tie, then beam up at him with the sweetest smile.

Two men, both dressed in light gray suits, hold each other close, one leans in for a sweet kiss as they pose in the picturesque hallway for a photographer.

These couples aren't just going through the motions, they're in love. Every gesture, every glance confirms what I'm pretending. Their marriages will be real. Ours will be... something else.

My pulse kicks up a notch causing my heart to pound in my chest.

I spin around, and crash straight into Rory's chest.

"Hey, Wildflower." His warm hands wrap around my upper arms. "You trying to bail on me?" His brows lift in question, but I can see the amusement in his eyes.

It's what I need right now. To make light of a situation that is starting to feel too heavy.

Rory looks handsome in a deep blue suit. His crisp white

dress shirt contrasts with his golden skin and when his lips stretch across his face, I'm the one who is about to melt.

I swallow hard. A flash of annoyance at how damn handsome he looks swirls through my blood. That's not a normal thought to have on your wedding day. But this isn't a normal marriage. With every charming smile and sweet gesture from Rory, I'm starting to wonder if I'm misjudging my ability to hold him at a distance.

"No, I'm not running. We made a deal and I'm here to fulfill it."

With his hands still holding me up, Rory's eyes scan the length of me.

"Wow, Summer. You're stunning."

If I hadn't felt pretty before, I do now, and that only adds to my confusion.

I hate the effect Rory's words have on me. The way his eyes lighting in approval makes my stomach flutter with excitement. How it used to be that way with Tripp until I realized he only wanted me by his side to show me off. He didn't actually care about me.

"Yeah, well, Winnie wouldn't let me wear a t-shirt and biker shorts."

Rory chuckles, turning me toward the courtroom door and opening it for me to enter.

"You could've shown up in a trash bag, and I still would've said 'I do' without blinking."

"You're only admitting your desperation," I tease as he takes my hand. He pulls me along toward the front of the room where the judge is seated behind the plain wooden bench talking with another couple.

The air carries a faint scent of old paper and lemon-scented floor cleaner.

Rory's lips twitch in amusement, before he shakes his

head. "Nah, it's because it doesn't matter what you're wearing. You walk into a room, and I notice. Every damn time."

At his words, I nearly trip down the court room aisle, but I don't fall because Rory's got me.

Of course, he does. Winnie had warned me, hadn't she? Rory's *that* guy. Helpful and sweet. Always doing good deeds. He'd probably marry any random woman that needed insurance. I just happened to be directly in his path.

At the sight of the generic courtroom, my anxiety eases.

There's no need for flowers or silk bunting. No music or choreographed entrance. No bridesmaids or groomsmen.

The North Carolina state flag in one corner and the American flag in the other, both faded by time, are the only backdrop. At the front of the room, the court stenographer sitting next to the judge, barely glances up as she types. The monotony of it all helps reassure me what kind of arrangement this is; completely transactional.

"The court has reviewed the terms of your agreement. All assets and responsibilities are divided as stated, and there are no further disputes. Mr. and Mrs.—well, not Mrs. anymore, I suppose—your divorce is finalized as of today. Best of luck to you both."

The couple in front of us are getting a divorce.

Good.

I mean, I'm not happy for their failed marriage, but it's a good reminder of what will ultimately become of me and Rory after the Olympics.

"Next," the judge calls out and Rory guides me toward the bench where the placard reads *Judge Clayborn*.

On the way, my eyes skim over the handful of people sitting in the audience. I recognize Logan, Charlie, and Eli. Then, there's Winnie, with her hand at her chest, discreetly giving me an enthusiastic wave.

As the judge announces why we are gathered here today, my palms start to sweat.

"Are you exchanging rings?" Judge Clayborn asks.

Rory reaches into his suit jacket pocket.

When he holds up the ring he has pinched between his fingers, my eyes bulge.

The ring in Rory's hand is gorgeous, but completely unexpected.

"I thought we decided on the ones from the quarter machine in front of Rowley's Hardware?"

"This is more convincing," he whispers.

I shake my head. "It's too much. More than what I got you." Reaching into the pocket of my dress, I produce the black rubber ring.

He grins at it. "You didn't follow the rules, either?"

I roll my eyes. "It was like nine dollars."

"I love it."

"You don't even have to wear a ring. A lot of guys don't. But, if you wanted to, I thought this kind made the most sense with swimming and all your training activities."

"Hell, yeah." Rory's smile is captivating. "I'm going to wear it."

"Okay. Whatever you want to do."

I shrug it off, dizzy from the heat.

We turn our attention back to Judge Clayborn.

"Rory, do you take Summer to be your lawfully wedded wife?" he asks.

"I do." Rory's voice resonates loud and clear.

"Summer, do you take Rory to be your lawfully wedded husband?"

My throat is suddenly tight. My lips part to utter the words, but nothing comes out.

"Summer?" Judge Clayborn prompts.

"I-I do," I finally manage the words.

"Rory, please place the ring on Summer's finger and repeat after me."

Rory nods and reaches for my hand. I want to will it to stop shaking, but my body is off the rails, doing things I've not instructed it to do.

Trembling hands.

Racing heart.

Throat tight and impossible to swallow past.

The ring on my finger, though delicate, has an unexpected weight to it.

As Rory recites his vows, it takes everything in my power to stay rooted to the spot. To not fidget under his thoughtful gaze.

It's just for show, I repeat to myself. But in my head, it's become more of a chant set to the tune of "Here Comes the Bride." So much so that I'm afraid I'm going to blurt it out in the middle of the ceremony.

Somehow, in the chaos of all that, I manage to repeat the vows after Judge Clayborn.

"...for better or worse, in sickness and in health..."

We sign the marriage certificate and I breathe out a sigh of relief that this stressful moment is over.

We did it.

"I now pronounce you husband and wife," Judge Clayborn announces to the handful of people in the tiny courtroom.

"Okay, so we're good to go?" I ask, glancing around at the smiling faces, my feet ready to rush for the door.

Judge Clayborn smiles from his perch, then nods to Rory. "You may kiss your bride."

You may kiss your bride.

I've been to weddings. I've seen them on television. I

know the gist of the ceremony, yet I'd completely forgotten about this moment. We hadn't discussed how we'd handle it. I'm just about to tap my cheek to cue him for a polite, harmless kiss, but the way Rory's lips slowly tilt into a devilish smile makes it impossible to focus.

His hands lift to frame my face. The firm pressure of his fingertips as they slide against the base of my neck causing heat to coil low in my belly like a struck match.

His eyes search mine, the moment stretching out between us, thick with something unspoken but undeniable.

Then, his mouth claims mine.

It starts out soft. Gentle. Almost reverent. But there's a tension beneath it, a tether pulled tight. Just when I think he'll pull back, he doesn't. He deepens it, mouth firmer, kiss hungrier, like he's not acting. Like he means it.

His thumb brushes over my cheek, coaxing me open for him—and I do, helplessly, willingly.

My thoughts scatter as my body takes over. My fingers move to grip the lapels of his suit jacket, dragging him closer.

I feel the slide of his mouth, the press of his chest, the possessive tilt of his head. We're kissing like we've been waiting for this for years.

Tasting.

Teasing.

Devouring.

Somewhere in the background, there are cheers, laughter...maybe applause? But it all fades beneath the rush in my ears, the heat of my skin, the low hum building between us.

My body sighs into his. Maybe that was an actual sigh escaping my mouth. Or maybe it came from Rory. I can't tell where he ends and I begin.

He pulls back slowly, reluctantly, like he doesn't really want it to end. I'm still holding onto him, unsteady and wrecked from a single kiss.

We should've done that before so I knew what I was getting into. So I could mentally prepare myself for the fact that *my husband* kisses like he has something to prove.

My lashes flutter and my lungs drag in air that doesn't feel like enough.

I've never been kissed like that. Now, I'm questioning if I've ever been kissed at all.

Finally, I'm able to open my eyes and focus on Rory. His lips are flushed, his breathing a little uneven, but that familiar golden retriever grin flickers back into place.

While my brain is spinning its wheels trying to figure out what just transpired, Rory isn't fazed at all. It's almost like he knew this would happen.

"I object," I whisper.

Rory just grins knowingly. "We're already past that part, wife."

nineteen

. . .

Summer's eyes meet mine, and I catch a flicker of electricity still crackling there before she diverts her gaze from me.

The world carries on around me, but I'm stuck replaying that kiss on a loop. I don't know how to exist in the world now that I've kissed Summer. Now that I know the feel of her lips, nothing's the same.

Judge Clayborn hands us a copy of the signed marriage certificate.

Winnie rushes over and throws her arms around Summer, squealing excitedly.

Logan offers me knuckles and Eli squeezes my shoulder. Charlie, who I could hear sniffling during our vows, blows his nose loudly into a tissue.

"Thanks for being here, seriously," I say, voice catching a little.

"Are you kidding?" Logan asks. "We wouldn't have missed it."

"It was beautiful," Charlie says, wiping a tear.

Logan and Charlie head over to talk with Winnie and Summer. I'm about to follow them when Eli grabs my elbow.

"I thought this was a platonic arrangement between you two." Eli lifts his brows.

"It is."

"Yeah, nobody kisses a friend like that."

I give him my most convincing smirk. "We're committed to the arrangement, that's all."

"That looked like commitment all right."

"You know how persistent my parents have been with the whole Daphne thing. I needed to do something. Besides, now I can focus on training with no distractions."

Glancing past Eli, my gaze catches Summer's legs, the hem of her dress just skimming the tops of her thighs. That glimpse of skin lights me up from the inside out.

"No distractions, huh?"

I meet his shit-eating grin. I could tell him it's all part of the act. What man wouldn't look at his wife like I'm looking at Summer? But Eli knows me too well. All I can do is ignore him and try not to fall in love with my wife. I promised I wouldn't, after all.

We file out of the courthouse, the rest of the group heading in one direction, while I lead Summer toward my Jeep.

I help her in, then walk around to the driver's side.

"You kissed me," she says, more surprised than angry.

"Judge Clayborn did say, 'you may now kiss your bride.' What was I supposed to do? Shake your hand?"

"There's a difference between sealing a marriage contract and what you did in that courtroom."

I glance over at her in the passenger seat.

I can see where my fingers teased her once soft hair into disarray. Where her lips are still swollen from our kiss and parted in exasperation but with the faintest hint of lingering desire.

It's true, I'd gone in for the kiss, but she kissed me back with just as much force.

I can't help the smug smile that slides over my face. She's right. When I leaned in, I figured I'd give her a simple kiss on the lips. A kiss to be convincing but nothing obscene. But once my mouth was on hers, it wasn't so simple.

Am I satisfied to see Summer flustered?

I'd be lying if I wasn't.

She hides behind indifference, so seeing her rattled makes me feel less alone in this.

Whatever this feeling is.

Desire.

Protectiveness.

She taps her fingers against her leg, and I notice the way her ring sparkles in the sunlight. My eyes shift to my hand on the steering wheel. The ring she placed on my finger. It's solid, not flashy, but it means something.

Possessiveness.

I want Summer. There's no denying it. From the way she responded to that kiss, there's a good chance she wants me, too. But there's a reason she put rules on our marriage.

Probably the same reason she's got her guard up most of the time. A sledgehammer won't get me through her walls. I'll need a chisel...and time.

With my left hand on the wheel, I place my right arm behind the passenger seat and lean close.

"I'm not sorry I kissed you like that. But I won't do it again, unless you want me to."

"Why would I want you to kiss me again?" she scoffs, but her gaze drops to my lips before returning to my eyes.

"Because you liked it. And it was fun." My lips twitch in amusement, causing her eyes to land there for a second time.

"Ha! You're the one who liked it."

"You're right. I did. And I'd do it again, anytime you want."

"We have rules," she reminds me, but I don't miss the way her breath hitches.

"You're right." I nod, pulling back to start the car. "You hungry?" I ask. Then clarify, "For food."

She sighs. "Starving."

twenty

. . .

After our courthouse wedding, we made the mistake of eating at The Salty Pirate, where Darcy spent the whole time making over-the-top gushy faces at me. Alice ended up covering for me and even though Rory tried to pay, Mick and Alice insisted our meal was on the house.

After lunch, Rory helped me get my van prepped to move to his house. He'd had Charlie drive his Jeep back to his place so he could drive with me in the van. This morning, I packed a suitcase for his house, which feels odd considering my van will be parked in his garage.

It occurs to me now that I have no idea where Rory lives.

It's one thing I forgot to ask about in the whirlwind that was us getting married. Now that we're on the way, I'm anxious to see where I'll be living during this fake marriage. With anticipation, my right thumb and index fingers rotate the wedding band Rory put on my left hand earlier. My thumb glides over the facets that hold each tiny diamond. I love the simplicity of the band while the small glittering diamonds give it a touch of glamour. I can't deny it's a beautiful ring, but I am still not sure how I feel about wearing it. I knew Rory and I were joking about the quarter machine rings, but that doesn't mean he needed to spend thousands of dollars on a ring for a marriage that won't outlive his swimming career.

I lift my gaze from the ring to watch as he makes a left on Driftwood Drive, then at the end of the alleyway, which is a dead end for beach access, he comes to a stop.

"This is it." He motions out the passenger window to the back of a gray house. I can't see the house yet, only the garage that's attached to it, but it's clear from the location that he's got beach front access.

"You live on the beach?" I ask, hugging Edgar to my chest.

"Yeah. It's an investment property I bought years ago with my first big sponsorship deal."

I nod as he opens the garage door with his phone, then pulls my van into the spot next to his Jeep.

"We're home." He gives me a huge grin, and scratches Edgar behind the ear. "Should I carry you over the threshold?"

I shake my head, and give him a wry smirk. "That's not necessary."

He shrugs, aiming that sincere, playful grin of his me. "If you wanted me to, I would."

It's words like those that make me question if I've made a terrible mistake. If this arrangement with Rory is dangerous. He's too sweet. Too unguarded and accommodating. Also, in the rush to get married, we didn't talk about any of the things that couples should talk about.

"No." I wave him off, reminding myself that we don't

need to do any of those traditions because none of this is real.

That kiss sure was, my brain chimes in to remind me for the millionth time since it happened.

I'd be lying if I said I'd never thought about kissing Rory. Or stared at his lips once or twice when he wasn't looking. But I'd never planned to act on it. Now I have to live with the knowledge that Rory is a phenomenal kisser and there's nothing I want more than to kiss my fake husband again, but I can't and I *won't.*

You can't change other people; you can only change the way you react to them. That's what my therapist always told me.

Since I can't stop Rory from being sweet, thoughtful, and *gorgeous,* I'll have to change the way I react to him. No more melting body or flutters of my reproductive organs.

I need to set a precedent. Rory and I are all business. And it starts the moment I walk into his house.

Rory grabs my bag from the van and makes his way toward the door.

Chivalry alert! I slam the van door shut and setting Edgar down on the garage floor, rush to catch up with him.

"I can carry my own bag," I say, hot on his heels.

"I got it." He turns to smile at me and that one curve of his lips nearly knocks me on my ass.

Rory keeps moving forward, but determined to keep things on an even playing field, I reach for the handle of my bag and yank.

Except that wasn't the handle, it was the zipper, and my pull on it has the entire side of the worn leather bag gaping open. My belongings, which I had hurriedly packed this morning, are now spilling out the side.

No neat and tidy packing cubes for this girl. Just loose

items stuffed in a bag. A pair of socks, a notebook, my toiletry bag, and oh that's right, my trusty pickle vibrator that I've nicknamed Big Dill.

Any hope of stuffing Big Dill back into my bag unnoticed is foiled when I see he's covered in sand. Sand and silicone aren't a good combo. But that's what you get from the garage floor of a house located on the beach. So, I do what must be done and wrap one hand around Big Dill, then vigorously move it up and down the length to dust the sand off him.

I turn to find Rory watching me, that curious grin of his splashed across his face.

"Is that—"

"Yes, Flipper. It's my vibrator."

His lips quirk. "It's a pickle."

"I like pickles, remember?"

"I can see that."

I stop the jerking motion I was using to sweep the sand off Big Dill and swipe my hand against my leg to release the excess sand.

Rory takes the vibrator from my hand and examines it. He clicks it on and pushes the settings button, switching it between the different types of pulses. I'm cool as a cucumber watching Rory explore the toy I use to masturbate with. Yup, I refuse to acknowledge the way my pulse thrums at the sight of his long fingers handling Big Dill because it's totally normal to have my new fake husband examining my vibrator.

"Shouldn't it be bigger?" he asks, with focused concentration on my pickle vibrator.

Rory's hands make Big Dill look more like a little gherkin. But that's fine because where I'm concerned Big Dill's specialty isn't penetration, it's clitoral stimulation.

"Trust me. Big Dill gets the job done."

"Big Dill?" Rory's smile widens and his eyes crinkle with amusement, like they know all my secrets. "Summer... that's—"

I refuse to be embarrassed. Big Dill is hilarious, and makes me happy, in more ways than one.

My ex never treated my pleasure like it mattered. I refuse to let my *fake* husband do the same.

"It's what?" I snap, a little too sharply. Old wounds rise to the surface before I can stop them.

My relationship with Tripp left me feeling unwanted. Undesirable.

With him, intimacy was always on his terms. I felt like a toy—something he could use—but never truly seen. Most of my attempts to show affection were brushed off, met with irritation, or outright rejection. At first, I blamed bad timing. Then, I learned he controlled everything, and I internalized the idea that his needs mattered more than mine.

His ties to my parents only made it worse. They wanted it to work, so if it wasn't, clearly I was the problem. *I* had to fix it. But you can't fix a one-sided relationship.

I know I'm not undesirable but the safest way to avoid repeating that pain is to keep my guard up. Keep my needs private. Take care of myself. With the help of Big Dill, of course.

"It's normal." I mutter. "I have needs. You have needs. Everyone has needs. Ugh, why am I even explaining this to you?"

Rory shakes his head, a soft smile playing on his lips.

Those full, firm lips.

Focus, Summer.

"You don't have to explain," he says. "I get it. Self-care is important."

It takes a moment for me to comprehend his words. To hear that he understands me and he's not making fun of me. I'm used to everything I do causing a fight, because with my ex, it did.

But Rory isn't fighting with me. In fact, the way he's looking at me with equal parts curiosity and amusement, and a smoldering look that's so fucking hot I think my body is going to burst into flames is confusing me.

As I stare up at Rory's handsome face, I start to question my 'no sex' rule. My brain does me a solid and reminds me: *Hey, remember? You're bad at intimacy. And sex.*

Right.

Tripp told us so.

Tripp's an idiot.

Well, both things can be true.

But also, I have no other experience to disprove him. And I don't want to make a fool of myself with Rory, so yeah, self-care it is.

I shake off the vivid mental image of Rory pressing me against the wall and dropping to his knees before it can finish playing out.

"That's right, I don't," I say, a little too firmly.

"And if you hadn't cut me off," Rory adds, "I was about to say that I think Big Dill is hot. And sexy. And fucking hilarious."

He casually brushes the rest of the fallen items off and places them back in my bag, as if we're not standing in a storm of innuendo and tension. I clumsily wedge Big Dill between some clothes like I'm trying to hide a crime scene, and Rory zips the bag closed like a gentleman.

After all the erotic visuals dancing in my head, I'm ready to dive under a cold shower to cool down.

Rory reaches for the door handle, but then stops and turns back toward me.

"Welcome home, Wildflower," he says, "I hope you and Big Dill will be very happy here. And Edgar, of course."

Those blue eyes twinkle with mischief. It's my favorite thing about them.

Dangerous, I remind myself.

But we agreed to the rules.

This is a marriage of convenience—nothing physical.

Just stick with Big Dill, he'll take care of it.

Inside, Rory walks me through the mudroom and laundry area, then into the living room. When I catch the view from the sliding door in the dining room, something stirs in me. It's like I've been here before.

With Edgar on my heels, I slide the door open and step outside. The moment my feet touch the path, I know exactly where we are. It's one of my favorite spots to bring the dogs.

From here I can see the dock where Cal sits every day. I rush down the path to the beach, heart pounding. When I turn around and see the house—it hits me.

It's the gray beach cottage with the yellow door.

The one I fell in love with that first week in Coral Cove.

The one I've sketched and painted over and over.

"Summer? You good?" Rory calls.

"I'm fine. Just looking at the water." Which makes no sense because my back is to the ocean, but Rory doesn't call me on it.

"You want the rest of the tour?" he asks, scooping Edgar into his arms.

"Sure."

I follow him in a daze back into the house.

I can't believe he lives here.

I can't believe *I* live here now.

"It's not a big house," he says as we walk through the kitchen and dining area. "But I had it updated a few years ago, and it's home now."

I nod, taking in the white oak floors, stone countertops, and soft beachy paint colors.

The space is modern, but warm. Thoughtful.

In the living room, there's an oversized sectional and a pair of deep linen armchairs facing a big screen television. A gaming system is tucked in the console; a Victrola vintage record player sits on top.

Floating shelves line the wall near the TV. Mystery novels and sports biographies make up most of his collection, with a chunk of sea glass serving as a book end.

While Rory being in my van had felt overwhelming, he seems to relish in my exploration of his things, watching me peruse his space with an easy smile.

It hits me. He probably renovated this place with Daphne.

As if he reads my mind, Rory says, "Whitney helped. She's got a good eye. She thought about majoring in architecture and design but her swim schedule made it impossible."

"She did a great job." I nod, relief flooding through me that I can enjoy the space without feeling like I'm in his ex-girlfriend's house.

"I cleared this area so you can put some of your plants here." He motions to an empty shelf in a sunny corner of the dining room.

"You did?" I ask, surprise lifting my brows.

"Yeah, you can't leave them in your van. They won't get any sunlight."

I know he's right, but I hadn't expected him to anticipate the need and have the space ready for me.

"Thanks."

He nods, motioning me down the hallway.

"This is the primary bedroom."

He flips on the light to reveal a bedroom painted in a soft gray. A huge Bird of Paradise plant in the corner adds the perfect amount of greenery.

A cozy chair with a rustic floor lamp sits in the corner. On a dark wood dresser rests one of my paintings.

My gaze snaps back to the painting. No, not just one of my paintings. *The painting.* The one of this very beach house that I'd thought about not giving up, but ultimately decided to part with.

"Where'd you get that painting?" I ask, pointing toward the dresser.

"I found it. It's one of those Coveys everyone has been talking about."

His eyes search mine, and I do my best to keep any emotion off my face.

"You know, the anonymous artist that leaves paintings around town for people to find?"

"Yeah."

"I was surprised to find a painting at all, let alone one of my house."

I swallow hard, emotion rising. "That's wild."

"I heard he mostly paints beachscapes so this was the first painting of a structure."

"He?" I question, my defenses rising. "Why do you think the artist is a 'he'?"

Rory shrugs. "I guess I hadn't thought about it. I just said 'he' out of habit." He chuckles. "Going forward, I will refer to the anonymous Covey artist as 'they.'"

"Hmm." I set the painting back on his dresser. "You

should frame it. Something simple. A tray frame in coarse-ground wood would look nice."

Rory moves to stand beside me, and I'm suddenly aware of the heat from his body. His fingers brush mine as he takes the painting from me.

"I have no idea what you just said. You'll have to help me remember that." He smiles, and suddenly the air between us is thick.

I clear my throat loudly. "Okay, so you said this place has two bedrooms?"

Rory sets the painting back down on the dresser, and I follow him across the hallway. He opens the door to the room, revealing a smaller bedroom.

But there's no bed inside it.

Instead, there's a large easel in front of the window facing the beach. There's also a small work table, a supply organizer with drawers, and a couple shelves for storing canvases.

"What is this?" I ask, the shock evident in my voice.

"Your studio."

My head whips around to look at Rory. *Does he know?*

"Rory."

He shrugs. "Call it a wedding gift."

"For our fake wedding?"

"The wedding was real. The marriage is fake."

"You know what I mean."

I don't know what this room used to be, but it definitely wasn't an art studio.

"Why did you do this?" I ask, still in shock.

"I want you to be happy here. You said painting makes you happy."

He motions to the opposite corner of the room.

"My cold plunge is still in here, so I'll need to use it from time to time."

As thrilled as I am to finally have a dedicated space to paint, I'm just as nervous Rory might find out I'm the Covey artist. The anonymity has given me more confidence in my art. It's allowed me to put my art out in the world without being tied to it and risk the kind of judgment I received in the past.

"Wait. There's only one bed in your house?" My head whips back in his direction. "So where am I supposed to sleep?"

He motions across the hall. "With me."

The idea of sleeping next to my husband shouldn't be surprising, but it still throws me.

"Rory..."

"We slept together in your van."

"That was different."

"How?" he asks.

"Because now we're married."

He laughs and I kind of hate how good it sounds.

This would be a no-brainer for a regular married couple, but our arrangement is not typical and I don't want to lose sight of that.

Scratch that. I'm terrified to lose sight of that.

I have no doubt that Rory is perfect husband material, but I'm not the wife for him. Not long term anyway. I have too much baggage. Too many insecurities to be a good partner.

He sets my suitcase down by the closet before opening it to show me where extra linens are kept.

"And look." He pulls open the small drawer in the bedside table. "The perfect spot for Big Dill."

"Thanks," I reply flatly, fighting a smile.

But then the mental image of me lying on Rory's bed, pleasuring myself with Big Dill emerges and I break out in a sweat.

My eyes lock with Rory's and I swear he's thinking the same thing.

For a moment, we stand there staring at each other. The air between us hums with unspoken possibilities.

"Okay, thanks for the tour." I turn and nearly trip over Edgar.

Clearly, he doesn't have any issues with our new home. He's on the rug at the foot of Rory's bed, legs up in the air, rolling around on his back.

"He found a comfy spot," Rory says, dropping down to rub Edgar's belly.

Seeing Edgar stretched out on the floor fills me with joy. That little guy has my heart and I can't imagine not having him by my side.

I lower down next to Rory to give Edgar some love.

"Hey," Rory says softly, his finger lifting my chin until I meet his gaze. "I want you to be comfortable here. It's your home now, too."

Rory's fingers slide along my jaw. It's the same way he cupped my face at the courthouse when he kissed me. I could so easily lean into his touch, drop my lips to his and see where this attraction takes us, but I won't.

Remember the rules.

I pull back and Rory drops his hand.

A moment later, he stands, then grabs a duffel bag from his closet and starts tossing items inside. He looks up to find me watching him.

"I've got a pool workout, then relay practice."

"Oh. Right. Of course."

Mentally, I shoo away the rush of disappointment. It's

not like I thought we'd be spending the day together. This marriage is for convenience and we're still going to live our separate lives.

"I'm sorry I have to rush out when you just got here."

"It's fine. That's the whole point of this, right?" I cross my arms over my chest and shrug nonchalantly. "You don't have to tell me where you're going. You don't even have to say goodbye when you leave."

I busy myself by dusting a piece of lint off his comforter.

"Summer?"

He draws my attention back to him just in time for me to see him throw his duffel over his shoulder before leaning in close. His proximity has me pinned to the dresser behind me, my heart racing at the thrill of him in my space.

"Yeah?" The word slips out breathless.

"I'll never leave without saying goodbye." There's sincerity in his smile, but the heat in his eyes is what makes my stomach flip.

"Sure." I clear my throat. "Whatever you want to do."

"I'll let you get unpacked."

"Okay." I nod, offering a limp wave as he turns. "Bye."

Once he's gone, I can finally breathe normally.

I flop onto the bed and bury my face in his comforter.

He smells like fresh linen and salt water, with a hint of oak. Clean. Crisp. Masculine.

And devastatingly arousing.

Big Dill is definitely going to have his work cut out for him.

twenty-one

. . .

RORY

With a signed marriage certificate and the satisfaction of Summer moved into my house, I breeze into the aquatic center like a man ready to take on the world. I toss my stuff in my locker, then get dressed for the team's pool workout.

Eli appears beside me, clapping a hand on my shoulder. "Owens is looking for you."

I nod, throwing on a t-shirt before making my way to Coach's office.

"Eli said you needed to talk to me?" I ask, my hand braced on the door frame.

"Sit down." He motions to the chair across from his desk.

"If this is about Summer—" I start, but Coach shakes his head, cutting me off.

"Connor Fisk is joining the team."

The name alone kicks up my pulse. It's not a full adrenaline surge, but a steady drumbeat of tension followed by a hollow drop in my chest.

Coach Owens isn't known for being a jokester, but he has his moments. Maybe this is one of them?

"You're kidding." I blink; certain I've misheard him.

"I know there's history between you two," Coach continues. "Some bad blood."

I mentored Connor through a program at UC-Berkeley when he was training with the Bay City Barracudas. He was a lonely teenager; reeling from his parents' divorce. I thought he was a good kid who needed guidance navigating sponsorships and the business side of swimming.

My jaw tightens remembering Connor's betrayal. It's been seven years, and we've crossed paths at every major meet, but showing up here to train with the Current is fucking ballsy.

"You could say that." I stretch my jaw, trying to loosen it from the tension settled there. "Why does he want to train here?"

Owens' brows lift in question.

Not every coach-athlete combo works, but Owens is known for bringing out the best in everyone.

"Point taken."

Owens nods, arms crossed. "He cut ties with Ryland Jenkins a few weeks ago and came to me looking for a supportive team dynamic."

A scoff escapes my throat. "That's interesting. Fisk has been a loner for years. He hasn't been part of a training team since college and seems perfectly content in his glass tower."

Owens' gaze softens. "He's had a rough couple of years since his mom passed."

I sigh, pushing a hand through my hair before leaning back into the chair. I'm not an asshole, so of course I feel bad to hear about Connor's mom. My mom is a lot to deal with, but I couldn't imagine her being gone.

"This isn't about you and Connor. It's about the team."

I get it. I do. But that doesn't mean it doesn't feel like a betrayal.

Owens isn't only my coach, he's like family, so I'm surprised he's made an official decision without discussing it with me first. I can't help but feel like the decision was made without my input because I might not be here in the next year. Out with the old, in with the new.

"I know what you're thinking. Connor isn't a replacement. He's an addition."

"As my coach of twelve years, I respect your decisions, but this isn't going to be easy."

"I'm not expecting you two to be best friends, but you are the team's captain and with that comes a responsibility to be an inclusive leader."

"When's he coming?" I ask.

"He's already here." Coach nods toward the hallway, an indication that Connor is somewhere in the aquatic center.

I'm even more blindsided.

"Seriously? Why didn't you tell me this yesterday?"

"I didn't want to ruin your wedding."

"How thoughtful of you." A tight smile strains against my lips.

He motions to the wedding band on my left hand. "Congratulations."

"Thank you." I fidget with the wedding band, twisting it around my finger. It's foreign, yet comforting.

"Now go get your warmup in."

I stand and exit Owens' office.

My close friends on the team know about my issue with Connor. The media thinks we're rivals because he snagged a sponsorship deal that had originally been offered to me. Some say I'm bitter because Connor is younger and will likely eclipse my record for all-time most Olympic medals, but my issue with Connor has nothing to do with hardware, and everything to do with honesty and integrity.

Out on the pool deck, I walk over to lane four. My lane.

At the other end of the pool, I can make out the swim cap of another swimmer warming up in it. I yank off my shirt, pull on my cap and goggles, then dive off the blocks.

The water is a cool balm to my heated skin. I slip through it easily, fine-tuned muscle-memory easing me into the warmup. After a few strokes, I can sense the other swimmer's approach. With both of us plowing forward through the water, we create two opposing high-pressure zones. When we meet in the middle of the pool, the pressure waves collide. The water flow between us is unpredictable as our bodies move through the turbulence of each other's wake.

Breathing to my left, I catch a glimpse of the swimmer's face breaking the surface beside me.

Familiar, but unwelcome.

Connor.

Even before our eyes connected, I knew it was him by the sun glinting off his inky sleeve rising out of the water.

Connor is known as the bad boy of swimming. He's not into drugs or partying, those wouldn't mesh with our rigorous training, but he's known for going through women like swim caps.

The upsurge of water his body creates as we move in opposite directions has my body responding with a rush of adrenaline.

We're warming up, yet when I make the turn, I clock my time well above a casual warmup pace. I shoot off the wall, and a handful of strokes later, we meet again. This time I'm prepared for him and right before we pass, I tilt my chest and angle myself downward, seeking out the small pocket of calmer water underneath Connor's wave.

On the next lap, my pace increases again. I know it's fucking stupid and I'm going to regret every second of this when I'm drained before the main set, but I can't help it. I push on, picking up speed with every turn, keeping my momentum with every pass until I find myself directly behind Connor.

The next turn, I'm right on his heels as he pushes off the wall.

This isn't the inclusive leadership that Coach talked about but it's what I need in this moment.

As we ease into the final stretch of the warmup, I glide past Connor and into the wall.

At the pool edge, we surface, each of our arms draping over the opposing lane ropes to rest. Connor lifts his goggles to his forehead.

Connor smirks. "Didn't know you still had it in you, old man."

"You shouldn't have come here, kid." I wipe the water from my mouth, every muscle in my body heated from our fast-paced warmup.

Charlie appears on the deck. "Hey, did you hear—" He stops short when his eyes find Connor.

"Yeah, I did," I finish for Charlie, whose brows are lifted in shock.

Connor looks from me to Charlie, then back.

There's a waiver of uncertainty before his self-assured grin returns.

"Why so serious, Shields? I'm just here to swim, man. Let's not make this more complicated than it has to be."

Connor wants to make this easy on himself and brush over our past? Well, I'm not going to give him that.

Grasping the backstroke wedge, I pull myself up to tower over Connor.

"You can act like we're good all you want, but the fact is, I haven't forgotten what you did. You crossed a line, and just because you're here doesn't mean I'm going to ignore that fact.

"You're here to swim," I say, keeping my tone calm but firm. "And that's all I need from you. Keep your head down, and don't get in my way."

At my words, Connor's jaw clenches. I expect him to argue with me, but instead he gives a terse nod.

"Gentlemen, I'd say you're warm now." Coach Owens appears at the top of our lane. "Four hundred freestyle at eighty percent effort. We're going at the top."

I pull my goggles down and when the clock hits the zero, I push off the wall.

With every stroke, I feel Connor on my heels, but I refuse to let him distract me. Instead, I use his presence to solidify my goals.

Push harder.

Be better.

Win.

twenty-two

. . .

SUMMER

I love my van but having space to move around is something I haven't had for a long time. Also, Rory's gigantic shower is beyond luxurious. Dual waterfall shower heads, a steam shower system, and adjustable body jets. I'm not sure how he gets anything done. I could be in here for hours.

After my shower, I towel off and pull on a tank top and underwear. I'm about to pull on shorts but then I glance at the clock. I don't know exactly what time Rory will be home, but it can't be for a while, so I take advantage of the alone time and walk around the house in my underwear. That's something I haven't done in years.

There's not enough time to paint before Rory returns, so I decide to explore the house instead.

It feels odd to be in Rory's house without him but he told me to make myself at home.

In the closet, I browse through Rory's clothes. There's a wide array of athletic shorts and t-shirts, polos, and slacks.

He's got a large collection of suits. I sift through them, noting the one he wore to our wedding earlier.

I've never lived with a guy before. Tripp and I dated for three years but I lived in on-campus housing with Scarlett while he had his own apartment.

In the dining room, Edgar is living his best life sprawled out in front of the large sliding glass window. When I pull the shades closed so I don't flash anyone who walks by, he groans at me.

In the refrigerator, I find an insane amount of food. Premade meals, protein shakes, fruits, and vegetables. Pickles.

I stare at the jar of pickles. It's my favorite kind. Brand new. Unopened.

A coincidence? Or, did Rory buy them for me?

The thought sends my stomach aflutter, so I close the door before I can get carried away.

I pour myself a glass of water, and lean against the kitchen island to drink it. When I lift the glass, my wedding band sparkles, catching my eye. Holding my hand out in front of me, I inspect the foreign piece of jewelry.

That's when my eyes land on Rory's record player across the room. When I saw it earlier, I'd been excited. I used to have one in my apartment, but had to downsize when I moved into my van.

Listening to music has always been enjoyable for me, but there's something about the sound quality of vinyl that hits different. It's warm and textured, the music somehow softer around the edges. Even the faint crackle and pop from the needle settling into the groove is so satisfying.

I walk over and drop to my knees on the floor to check out Rory's collection of records.

Bruces Springsteen, Hozier, Radiohead, Tom Petty, The Rolling Stones.

We hadn't talked about it, but it's interesting to see Rory's taste in music is similar to mine. Eclectic, classic, with some pop hits thrown in. I smile because he's also got ABBA and Taylor Swift next to Frank Ocean and Nirvana.

My fingers stop on a record I remember my grandmother playing often. Fleetwood Mac—*Rumours*. Carefully, I slide the record out of the sleeve and load it on the turntable, then flick the on switch and move the needle to the rotating vinyl.

There's a moment of static, then Stevie Nicks' raspy voice fills the room. It's whiskey-warm, a mix of gravel and velvet. I let her natural vibrato serenade me while I explore the kitchen.

I'm not a great cook, but I wouldn't mind learning to do more now that I have a full kitchen at my fingertips. This time I stop in front of Rory's refrigerator to look at the magnets clinging to the stainless-steel finish.

A giant taco-shaped one that says "Tacos Are Life."

A bottle opener magnet.

A Carolina Current Swim Club magnet.

A polaroid of Rory and his teammates tucked under a "I got crabs in Charleston" magnet.

There's also a bunch of refrigerator letters you can spell words and phrases with. Most are pushed around haphazardly, the only readable phrase is "IN HARD, OUT WET."

"Is that a swimmer thing?" I ponder out loud.

There's a crackling pause between songs, then "Go Your Own Way" starts playing.

I'm reminded of how Scarlett and I would belt this out in our dorm room. It was my anthem for most of my senior year, as I yearned for a life far different from the one my parents were dictating at the time.

I grab my phone off the counter and text Scarlett.

Listening to Fleetwood and missing you

She responds immediately with a video of us singing together. I laugh watching our younger selves belt out the song while dancing around our dorm room.

SCARLETT

Miss you like crazy. I need to come visit.

A moment later another text comes in.

SCARLETT

Don't forget the microphone

I glance around Rory's tidy kitchen, my eyes landing on a utensil canister sitting on the counter. After a quick perusal, I select a whisk as my microphone of choice.

When the chorus hits again, I'm dancing around the house, belting the song at the top of my lungs. My hair, mostly dry now, but wild and wavy, is giving Stevie Nicks vibes.

My movements aren't graceful and I know I'm off tune, but there's no one here but Edgar to witness it.

Edgar is disturbed. He's never seen me like this. There's no space in the van and the proximity to other people at the RV park wasn't ideal for private concerts.

As the song hits the guitar solo, I turn the whisk into a guitar, giving it everything I have. I'm bouncing on my toes, playing my air guitar.

I'm mid-spin when I spot the audience: a wall of broad shoulders and horrified expressions.

My instinct is to shriek and dive behind the couch. While I'm cheek to the carpet, I notice Edgar lying on the rug nearby doing absolutely nothing to help me during this home invasion.

Rory was right. Edgar's guarding instincts are non-existent.

"Summer, it's just us," comes a deep, but soothing voice from the doorway. "We didn't mean to scare you."

Slowly, I peek my head over the couch to get a better look. I recognize Eli, Logan, and Charlie but there are a few others hovering behind them. A moment later, the group parts and Rory appears.

At the sight of him, I rise from my flattened position. Still holding the whisk, my face burning.

He's freshly showered, hair still damp with a dusting of scruff on his jaw. His eyes sweep the room and land on me.

"Well, this is the end of my sanity."

twenty-three

· · ·

RORY

I walk over and grab the blanket off the back of the couch to cover Summer.

"It's just underwear." I can tell she's trying to shrug it off, but secretly she wants to melt into the floor.

"You're kind of...on display." I motion to her chest without dropping my eyes there.

Her eyes widen, and she pulls the blanket tighter around her.

"Oh my god, did they see?"

I want to reassure her, but there's no doubt that they did. It was the first thing my eyes had connected with when I walked in the door. Those tight nipples pressed against the soft cotton of her tank top.

I wonder if there's a medical spa service for extracting the image of my wife's nipples from these guys' brains. I'd spare no expense for that procedure.

"Possibly."

If it were me walking in alone, I'd chuckle, but there's nothing funny about my teammates seeing my wife half naked.

"We didn't see anything," Charlie says, covering his eyes.

"That's a lie." Logan claps. "Encore!"

I glare at him and his clapping dies mid-beat.

After a tough practice, I'd been slow to shower and the guys had gotten to my house before me. I'd texted Summer, but it's clear she didn't get the message.

"What? I like to dance around in my underwear, too." Logan motions to Eli. "Eli's seen me before."

Eli shakes his head. "Unfortunately, yeah."

Logan keeps talking. It's what he does in these situations. "Most people don't realize air guitar is all in the wrist, but man, you nailed it."

Eli holds up the bags in his hands. "We brought dinner. It's a Tuesday night tradition."

"Oh, shit. Do you think because Summer's here now, Tuesday nights aren't taco night anymore?" Charlie asks.

"Fuck that. I'm eating those tacos and I'm eating them while they're warm," Logan growls. Snatching a bag out of Eli's hand, he walks over to the dining table, dumps the bags' contents on the table, unwraps a taco and yells, "Let's feast!"

I'm about to tell Logan to collect his tacos and get the fuck out of my house when Summer clicks off the record player, then disappears down the hallway. She's my priority, so I follow her into the bedroom.

"I'm sorry about the guys barging in. They've always walked in unannounced. They should have knocked."

"Yeah, that would have been nice." She drops the blanket on the bed, then reaches in a drawer to pull out her work skirt. Before I can stop myself, my gaze trails down the back of her legs. Those tan, toned legs that already had me off my game at the courthouse.

I drag my eyes away. I need to stop eye-fucking my fake wife.

This isn't high school, and she's not some crush I can't stop staring at. She's Summer. Independent, untouchable Summer.

And she's trusting me. The least I can do is pretend I'm not undressing her with my eyes.

"Logan is moodier than I remember him being."

"Yeah, he gets cranky when he's hungry." I motion toward the noise my friends are making in the living room. "I can tell them to go."

"No, don't. It's tradition. You guys had all this going on before I came into the picture and I don't expect anything to change."

"But things are different now." The words fall from my mouth without a thought.

Summer blinks ups at me. "We got married six hours ago. They shouldn't be. You guys can pretend like I'm not here."

I keep my focus on her face, ignoring the hot-blooded instinct to drop my gaze to her chest where her nipples are still pebbled beneath her tank top.

"That's impossible."

"It shouldn't be. Isn't that the goal of our arrangement? To keep your routine?"

I lean against the bathroom doorway, watching her pull her wavy locks into a ponytail. My eyes scan the length of her, stopping at the curve of her ass.

She clears her throat. "I can see you in the mirror."

"The rules never said anything about not looking at you."

"Maybe they should." She turns to face me and now she's right there.

"I liked seeing you like that."

"Like what?" She crosses her arms defensively. She thinks I'm talking about her being braless.

"Carefree. Content."

It was the same version of Summer I saw a few nights ago when she was eating her burger and making little sighs of satisfaction.

I'd mentioned it to her then, and now the same look she gave me that night is sliding over her features. It's like she thinks she's in trouble for enjoying life. For being happy.

But while I'd enjoyed her display of joy and contentment, I'd been caught off guard by the possessiveness I'd felt.

"I've got to admit, I didn't like the guys seeing you like that."

"Why?" she asks, her breath hitching.

"Because you're *my wife*."

"Your *fake* wife," she reminds me.

"Still mine," I say. It's half a joke, but I feel the truth of it in my gut.

She narrows her eyes at me.

It's another silent standoff, like the one in her van last week. Another conversation of me wanting to protect her while she asserts her independence. I like it more than I should.

She's the first to break eye contact. Brushing past me without a word.

I follow her lead, the tension between us crackling but unspoken as we head out to the living room where the guys are packing up the tacos Logan unceremoniously dumped on the table.

"We can leave now," Finn says. "Logan ate five tacos which should be enough to sustain him for the drive home."

Summer shakes her head. "You guys stay. I have to leave for work anyway."

"Thanks for letting us stay," Charlie says, chowing down on a taco. "We figured with what happened at practice Rory would need taco night."

"What happened at practice?" Summer asks, turning her attention back to me.

"Nothing," I'm quick to say.

"Connor Fisk showed up," Logan says, sounding far less combative now that he's buried in tacos.

"Who's Connor Fisk?" she asks.

When Logan goes to answer her question, I give him a sharp nod.

"Just a guy on the team," Logan says before starting to inhale another taco.

It's not that I don't want Summer to know about Connor, but now is not the time.

"Can I give you a ride to work?" I ask, watching her slip on her tennis shoes and grab her purse off the hook by the door.

"Stay in your lane, Shields," she says, reaching for the door handle.

"What's that supposed to mean?" I call to her retreating back.

"You're the swimmer, you should know." She waves without looking back.

I know what it means, but where Summer's concerned, it doesn't feel like an option.

Logan places his key to my house in my palm.

"We still know the front door code," Charlie says.

"Thanks for the reminder to change that, too."

"Can we still come over for Madden Mondays?" Xio asks. He's nineteen and the youngest on the team. He's like a little brother to most of us, eager to hang out and for the most part, takes our teasing in stride.

"Yes, but you'll have to knock."

His face lights up at the knowledge that our team gatherings aren't changing.

"This feels like a breakup," Charlie says, removing his key from his keyring.

"Why'd you have to go and ruin everything by getting married?" Logan pouts.

"You know why," I mutter.

"But if it's for show, then Summer's more like a roommate, right?" Xio asks.

"You told him?" I direct my question to Logan.

While I'd told Eli, Logan, and Charlie about my arrangement with Summer, I didn't plan to share the details with the entire team.

"Actually, I told him." Finn nods from the chair where he's got his nose in his phone.

"Who told you?" I ask.

"Shit. He must have overheard Eli and me talking about it."

Finn smirks, his eyes still focused on his phone. "If I had a roommate that looked like Summer, we'd be fucking."

Logan lets out a low whistle and Eli flicks Finn on the back of the head before I reach out and yank his phone out of his hands.

"What the—" Finn looks up at me.

My eyes sharpen on him. "That's my wife you're talking about."

"Oh, shit." His eyes widen with the realization that he spoke before his brain even processed what it was saying. "Sorry," he mumbles, sinking farther into the chair.

"Rory and Summer's relationship is off limits," Eli announces. "We're a team and we support each other."

"And if we find out you're talking about them, you'll be sent to Spruce to get your asshole waxed," Logan chimes in.

"Wait—what?" Xio blurts, panic creeping into his voice.

"It's a special brand of torture that will help you remember to keep your mouth shut."

"Why your asshole?" Finn asks.

"Because it hurts like hell, that's why." There's an annoyed edge to Logan's voice.

"How do you know?" Xio asks.

Logan shakes his head. "No more questions."

"You said we're a team." Xio motions to the group. "What about Connor? Are we supposed to hate this guy or just ignore him?"

After practice, I'd sat in the ice bath to help with my knee and shoulder stiffness. Making sure Connor knew his place had made me train harder than I would have normally. When Coach had us at eighty-percent, I was giving close to one-hundred. It's not sustainable but I needed to set a precedent today.

Even if I have nothing to prove, Connor joining the Current is a punch-in-the-gut reminder that everything's changing, and my time in the pool might be running out.

"Yeah. What do you want us to do about Connor?" Charlie asks.

"Still can't believe he showed up. And that Coach agreed to train him," Logan says.

Eli grabs a taco from the pile. "I can't speak for Owens but he must see something in the guy."

"He's a phenomenal swimmer," Xio says, his gaze far-off like he's starstruck. "His Paris swim for the two-hundred individual medley was flawless."

Logan nods. "Shitty character and self-centered, but Xio's right, there's no debating his skill."

With all the back-and-forth comments, I finally respond. "You guys don't have to ice him out on my account."

Logan shakes his head. "We won't have to do anything, Connor is a lone wolf, he'll keep to himself."

Logan is right. Connor's career has been built off his egoism. He's always put himself first, disregarding how his actions affect others. While swimming is an individual sport, the grueling training and strict lifestyle makes it important to have a support system and team that you can rely on. Owens mentioned that Connor was looking for a team dynamic, but unless he changes how he interacts with others, he's not going to benefit from the close-knit training group we have at the Current. And while I'm the team captain and enjoy helping others, I put my effort and mentorship into Connor once and I got burned.

Xio sighs.

"What's going on, kid?" I ask.

He wrings his hands together. "I'm worried about my spot on the four-by-one-hundred freestyle relay. With Connor here, I know he'll knock me off the relay team."

Logan smirks. "Don't you worry about that. Connor doesn't do relays."

Xio tilts his head in confusion. "What do you mean?"

I turn to Xio. "Logan's right. He could anchor any relay team he wanted but he never does."

"Why?" Finn asks, joining the conversation.

"Lone wolf," Logan responds, still chowing down on his taco.

"So even though he could medal with all of the relay teams, he chooses not to?" Finn questions.

Their confusion is warranted. It doesn't make sense to not lend your talent to a relay team, but that's just another thing that bugs the hell out of me about Connor. And another reason why I'm dumbfounded that he joined the Current.

We finish the tacos, all sixty of them, then after a few games of Madden, the guys leave.

Once they're gone, I pull Edgar into my lap, then check my email, before responding to some questions Vivi has for my social media. I send her a picture of me and Summer from the courthouse ceremony. My arm around Summer's waist while she's staring up at me with a soft grin. It had been right before I kissed her. Right before everything shifted and I realized I was in way deeper than I meant to be.

I drop my phone and let my eyes close.

Even half-asleep on the couch, all I can think about is the way she looked at me today, and how damn much I want to see that look again.

twenty-four

. . .

Déjà vu hits the second I step out the back door of The Salty Pirate Café and spot Rory. My arms immediately cross over my chest. Not because it's cold, because I'm annoyed. Mostly at Rory, but partially at myself for the rush of excitement at seeing him there.

"You don't have to walk me home," I say, giving him my best side-eye as I head for the dumpster with the bag of trash in my hand.

Rory follows, lifting the lid of the dumpster so I can throw the bag in.

"I know, but I didn't want you to get lost." He shoves his hands into his pockets, lips curving into the butterfly-inducing smile I know all too well.

When Rory smiles at me I get flustered. To hide my reaction, I overcompensate and become mean.

"What are you talking about? I've been in Coral Cove for months."

"Yeah, but you just moved into my house today, so technically you've never walked home from the café to our place before."

"Our place?" My brows lift.

"Used to be mine. But you live there now. Mine plus yours equals ours."

He's logical. He's sweet. And he's exasperating.

All I can do is shake my head.

"Did you have a good shift?" he asks, motioning for us to start walking.

"Yeah, we were busy as usual."

Habit has me moving in the direction toward the RV park, but Rory takes my hand to pull me in the opposite direction.

"It's a good thing I'm here." He chuckles. "You're already lost."

"Or maybe you're a distraction and I'd be fine without you," I mutter, pulling my hand from his, knowing full well my brain has a tendency to get sidetracked when he's nearby.

He lets my hand go, but his fingertips on my back steer me in the right direction.

Once we're making our way down Wavecrest Way, our bodies naturally fall into a rhythm that feels effortless, yet I'm hyperaware of the space between us, or more accurately, how little space there is. As we stroll down the narrow sidewalk, our arms brush every now and then, and each time, my skin tingles like it's remembering something that my brain refuses to acknowledge.

Like the kiss I've been replaying in my head since this morning.

You're attracted to Rory. You like him. It taunts me.

That's when I notice he's humming a familiar tune. It's "Go Your Own Way."

"What?" His grin is all innocence. "It's catchy."

I narrow my gaze.

"Logan did a repeat performance after you left."

My jaw drops. "In his underwear?"

"No, he kept his clothes on."

"God, that was embarrassing."

"You don't have to be embarrassed. It was adorable."

All I can do is shake my head as I relive the humiliation that was Rory's teammates walking in on me singing in my underwear.

"Just so you know, I collected the guys' keys and told them they had to knock from now on."

"Thank you."

We walk in silence for a beat, the air outside heavier than it was earlier. A breeze picks up, stirring the hem of my skort and carrying the scent of salt into the air.

The wind blows the loose hairs from my ponytail into my face, so I lift a hand to smooth them back.

"Who's this Connor guy?" I ask.

"Connor Fisk." The name comes out on a sigh. There's a beat of silence before Rory continues. "I mentored Connor when he was in high school and I was in college. I recognized his talent and I wanted to help him navigate the industry. There was a sponsorship opportunity that came up. A flashy and lucrative brand deal but the company's practices were questionable. I turned it down and advised Connor to do the same. He didn't listen. Took the payout, then became this guy I didn't recognize."

"So, he went to the dark side?" I ask, using the only analogy I can think of for this situation...*Star Wars.*

Rory laughs, and the sound resonates in my chest.

"Yeah, I guess you could say that."

"Connor is Darth Vader, and you're Luke Skywalker."

"Except he's not my father."

"And you don't have a crush on your sister."

He laughs. "Speaking of Whitney, she'll be here next week."

"That's exciting. Does she have a place to stay?"

"She's moving in with Winnie."

We walk up the steps to the side porch. While I'm waiting for Rory to unlock the door, I study him. His t-shirt is stretched against his strong, broad back, his shorts hugging his tapered waist at the same time straining against his sculpted ass. Wind-blown and tousled, his thick, wavy hair has me yearning to run my hands through it. And then there's the way his long, steady fingers grip the key before shoving it into the keyhole with such force and precision that I nearly gasp with longing.

The image of Rory's hard, muscular body hovering over me, pressing me into the mattress and whispering in my ear. *That's it, Wildflower. Let me fill you up.*

"What did you tell Whitney about us?" I stutter, trying to redirect my thoughts.

He opens the door and flips on the hallway light before motioning for me to enter. Once I'm inside, he closes the door behind us and locks it.

Rory slips out of his sandals while I move to toe-off my tennis shoes.

A teasing smile plays at his lips. "That you fell madly in love with me and begged me to marry you."

I gasp in horror, then threaten him with one of my shoes. "You take that back or I'll call Daphne right now and tell her everything."

Rory lets out a small chuckle, shaking his head. His

hand brushes over the top of his thick, sandy-blond hair. I bite my lip watching his fingers tease through the strands, wishing they were mine.

"I told her that our marriage was quick, but necessary."

"Necessary, how?" I need to know what information Rory has divulged so I'm not caught off guard.

"I didn't give her details, only that it made sense for both of us."

"Hmm." I drop the shoe to its match on the floor and walk farther into the house.

Edgar is there in the living room curled up on the rug as if he's been doing it for years. I scoop him up and carry him down the hallway with Rory following behind me.

Inside Rory's bedroom, he pulls out his phone.

"Vivi sent me this for our approval." Rory hands me the phone and I see a picture of us at the courthouse. "We're spinning it as a one-month anniversary post."

I scroll to the next photo. It's one of us kissing after the judge had pronounced us husband and wife. I've thought about our kiss countless times today, but recalling how it felt and seeing how we looked are two very different things. This photo offers me a glimpse into just how much I liked kissing Rory. And how easy it will be to convince anyone who sees it that we are really together.

The visual of us alone is enough to spur tiny rivulets of pleasure to build in my belly.

Flooded with the memory of kissing Rory and the visual evidence of how hot it really had been, my blood surges, causing a flush to creep up my neck. My brain desperately struggles to keep the awareness of it off my face.

"You were really into our kiss today, huh?"

I tilt my head. "Excuse me?"

"For the photos," he says, smirking now. "Hands gripping my jacket. I think you even sighed into my mouth a little."

I can't hold it back any longer. Heat rushes to my face. Embarrassment or annoyance, it doesn't really matter at this point. "That was *you* sighing."

"Oh, I definitely didn't sigh. But you?" He gives me a knowing grin. "You were enjoying yourself."

"I was selling it," I bite out.

"Uh-huh. Whatever helps you sleep tonight."

My face pinches into a scowl, but there's no real venom in it. If anything, I hate how much I like this, how easy it is to fall into a playful back and forth with him.

"You need anything?" he asks, quieter now.

I hesitate, feeling the weight of the moment. He's being genuine, not teasing, not cocky, just *him*. And for some reason that feels more dangerous than anything else.

We got married today so I can use his insurance. He moved me into his house. What more could I possibly need?

He pulls his t-shirt off and yanks back the covers. His athletic shorts hang low on his waist and when he leans over to adjust his pillow, I swear I can see the outline of his cock against the soft material.

A few ideas spring to mind but I push them away.

"No, I'm good."

I set Edgar down in the bed that Rory bought for him, then head for the bathroom to get ready.

After brushing my teeth and washing my face, I flip off the light and return to the bedroom.

Rory's king-size bed is huge compared to the small loft bed we slept on in my van, yet seeing him lying in bed with the sheets bunched at his waist, the smooth skin of his torso partially highlighted by the light from the bedside lamp, I'm suddenly overwhelmed.

"Do you have extra pillows?" I ask.

"How many do you need?"

Rory pushes back the covers to stand and reveals himself in a pair of black boxer briefs.

They're just tighter versions of his usual shorts, but my brain was not prepared and now I'm struggling to look at or think about anything else.

"What?" I blink, finally pulling my gaze from the space between Rory's thighs.

"Pillows." He chuckles. "How many?"

I need to build a fortress. A pillow wall between me and Rory and these dirty thoughts I'm having.

"All of them."

Another loud, echoing boom of thunder detonates overhead, rattling the windows.

I hate thunderstorms. A gentle rain is nice, but resounding thunder and the hard pelting of rain against the roof is a big nope for me.

Logically, I know there's no imminent threat. I checked the radar on my phone and it's just a thunderstorm, but I can't calm down. With sleep nowhere in sight and Rory snoozing soundly on the other side of the pillow wall I created, I crawl out of bed and sneak past Edgar, who's oddly not disturbed by storms.

Out in the living room, I turn on the lamp by the couch. With the room illuminated, I can see all my plants lined up on the shelves that Rory had cleared for them.

I randomly select a book from Rory's collection, pull the blanket off the back of the couch and wrap it around me.

As the rain pours down outside, I open the book and reread the first page seventeen times. My brain is looking for a distraction, but the words aren't pulling me in.

"Can't sleep?"

The voice behind me has me jumping higher than the last boom of thunder.

It's Rory, leaning against the doorframe. The view of him in his boxer briefs just as enticing as it was earlier.

"What gave it away?" I ask, closing the book.

He walks around the couch and drops down next to me. Even from a few inches away, I sense how warm and solid his body is.

"I didn't peg you as a storm worrier."

"I'm not. I just hate how unpredictable it is."

Another crack of thunder shakes the house, and I can't help but flinch. Rory takes the book out of my hand.

"Come here."

My eyes narrow at his motioning gesture. "Come here, what?"

"You're not going to sleep, so you might as well get comfortable."

He shifts, opening his arms like it's the most natural thing in the world. My body is walking the line between the adrenaline rush from the storm, and exhaustion from the day. After a moment of hesitation, I give in. His arms come around me, strong and solid, while his heartbeat is a steady drum against my cheek.

Why is he so warm and inviting and annoyingly irresistible?

"This is silly. I don't need to be comforted."

Rory's chin presses against the top of my head. "That's why you're clinging to me like a baby koala?"

"This isn't clinging. I'm simply existing on top of you."

"Mmhmm. Whatever you say, wife."

Another crack of thunder and his arms tighten around me. His hand starts to rub slow, soothing circles against my back. It reminds me of the night my van was broken into.

"Have storms always bothered you?" he asks.

Those slow, absentminded circles have me in a trance.

"No. I used to love them, actually."

"What changed?"

I shrug, my shoulder nudging against his chest.

"I don't know. Somewhere along the way, they started making me feel...trapped."

Somewhere along the way was the summer after my sophomore year, when Tripp and I had been dating for a few months and everything started to shift.

Above me, his voice is gentle. "Trapped how?"

"Like you know something is coming, but you can't stop it. You just have to sit there and take it."

"You felt powerless?"

An uncomfortable lump in my throat makes it difficult to swallow.

That's exactly how I felt in my old life.

"And unwanted," I murmur, giving voice to the hurt that I experienced with my ex.

Beneath me, Rory stiffens slightly, and just for a second his fingertips falter on my back before resuming their lazy circles.

But I'm all too aware that he's pulling at a thread that I don't want to unravel.

Pushing off his chest, I sit up and move away.

"You should get some sleep."

From the opposite end of the couch, Rory stares at me, his eyes narrowing slightly.

"I'm not going anywhere." His voice is low and firm. I can hear the frustration in it.

He shifts over until his thigh presses against mine. With those blue eyes boring into mine, his hand cups my jaw.

"I don't get it, Summer. You've got this idea in your head that you're hard to want. And I'm trying to figure out what idiot made you think that, so I can prove them wrong."

Tripp. He's the idiot. My brain knows this. For years, it's been trying to reassure me that the lack of intimacy in my relationship was more about him than about me. But there's a sneaky part of my subconscious that doesn't believe it.

Then, there's the fact that I have no new experiences to wipe Tripp from my memory. No counter evidence to his rebuff.

Tripp once controlled so much of my life, it's been years since we were together, and I'm tired of letting him still have an impact on me this way.

"My ex. We met in college and my family loved him. That should have been the first sign, but back then I was still the perfect, obedient daughter."

Rory's jaw tenses. "Did he—"

I shake my head. "No, he wasn't abusive. He was all about appearances, just like my parents. He told me what to wear, how to act."

I swallow, holding the tears back.

"What else, Wildflower?" Rory strokes his thumb over my tattoo.

"It's stupid." It's what Tripp used to say to me when I'd try to explain how I was feeling. I hate that I still use that word when I don't know how to explain how I feel.

"Nothing about how you feel is stupid," Rory assures me.

The way he's looking at me right now makes me believe that.

"He didn't want me. You know?"

A rush of breath flows from Rory's mouth and he immediately shakes his head.

"I don't understand how that's possible."

I roll my eyes, remembering how serious Tripp was about everything. Everything except me.

"He had this thing about his hair." I half-laugh, recalling Tripp's incessant need for perfection. Not a hair out of place.

"What was that?" Rory prompts.

"He hated when I touched it. Even when I tried being affectionate, he'd scold me like a child. It sounds silly, but after all those years with my ex, I struggle with showing affection. I just shut down and keep my distance, too afraid I'll make the wrong move."

"Summer, that's fucked up."

I shrug, not sure how else to respond. I'm already feeling like I've revealed too much. I've let Rory peek at my insecurity and I wish I could take it all back.

Rory stands from where he's been sitting on the couch and moves in front of me.

I glance up at him. He's massive. Those broad shoulders and long, muscular arms of his appearing almost wing-like. At least that's what Scarlett had planted in my head when she'd sent me a picture of Rory at a competition comparing him side by side to a character in the romantasy series she's currently reading. I'm not a fantasy reader, but I'm starting to understand the appeal of someone who is otherworldly. That's how Rory seems to be. Perfectly sculpted from stone.

He drops to his knees, settling in at my feet.

"What—" I start, but in the next moment, his intentions are clear when his hands gently wrap around my wrists before slowly guiding them to the sides of his head.

The moment my fingertips touch his hair; I'm startled by how intimate it feels.

My eyes find his and he nods in reassurance before giving me that devastatingly handsome smile of his.

"Get in there, Wildflower. Mess it up real good."

When I don't move, Rory guides my hands through his hair and gives them a shake, causing the sides of his hair to stick out.

A surprised laugh escapes from my throat. And a piece of the armor I've secured around my heart weakens at his gesture.

"You look wild."

"Good. Now show me what you can do."

It's hair. On his head. Yet dipping my fingers into Rory's thick strands sends a wave of pleasure coursing through my body that I haven't felt in a long time. It's more than just contact. It's connection.

His hands remain on my wrists for a minute, then he drops them to the couch on either side of my hips.

I'm like a child being given a paint set for the first time. I want to explore and discover all the possibilities.

I push through the strands, lifting them upward until Rory looks like he's been shocked by electricity. Then, I smooth it out again before teasing the center up into a mohawk. Before long, my exploration has his hair a mess, sticking out every which way.

As my fingers comb through his hair, I find myself relaxing. I start to play with different pressures. Applying more weight to the pads of my fingers near the sides and crown of his head, before easing off and using my fingernails lightly against the back of his head.

Pretty soon I'm lost in the feeling of freedom and my curiosity takes over.

My hand slides to the back of his head, loving the feeling of his hair running between each finger before I scissor them together and give a light tug.

A muffled whimper slips past Rory's lips. It's raw and unguarded, the same way I'd felt a moment ago when I'd pulled his hair. At the sound of him, my nipples harden and slickness gathers between my thighs.

Rory's low whimper settles between us and my eyes go wide with uncertainty.

"I'm sorry."

My fingers release his hair, my hand immediately withdrawing, but Rory catches my wrist.

He shakes his head. "Don't be. I liked it." His voice is still trembling with the weight of pleasure.

He's telling me it's okay. He liked it, but I've never heard a man make that sound before. And I've never been this turned on before, either.

"Okay." I nod, pulling away to busy myself with folding up the blanket, before standing to return the unread book to the shelf. "Thanks for that. It was nice." My words come out in a rush before I quickly retreat down the hallway.

When I get back to the bedroom, I jump into bed and pull up the covers. Shoving my hands under my cool pillow, I take a shallow breath.

Oh my god. What was that?

It was supposed to be amusing. Me messing up Rory's hair as consolation for my ex's inability to ever let me touch his. But the way my body responded. The sound Rory made when I tugged his hair. It all felt like more than that. It was electric and terrifying and I want to do it again.

A moment later, I hear Rory enter the room. On the other side of the pillow wall, the bed dips with his body weight and I hear the rustle of the sheets as he pulls them up.

He sighs. "You know, Wildflower, I think you just ruined me."

"What?" The single word is muffled into my pillow.

"The feel of your hands in my hair. Nothing has ever felt that good."

"I'm glad you liked it." The darkness covers up my cringe. What am I saying? "Goodnight."

"Goodnight, Summer."

twenty-five

. . .

RORY

After three hours of dryland training and swim practice, followed by a high-protein meal and ice bath, I spend an hour with Coach reviewing this week's training goals and the upcoming meets. Then, video analysis of my recent breaststroke form to evaluate how my rehabbed knee is performing, and a check-in with the team's dietician.

Now, after a strength training session in the weight room, I'm toweling off from my shower.

It's my usual Friday routine. Same grind. Same goals. Same sore body.

But ever since Summer and I got married, nothing feels the same.

I'm here doing the work, pushing my body through every set and rep, but my mind keeps drifting back to her.

Every spare second, I'm back on my couch holding Summer during that thunderstorm. Recalling how she'd looked at me like I was the safest place in the world while the rain pounded against the roof. And then, she'd told me about her ex, how he used to hate it when she touched his hair. How he made her feel like she was too much in even the small way she wanted to give love.

So, I'd let her run her hands through my hair.

The way she'd started out so careful, so tentative, before she got bolder. Her fingers finally threading deeper through my hair, tugging, and exploring. I'd loved watching her confidence grow. Not to mention how amazing it had felt to have her hands on me. Even the softest touch from her had wrecked me.

Now, I notice everything about her.

The way she hums when she's sketching in her notebook. The way she tugs the sleeves of my hoodie over her hands when she's cold. The way she kicks her toes against mine under the table like she doesn't even realize she's doing it.

She's driving me crazy without even trying. Every small, unguarded thing she does just makes me want her more.

And lately, it's getting harder to pretend I'm not dying to be the one she turns to for *everything*, not just comfort after a storm. I want to be the one who shows her exactly how much she's wanted. How much she's already mine.

"You good, man?" Eli asks. "You're awfully quiet today."

He's right. He's typically the quiet one, while I go full podcast mode on him. But today, Summer's presence in my head has me turning inward.

"Just tired." I try to play it off.

"That's never stopped you before." He smirks, drying his hair off with a towel.

I meet his assessing gaze. "I'm fine."

"I know that look. This is about your *wife*."

"Don't say it like that."

"Like what? Like *wife*? 'Cause that's what she is." He studies me a moment. "It's only been a week. Is there already trouble in paradise?"

Eli is my best friend and he's the one who understands me the most. He also understands relationships. He was set to propose to his college girlfriend, Blair, but they ended up breaking up instead. Even though he hasn't dated anyone seriously since, he's more knowledgeable about relationships than Logan and Charlie.

"You know that we're not really together, and our arrangement has rules."

"Yeah, you told me." He dries his hair with a towel. "You also told me it wouldn't be a problem." He shakes his head. "You're so fucking screwed."

"I was expecting a more motivational pep talk. You know, something along the lines of 'You got this, man. I'll help you through it.'"

"You got this, man. Your *hand* will help you through it." Eli grins.

We look up to see Connor exiting the showers. He's kept to himself since that first day, and for my part, I've done my best to ignore him. We've got a meet in Fort Lauderdale in a few weeks and I'm curious to see how Connor's presence affects the team's results.

How his presence affects *me*.

We get dressed, then Eli and I head for the locker room exit.

On our way out, we run into Charlie. "What are you guys up to tonight?"

"Rory here is in need of a distraction."

"From what?" Charlie asks.

Eli smirks. "Longingly staring at his wife's lips."

Charlie nods knowingly. "How about you have people over tonight? Do a bonfire on the beach."

I nod at Charlie's suggestion. "That could work."

We're on our way toward the front door when we run into Vivian.

"Eli, I need to talk to you," she says.

Eli sighs like he's been avoiding Vivi and he just got caught. "It doesn't matter what the payout is, the answer is no."

"Seriously?" Vivi turns to gape at me. "Will you talk some sense into him?"

I shrug, because there's nothing I can do.

I get that Eli wants to keep a low profile, but it's not like we're celebrities that can't walk down the street without getting mobbed. And while it's important to do the research and be selective about our brand endorsement deals to understand who we are aligning ourselves with, Eli hasn't done a campaign in years. We call him the endorsement snob.

"First off, it's annoying that you're shooing me away like a car salesman even though you don't know what I wanted to talk to you about."

Eli nods apologetically. "I'm sorry, Vivian."

"Apology accepted. Now if you had checked your emails, you'd have seen I was trying to tell you that you've been named *All Sports* Sexiest Athlete of the Year." Vivi claps then wraps her arms around Eli in a celebratory hug. "Congratulations."

Eli stands stock still, simply patting Vivi on the back during her moment of celebration.

"Why aren't we celebrating?" she asks, clearly annoyed with our lack of enthusiasm.

I clear my throat. "*All Sports* is the magazine that you know who works for."

Vivi's eyes widen when she understands what I'm telling her. Eli's ex, Blair, is a Brand Partnerships Manager at *All Sports*. His nomination likely had nothing to do with her because she's responsible for securing advertisers and sponsorship deals, but that doesn't matter.

Vivi sighs. "You have to say yes, or I'll cry. I've always wanted one of my clients to be picked."

"Hey, what about me?" I ask, rubbing my chest while attempting to sound hurt.

"You got the title six years ago. I wasn't the PR manager then."

Eli groans. "I'll think about it."

"Hey, Viv. Bonfire at my house tonight. Tell everyone."

"Did I hear someone say bonfire?" a voice calls out.

I turn to find Whitney darting toward us.

She's weighed down by a large backpack, its weight swinging wildly with every hurried step she takes, but that doesn't stop her from launching herself at me.

"Hurricane Whit...incoming!" she calls out.

Catching her midair, her impact is solid, but I hold my ground. I squeeze her tight. Feeling the solid strength she's built over the last four years, a flash of pride hits me. My little sister isn't so little anymore.

Vivi laughs at the sight of us.

"It's good to have you home," I say, as Whitney finally drops to her feet.

"Thanks! It feels good to be here."

She shoves a strand of hair out of her face and smiles up at me with the same stubborn sparkle she's had since she was five years old and convinced me she could swim out to the sand bar without floaties.

"You look good," I add, studying her. "Not too worn out from the season."

"Give her a week with our training program," Charlie teases.

Logan, who just exited the locker room, catches the scene and jogs over, grinning.

Behind him, Connor walks by, his eyes on the group. No, not the group, on Whitney. Protectiveness surges through my veins and every brotherly instinct I have kicks to life like a starting gun. Connor's got a reputation for being a loner in the pool, but from what I've heard, it's the opposite where women are concerned.

I lift my chin in his direction, giving him a hard look.

It's not an invitation, it's an order. *Move along.*

"What's on the agenda today?" I ask, redirecting my attention to Whitney.

"I just got myself settled into Winnie's house and I'm meeting with Alex for weight training."

"Winnie's house?" Logan lets out a low whistle and shakes his head. "Good luck surviving all her rules."

Whitney laughs. "Not eating on the couch isn't the end of the world."

Logan lifts his brows, looking personally offended. "Speak for yourself, Whit. Couch snacks are sacred."

Whitney ignores him and flashes me a curious smile. "Oh, and I can't wait to meet my new sister-in-law."

"That's right. You haven't met Summer yet." My chest tightens with a strange mix of excitement and nerves. Whitney's opinion matters to me, and Summer's quickly taking up residence in my thoughts and if I'm going to admit it, my heart.

What if they don't hit it off?

"You're going to love her," I add quickly.

"She's really great," Vivi adds, saving me.

Whitney lifts a brow, but she lets me off the hook. "I'm sure I will." Then she turns to go. "Gotta head to my training session."

"Before you go, I'm having people over later. Bonfire on the beach. You in?"

"For sure. Text me." She waves, then moves toward the locker rooms.

"I've got a meeting. I'll see you guys later." Vivi's eyes drop to her phone as she walks toward the offices.

Charlie, Logan, Eli, and I keep walking toward the exit.

"You mentioned Summer is asthmatic," Eli says. "Isn't smoke a trigger for asthma?"

Oh shit. Is it? I can't believe I didn't even think about it.

"Yeah, I guess you're right."

The more I think about it, the worse I feel. How am I supposed to be a supportive husband if I don't know even know what her triggers are? Sure, I could Google it, but that's not the same thing as knowing what Summer needs specifically.

Now, I'm recalling Summer has a doctor's appointment today.

Thanks to the Current's staff, they managed to fast-track her insurance application but first-time applicants have to do a full health exam. With how stubborn Summer was about getting her prescription filled, I can only imagine she's not going to be the easiest to talk to about her triggers and limitations, but getting the information straight from her doctor would be helpful. It would put me at ease, that's for sure.

I glance at my watch. She should be there now.

"I've got an appointment, but I'll let you guys know about the bonfire later."

After exiting the aquatic center, I head straight for my car, and then Coral Cove's medical center.

twenty-six

. . .

After taking my vitals and paperwork, the nurse left me in a paper gown to await the doctor.

As I wait, I stare at the muscular system chart on the wall of the doctor's exam room I'm sitting in. The human body sure has a lot of muscles. The chart makes me think of Rory and his sculpted physique. I scan over the laminated chart. *Yep, he's definitely got that muscle...and that one.*

I'd felt them all the night he wrapped his arms around me on the couch.

This morning, I'd been thankful Rory was already gone to practice when I woke up to walk the dogs. I've been keeping a bit of distance since the storm last week—the night I buried my hands in his hair.

That moment's been replaying in my mind more than I'd like to admit. I haven't touched him like that since, not because I don't want to, but because I want to *too much*.

After the walk, I spent the rest of the morning painting. The memory of the thunderstorm, the wildness of the rain and the tension between us, still lingers in my mind and my brushstrokes.

The door opens, pulling me from my thoughts. The nurse pops her head into the exam room. "Mrs. Shields, your husband is here."

"Rory?" I question as if I need to confirm which husband she's referring to.

"Your husband," she confirms.

"Right."

"Would you like him to join you?" Her smile is pleasant and easygoing. I'm sure this is a regular occurrence, husbands supporting their wives at the doctor.

I glance down at the paper gown I'm wearing.

Absolutely not.

But I keep that answer to myself because I don't think that's a normal response.

"Did he say if he needs something?" I ask.

"Just a minute." She closes the door. While I wait for her return, I swing my legs, my heels bouncing off the metal exam table below me.

A minute later, she's back.

"He has some questions for the doctor."

"What kind of questions?" I ask.

The nurse sighs. "Just a moment."

Her pleasantry appears to be waning with each round of telephone, so I motion her back.

"You know what, never mind. Just send him back."

A minute later, there's a knock on the door, and it opens with Rory standing behind the nurse.

"Hey."

I've seen him freshly showered nearly a dozen times now. That seems to be his typical state of being, but it never gets old. His thick tousled hair half damp while I can still see the light imprint of goggle marks around his eyes. If I leaned into him, I'd get a whiff of his eucalyptus body wash and the faint hint of chlorine. Finding myself shifting in his direction, I pull back until my spine is stick straight.

"What are you doing here?" I ask.

"Moral support." He grins. "And I realized I don't know much about your asthma, so I thought it would be best to educate myself. You know, since we're married now."

"That's why you're here?" I ask, annoyed he came all this way for something I could easily explain. "I can tell you anything you need to know."

"That's true, but you are the person who didn't think filling your inhaler was important, so forgive me if I want to hear the answers from a professional." He combs a hand over the top of his hair, and I watch in amazement how the bicep in his arm flexes so fluidly.

That one is especially well developed.

Refusing to be distracted, my brain refocuses on his words.

"That's rude. Don't you think I would be the best person to talk to about *my* specific condition?"

A knock on the door interrupts our conversation, but it doesn't stop me from stewing over Rory's insinuation that he doesn't trust me to tell him about my condition.

"Good afternoon, I'm Dr. Lasgo," she extends her hand to me.

"Summer."

"Nice to meet you."

Rory stands and shakes Dr. Lasgo's hand.

"I'm Rory. Summer's husband."

I shoot Rory a sharp look, but he just lifts his brows, unbothered. *What? I am.*

"Nice to meet you both. I see this visit is a physical exam requested by your insurance carrier."

"Yes." I nod.

"And I have some questions." Rory raises his hand like he's a student trying to get the teacher's attention.

"Sure." The doctor motions to Rory while she types on her laptop. "Go ahead."

"Would a bonfire with smoke be a trigger for Summer's asthma?" Rory asks.

"Smoke definitely can be a trigger. I think the most important thing is that Summer is consistent with using her inhaler, which I think she noted was out of date and at one time even empty." She reviews her notes on the computer.

"Yeah, that was not cool." Rory narrows his gaze at me.

"I'm taking care of it now." I motion to the exam room.

"Any other questions or concerns?" Dr. Lasgo asks, looking between us.

"What about exertion?" Rory asks, typing something into his phone. "What type of activity, if any, is off limits or needs to be monitored?"

My annoyance grows because I could have easily answered these questions.

"Again, that's Summer's call. There's no activity I would limit as long as she's got her inhaler on hand and has been using it regularly. Mild, daily activities like walking, hiking, and moderate aerobic exercise should be fine."

Rory glances down to his phone again.

"What about sex?" he blurts out.

My eyes bulge at Rory's question, but Dr. Lasgo doesn't

miss a beat. "Sex is not an activity that would need to be limited or refrained from. Again, it's Summer needing to monitor what she feels is a comfortable situation."

I shoot Rory a glance. *Are you done?*

Dr. Lasgo continues. "Though there are some intimate situations that could be triggering. Choking or breath play are not recommended."

"Got it. No choking or breath play." Rory looks so serious as he types on his phone.

Is he taking notes? I watch his brows crease with concentration. Yeah, he totally is.

"Certain positions that put pressure on the chest or abdomen that could make breathing more difficult should be refrained from. Also, temperature and humidity changes like a steamy shower could irritate the airways so use caution and monitor Summer's breathing in those situations."

While Rory nods and takes notes on his phone, I'm seriously considering climbing under the table.

"Strong scents, like scented candles, certain types of massage oils and lotions, sometimes contain ingredients that trigger asthma symptoms. Even unwashed bedding that contains dust mites could be an issue."

Rory looks up from his typing. "This is very helpful."

"If you have any further questions, you can give the nurse line a call."

"Can I get that number?" Rory asks.

Dr. Lasgo pulls a card out from the plastic holder on the wall and hands it to Rory.

"There you go."

"Thanks."

The doctor goes through the exam. Easy stuff like

listening to my lungs and checking my ears and throat. Then, she examines my wrist that was injured in Rory's skateboarding debacle.

"Is this still painful?" she asks, gently manipulating my wrist.

"A little bit tender but not like it was."

Dr. Lasgo nods. "I'd say you can stop using the brace. Take it easy but see how it feels to get full range of motion."

"Okay." I nod, happy to be rid of the brace.

"Now, Summer, I see you checked the box for birth control. That's something you would like to discuss at this visit?"

At Dr. Lasgo's words, Rory stands, nearly knocking over the tray beside the exam table. "Should I be here for this?"

Dr. Lasgo smiles kindly. "I think family planning conversations are important for both parties."

"Family planning?" Rory sits back down.

I'm about to disagree with Dr. Lasgo but it might be weird if I ask for Rory to leave. I mean, can it really get any more awkward than the choking and breath play comment?

"What is your current form of birth control?" Dr. Lasgo asks.

"Um, condoms?" It's a safe answer. It's what most people use. Most people who are having sex, which Rory and I are not.

"Is there any chance you could be pregnant?"

Do not look at Rory. Do not look at Rory.

"No." I shake my head.

"Have you ever been on oral contraception before?" the doctor continues.

"Yes. In college. About four years ago."

"Was there a reason you stopped taking the medication? Any side effects you were experiencing?"

Let's see, I broke up with my boyfriend who was cheating on me and swore off guys so birth control wasn't really on my mind. Until now.

Until Rory. The words float from the back of my brain where classified information is stored.

"No side effects. Just an insurance thing."

"Are you interested in a low-dose estrogen pill? Or would you like to discuss other options?"

"The pill is fine." I'm dying to move this conversation to something else.

"Okay. There shouldn't be any interference with your medications. Do either of you need STD screening while you're here?" Dr. Lasgo looks at me before shifting her gaze to Rory.

Kill me now.

For all the willpower I've exercised to not look at Rory, my eyes lock onto his.

"No. I'm good."

Rory nods his head. "Same."

"I'll get your prescriptions updated and sent over to the pharmacy."

"Thank you."

"It was nice to meet you both." Dr. Lasgo nods to us both before leaving.

Across the room, Rory is still as a statue.

I hop off the exam table. "I need to get dressed."

He nods. "Okay."

"So, you need to leave."

"Got it." He nods, heading for the door.

I get dressed, then find Rory, who wasn't chased away by the awkwardness of the previous conversation, waiting for me in the lobby of the medical center.

When I move toward the exit, he follows.

"You could have asked me those questions. I know all the answers. I know what level of exercise and exertion I can handle. I don't need you watching out for me. Trust me, I've had enough of that in my life."

"I get it, but I hate feeling helpless. Watching you wheeze and not be able to breathe properly was scary as fuck and if there are things I can do to accommodate you, then I will. But I need to know what they are."

"Asking questions about exertion...and sex *positions*?"

"Hey," he gives me a look, "I asked about sex. Dr. Lasgo brought up the specific triggers. Now we know choking is off the table."

I try to calm my racing heart while imagining Rory's large hands wrapping around my throat. His fingers applying firm, but gentle pressure.

"Choking was never on the table."

"Maybe a light hand necklace would be okay."

"*Rory.*"

He shrugs. "Sex is a part of life."

"Not *our* lives," I remind him, ignoring the dull ache between my thighs that this conversation has brought on.

"Yeah, I get that. Loud and clear."

The conversation in the exam room had triggered the memory of Tripp using my asthma as a reason to not touch me. He didn't want me to get worked up. I was too fragile and needed to stay calm. He'd even tried to convince me that's why he cheated. Like he was being considerate of me by fucking other women.

"By the way, I'm paying for the birth control with my own money," I say, glancing both ways before I cross the street to the parking lot.

I'll take advantage of Rory's insurance and prescription

discounts, but I need to keep as much independence in this relationship as I can.

"I already had them bill it to insurance. The balance gets automatically paid by my account."

"You're impossible, you know that?" I huff, turning to look at him while I wait for him to unlock the car.

"I prefer to view myself as a devoted husband." He opens the door to his Jeep for me, then climbs in and starts the engine.

"I was thinking of having some people over for a bonfire on the beach tonight. Are you okay with that?"

"It's your house. You don't have to ask me."

"It's our house," he says so matter-of-fact it surprises me. "And I'll always check with you."

I stare at him for a second, lips parting before I can think of a response.

"Fine," I say eventually, pretending to roll my eyes. "But only if there are s'mores."

"It wouldn't be a bonfire without them."

"Then I guess I'll allow it," I say, failing to hide my smile.

Rory hums, satisfied, and puts the Jeep in gear. We drive a few blocks in comfortable silence.

"Oh, by the way, I already picked up some dark chocolate for the s'mores."

I glance over. "From the grocery store?"

"No, that little place off Highway Seven. The one with the tiny parking lot and the sign that just says 'Cacao.'"

My eyebrows lift. I've only been there a few times because it's next to a gas station on the far end of Coral Cove and not convenient to get to.

"You went out of your way?"

He shrugs casually, eyes still on the road. "You

mentioned once that it was the best dark chocolate, smooth and not too bitter."

I blink at him. That's it. No big speech. No bragging. Just...he remembered and took action.

I turn toward the window, pretending to look at the ocean, but really I'm trying to calm the flutter in my chest. Because maybe this is what it feels like when someone really sees you.

twenty-seven

. . .

RORY

After Summer's doctor appointment, I went with her to walk her afternoon dogs, then dropped her off to work at the café.

I clean up the house, which takes longer than usual because Summer's stuff is sprawling all over the house. Her van always appeared tidy, but maybe that's because there was less space for things to roam.

A trail of her books on the coffee table.

A chipped mug full of paintbrushes on the kitchen counter.

Her favorite oversized cardigan tossed over the back of the couch.

A pair of flip flops abandoned by the front door.

And hair ties, so many hair ties, around doorknobs, next to lamps and every surface in between.

I cheerfully put things back in their place because damn if I don't get off on it. Summer's chaos tangled up with my calm makes this place feel more like home.

Then, Edgar and I nap on the couch for an hour before I have to hop on a zoom call to record a podcast with Lane Talk, a swimmer-focused podcast that discusses training, competition, and balancing life outside the pool.

For me, podcast interviews are easy. Talking with people and talking about swimming are two of my favorite things, so it's not until the hosts, Cullen and Patrick, bring up my marriage that I'm thrown off.

"Speaking of life outside the pool, we got a lot of questions from fans about your recent wedding," Patrick says.

Cullen laughs. "There are a lot of broken hearts out there."

"Before we get into it, first we should say congratulations."

"Yeah, congratulations," Cullen echoes.

"Thank you," I say, wishing I'd taken a look at Vivi's email prep for this.

"Now, I'll cut to the chase and ask all the burning questions listeners want to know. How is married life? And when did a busy guy like you find time to fall in love?"

"Married life is great. No complaints."

Except I may be falling for my fake wife.

"Your wife is listening, isn't she?" Cullen teases with a hearty laugh.

"No, she's at work, but I think she'd agree we're having fun."

"But seriously, what shifted? You've always been laser focused and now you're suddenly married. Was it love at first sight?" Patrick asks.

"I don't know if it was first sight, but it didn't take long." I hesitate, making sure my words are carefully crafted, but I can't help the smile that tugs at my mouth when I think how Summer and I met, and the way I was immediately drawn to her. "It was easy with her. And nothing in my life has ever felt easy."

Cullen's brows lift. "Sounds like you're a goner."

"She's someone who gets it. All of it. The pressure, the quiet, the weird schedule. And she makes all of that feel a little less heavy."

From the looks of Cullen and Patrick's faces, I nailed it.

They move on to ask about my training focus and upcoming competitions, but I'm only halfway listening. I'm still thinking about my responses to their questions about Summer. And all I can think is that for a fake marriage, everything I just said felt pretty damn real.

Eli was right. A bonfire with teammates and friends is the best way to keep myself distracted from thinking about Summer. Although I'm finding my eyes tracking her every move, which would be much easier if we were alone in the house, not mingling in a large group of people gathered around a roaring fire.

Through the flames, I can see Summer talking with Whitney. I look on as she takes a sip of her seltzer, nodding at something Whitney says before they both start laughing. Since I introduced my sister to Summer, they've been talking non-stop about art and design. I know it shouldn't matter, but I love that they're getting along so well.

"I'm just saying, *American Gridiron* is the same damn game every year. They just change the number and expect us to act impressed," Finn says, shaking his head.

Xio chuckles. "Yeah, and yet you still buy it."

"That's because I have hope, Xio. Maybe this time, it'll be worth it."

I can't help but grin at their conversation. "You really think they're going to fix *Dynasty Drive*?"

Finn grumbles, knowing full well I'm right but he's still going to continue to buy the game anyways.

Logan settles into a chair and crosses his ankle over his knee. "All right, pick one: you either get to be an Olympic athlete in your sport, or you're a pro gamer making millions. What's your move?"

Xio smirks. "Olympian, obviously."

Xio has been focused on making his first Olympic team this year. He's putting up impressive times and if he keeps it up, I have no doubt he'll make the team.

Finn shakes his head. "Pro gamer, easy. No early morning training. No ice baths. Just vibes and sponsorship money."

"You'd wash out in six months." Xio laughs.

"Okay, rude."

Finn mock-scowls because he knows that commitment isn't his strong suit.

"But true." Logan grins.

This is what I needed. A night with the guys on the beach talking about meaningless shit. Marrying Summer, then Connor showing up to train with the Current all in the span of a week has shifted the foundation of my once predictable life. But this feels good.

"Oh, shit," Logan murmurs under his breath.

"What?" I ask, half-chuckling as I reach for a seltzer water from the cooler.

"Connor's here."

My head jerks in the direction Logan's looking.

Sure enough, I can make out Connor's dark, messy hair

and arrogant grin through the flicker of the bonfire flames as he greets a group of people. But I refuse to give Connor the satisfaction of a reaction. It's clear from his actions since the moment he arrived in Coral Cove that's what he wants from me. So, I'll ignore him just like I've done at practice.

It's fine. Totally fine. No reason to tackle him into the bonfire.

Sitting back down, I crack open my water and take a large gulp, determined to not put any more energy into Connor's presence.

"Did someone change the music again?" Charlie asks, checking his phone.

"Hell no." Logan shakes his head. "We all know how protective you are of your curated playlists."

Eli chuckles. "Yeah, for a guy whose pre-race warm up song is 'Call Me Maybe,' you're awfully particular about setting the right musical tone tonight."

"'Call Me Maybe' gets my blood pumping like no other song can."

"Maybe if you're prepping for a middle school dance," I tease.

"Mock me all you want, but it's scientifically proven to boost performance."

"I'd love to see the science backing that."

My jaw relaxes and my mood lifts, until I catch Finn grimacing.

"What?" I ask. Before he can answer, I follow his gaze across the bonfire to where Connor is standing, but he's not alone this time. He's talking to Whitney and Summer, and my state of relaxation vanishes.

I know both women can hold their own, but seeing Connor near my sister and my wife sets off a primal instinct to protect what's mine.

Just the sight of them in the same proximity has me up out of my chair and moving in their direction.

As I approach, I see Connor holding Summer's hand. When her hand drops, it's obvious it was a handshake introduction but that doesn't matter to me. Every instinct in my body flares with irritation.

Seeing him near her twists something deep inside me. I can't shake the feeling that he's trying to get too close. He's testing me, pushing boundaries in a way that feels calculated. I'm sure it's just a part of his usual game, but that doesn't make it any easier to deal with.

"There he is." Connor motions with a lazy grin as I approach.

"Hey," Summer says with a soft smile. "I was just about to come find you."

I can tell by the look on her face that she's trying to diffuse the situation. But it's not her issue, it's mine.

"Connor." My tone is as sharp as the terse nod I give him. "Didn't expect to see you here," I say, wrapping a possessive arm around Summer's waist to stake my claim. Even though I'm focused on addressing Connor, I immediately notice how perfectly she fits against me. The curves of her body beneath the soft fabric of her dress, and the warmth of her body pressed against mine.

She relaxes into me and now my heartbeat quickens for a different reason. Not from the adrenaline of coming over to confront Connor, but the proximity of Summer and how she affects me.

When I turn my attention back to Connor, I see the glee in his eyes. He knows he's gotten a reaction from me.

Connor leans back slightly, like he's enjoying the discomfort he's stirring up. "Didn't realize I needed an invite. Team bonding, right? That includes me now."

I don't know if it's the way he keeps pushing or just the fact that he's here when he clearly wasn't invited, but my irritation is building.

"You don't get to show up here and act like we're all good. We're not. And team bonding usually works better when there's trust."

Connor's lips curl into that annoying half-smile.

"That's right. I forgot. Rory Shields is perfect. Your training, your medals, your life. Now," he motions to Summer, "the perfect little wife."

That's the last straw. I want to snap back at him, to let the anger loose, but it's not about him anymore. It's about her. Summer doesn't deserve to be reduced like that.

"Say whatever you want about me," I say, low and hard. "But you don't get to talk about her."

Beside me, Summer inhales sharply. Whitney's eyes go wide, but there's a knowing smile on her face.

Connor's smirk doesn't falter.

"Am I not being clear? Don't fucking talk about my wife."

"Whatever you say, golden boy." Connor's voice drips with bitterness.

Connor's older now, but it's clear he's still the same punk kid with an attitude. Thinking he can do whatever the hell he wants and screw everyone else.

Beside me, I feel the presence of Charlie, Eli, and Logan.

"Rory," Eli says, eyeing me with a knowing look. "Everything good over here?"

At my friends and teammates' arrival, Connor's smirk turns humorless. "Must be nice having people in your corner when it counts. Not all of us have had that luxury."

With that, Connor steps back and walks off.

I want to clap back at his declaration. Years ago, I was in

his corner, but that changed due to actions of his own doing. He doesn't like the results of his own behavior, but I don't see him owning up to it, either.

"You okay?" Summer asks, drawing my attention to her.

I look down to find her staring up at me with a curious expression. It makes me wonder if I took the protective husband thing too far.

With Connor gone, there's no reason to still be holding her snug against me, but I desperately want an excuse to keep her there.

Does simply loving the feel of her there suffice?

"Let's go grab the stuff to make s'mores," Whitney says to Summer.

"Yeah, okay." Summer nods before shifting out of my hold to leave with Whitney.

With them gone, the guys usher me back toward our chairs on the other side of the bonfire.

"Dude," Charlie claps me on the back as we walk, "you skipped the jealous boyfriend phase and went straight to 'that's my wife' energy."

The curious smirk from Eli has me thinking I'm already in too deep.

After s'mores are consumed, and the bonfire is put out, we make our way inside. Most of the guys and Whitney are playing video games while Winnie starts a drinking game for the remaining group—those who don't have swim practice tomorrow.

"Hey," Summer says, walking over with rosy cheeks and a lazy smile. She drops down onto the arm rest of the chair, her knees brushing against my thigh. "Some of the ladies are going to go out."

Summer's tipsy. But I have to admit, as long as she's safe, I like seeing her let loose.

"You going to go?" I ask, knowing no matter how much I want Summer to myself, I know what she needs. To make her own choices and feel supported.

"Yeah. I think I will."

"Okay. You have the key and the door code to get in?"

Summer nods.

"You're not going to miss me too much, are you?"

I chuckle softly. "I'll try to survive without you."

"Hmm."

I expect her to stand and walk off, but she sits there staring at me.

No, staring at my lips.

I slide my hand along her jaw and dip down to place a kiss on her lips. She tastes like chocolate and marshmallow and contentment. Before I pull her into my lap and kiss her the way I really want to, I release her.

"What was that for?" she whispers, dazed.

"Something to think about while you're gone."

twenty-eight

. . .

After leaving Rory's, we walk to The Fat Pelican where Winnie heads straight for the bar and orders tequila shots.

"I was going to get this round," Darcy pouts.

Winnie wraps her arm around Darcy's shoulders. "Don't worry. There will be more."

And there are more.

At least two. Then a beer is pushed into my hand by Cora and we hit the dance floor.

I'm not normally a big drinker, but I use the buzzy, tingly feeling to let the tension-filled moments of the day melt away.

The awkward conversation with Rory about sex in the doctor's office earlier.

Rory's arm wrapped possessively around me on the beach. And how much I liked it.

Oh, and that kiss he planted on me before we left the house? Running on a loop in my brain since it happened.

I try to shake it off, close my eyes, and focus on the beat of the music. The thumping bass trying to drown out everything else. But no matter how hard I try, the feel of Rory's lips on mine keeps sneaking back into my thoughts.

It wasn't the kiss itself. Okay, maybe it was.

I recall the way his lips had been tender, yet firm, like he wanted to make sure I remembered it. The way I'd been desperate to lean into it for just a second longer. And how obnoxiously handsome he'd looked doing it. That stupid, smirky, too-perfect grin he wore afterward only made it worse.

I need to focus on that.

Rory's too good looking. Too patient. Too understanding.

I've married a walking green flag of a man. A charming, irresistible nightmare if there ever was one.

And I'm undeniably attracted to him.

The thought has me going stiff in the middle of the crowded dance floor.

"You okay?" Darcy yells over the music, a worried look on her face. "Are you going to be sick?"

I furiously shake my head, as I force those unwanted thoughts to the back of my brain and start dancing again.

Around midnight, Winnie corrals us to Sully's for a late-night slice of pizza, then into the car service that she coordinated to pick us up, also known as her brother, Eli, in an SUV.

"Did you ladies have fun?" Eli asks.

"It was a blast." Winnie giggles from the front seat.

I know I'm drunk because I offer up the information about Eli and the rest of the guys seeing me in my underwear last week.

Eli tries to comfort me. "It wasn't a big deal."

"No, that is. I would have died!" Darcy shrieks.

As we make the rounds to drop everyone off, the SUV is a cacophony of women singing offkey and talking loudly over each other, but Eli drives us with the patience of a kindergarten teacher.

"Summer, this is you," Winnie says, hopping out to let me get by her. I half expect to see my van, but when I look up, it's Rory's beach house.

Somewhere between that last tequila shot and devouring a slice of pepperoni and mushroom pizza the size of my head, I'd almost been able to forget the man I'm coming home to.

Winnie wraps me in her arms, laughing when we both tip sideways, nearly falling.

"This was the best night." And I mean it. I haven't had fun dancing and hanging out with friends in the longest time. Scarlett travels the world for work so girls' nights are not a common occurrence.

"I had so much fun with you. We have to do it again soon." She squeezes me one more time before setting me on course to walk up the path to the front door.

After two attempts, I open the front door, then wave to Eli, Winnie, and Cora who have been patiently waiting at the curb.

Once inside, I catch my breath against the door. Then, with one hand against the wall, I reach down to unhook the ankle strap of my sandal. But in my condition, this really isn't a standing-up kind of task. I sway a bit as I hop from one foot to the other, but eventually give up. I'm so tired, I'll probably just sleep in them.

Sleep. That sounds nice.

I need to lie down, but the bedroom is so far away. And then there's the fact that Rory is in there and the whole reason I consumed so many drinks tonight was so I could forget that I'm attracted to him. Clearly, it backfired because now all I can think about is how his naked torso must look with the soft sheets gathered around his narrow waist. The same way he looks every night when I stare longingly at him. He's probably got one muscular arm stretched overhead with those full, commanding lips of his barely parted while he breathes peacefully.

Yeah, I can't go in there now. In my condition, the pillow wall won't keep anyone safe tonight.

I push off the door, and stumble forward. The couch has got to be here somewhere.

It's late, and I know Rory has an early morning workout, so I'm trying my best to be quiet, stealthily creeping through the dark living room, but I misjudge the space and bang my knee into the side table by the couch.

"Fuck a duck!" I exclaim, biting my lip to help divert attention away from the excruciating pain in my knee. I can't imagine how much it might hurt if I didn't have a fifth of tequila coursing through my veins. "That's definitely going to leave a mark," I mutter.

"Summer?" a deep, yet groggy voice murmurs.

The voice is so close and unexpected that I jump, but the fact I'm already hopping on one heeled-sandal foot has me thrown off balance. I pitch forward and land with a thud on the carpeted living room floor.

At this point, it would be less painful if I just crawled on the floor.

A light clicks on and my eyes adjust to find Rory scrambling to hover above me. He's shirtless, of course. My eyes devour his broad, curved shoulders, then travel downwards to the hard planes of muscle that make up his chest and torso. Don't get me started on his brilliant blue eyes and the soft, sleepy smile he's giving me.

"Are you okay?" he asks, throwing my arms around his neck so he can lift me off the floor.

I mumble something half coherent, my brain too busy processing the feel of his skin against mine.

He drops onto the couch with me in his arms.

Thank god. I finally found the couch. And Rory. It's a win-win for all the pain my body has experienced in the last two minutes.

I should release him but I don't want to. He's sleep warm and oh so cozy. It's taking all my will power not to nuzzle into his neck.

"Wait. Why were you on the couch?" I ask, trying to collect my thoughts. "I thought you'd be in bed asleep."

"I couldn't sleep."

"Why?"

He glances away, but I can just make out the slightest flush of his cheeks in the dim lighting. His eyes find mine again.

"Because you weren't here. My brain can't relax until I know you're home."

I have zero control of the giddy smile that creeps across my face. His announcement shouldn't make my pulse pound. It should set off alarm bells, but if there are any, I'm too tipsy to notice.

I giggle, which is a sign I'm drunk because giggling isn't something I make a habit of doing. Laughing dryly. Cackling, and scowly stares, yes. Giggling like a school girl? Not my thing.

His hands grip my waist and my entire body starts to tingle.

Cue more giggling.

"Did you have a fun night?" he asks, fixing me with his magnetic gaze while his large hands brush my wild hair away from my face.

"Yes. Until I slammed my knee into the table."

His hand grazes over my injured knee, his thumb circling the bruise forming there.

"Is your wrist okay? From falling?" He checks it out next, but there's no pain anywhere. I feel great. There must be narcotics in his smile.

"Yeah, I'm good."

After his inspection of my wrist, he shifts me off him and onto the couch. I pout at the loss of contact, but he's too busy examining my puffy knee to notice.

"Just a sec."

He leaves me there for a minute, but comes back with one of his ice packs wrapped in a towel. Lowering down in front of me again, he wraps my knee up with the ice pack before his hands lower to my feet where he starts to take off my strappy sandals.

"You know, Wildflower, if you wanted me on my knees, you could've just asked." He winks, and my belly swoops.

I want to maul this man.

That's the tequila talking, I'm sure.

Or my brain recalling how hot it had been when he'd been so possessive over me at the bonfire earlier. I'd never felt that kind of protection before. I liked it. A lot.

Or it could also be the fact that I think I'm starting to develop the tiniest of crushes on my husband.

Husband, husband, husband.

My brain chants it over and over until all meaning of the word is lost.

But that doesn't work. None of this works if there are feelings involved.

"You want to get ready for bed?" he asks.

I remind myself what we're doing here.

It's temporary.

Convenient.

Not romantic.

All those reminders, but my silly, alcohol-soaked brain doesn't care.

You need to care, or this is going to hurt a lot more than a bruised knee.

twenty-nine

RORY

Summer is seated on the kitchen counter wearing an oversized t-shirt that says *I Can't Make Everyone Happy, I'm Not a Taco*. Her bare legs spilling over the marble edge where they dangle against the cabinets below.

"Nice shirt," I say, handing her the water and two ibuprofen I already grabbed from the bathroom cabinet before lifting the ice pack she's got settled onto her knee to examine her bruise.

"Wish I could say the same to you." She gives me a wry smile, her eyes dropping to my abs before making a slow perusal upward.

I've never seen her tipsy before, and this version of Summer is dangerous. One minute she's giggling and stroking my chest, the next she's glowering at me.

"You're a problem, Rory."

I raise a brow, amused. "Oh, yeah? What'd I do this time?"

"You walk around all tall and gorgeous and stupidly nice, and you think it's no big deal, but it is a big deal! Do you even know what it's like having to live with you?"

"Just to be clear, you're mad at me for existing?"

"Yes!" she snaps, pointing at me. "Because I did not sign up for my fake husband to be so—so—"

"I mean, technically, you did sign up for it."

Summer groans, dragging a hand down her face. It's clear, she's not appreciating my teasing tone.

"I mean, what's it like walking around like this all the time?" she asks.

"Like what?" I ask, curious where this is going.

"Your abs, Flipper. Your ridiculously fit swimmer's body. The whole *thing*."

I swear her eyes drop past the waistband of my shorts.

That's interesting.

I can't help the wide grin that pulls across my face. "So, you've been looking."

She makes a face that I've never seen before. It's a combination of annoyed and relaxed. Like she's bothered by my appearance but also at peace with it.

"I've been forced to look. It's all right there." She motions to me.

"And if I put a shirt on, you'll be totally fine? No distractions. No problems."

"It would help," she murmurs. "But there's still your face."

"What's wrong with my face?" I run a hand along my jaw, looking for the issue.

"Nothing. That's the problem."

I shake my head, holding in a laugh. "You're going to have to be more specific. If I don't know the problem, how can I fix it?"

"There's nothing to fix. That's the problem, Flipper. You're gorgeous. Your smile is perfect. And that dimple is obnoxious. It's always winking at me. Also, those eyes of yours are too mesmerizing." She drops her head back against the glass cabinet.

For the first time since we met, Summer's guard is down. If this is a dream, I don't want to wake up.

I know it's best to keep our situation light and playful, but the lust in her gaze is palpable and fuck if it's not wreaking havoc on my restraint. Pushing off the island, I close the space between us. My hands drop to the counter on either side of her hips.

"So, let me get this straight," I drop my voice low, "because I don't want to put words in your mouth, but you're annoyed that I'm too good looking?"

There's a beat of silence, Summer's eyes shifting sideways like she's thinking hard about my question. Finally, her gaze meets mine.

"Yes. It's frustrating. I never planned on getting married in the first place and now, I have to deal with a hot fake husband?"

She stares at me defiantly before raising her glass between us and chugging it down. When she lowers it, her upper lip is wet. Instinctively I swipe my thumb across it. Those plush lips that I've been thinking about since our wedding day kiss.

"And I'm too nice to you?"

"Something like that."

She has no idea how much nicer I want to be. How much more I would give her if she'd let me.

"I'm sorry to put so much strain on you," I say, taking the water glass from her. "So, tell me, wife, what do you want me to do about it?"

Her glare is sharp, but it softens as her eyes flick down to my mouth for half a second too long. It's not an invitation but it's sure as hell an indication of what she's thinking about right now.

My hands find her hips, gripping her there and pulling her closer to the edge of the counter. Closer to me.

"I want—"

She pulls me to her and crushes her lips against mine. She doesn't say the word, but she tells me with her mouth.

You.

As my body floods with the relief of having her like this again, I groan.

Summer's hands push into my hair. And fuck, it feels amazing.

This kiss is different than our wedding day. It's deep and unrestrained because now we're prepared. It's different than the kiss I'd planted on her before she left for the bar earlier because there's no audience. No one to see how my hand wraps around her neck, angling her where I want her, my fingers applying a slight pressure without restricting her breathing. No one around to hear Summer's gasps of pleasure when I pull her center flush against me. No one to witness the wild frenzy of a fake couple lost in a real kiss.

Just when I imagine us staying here all night, Summer pulls away abruptly, breathless and staring at me like she just made the biggest mistake of her life. I can see the wheels turning in her head. She's looking for an escape route.

"I need—I need to go to bed."

She's right. We both do. My alarm is only hours away. But when I'm tired tomorrow, I'll know it was worth it. She's worth it.

"Yeah, let's get you to bed."

I lift her off the counter, expecting to set her on her feet, but she wraps her legs around my waist. Then, her arms around my neck, turning to nuzzle her face into it. She clings to me and I love the way it feels to have her in my arms.

Fuck. If I had to choose my favorite between kissing Summer and holding her in my arms, I'd be hard pressed to decide.

In the bedroom, I pull back the covers on her side and slowly lower her into bed. Then, grab the blankets and pull them up over her.

"You didn't have to do all that," she murmurs.

I brush a strand of hair off her face. "Yeah, well, husband duties."

"Rory?"

"Yeah, Wildflower?" My thumb finds her wrist to trace over her tattoo. When she doesn't respond, I shift my gaze to her face. I expect her eyes to be closed, but she's staring back at me. "You okay?"

"Hmm, just tired."

"Get some sleep."

She nods, her eyes closing, and I click off the light before settling under the covers on my side.

Now that Summer is home next to me, I can sleep.

thirty

. . .

SUMMER

When I wake up, my mouth is dry and my head feels like someone shook it like a snow globe. Delighting in thrashing it about just to see tiny pieces of white plastic flutter to the bottom.

Slowly, my eyes open to find I'm sprawled horizontally across my bed.

Scratch that. Rory's bed. It's technically his and I'm just crashing in it.

His California King is the size of a small island, yet I managed to take up the entire thing last night.

Either I shifted into this position after he left, or he never slept here at all. I'm not certain because it takes me a moment to piece together everything that happened last night.

Ladies' night. Too many drinks.

Bumping my knee and Rory leaning against the kitchen counter, shirtless and smiling.

The details of it all are fuzzy. I don't remember exactly what I said, but from the way my heart starts racing with hangxiety—the anxiety of being hung over due to uncertainty of one's actions from the night before—I've got an inkling it was more than I'd ever planned on divulging.

My fingertips trace over my dry, puffy lips and I get the vague sense that they were used for more than just spilling secrets.

My stomach clenches as the memory crashes in.

Oh god. I kissed Rory.

I close my eyes and recall the moment his lips were pressed to mine. My tongue exploring his mouth as I held him to me, my limbs wrapped around his body like I was holding on for dear life.

And it was even better than I'd remembered from the courthouse. And the kiss I'd been thinking about at the bar all night.

Damn it. And damn that tequila.

"Morning, Wildflower."

My heart leaps to my throat as I whip my head up to find Rory leaning against the doorframe to the bathroom.

Keeping my aching head in mind, I slowly lift to a seated position on the bed and turn to face him.

I hadn't heard him but it's clear he just got out of the shower. His hair is damp and his naked torso is brilliantly displayed with only a white cotton towel wrapped low on his waist. My eyes take in every inch of his bare skin. And there are lots of inches.

Rory's standing there shirtless, looking like a fucking thirst trap and it sends a spike of irritation into my blood. If he wasn't so damn gorgeous and flaunting himself all the time then I wouldn't have the very complicated issue of wanting him.

When my gaze finally reaches Rory's, he pins me with an infuriatingly knowing look in his eyes.

I'm so screwed.

"How are you feeling this morning?" he asks.

"Good." It's a stretch but telling him I'm anxious makes the situation even more difficult. "How was practice?"

"Hard, but it felt good to push myself."

This is good. Small talk is good. If only we could stick to that for the next few months, we'd never have to discuss what happened last night.

"Summer—"

"I gotta pee."

I flip the covers off and rush toward the bathroom. When I pass by Rory, I get a whiff of his clean scent which causes my heart to race even more.

He moves aside so I can pass, and I shut the door behind me.

It wasn't a lie; I do have to pee. But now that I'm in the safety of the bathroom, away from Rory's perceptive gaze, I think I might never leave. It's either take up residence here or face Rory. I'm thinking I could make it a few days at least. I've got running water and a toilet.

After I finish my business, I down a gallon of water, then brush my teeth.

I'm about to dive into an *All Sports* magazine that's sitting on the counter to lay low when the smell of bacon infiltrates the space. My stomach growls at the heavenly scent and I realize Rory is luring me out of hiding with the promise of breakfast.

Damn. He knows all the tricks.

I crack the bathroom door and find the bed is made but no Rory in sight. In the distance, the sound of bacon sizzling on a frying pan can be heard.

Rory's so damn domestic; it makes my nipples hard. I glance down at my t-shirt and sure enough, my nipples are waging war against the worn cotton. I grab the nearest hoodie and yank it on before padding out to the kitchen.

As I'd presumed, Rory's there in the kitchen cooking. He's got a t-shirt and shorts on now. Thank god he's not a weirdo who fries bacon without a shirt on. Still, the visual of his muscular arms pressing against the sleeves of his shirt is enough to make my heart trip over itself.

"New marriage rule," I say, trying for casual as I walk past him. "You have to wear a shirt at all times. Preferably a turtleneck."

Rory's lips quirk into an exaggerated smile. "All times, huh?"

"Yes."

"I recall a similar conversation last night."

"About last night—" I begin.

He lifts a brow. "Which part?"

"I don't need a recap."

"You sure? Because you were very talkative."

At his teasing grin, my stomach drops, but I refuse to offer up information he doesn't have. I need to know what Rory knows so I can do damage control. Get this fake marriage back on track.

"Yeah? What did I say?" I ask defiantly.

My eyes narrow as I watch him turn off the burner then slowly make his way over to me.

His proximity is making me twitchy with nerves, but I can't show him my weakness.

"Something about me being too gorgeous and how it was annoying for you to deal with having a hot, fake husband."

"Right. That." I clear my throat, hoping that's the worst

of it. "That was the alcohol talking. I wasn't in my right mind, so anything I said should be disregarded."

He studies me a moment.

"Isn't it usually the opposite? Anything said under the influence tends to be closer to the truth? Drunk words are sober thoughts. That sort of thing."

I know what he's getting at. Alcohol lowered my inhibitions enough to be honest.

I am attracted to Rory, but I'm the one who came up with the rules for our marriage so, attraction or not, I need to enforce them.

"It was a mistake," I blurt out. Kissing Rory wasn't a mistake but it's all I can think of right now.

He doesn't move. Doesn't even flinch at my words. Either he knows I'm full of shit or he agrees. I'm not sure which one is more terrifying.

"Hmm." Rory leans against the built-in cabinet on the opposite side of me. "What about my rules?"

"What rules?" I ask slowly, buying myself time to remember if we discussed any other rules last night.

"You're not the only one who can make rules."

I'm guessing we didn't and he's trying to assert his authority now.

My eyes narrow at his mischievous smirk. "Fine. What?"

"You can't wear those little shorts anymore." He motions to my overly worn, softer than a cloud sleep shorts.

I gasp in outrage. "What do my sleep shorts have to do with anything?"

"I think it's only fair."

"Fine. Then you can't stretch in front of me. No more of that lunging thing with all the pelvic thrusting."

"I have to stretch or my hip flexors get tight."

"Then you'll have to do it in private."

His eyes narrow with suspicion. "You know you're only admitting to watching me."

"It's hard not to notice." I lunge forward in an exaggerated movement to show him how obnoxious it really is. My head spins, and I have to reach out to the counter for balance.

Once I'm upright again, Rory stalks closer, pining me with a fierce look.

"You can't wear that perfume anymore." He dips his head closer to me. His nostrils flare, as if he's smelling it right now. "The one that smells like sun-warmed skin after a day at the beach, and jasmine, and honey."

"I don't wear perfume. That's just how I smell."

His brows drop. "Well, that's inconvenient."

I glance around for some idea for another rule that will make him think again.

"You can't stand close to me."

Rory takes another step toward me. "Define close."

When I step back, my butt hits the counter. "This." I point a finger at his chest. "This is too close."

Edgar appears at our feet, looking back and forth between us, like he's the referee to our sparring match.

"Do these rules happen to be because of what you said last night?" he asks, eyeing me curiously.

"No." I'm quick to respond, but the reality is I'm losing control of the situation.

"Hmm. Okay." He nods contemplatively, then pins me with a heated look. "I have a confession, but I wanted to tell you when I knew you'd remember."

"Tell me what?" I swallow hard.

He moves closer, completely ignoring my proximity rule.

"This was supposed to be simple. An arrangement. Fake. But when you smile at me, I feel it in my chest. And every day, it gets worse. I notice everything about you. How you chew your lip when you're thinking."

At his words, I release my lower lip from between my teeth.

"How you sigh when you're falling asleep. And I sure as hell can't sleep next to you without wanting to touch you. And god, Summer, I want you. In every way. I don't know how to turn it off.

"Before we got married, you made it clear you didn't want anything to happen between us, and if that's still what you want, I'll have to live with it. But fuck, that's not what I want." His gaze drags over my face, slow and deliberate. "I want you, Summer. Nothing has ever felt simpler. And last night wasn't a mistake. It was the furthest thing from it."

My pulse pounds at Rory's words.

He wants me.

He says it like it's a fact. Like it's inevitable.

I scowl in disbelief. This isn't how this was supposed to go.

"You can't just say stuff like that."

"Why not? Because you don't want to hear it? Or because you do?"

His prodding has my defenses sounding the alarm.

"This was never part of the deal, Rory."

"Things change."

"Not this. Not us." I force myself to hold his gaze, even as my chest begins to tighten and my breathing becomes shaky. "You don't actually want me. You're just caught up in whatever this is." I motion between us. I'm realizing it's easy to start to feel things for someone you're living with and married to, and who looks at you like they want to know every part of your soul. But it's not real, right?

Rory exhales through his nose, his gaze darkens. Then,

he reaches out to tuck a piece of hair behind my ear. Slow. Gentle. His fingers graze my skin, and my breath catches at the contact.

"You really don't think I want you?" he murmurs.

I can't answer, my throat is starting to close.

My breaths are becoming more ragged.

Suddenly, the only sound between us is my wheezing.

Rory steps back and rushes toward the front door where my purse is sitting on the console table. A moment later, he returns with my rescue inhaler. He hands it to me and watches as I slowly inhale the medication.

We stand there for what feels like forever. Rory monitoring my breathing while I focus on keeping my guard up.

With my asthma triggered, I expect him to back off the conversation. It's what my ex would have done. No, that's not true. Tripp wouldn't have even bothered to start the conversation in the first place.

Once my breathing has evened out, Rory moves in closer again.

"You're running."

I inhale deeply, then give him my best glare. "I am not."

"Yeah?" He shifts closer to me, to where he was before he'd given me space to take my inhaler. "Then look me in the eyes and tell me you don't want me, too."

This conversation has taken a turn I can't handle.

"I want—" My stomach lets out a vicious growl. "Bacon."

Rory grabs a piece from the pan and hands it to me. It's cooked perfectly, deep golden brown with crisped edges and a slight glossy sheen from the rendered fat.

"Summer." His voice is softer now. "Why are you fighting this so hard?"

Because I know what it feels like to be wanted for the wrong reasons.

The thought is so loud in my head, I wonder if I've said it out loud.

I glance up to find Rory looking at me. Steady. Patient. Like he'd stand here all day if he had to.

And something in me cracks open.

"My ex didn't want me. I mean, he wanted me as a girl-friend. He liked having me around, liked showing me off, liked that I fit into the life he wanted." I pause to finish the piece of bacon. "But when it came to other things, he just wasn't into it. Into me.

"I kept trying to fix it. I kept thinking maybe I just wasn't enough, or maybe if I did something differently—" I shake my head, remembering all those feelings of rejection. "And by the time I figured out it wasn't me, I didn't want to try anymore."

Rory's shoulders are tense, his jaw tight.

"I want to kill him."

"What?" I blink.

"I want to kill him," Rory repeats. "For making you feel like you weren't enough. For making you second-guess something that was never your fault."

"You don't have to—"

"You are enough." His voice is low and firm, like he's desperate for me to believe it. "You always were."

His words soothe a part of me that I'd thought was buried under the rubble of my past relationship.

He kisses me softly on the lips. It's nothing like our kiss last night, but it's confirmation of everything he just said.

He wants me.

On his wrist, Rory's watch buzzes.

Slowly, he pulls back, checking his watch. "I have to go."

"Go?" I blink, confused at the sudden change of events,

and how much effort it's taking trying to recover from such a soft kiss.

His mouth quirks up at the corner. "Coach wants to meet. I've got video analysis, then a nutrition check-in before weights at eleven."

I've seen Rory's schedule. I know it's packed, but it always amazes me how much he accomplishes in a day.

He loads up a plate of eggs and bacon, then sets it at the counter for me.

"I've got to head to Charleston tomorrow for a couple days for a campaign shoot for Hydra-Fuel. I just got the details from Vivi."

My eyes widen. "That's huge. Congratulations."

He nods. "Would you come with me? There are a lot of art galleries and other fun things to do." He swallows. "I'd love it if you came."

My heart pounds with his request.

He had me at art galleries...but there's the small issue of spending more time alone with Rory.

At least here I've got my schedule and he's got his. I can pretend I'm not losing my mind over him. But two days in Charleston, just us? That sounds terrifying.

"I don't know. I'd have to check with Alice. See if someone can cover my shifts." Or not mention anything to her and say I couldn't get off work.

"Okay. We can talk later."

Rory presses his lips to my temple. It shouldn't light me on fire the way it does.

And when the door closes behind him, I breathe out a sigh of relief that I don't have to answer any more of his challenging questions right now.

With Rory gone, I finish eating the breakfast he

prepared for us, then Edgar and I head out to the beach to paint.

It's a picturesque day and even with my woozy head, painting with the sunshine on my face immediately lightens my mood. Or maybe it's the fact that even though things are unresolved between me and Rory, telling him about my ex had removed a weight from my shoulders.

Look me in the eye and tell me you don't want me, too.

I'd been too afraid to respond. Too afraid to find out what happens if I admit the truth.

thirty-one

. . .

RORY

He didn't really want me.

Summer's words have been replaying in my head all day. She had shared about her ex before, but I didn't know the extent of their relationship and how he had treated her. Now, I can't get it out of my head.

When she'd whispered those words earlier, they'd dug into my chest like a hook, pulling tight.

I've never felt this protective over someone. Never felt the rush of anger that came with learning the woman I care about had been treated poorly by another man. And how badly I wanted to track down the guy who made her feel like she wasn't enough and wreck him. Not just for hurting her, but for making her second-guess herself. For making her believe she wasn't worth wanting.

But this isn't about the past. It's about Summer.

Now I understand why she keeps pushing me away. Why

she insisted on no sex or intimacy in our marriage. Why she throws up walls every time I get close.

She doesn't trust it.

She doesn't trust *me*.

And now I need to figure out how the hell I'm going to show her I'm not like her ex.

I could be patient. Give her space. Make sure she doesn't feel pressure to take this further before she's ready.

But the truth is, I don't want to wait.

Not because I'm desperate for more, even though I am, but because the more time I spend with Summer, the more I see how she holds herself back. And not just from me.

From everything.

She's made herself smaller by downplaying her talent, and her beauty. Pretending she doesn't notice the way people look at her like she's something special, because it's safer not to.

I know what it's like to be wanted for the wrong reasons. Valued only by who you know and what you can do for people. I've spent my whole life navigating it.

I want Summer, and whether she comes with me to Charleston or not, I'm going to show her how much more she deserves. More than whatever that guy before me made her believe was all she was worth.

She doesn't have to be ready right now, but I'll be here when she is.

thirty-two

· · ·

Darcy forced me to come to Charleston. I made the mistake of mentioning it in passing at work and she immediately volunteered to cover my shifts. Then, she proceeded to send out a group text to Winnie, Cora, Whitney, and Vivi and she had my dog-walking shifts covered in less than twenty minutes. She's dangerous.

After Rory's morning practice, and my walk with the dogs, we dropped Edgar off at Winnie's and Whitney's house, then drove down to Charleston. We checked into the condo where we're staying, then Rory had a few meetings before we grabbed lunch.

After lunch, we walked down King Street, checking out the shops there before we drove out to the warehouse where his Hydra-Fuel sports drink campaign shoot is taking place.

I glance at my watch, checking the time.

"You got a hot date?" Rory jokes, walking over shirtless and in a pair of athletic shorts.

"If I did, would you be jealous?" I tease.

He brushes a loose hair out of my face. "Jealous? Nah. I'd just feel bad for the guy when he realizes you're obsessed with your husband."

"Obsessed?" I laugh. "That's a stretch."

We haven't mentioned the conversation we had in the kitchen yesterday and I'm hoping Rory is going to just let it go.

"There's an exhibit at a gallery I wanted to see. It closes at six."

"Then I'll make this quick, so we can go."

"It's okay if we miss it."

"Trust me, I'm a professional. We'll make it."

"Time to get lubed up." Vanessa, the photographer's assistant, appears with a bottle of oil in her hand. She looks between me and Rory, then hands me the bottle of oil. "I'll let your wife do the job." She winks before rushing off.

"I thought oil and water don't mix," I say, staring at the bottle of oil in my hand.

"I'm not getting in the water, but they want me to glisten." He smirks before his eyes drop to the bottle in my hands, and his smile morphs into one of sincerity. "If you don't want to, I can tell Vanessa—"

"It's okay. I can do it," I rush out, knowing it might seem odd if I'm his wife and I refuse to oil him up.

I squeeze out the oil, then place my hands against his back. I'm starting there because it's far less intimidating than his front with his washboard abs and those magical V muscles.

"They only gave you one bottle?" I ask, sliding my hand down the back of his sculpted arm. "Have they seen how much surface area needs to be covered?"

He rolls his shoulders back and groans.

"This okay?" I ask,

"More than okay. My gorgeous wife is rubbing me down with oil. What's not to like?" He shoots me a wink over his shoulder.

"You're enjoying this too much."

I make my way around to the front of his body.

"Every fucking second." Rory winks. "Don't forget the abs. The abs are very important."

I make a show of squeezing more oil out and slathering it on him, my oil-covered hands slipping over his carved muscles.

Beneath my palms, Rory's muscles contract. The deep, sloping lines on his lower abdomen are dangerously captivating. When my fingertips dip just beneath the waistband of his shorts, his stomach quivers. It's a fascinating movement, one I'm dying to see again but the area is already fully covered, so I move upward, determined to finish the job without embarrassing myself.

When my hands move over his chest, Rory makes his pectoral muscles dance, one side, then the other. I look up to find him smirking at me.

It's that lighthearted smirk of his that makes me forget to be intimidated, and has me reaching up and lightly pinching one of his nipples between my fingers.

As I tease over his pebbled nipple, a gravelly groan rises out of Rory's throat, startling me. The sound isn't playful or teasing, it's feral, like a wild animal rattling around in its cage. Just like the night I put my hands in his hair, it's like no sound I've heard before, so I immediately second-guess myself, and start to pull my hand back.

"Sorry, I shouldn't have—"

Rory quickly covers my hand with his, holding me to his warm, slick skin. When he lifts my chin with the finger of his other hand, the passion in his eyes has me weak in the knees.

"Don't be sorry, Wildflower." The thumb of his hand holding mine grazes the tattoo on my wrist. "I like your hands on me."

There's a beat of silence between us. Me recovering from the embarrassment while Rory looks at me like I'm made of glass and could shatter at any moment.

"Okay, Flipper. You're a greased eel now." I pat the center of his chest as to not be near either nipple.

The brand manager appears beside us. "We're ready for you." She gives me a towel to wipe my hands on. "There's a restroom in the hallway to wash up."

As I follow the brand manager's directions toward the restroom, I feel Rory's gaze lingering on me. Like a touch between my shoulder blades. A sizzling heat I can't ignore.

Inside the restroom, I close the door behind me and lean against the sink, my chest rising and falling too fast for what was technically just a massage.

Except it wasn't just a massage.

Not when his skin was so warm under my palms.

Not when his body reacted to my touch like that.

Not when he looked at me like I was something he craved.

My hands still smell like the coconut-vanilla oil. I lift them to my face like a lunatic and breathe in, remembering the exact way his stomach quivered when I skimmed just under the waistband of his shorts. The way his nipple pebbled beneath my touch. The way he groaned, not in amusement, but with hunger.

And then the way he looked at me. Not like he was teasing. Not like he was waiting for me to pull away. But like he was holding himself back. For me.

The ache I've been ignoring sharpens low in my belly, and I press my thighs together as I grip the edge of the sink.

He likes my hands on him.

He wants more.

And god help me, I do, too.

Rory was right. He is a professional, breezing through the shoot with charm and ease. Even the poses where he needed to look serious, he had no trouble pulling off an intense stare that made my stomach flip.

He showered to get the oil off, then we headed to Chalmers Street for the art exhibit I want to see.

The gallery is housed in a historic building on the cobblestone street, its brick façade softened by the climbing ivy and adorned with wrought-iron accents. Large, arched windows allow passersby to catch a glimpse of the art inside. A black and gold sign hangs above the door, reading "Lowcountry Collective."

It's the type of gallery I've longed to see my art displayed in.

Inside, the gallery itself is sleek and minimalist. High ceilings with skylights flooding the room with natural light, while hardwood floors and white walls are a neutral canvas for the art on exhibit.

As we walk through the small gallery, seeing the art on display is a mixed feeling. I love looking at art. Studying it and seeing how other artists bring their visions to life, but the feeling that I'll never get to this point has my stomach tying itself in anxious knots. My fingers itch for a pencil or a brush, even as that old whisper of doubt slides in...*you're not good enough.*

Rory's hand brushes mine as we walk, and I glance over to see him studying the piece in front of us with a thoughtful expression.

"What do you think this one is about?" he asks, tilting his head toward the large canvas layered with chaotic brush strokes of indigo and rust.

I blink at him. "You're actually trying to interpret it?"

"Of course, I am." His brow furrows. "I feel like it's about tension. Like the colors are fighting but also sort of relying on each other to be noticed?"

My jaw drops slightly. "That's—" I shake my head, stunned. "That's actually really good."

Rory shrugs like it's no big deal, but a little smile tugs at his mouth. "I've been trying to see things the way you do. You light up when you talk about art. It makes me want to understand it."

Something in my chest squeezes tight. I turn back to the painting, pretending to study it again so he doesn't see the tears welling in my eyes.

When he slips his hand into mine—casual, easy—I let him. Because even though I'm standing in a gallery full of art, none of it makes me feel as seen as the man beside me.

thirty-three

. . .

RORY

My hands grip the edge of the pool and I stand to yank off my goggles.

Keeping up with my workouts when I'm traveling is a must, so when the campaign was booked, Vivi made sure they put us up in a condo with a lap pool.

While I catch my breath, I look over at the lounger Summer had been sketching on earlier, but she's gone. I pull my swim cap off, then climb out of the pool and grab a towel before making my way back up to the condo.

"Summer?" I call, toweling my hair off as I walk into the living room.

There's no reply, so I move toward the bedroom.

As I get closer, there's a faint moaning sound, and I wonder if she's okay.

I make my way to the doorway. The bedside lamp is on, casting a warm glow across the room. That's when I see her.

There, spread out on the bed in only a t-shirt, is Summer, with her hand between her legs.

At first, I think I must be seeing things.

What I want to see, not reality.

But the longer I stand there expecting the image of Summer pleasuring herself to disappear, the more I realize it's not a mirage.

Her shirt is damp where her bikini used to be but she must have taken it off because beneath the soft, wet cotton, her nipples are stiff peaks. Her lips are parted. The bridge of her nose pinched and wrinkled in frustration.

I'm too enraptured to leave. I know I should give her privacy but everything about the sight of her is holding me to the spot. The tuft of light curls gathered at the apex of her thighs. Even from this distance I can see the glistening of her arousal.

"*Rory.*" She moans, her eyes still shut. "*Oh, please.*"

Fuck. Hearing my name as a plea on her lips will forever be etched into my brain. It'll haunt my dreams.

This woman, *my wife,* with her flushed cheeks and fiery soul, is touching herself to the thought of me. The knowledge sends a potent rush of chemicals through my veins. Drawing most of my blood supply south, my cock strains against the confines of my wet jammer. The surge of desire has my fingers gripping tighter on the towel around my neck. Even my balls ache at the sight of her.

Fuck.

I can't look away. My hand reaches out to steady myself on the wall, but the wall isn't there and my fingertips bump into a small anchor figurine on the upright dresser instead. As it skirts along the surface of the dresser, I try to catch it, but I'm too late and it hits the wooden floor with a clank. The disturbance has Summer's eyes flying open, her body springing upwards. Before she sees me, I try to get behind the door, but it's impossible to hide my large frame quick enough.

"Rory?" she calls out, my name on her lips trembling with uncertainty this time.

I'm caught, so I walk back in the room, with the towel draped casually over my shoulders.

"Sorry." I reach to pick up the brass anchor figurine and put it back in its place. "I heard my name and thought you needed me."

Giving her a moment to recover from my sudden appearance, I take my time, slowly dragging my eyes from the anchor figurine across the room to her. But she hasn't moved to cover herself. She's still spread out on the bed, her t-shirt barely concealing her sex. Beneath the hem, without her fingers blocking my view, I can see she's swollen and so fucking slick.

The sight of her there is exhilarating. I've never seen anything more beautiful in my life. Not because she's wet and touching herself, but because of the way she's raw and unabashedly sexy.

My eyes drop to the space between her thighs again.

Damn. She was close and I interrupted her.

I clear my throat, but my voice still comes out like gravel. "Do you need me, Wildflower?"

Her lust-filled gaze traces down the length of my body, stopping at what I know to be the large bulge in my jammer.

Jammers are good for streamlining but they're shit at hiding erections. Not that I'm trying to hide it. I wouldn't bother to deny my attraction to Summer. Clothes, no clothes. Smiling or scowling. I want her. It's irrefutable.

But I've had to be careful with her. While I'm hanging by

a thread with my desire for her, I know she needs to make this decision on her own.

She licks her lips. "I—" She hesitates, before her gaze meets mine again. "Will you talk to me?"

Her eyes fall to the spot on the bed beside her, then back to me.

"Yeah." *I'll do anything you need me to.* It's the truth. In this moment, and all the ones after with her. But Summer isn't ready to hear that. I wonder if she will ever be ready to hear the truth of how I feel about her. That my emotions already overstepped the line we figuratively drew when we came up with this arrangement. Each day with her is making me both thankful and regretful for our agreement. If this is as close to touching her as I'll ever get, then I'll take it.

I find my place on the bed beside her. Lowering down to my side, I tuck my arm underneath the pillow, then rest my head on it.

She settles back down on the bed and the scent of her drifts over me. Coconut sunscreen and citrus shampoo with a hint of sweat and the muskiness of sex. Her sex. My gaze follows her hand as she inches up the hem of her t-shirt, and her fingers return to her center.

"What should I talk about, Summer?"

"Anything. I just need to hear your voice."

The way her voice pitches on the word need makes my chest expand with pride. I need to stroke myself like I've never needed a release but I hold back, focusing on my beautiful wife.

"I have to admit I saw your pretty pussy from across the room. I bet you're so soft and smooth."

"Hmm." She bites down on her lip, then slowly releases it. "Tell me what to do."

"Be a good wife and show me how you like to finger-fuck yourself."

She nods, letting her hand drop between her legs again.

"Slip a finger in."

Her wrist arches with the movement.

"Now rub your clit with your other hand."

"Rory. Yes."

Her hips lift, rocking in rhythm to her fingers. I can hear how wet she is and it's taking everything in me to not slide a hand between her legs and feel her.

"That's it, Wildflower. Fuck that pretty cunt until your fingers are soaked."

Her soft pant indicates she likes what I'm saying.

My cock begs for me to join in on the action, but it'll only distract me from watching her. And I fucking love watching her touch herself.

"You're such a good wife, Summer. Letting me see you like this."

"I wanted you to see me," she admits on a gasp and I wonder if her pleasure is making her say things she wouldn't normally.

"You did?"

She bites down on her lower lip and nods.

"I'm glad. I like the show, baby."

And fuck, I do.

All I can do is stare as her chest rises and falls. Her nipples straining obscenely against the cotton of her shirt.

"You're so god damn beautiful."

Another cry and she comes hard, the soles of her feet pressing into the mattress while her hips lift off the bed. I'm entranced by the way her face pinches tightly before going slack.

Fuck. I haven't even touched her and I already know I'll

never be the same man after witnessing Summer find her release.

We lie there for a moment, Summer's breathing evening out while I commit every sound of her climax to memory.

Her hand drops from her center and onto the bed between us. My restraint is at its breaking point. I can't fucking help myself. I reach for it and press her fingers into my mouth. She turns to me, her eyes wide, watching as I swirl my tongue over her digits, sucking every drop of her off.

She tastes even sweeter than I imagined.

"Fuck, Summer, you taste like wildflowers and sweet tea."

She lets out a puff of laughter, throwing her other arm across her forehead as she giggles. Like she's exasperated while also turned on.

Now that I've tasted her, I'm thoroughly fucked.

With Summer still in a daze, I press a kiss to her palm, then roll off the bed. There's only so much a man can take, so I head for the bathroom to shower. Ultimately, I know I'll be fucking my hand with the taste of my wife still on my tongue.

As the hot water beats down on my back, I brace one hand on the tile and try to steady my breathing. My other hand is wrapped around my cock, my hips thrusting into my tight fist to the memory of Summer pleasuring herself.

It's not a new occurrence but now that every fantasy I've

ever had about her has been permanently upgraded by the real thing, I can't help myself.

I watch my climax rinse down the drain, then finish my shower.

By the time I return to the room, Summer's curled beneath the covers, her peaceful face telling me she's already drifting off to sleep. I want to climb in beside her, pull her against me, hold her all night. But I know myself too well.

So, instead, I grab an extra blanket from the closet and crash on the couch.

There are lines I won't cross, not while she's still sorting out what this marriage means to her. And while she let me in tonight, she trusted me. I'm not about to rush her past that.

She deserves everything, including my patience and the space to want more because she's ready, not because the moment got the better of us.

Even if sleeping out here with a hard-on and the taste of her still on my tongue is its own kind of torture.

Because she's worth every second of the wait.

thirty-four

. . .

SUMMER

It's been four days since Charleston. Four days since I touched myself in front of Rory, and he hasn't brought it up. Not once.

He's been polite. Respectful. His usual charming self.

It's as if I didn't fall apart under his voice, then watch him lick me off his fingers. And it's driving me insane.

Every time he brushes past me in the kitchen, every time I hear him laugh with Whitney from the porch, or he splits his chocolate banana protein shake with me because I need fuel to paint, I feel it all over again.

I've thrown myself into painting. Kept myself busy with a few extra shifts at the café. Anything to keep from looking at him like he's the answer to every problem I've ever had.

But tonight? Tonight, I have to put on a dress and walk into a country club ballroom for a swimming charity gala and pretend I'm not coming undone every time he looks at me.

Walking in to The Golden Lane Project gala, the scene is reminiscent of many I recall from my old life. An opulent venue with sparkling chandeliers hanging from high ceilings. A string quartet is playing in the background while waiters glide though the ballroom with trays of champagne.

A waiter stops beside me and I take the offered champagne. My head is clear again after my fun last night and I know I need to keep my wits about me, but it gives me something to do with my restless hands.

That's when I see him.

Across the room, talking to a group of people, is Rory looking heartbreakingly handsome in a black suit.

He'd needed to come to the event early to meet with the foundation chairs so he'd gotten ready and left even before I'd gotten home from visiting Cal with the dogs.

I take a moment to watch him. His charismatic smile, the way he's genuine and engaged. He's mesmerizing.

Suddenly, his eyes find mine and his smile widens. I watch him excuse himself and make his way over to me. As he advances, his confident stride and sexy grin cause my heart to stutter. It's like watching a tidal wave approach. Fascinating and eloquently beautiful, even though you know it's got the power to destroy you.

He greets me with a kiss on the cheek, but the way he possessively places a hand on my waist to pull me toward him provides the overwhelming crash I'd anticipated.

"You look..." He shakes his head like he's lost for words. "Stunning."

His touch is gentle, but there's heat beneath it. A smoldering, patient heat that sits low in my belly. And when his hand slides to my back and his fingertips graze the exposed skin of my backless dress, it's effortless, like his hands were always meant to find my skin.

As he leads me around the room, introducing me to people, his hand never strays far. Sliding from the small of my back to my lower hip, then grazing my arm before brushing my waist with the kind of ease that sets every nerve on fire. I should be focused on smiling and nodding, but all I can think about is how those same hands might look pressing my thighs open.

Finally, we stop at a standing table with Winnie, Whitney, and some of Rory's teammates, and I'm thankful for the support. I'm already overheated and we've barely touched.

There's a large crowd of people near the tables on the far side of the room, and I notice Rory's parents are among them.

"What's going on over there?" I ask.

"Oh, didn't you hear?" Winnie's eyes light up. "There's a Covey up for bid."

"What?" My heart stops.

Suddenly, I feel naked. Exposed.

I glance down to make sure I'm still fully clothed because the thought of something I painted being up for silent auction at one of the largest galas in North Carolina is sending me into a spiral.

"Well, it was in the silent auction," Logan says, "but so many people were bidding on it, they're planning to move it to a live auction."

I'm stunned at Logan's response. That can't be right.

"Let's take a look." Rory's hand finds the small of my back again as he urges me forward.

Once we're closer, I see the painting. They've moved it to an easel on the stage. It's one of my larger pieces. I'd started it small, but the scene demanded more space.

It's a golden-hour ocean scene. The first painting I'd done after meeting Rory.

The sun is low in the sky, casting a warm, golden reflection across the water. The edges of the painting are a deep blue, with the color fading into warmth the closer the water is to the setting sun. From where we're standing it's hard to see, but I know it's there. The barely visible silhouette of a swimmer in the distance.

While I'm standing frozen in front of my own work, Rory's parents approach.

"Mom, Dad." Rory's voice is warm and steady. "You've already met my wife, Summer."

"Right." His mom gives me a quick glance, but seems unbothered and distracted.

I don't know what I expected from Rory's parents tonight, but they're acting even more strange than the night I announced we were married.

"How is your evening going?" I ask, trying to keep things light.

"If you must know, Lucinda Boswell is getting on my last nerve. She kept outbidding me in the silent auction for this painting."

"Oh?" My heart skips a beat. Rory's mom is bidding on my art? That's the last thing I would have expected.

"You know the anonymous beach artist." She motions toward the stage. "It's up for auction. I had told Lucinda how much I wanted it and now she's on a mission to claim it for herself."

Not just bidding, fighting over it.

As more people gather, Whitney joins us and greets her parents.

"How can they tell it's really a Covey?" Whitney asks.

"See the little signature on the bottom right corner." Winnie points to the bottom of the canvas.

Whitney squints to see the small marking I make on all my paintings. "Yeah, but couldn't someone fake that?"

My pulse quickens at the conversation. I know it's real because I painted it, but they're right, someone could mimic the style and try to pass it off as one. My fingers tighten around the stem of my champagne glass.

Rory must notice my nerves, because his grip tightens on my waist.

"You're awfully quiet," he whispers, pulling me in closer before taking a sip of his soda water with lime. "Do you like the painting?"

I swallow and nod. "Yeah, it's..." My words trail off because it's hard for me to talk about my art even if no one knows it's mine. Just seeing it sitting up there in front of all these people is making it hard to breathe.

To calm my nerves, I take a sip of champagne.

"We'll start the bidding at seven thousand dollars," the auctioneer announces.

The champagne I just attempted to swallow sprays from my mouth. Coughing loudly, I clutch my burning chest.

"You okay?" Rory looks down at me, concern in his eyes as he rubs my back.

"Fine." I nod, still coughing as I try to recover.

The bidding takes off fast. Rory's mom and another woman across the room who must be Lucinda Boswell go back and forth while more paddles rise. With each paddle lift, I'm growing increasingly uncomfortable. I'd never imagined to hear such large dollar amounts associated with my art. When the bid reaches twenty thousand dollars, I want to tap Rory's mom on the shoulder and tell her I'll paint her something else, but that would give me away, and I'm not ready for that.

"We have an anonymous bidder that will match any bid," the auctioneer announces while out of the corner of my eye I see Rory pocket his phone.

There's a flurry of chatter in the room.

Rory's mom scowls in Lucinda's direction, but it's clear someone wants it even more than they do.

"Twenty-two thousand?" the auctioneer calls, looking into the crowd.

We watch Lucinda shake her head, indicating she's out. Maybe it's the fact that her friend won't end up with the painting, either, but Mary Ann drops her paddle to indicate she's also done.

"Sold for twenty-two thousand dollars," the auctioneer announces ecstatically.

I stand frozen, my jaw on the floor.

Rory leans close again. "That was fun."

"Can you imagine?" Mary Ann says, fanning herself with her auction paddle. "Twenty-two thousand dollars for a painting by some anonymous beach rat."

My heart stumbles. *Beach rat?*

"I think it's beautiful," Rory says calmly, pulling me in tighter like somehow he knows I need the reassurance.

"Mm," Mary Ann hums, clearly distracted by her own irritation. "Let's just hope Lucinda's out of town when the next one comes up."

If Rory's mom knew I was the artist, would she still want it?

Rory's father's voice cuts through my thoughts. "Son, I

hope you were smart about this and signed a prenup." He motions to where Rory's hand is resting on my hip.

"Oh, don't worry, Mr. Shields," I say sweetly, turning toward him with a practiced smile I haven't used in years. "I don't want Rory for his money. I'm here for other things, if you know what I mean." I punctuate it with a cheeky wink.

Beside me, Rory lets out a laugh, his eyes dancing with amusement, and I can't help the rush of satisfaction that floods my chest.

But under it all, beneath the glamour and the glitter and the jokes, I feel something else.

His touch on my hip.

The heat simmering between us.

And the knowledge that tonight, something's going to give.

thirty-five

. . .

RORY

The moment we walk inside the house, Summer steps out of her heels and rushes toward the bedroom. After dropping my keys on the counter, I pull at my tie and follow her down the hallway.

The car ride home had been quiet, but she hadn't seemed upset. More distant, like she's in her head. The same way I've been in mine.

After seeing my parents at the auction, I'd needed to head straight to a media panel with Connor.

The panel was fine. Connor had been professional, which was better than I expected. But while I answered questions about team chemistry and upcoming meets, all I could think about was Summer.

For me, I'd been holding it together all damn night.

Touching Summer, having her hands on me. Kissing her in front of everyone and pretending like it didn't wreck me every time our lips touch had become too much. My plan to show Summer how much this chemistry between us isn't just for show only resulted in whittling away what little restraint I have left.

When I walk into our bedroom, I expect Summer to have already changed. But I find her in the closet, standing there in the ocean blue gown that's been slowly killing me all night, staring at her reflection in the full-length mirror. It feels like she's been in her head since the auction. For some reason the Covey painting rattled her. Maybe it's an artist thing. But if my suspicions are correct, there's more to it.

"Hey, Wildflower," I say softy, reaching up to pull my tie off.

"Did I do okay tonight?" she asks, an unreadable expression on her face as her fingers reach up to start unzipping her dress.

"What do you mean?" I ask, tugging off my cufflinks.

"Do you think we were convincing? That people believed we're a real couple?"

"Summer, you were great. Why are you—"

"What about you?" she cuts in, unclasping her necklace and turning to set it on the closet island.

I let out a slow breath, unbuttoning my sleeves while trying to figure out what the hell is going on.

"What about me?"

"You looked at me like you meant it," she says, her voice going quiet. "Like it was real. You touched me like you meant it. It felt—" She swallows, her eyes darting away before finding mine again. "It felt too easy."

At Summer's words, my chest tightens.

"That's because I wasn't pretending."

I take another step toward her.

"Nothing was fake tonight, Summer. I don't have to fake it with you."

At my words, something in Summer's expression shatters. I've seen it before. She's overwhelmed and freaking out.

Because while she'd expected to play pretend tonight, she'd felt it just like I had.

"Wildflower—"

"I never—" she blurts, but quickly snaps her mouth shut. I watch as her hands curl into fists by her sides. "I've never—" she tries again, voice shaking with frustration. "A guy has never made me finish before."

There's silence as I take in Summer's words. I think I might have stopped breathing.

"I don't know why I said that." Her palm presses to her forehead and a soft, nervous laugh bubbles up her throat.

"You're serious?" I ask.

She nods.

"Not once?"

Summer slowly shakes her head in confirmation.

The anger and disbelief I had when she told me about her ex not wanting her returns. *What the actual fuck is wrong with that guy?*

When our eyes lock, I see her insecurity reflected to me, but I also see the desire.

"You keep looking at me like that, Wildflower," I say, my voice low, "I'm going to do something about it."

She swallows thickly, her eyes never leaving mine as her tongue peeks out to wet her bottom lip.

"I don't even know if I can. It might take me a while. It's only been me and Big Dill for years."

That's right. Big Dill the pickle vibrator. Lucky bastard.

"But in Charleston when you talked to me while I touched myself, it surprised me." Her voice is softer now. More vulnerable. "You didn't even lay a hand on me and I

—" She breaks off, her breathing coming harder now. "I came so hard I saw stars."

I step closer, hand itching to touch her but waiting. "I remember every second of that night."

She nods. "I want to feel that again."

"If this is what you want, Summer. If you're asking me to make you come, then I'll spend as long as it takes to get you off."

My words are steady, but my head is spinning with her confession. No other man has had the pleasure of seeing my wife's face when she comes? Fuck if this night didn't take an unexpected turn.

My anger at her ex morphs into smugness, and I can't stop smiling.

"Why are you smiling like that?" she asks.

"I'm going to be the only man to make my wife come."

Her eyes widen, and I can see uncertainty seeping back in. "I don't want you to be frustrated if I can't. If it takes too long."

I hate that she feels like she's a burden. It makes me fucking livid.

"Stop acting like you're a burden, Summer," I growl. "Pleasuring you is going to be my goddamn privilege."

But then I realize she never asked me. She never said the words.

"I need you to say it, Wildflower." I brush her hair behind her shoulder, then drag my fingertips over her collarbone.

"Say what?" she asks.

"What you want me to do."

She looks like a deer in headlights. Caught between the high beams of desire and self-doubt. My other hand reaches out to take hers, to softly run my thumb over her knuckles before giving it a squeeze. I'm reassuring her this isn't a test but something I need from her so I can give her what she needs.

Her eyes drop to where our hands are joined, then she takes a step closer until our chests are brushing against each other, her eyes downcast for a moment before she turns to look up at me.

"Rory?" She sighs, her eyes fluttering closed before they blink open again.

"Yeah, Wildflower?"

"I want it to be you. Please make me come."

thirty-six

· · ·

SUMMER

I can't believe I told Rory that no guy has made me come before. It's the truth, but I'd never planned on sharing that insecurity.

When I told him, I think I actually saw his chest puff up, like he was excited for the challenge and determined to make it happen.

Then, he asked me to say the words. To make it clear to him what I'm asking for.

I've already made it this far; there's no turning back now.

"I want it to be you. Please make me come." It comes out needier than I'd expected. More desperate. But that's what I am. Desperate for Rory to touch me. To make me come undone. Because if there's anyone I trust to be out of control with, it's him.

Rory's hands slide over the smooth fabric of my silk gown, skimming down my sides until they rest on my hips.

"This dress has been killing me all night. Maybe I'll leave it on to prove a point."

"What point would that be?" I ask.

His hands gather the material of the dress until I can feel cool air on the back of my legs. "That it was never the dress driving me wild." His voice is low and rough. "It was *you*."

Rory's words send a delicious shiver down my spine. I've never been this desperate for a man to touch me. I'd all but thought I'd lost that side of myself.

In the next moment his mouth captures mine. This kiss is different than the others we've shared. It's the honesty of two people admitting they want each other and I've never felt such a rush. Our lips fuse together and Rory owns every inch of my mouth.

His hands explore my body. My waist, my hips, then finally those large hands grip the flesh of my ass to pull me tighter against him.

I sigh into his touch. I haven't been touched in so long. And never like this.

"I want to see all of you," he growls between kisses.

Slipping the straps off my shoulders, the dress flutters into a puddle at my feet, leaving me in nothing but a thong.

"*Summer.*"

My heart slams against my sternum as Rory's heated gaze pours over my naked body.

"You're exquisite."

With his hands around my waist, he lifts me up onto the closet island. The marble beneath me is cool in contrast to my scorching skin.

Stepping between my parted legs, Rory's hands lift to cup my breasts while his thumbs trace circles over my nipples. I gasp at the feeling of his warm hands; how big they are and how good it feels. Then, I find myself arching my back to get closer.

"You're so fucking pretty, Wildflower. Do you like having your tits played with?" he asks, dipping his head down to pull a nipple inside his mouth. It's warm and wet, and his tongue is masterful as he swipes across my nipple before sucking it between his lips.

"Mmm. I don't know. I mean, this feels amazing. I like it. But no one's done it before."

Rory's hands stop moving but they remain on my breasts, holding the weight of me in his palms. When his gaze lands on mine, I see the fire blazing in his pupils.

"You asked me to make you come, and I will, but damn it, Summer, every inch of you deserves to be worshipped." He drops a kiss to my neck. "And that's what I intend to do."

I'm not exactly sure what that entails, but the look in Rory's eyes tells me there's no room for discussion. He's got an agenda, and the agenda is me.

He lifts me off the counter, my legs automatically wrapping around his waist, while my breasts press against the soft fabric of his dress shirt. The simple feel of his firm hands against my bare back sends a rush of arousal between my thighs.

Gently, he sets me down on the bed, then hovers above me like a Herculean god here to assert his will.

I'm mostly naked and he's still got his shirt and pants on.

"Are you going to take off your clothes?" I ask, propping up on my elbows to see more of him.

"Do you want that?" He smirks. "Or is it against the rules?" He motions to the walk-in closet. "I'm sure I have a turtleneck in there somewhere if that's what you're into."

"Funny."

"It was your suggestion."

My lips press together, trying not to laugh as I shake my head. "Take off your shirt, Flipper."

With torturously slow movements, Rory starts to unbutton his shirt. He's toying with me. For all the times I've seen Rory walking around with no shirt on, there's something extremely erotic about watching him undress. The way the fabric slides over his shoulders. The ripple of his abdomen as he moves to pull one arm out, then the other. He hasn't even touched me and it feels like my orgasm is imminent.

"Is that what you wanted, Wildflower?" With strong arms bracketing my head, he hovers above me, then drops a kiss to the corner of my mouth.

"Yes, and I want to touch you," I find myself saying.

The corner of his lip quirks up. His knowing glance tells me everything. All my exasperation at him for being shirtless was merely frustration with myself for reacting to him. For wanting him. And even when I oiled him up at the campaign shoot, I'd felt hesitant. Unsure.

"I'm yours to touch."

His words soothe me. They give me a sense of belonging that I've never had.

Lifting my hand from the bed, he kisses my palm, then places it against his chest.

My palms flatten against Rory's pecs, appreciating the sturdiness of him. Shifting my eyes to his face, I stare up at him, watching his reaction as my hands map over his heated skin. When I reach the waistband of his pants, his jaw tightens and he lets out a restrained puff of air.

I'm going for the zipper on his slacks when he moves forward, pushing me back onto the bed.

"My turn."

His lips are everywhere. My neck, my collar bone, my breasts.

Rory's mouth has found its way back to my chest. Showing me, for the first time, what it feels like to have a man put my pleasure above his. To take the time to explore my body. With every touch my senses heighten, my heart rate kicks up and my breathing becomes shallow.

"Did you use your inhaler today?" he asks, chin propped on my belly button as he settles himself between my thighs.

"Yes."

"That's my girl." He presses a kiss to my stomach, then pulls my thong down my legs and tosses it aside. "Now I can give you exactly what you need."

When he says it, I believe him. I always thought I needed to be in control, but I don't want that right now. Not with Rory.

So, when his palms press my thighs open, I let my knees fall and expose myself to him. In such a vulnerable position, I could easily feel self-conscious, but I don't. Not with him.

Rory gazes between my thighs, then back up to my face.

"Look at you, Wildflower. Already so worked up, and I've barely touched you."

It's a teasing statement, but his tone is awestruck. Like a kid in a candy store who's just been told everything inside is for them.

The liquid heat pooling at my core is for him. And he knows it. Dropping his head between my thighs, he flattens his tongue and licks up my center. That single lick has my eyes rolling into the back of my head.

"Fuck, Summer." Rory groans against my center, before dipping his tongue inside me. "You taste like you were made to ruin me."

My breath hitches at his words.

"You taste like sin and summer, and I'm never gonna get enough of you."

With his molten gaze between my thighs, he slips a finger through my center, his knuckle bending to nudge at my entrance before moving upward to circle my clit.

Another soft tease up and down, but this time he sinks his finger inside me.

It's a simple motion, but I'm mesmerized by how erotic a finger can feel. How connected it makes us.

When I glance up, I see Rory watching me closely. Like he cares about my response. Like he's cataloging it and taking notes.

His hair falls forward, messy now from my hands.

I can't take my eyes off him.

I'm struck by the way his broad shoulders tense with focus. How the sight and feel of his hands gripping my thighs, firm but reverent, makes me feel like I'm something both precious and wild.

The slight crease between his brows, like he's concentrating harder now than he does at the starting block. Like I'm the thing he wants to win more than anything.

Watching him play with me only adds to the tension building between my thighs.

"You want more?" he asks, dipping his head down again to suck my clit.

"Yes." I sigh.

My fingers weave through his hair, tugging at the thick strands while he buries his tongue inside me. Just like the night of the storm, Rory lets out a moan. It's a soft whimper that I feel against my core. The telltale signs of my orgasm start to build.

"You feel that?" He presses two fingers inside me now. "How perfect you are around my fingers?"

His fingers continue to pump inside me, but he looks up from between my thighs. When our eyes meet, I'm done for.

Rory's eyes dark, mouth glistening, a smug little twitch at the corner of his lips.

The sight of him there between my parted thighs, the feel of his fingers stroking, his thumb circling my clit, it's too much.

All the pent-up emotion and need to hold back releases and my orgasm hits me full force.

"Oh, god. Rory."

My orgasm comes crashing down on me. Waves of pleasure pulsing as nerve endings fire off one after another. I gasp at the pleasure bearing down on me. And the surge of wetness between my thighs.

Removing his fingers, Rory licks through my center, like he's savoring me. My legs tremble as rivulets of pleasure continue to flow through my body.

Then, he's there, hovering over me to capture my mouth with a deep, sensuous kiss.

"You're so pretty when you come." He brushes my wild hair away from my face.

"Thanks?" I laugh, feeling weightless. My body is boneless but I manage to push myself up to sitting. "That was... intense. It's never felt like that before." I cup his jaw and press my lips to his. "You get a gold star, Rory Shields."

"I'll put it next to my medals. But only if it says makes my wife come so fucking hard she squirts."

"I did not squirt." I pause, wondering if that's what the extra wetness between my thighs was. "Did I?"

"Yeah. But don't worry, I licked up every drop."

Just staring at him makes my chest ache. I want to make him feel the same. I want a gold star, too.

I reach forward toward the button of his suit pants, but

he gently wraps his hand around my wrist to pull me back. A sense of déjà vu tickles my brain.

"You don't want me to touch you?" The familiar sting of rejection has me withdrawing. "I thought—"

Rory reaches for me, shaking his head. "That's not the issue. I want your hands all over me," he blows out a breath, "but I need a minute."

"Oh? Why?" I ask, still confused. I'd felt his erection on my thigh earlier. He seemed more than ready a few minutes ago.

He chuckles, his laugh filled with self-deprecation while his cheeks turn the faintest shade of pink.

"I already finished."

"You did?" I glance down at the crotch of his pants, the thick ridge of him still pressed against the zipper.

"Yeah, in my pants."

I blink once. Twice. That's not what I was expecting at all.

"Does that happen often?" I ask, curiosity making me blunt.

"No. It's never happened before." He laughs again, running a hand through his hair. "I've never been this turned on, either. Never been so completely wrecked by giving pleasure."

He pulls me close, holding me against his chest.

"It was you. You do that to me. Seeing your face when you came, the taste of your orgasm on my tongue. It was too much."

After holding me in silence while I process what just happened, he releases me to push off the bed, and moves toward the bathroom. A minute later, he returns with a wash cloth.

"You don't have to do that."

"You're right, I don't have to. I want to."

The look he's giving me is pure adoration. I soak it up because I'm too tired to fight it.

The warm cloth against my inner thighs and sensitive flesh makes me shiver with pleasure. When he's done, he tosses it aside and pulls me up toward the pillows.

"I had fun with you tonight. At the gala, and just now."

"Same."

"Thank you for trusting me. For letting me have you like that."

I don't know what to say. No one has ever thanked me for letting them give me an orgasm. Because no one ever has.

So, I focus on where my finger is tracing the tattoo on his shoulder blade. It's the five rings symbolizing the Olympics.

"When did you get this?"

"After my first games."

"How did you decide where you wanted to put it?" I ask.

"Because my shoulders carried the weight of everything I've endured to reach the Olympics. Every grueling set, every missed moment with friends, every sacrifice. But they're also my source of power. Every stroke starts there."

I smile, loving to hear the passion in his voice. "I thought you were going to say because it looks cool."

"That, too." He laughs, his finger tracing over the sensitive skin inside my wrist where wildflowers are inked. "What about yours?"

"They're wildflowers." I state the obvious.

"I know. They're a symbol of freedom and independence. Someone who refuses to be tamed."

My eyes narrow. "How do you know that?"

"I looked it up when I first saw your tattoo. After I gave you the nickname, I wanted to make sure it fit."

"Hmm."

"It fits you perfectly, Summer." He presses his lips against my tattoo. "Why here? The skin is sensitive. It must have hurt."

It did. But what's physical pain when you're hurting so much more emotionally?

The way Rory's looking at me has me thinking he can read my mind. He's too damn intuitive.

"So I could see it when I painted."

He smiles, the skin beside his eyes crinkling. "I love it."

We lie next to each other in contented silence, Rory brushing his fingers through my hair while I trace the lines of his carved muscles until a rumbling growl reverberates between us.

"Are you hungry?" Rory asks. I can hear the hopefulness in his voice.

"No, but I know you are," I tease. "You're always hungry."

"I don't want to get out of bed, but if I don't eat, we're going to be listening to my stomach growl all night."

I stretch my arms above my head, then curl my naked body back into the covers.

"Go get your snack. I'm going to take a power nap. I'll be good in ten."

"Goodnight, Summer," Rory says, pressing a kiss to my forehead.

"Seriously," I mumble, "wake me up. I want to return the favor."

"It wasn't a favor. It was a privilege."

God, he's so sweet. I drift off thinking of all the ways I'm going to enjoy having him. Just as soon as I get some rest.

thirty-seven

. . .

RORY

SUMMER

You didn't wake me up

> You were sleeping so peacefully. The
> softest, most delicate snore. I didn't have
> the heart.

SUMMER

Hmm. Still should have tried. I feel slighted
that I didn't get to touch you last night.

> I'm the one who's wounded here. You
> passed out and made me eat all the snacks
> by myself. Alone. Shirtless. Vulnerable.

SUMMER

Wow. I can't believe I missed naked snack
time.

> And I didn't get to watch you lose your mind
> again. So yeah, we both missed out.

SUMMER

How was practice?

Brutal. I think I left a piece of my soul in lane four.

I'm on break now. You want to meet up for a late breakfast?

SUMMER

Yes! I'm starving.

See you in a few.

~~~~~

Summer walks into the open-air diner in a bright pink sundress with the breeze tossing strands of her wavy blonde hair around her face. I don't think I'll ever get used to the feeling I get when she walks in a room. The quiver of delirious contentment I get when our eyes meet. The way my brain slows its usually chaotic pace.

That's her.

After last night, I'm even more excited to see her. To bask in the new stage of our relationship. I don't know exactly what that stage is, but I know I want to go deeper with Summer. I want it all.

I stand to greet her, wrapping my arms around her upper back to pull her close to me.

"Hi." I smile at her like a school boy with a crush.

"Hi." She smiles back, her arms wrapping underneath my arms until her hands reach my shoulders.

With a quick kiss to her temple, I release her. I know
~~~~~

part of Summer's issue with her ex was him showing her off in public but not wanting her in private, so that makes me uncertain on where she is with PDA. Like if eating her pussy last night means I can hold her hand in public now.

Instead of taking the seat across from me, she sits down on the bench next to me.

"One orgasm and we're sitting on the same side of the table?" I tease, remembering how she told me we would never be a couple who sits on the same side of the table at restaurants.

She lifts a brow. "Please. I'm just avoiding the sun glare."

I thought I was on the sunnier side but maybe the sun shifted. I glance across the table at the shady side I'd reserved for her. Still plenty of shade.

"Do you want me to move to the other side?" I ask as she peruses the menu.

Under the table, her knee brushes against mine.

"No."

The waiter stops by to take our order. I don't recognize him, so he must be new here. His nametag reads Justin.

"Steak and eggs, please." Summer closes her menu.

"How would you like the steak cooked?" he asks.

"Medium rare."

He nods, hesitantly scanning the digital menu before pressing a button.

"And the eggs?"

"Over easy, please," Summer replies.

Another frantic perusal of the screen to find the selection.

He collects Summer's menu and tucks it beneath his ordering device, then looks at me.

"And for you?"

"Good morning, Justin. How are you today?" I ask.

"Um, good." He smiles nervously. "It's my first day, so I'm trying not to mess shit up, you know?"

I give him a supportive nod. "You're doing great. I'm Rory. This is my wife, Summer."

He nods to Summer. "Nice to meet you."

"Are you new to Coral Cove?" I ask.

"Yeah, I just moved here with my boyfriend. He loves to surf and I'm along for the ride."

"That's cool. I come here a lot after practice, so you'll be seeing us regularly."

"Practice? What sport do you play?" Justin asks.

"I'm a swimmer. I train with the Carolina Current."

Justin nods, not certain what to make of that, I guess.

"He's being modest. He's the most decorated Olympic swimmer of all time," Summer says. Whether Justin is impressed or not, the fact that Summer's words are full of pride makes me smile.

"No shit? That's awesome."

Justin reaches out his hand for me to give him a high-five.

"Thanks."

"Oh, yeah. Can I get your order?"

"Yes, I'll have the three-egg scramble with turkey sausage and bacon, hash browns, and whole wheat toast. Also, a short stack of banana walnut pancakes with peanut butter on the side." I pause to consider my drink choices. "A black coffee and a chocolate milk."

"That's a lot of food."

"He's a hungry man," Summer responds, sipping her water.

"I'll get that out as soon as I can. As soon as the kitchen cooks it."

"Thank you." I nod and Summer bites her lip, trying not

to smile. "What? I've got to get in good with the wait staff. They're the gatekeepers between me and food."

"You're ridiculous."

"And yet you married me."

"Oh, right. That. Complete lapse of judgment."

"Even after last night?" I smirk, before leaning in to whisper, "I can still taste you on my tongue."

Summer's eyes widen. "Oh look, it's shady over there now."

She eyes the other side of the table and moves to stand, but I easily pull her back down next to me.

"Please stay. I like you here."

Her lips twitch but she stays seated and takes another drink of water. I slug mine back in two swallows, then roll my shoulders down my back, releasing a low groan as my aching muscles protest.

"You said practice was brutal. Why?" she asks.

I sigh, hating to admit the truth.

"I've been pushing myself to keep up with Connor. I mean, I can keep up with him. I can dominate him if I want to, but doing it every practice, every day. It's catching up with me. With my body."

"Is that normal? Pushing teammates to the point of fatigue? Or is this because you and Connor aren't on good terms?"

"The latter. The team challenges each other for sure, but not to the point of detrimental impact on our bodies."

"Are you going to talk to him, or just metaphorically beat each other up in the pool every day?"

"He leaves tomorrow for a tour as an ambassador with the Rising Tides Swim program."

"So, your body gets some time off from training with him. Shouldn't you be excited?"

"I am. But—"

"Wait. Isn't that the same program Whitney is an ambassador for?" she asks, her brows lifting with suspicion. "She told me about it at the bonfire. Was really excited to get the spot."

"Yeah, it's the same one."

Summer's eyes widen. "So, Connor and Whitney are traveling together for a week? Do you think—?"

I cut her off, laughing. "Never in a million years. Whitney is too focused to let a guy like Connor mess with her."

"Hmm."

"What's 'hmm?'"

"I don't know." She shrugs. "I didn't think I'd ever get married, even if it was fake, and here we are."

"I don't like what you're implying."

"That something might be going on between Whitney and Connor?" she asks.

"No, that Connor and I are similar in any way."

"You need to talk to him. Clear the air. You're a people person. You're trying to be best friends with our waiter, how can you not want to resolve things with Connor?"

I let Summer's assessment sink in.

She's right. I am usually a forgiving person, but with Connor, he's issued no apology, and shown no remorse for his actions. He's been a cocky asshole since he walked into the aquatic center a few weeks ago so I've responded accordingly. It's not like me at all. I secretly hate it but he's the one who entered into enemy territory waving a red flag, not me.

Our food arrives and we dig in. Summer slowly, while I do my best not to look like a cave man. I use the toast as a vessel for the eggs, then wrap a banana walnut pancake around a sausage link before dipping it in peanut butter.

Summer laughs. "Is it a game trying to see how many calories you can pack into one bite?"

"Maybe." I chuckle around my full bite.

She's been eyeing the last banana walnut pancake so I push it onto her plate.

She forks the remaining steak on hers and transfers it to mine. I devour it in a single bite.

"What's your schedule for the rest of the day?" I ask, curious.

"Lunch shift at the café. Then afternoon dog walking." She lifts her wrist up. "Today was the first day my wrist didn't ache so I texted Winnie she said I could ride my skateboard finally."

"Must have been the orgasm last night." I grin. "See? Even though I injured you, I healed you."

She nudges me playfully with her shoulder.

"Doubtful."

"Are you going to paint today?" I ask.

"Yeah, later this afternoon. I'm feeling a sunset session. They're one of my favs. Either sunset or early morning."

I glance down at her. "I'd love to see something you've painted sometime."

She bites her lip. "I don't know. Maybe."

All I can do is nod.

Summer hasn't shared the specifics of her art with me yet, so I'm trying not to push it too much. It's something she's had to guard in the past and I don't want her to feel that way with me. I want her to share it on her own terms.

I'm quickly noticing that for someone who said 'space' was their love language, there's none of it between us now.

Her thigh brushes against mine again, so I do what I've been dying to do since we sat down and lift her leg to drape it over mine. It feels like the most natural thing in the world.

The new angle of her leg shifts the hem of her dress, exposing more of her legs. My hand moves beneath the table to rest on her bare thigh.

"This okay?" I ask, loving the feel of her silky skin beneath my palm. Touching her thigh has my thoughts quickly returning to how it had felt to hold her open while I'd licked her pussy last night.

I'm certain she'll fight me on it. Toss out some sarcastic quip. But she quietly hums with approval, taking the last bite of the pancake.

"I'm not normally a sweets person, but that pancake was so good. I'm going to be thinking about it all day."

I lean down to press my mouth to her ear.

"I get it. Now that I've tasted you, it's all I've been able to think about."

My fingers wander farther up her leg, slow and measured, until they disappear beneath the hem of her dress.

At my advance, Summer's breath catches, but she doesn't pull away.

"Do you want me to stop?" I murmur, keeping my voice low.

She shakes her head. "No."

Hidden beneath the diner's deck awning, we're sheltered from the warm sun. The salty breeze flows through Summer's long hair, then wraps around us like a secret.

There are only a few other tables occupied on the deck, but I'm still aware we're in a public place. I keep my gaze forward, letting my palm slide over her inner thigh until my fingers find the edge of her underwear.

Just this secret touch beneath Summer's dress is enough to set my body aflame.

"You looked so pretty falling apart for me last night." I

dip my fingertip under the edge and trace along the seam. "I keep thinking about how soft you sounded. How sweet you tasted."

I notice Summer's left hand is curled around the edge of the bench, her nails digging into the worn wood.

"I'm going to take my time with you later. Spread you out on my bed and make you beg a little." My voice dips lower. "I want to hear that rasp in your voice when you whisper my name again."

"Rory." It's half a warning, half a plea.

I watch as Summer's lips press together and her cheeks flush with want.

My finger releases the edge of her underwear, then slipping out from under her dress, my hand finds a safe place back on her thigh.

"Later," I promise her, squeezing her leg softly above the knee.

"You're evil," she says calmly, placing her sunglasses back on her face.

I give her a heated grin. "No, now I'm motivated. I've got to give myself something to look forward to after two hours of sprint sets this afternoon."

"Hmm. Well, if you're going to leave me all worked up, maybe I'll go home and let Big Dill take care of me instead."

My cock surges at the thought of Summer lying on our bed, pleasuring herself with her pickle vibrator.

"Summer." Now it's my turn to plead.

"Yeah, have fun thinking about *that* during practice."

She stands up and steps over the bench to leave. I follow suit, but reach out to catch her hand and pull her back toward me.

The momentum of my tug has her pressed up against me. My hands find her waist, and I drop my mouth to hers in a slow, sensuous kiss. I've never wanted to ditch out on training as badly as I want to right now. But I can't.

When our lips part, my hand cups her jaw. "I'd never leave you wanting if I had a choice."

Her expression softens, a small smile pulling at the corner of her lips.

"Guess I'll find out later."

thirty-eight

. . .

SUMMER

Rory doesn't seem like the kind of guy who would get satisfaction out of edging his wife on a picnic table at the outdoor diner on a Friday morning, but that's exactly what he did to me. I'm still thinking about how badly I wanted him to yank my underwear aside and sink his finger into me. I couldn't care less who was there to witness it.

But he'd pulled back and vowed to properly take care of me later.

After we barely refrained from public indecency, Rory headed back to the aquatic center for a team meeting, weight training, a nutrition check-in, and a mobility workout.

I was exhausted just listening to all the different elements that go into his day. He'd clearly earned every bite of his two-thousand-calorie breakfast.

Now, I'm walking home from breakfast, my body still buzzing from Rory's voice in my ear, from the way he'd tossed my leg over his like he'd done it a hundred times. That's what had caught me off guard. The realness. The ease of simply sitting next to each other and eating a meal. Effortless conversation mixed with tender, teasing touches.

It felt good.

But this wasn't supposed to be real. It wasn't supposed to feel like anything.

And yet, the way Rory looked at me when he thought I wasn't paying attention.

The way he listened intently when I talked.

The way I'm already addicted to his touch.

It's making me forget that this is supposed to be temporary. That I made Rory promise not to fall in love with me. Because the truth is, I'm starting to wonder if I'm going to break my own rule.

While I'm walking, I pull out my phone to text Scarlett about last night.

> My fake husband fingered me last night and it was the most erotic experience of my life

SCARLETT

OMG! Details please.

> I can't even remember the details. The intensity of my orgasm wiped everything from my brain.

SCARLETT

God, I'm single as fuck. But yay for you! Hope your husband can introduce me to one of his hot swimmer friends.

Sorry 😞 And yes, if you come visit. Although I don't know which one. Eli is hung up on his ex. Logan is a player who gets hangry. I swear Charlie has a thing for the team's publicist, and Xio and Finn are just way too young.

SCARLETT

It doesn't matter anyway. I don't have time for a guy right now. I'm hell bent on getting this promotion.

You're going to get it! How was your trip to Fiji?

SCARLETT

Amazing! But you'll never believe it. My publication merged with Adventure Abounds!

Wait. Isn't that Wilder's publication?

SCARLETT

Yeah.

That's all you have to say about it?

SCARLETT

It's a huge company. I probably won't even see him. Btw, how's your art piece coming? The hot swimmer one that is totally not based off the obsession you have with your fake husband.

Watch it.

SCARLETT

So, you're not denying it?

I leave Scarlett's message unanswered. My brain has too much going on to form a plausible response.

Then, I text Rory a pickle emoji just to mess with him.

After my shift at the café, I revive my skateboarding skills by taking Paulie and Pearl for a 'walk' down the beachfront path and out to visit Cal at his resident fishing spot on the boardwalk.

"You know you don't have to feed me just to come say hi."

"I know."

But I want to. After so many years of others always expecting me to act a certain way or be something for them, I like bringing Cal food because he doesn't expect it. That's what gives me joy.

I know if I were to show up empty handed, because I've done it before, Cal would smile and we'd talk about his fishing and the weather and something else just as mundane and it would be perfect. Because Cal doesn't expect me to be anything I'm not.

It's the same way I feel when I'm with Rory.

The thought makes my chest pinch. For a moment, I feel like the wind has been knocked out of me.

Cal pats my hand.

"You'll figure it out."

"What?" I struggle to remember what we had been talking about before my brain took a dangerous turn.

On my way to return Paulie and Pearl home, we walk through downtown Coral Cove so they can get a treat at the pet supply shop. As we're leaving, the frame store next door catches my eye. Not just the store, but a frame displayed in the window. It would be perfect for Rory's Covey painting, so I return the dogs home, then head back to the frame shop to make a purchase.

The sound of Edgar's collar tag clinking from where he was curled up in his bed near the door alerts me to Rory's arrival.

I turn to find him standing in the doorway. Edgar is excitedly bouncing at his feet, so Rory picks him up and cuddles him close so Edgar can lick his face.

"Hey, buddy. I missed you, too."

While Rory's smiling down at the giddy pug, I take a moment to appreciate how good he looks. He's dressed in black joggers and a gray hoodie. To top it all off, he's wearing his blue Carolina Current hat backwards. Those tufts of hair that stick out from beneath his hat are my weakness.

Among other things.

I'd just finished cleaning up for the day.

I've been using the walk-in closet as storage for my canvases; using a fan to keep airflow and reduce humidity to help my paintings dry.

Earlier, I'd taken my easel out onto the deck and painted the beach as the sun set. Afterward, I'd turned my attention to the swimmer piece I'm working on.

The swimmer is mid-stroke, rising out of the water as seen from the end of the lane. It's exactly the way I'd seen Rory that day at practice right before Winnie drove me home from the aquatic center after examining my wrist.

The painting is nothing like the beachscape Coveys I've done, and while I'm still working to get the right proportions and shading on his body, it's been a fun challenge.

Rory sets Edgar down on the floor, his easygoing smile fading into hunger at the sight of me.

"Is that what you paint in?" he asks, voice hoarse.

"Yeah." My eyes drop down to the worn in, olive green canvas overalls. "When I'm in the house."

"You expect me to function with you looking like that?"

"Like what?" I ask, eyes narrowing.

I'd been wearing my bikini earlier, but took it off when I slipped into my overalls and neglected to put anything on underneath. I attempt to adjust the top part of my overalls to cover the side boob I know I'm sporting.

"Like a damn fantasy." He steps closer, and my body hums in response to his proximity, making me even more aware that I'm not wearing anything underneath these overalls. "Paint-splattered. Messy hair and glasses. And practically falling out of these overalls."

"I know. I'm a mess. I should go shower."

He shakes his head, a knowing smirk on his face. "Later."

It's a command. Like he's got a plan and while me showering is on the agenda, it's not what's happening now.

"Can I see what you've been working on?" Rory asks, moving toward the easel where the painting is.

My entire body tenses. It's a familiar sensation I've come to associate with the thought of showing someone my art.

But I fight against it. Because it's a step I want to take.

Showing someone my art. No, not someone. *Rory*.

I move to lift the cover off the swimmer painting, then step back.

Fidgeting with my hands in silence, I watch him take it in.

He blinks. Then turns to me and smiles.

"Summer, this painting is incredible. Your work is

incredible. And I'm not just saying that because I'm happy you have a thing for swimmers."

I laugh at his joke, but really my heart swells with his kind words.

He moves closer toward the canvas. "The detail work on this. You're extremely talented. I can't believe you almost gave this up."

"Thank you. That means a lot." I move to stand next to him. "I'm working on getting the right shading. I'm used to working with water in my paintings, but the way his face reflects in the pool is different than anything I've done before."

"What do you normally paint?"

"Um, mostly still-life." It's a vague response in order to not give away more details.

He turns to me with a mischievous smile on his face. "Would you paint something for me?"

"I don't know. What do you have in mind?" I ask curiously.

He grips the neck of his hoodie and pulls it off.

Shirtless is pretty much Rory's natural state of being, but it never gets easier to control my racing heart and sweaty palms at the sight of him. Or to keep myself from wondering what it would be like to lick his nipples.

Maybe that's why I'd been annoyed he hadn't woken me last night. I never got to explore him the way I wanted to.

I want to trace his nipples with my tongue. Tease him like he did me. Then slide my hand into his pants and fist his cock.

The thought has my nipples hardening against the soft cotton of my overalls.

Why am I so focused on nipples right now?

Oh, because my husband has the hottest nipples I've ever seen.

He steps forward, and I suck in a breath, remembering the thrill of having his hand beneath my dress at breakfast this morning.

"A mermaid, right here." He points to the space above his heart where his pectoral muscles are bulging, and his nipple is tight.

Call it my nerves, but a laugh breaks loose from my throat and Rory's smile gets bigger.

"Yeah, I'm thinking of getting another tattoo and want to see what it would look like."

My eyes roll toward the ceiling. "God, please no."

"A mermaid with a pink and purple tail and long blonde hair." He brushes one of the loose strands from my messy bun out of my face. "The wilder the better. And glasses. Don't forget the glasses."

I shake my head, but my smile persists because when Rory is smiling at me, I feel at ease.

"Didn't you know mermaids don't wear glasses?" I smirk.

"Mine does." His finger glides along one leg of my glasses before it teases along the shell of my ear. I disguise the quiver his touch causes as simply being chilled by the early evening breeze coming in from the cracked sliding door overlooking the beach.

Mine does.

How can two simple words make my heart race so uncontrollably?

"Fine. I'll do it if only to prove to you that you should definitely not get a tattoo of a mermaid on your chest."

"Where do you want me?" he asks.

Everywhere.

I glance around the room to determine where this

impromptu art session should take place, but the only place to sit is on the futon.

"Have a seat." I point to it and Rory follows my direction. Then, I rummage through my paints to see what I have for acrylics.

Finally, with a palette and assortment of paintbrushes in hand, I move to stand between Rory's legs to start my work. But with the first stroke of my brush, I realize we have a problem.

"The paint is going to run; I need you to lie down."

"Sure thing." He removes his hat, then drops to his back, lacing his fingers behind his head. I lean over him to keep working on the mermaid's tail, but now he's too far away.

"I need to get closer."

"So come closer."

His hands grip the sides of my waist and in one quick motion, he's got me straddling his lap.

"How's this?" he asks, grinning. "Because I think this is the perfect position."

It is the perfect angle for painting, among other things.

"You would."

"What can I say? I like this view."

I shake my head, trying to focus on keeping my hand steady. I've never had this issue before, but there's something about straddling Rory's hips and leaning into his naked torso that makes focusing on my art more challenging. Oh, and the fact that with every tilt of my hips, I can feel his rigid cock pressing at my center. That's making it nearly impossible to focus.

"Rory."

"Hmm?" His brows lift, a feigned look of innocence on his face.

"Behave."

"My beautiful wife is straddling me. It's out of my control."

"How's your knee?" I ask, hoping to distract us from how good it feels to have him beneath me.

"Good." He exhales deeply, like he's letting all the day's worries go.

"How was practice without Connor there?"

He chuckles. "I think I've gotten so used to pushing myself, it was hard to dial it back."

"So maybe it's been a good thing to have Connor challenging you?"

"Hmm. Still doesn't mean I like the guy."

Rory reaches up with one hand to brush aside a rogue hair, his thumb teasing along my jaw line as he sweeps it behind my ear.

"Stay still, Flipper, or it won't be a mermaid, just a blob."

That's when I get an idea. I put the finishing touches on the mermaid, then mix the black and white paint to create the perfect shade of gray before getting to work.

I do some shading work around the fins and tail, then finish it off with a blue eye, just one since the animal is in profile.

"There. I'm finished."

I climb off him to grab a hand mirror from the bathroom, then return to my position to show him my work.

"What's this?" Rory uses the mirror to check out the art painted on his chest.

"Your mermaid looked lonely so I gave her a friend. His name is Flipper."

Rory's gaze locks on mine. "Now all I need is a cute little pug floating on an inner tube between them and our little family is complete."

My heart pounds at his suggestion. To put Edgar in the

painting, and that we're a family. There's a niggling feeling in my ribcage. Whispers of questions that have started to grow louder in the back of my mind.

What would it be like to give this man everything?

But this is just playing around. It's temporary. The tattoo I'm painting and our marriage.

Right?

Rory's magnetic smile makes it easy to forget and for once, I want to keep playing along. To soak up as much of this man before he realizes there's more downside than benefit to me being his fake wife.

"Easy fix," I say, hopping off his lap to grab more paint from my basket. When I'm back in place, to work on adding in Edgar, Rory settles back into the pillows with his hands behind his head. His abs contract, displaying all eight of his distinct abdominal muscles, and with the shifting of our bodies, his joggers are now hanging obscenely low on his trim waist. Those V muscles on each side of his pelvis expertly defined and leading to the thick ridge beneath that I'm trying to pretend doesn't have me wired and wanting.

I want to write *mine* in paint across his chest. That's the tattoo he should get.

"If your parents didn't want you to pursue art, how did you keep painting?" he asks.

I glance up to find him studying me.

Now I'm feeling silly because I'm over here ogling him and he's trying to have a serious conversation. That's the power of Rory Shields, sexy and genuine...it's a deadly combination.

"I kept it a secret. I set up a little studio in my closet. Never talked about it or showed them pieces I was working on." My paintbrush hovers over his chest as I recall the memory. "Then, I came home one day, and everything was cleared out."

"*Summer*." Rory exhales my name, heavy with sympathy. Normally I would hate for someone to see my weaknesses, but I'm starting to realize that showing him this side of myself, the vulnerable side, isn't as scary as I'd thought. It feels good to be seen by someone. No, scratch that. It feels *wonderful* to be seen by Rory.

"You setting up this studio for me is the first real one I've had. My van was too small to keep anything set up permanently. So, this is the first time I've been able to have my art out in the open. To play and create without looking over my shoulder."

"I'm so sorry that you couldn't chase your dreams. I can't imagine what that felt like. I don't know what my life would be like without swimming. It's been my foundation. The only thing I've known. My parents, although they can be heavy handed and try to control my personal life, they've still been mostly supportive throughout my career."

I lean back and examine my work.

"Now it's complete."

Rory smiles and everything in my body turns to mush.

"If you're trying to convince me not to get this tattoo then you played it all wrong."

I lean forward, then lower my face to his chest, blowing a puff of air at the fresh paint. I watch as goosebumps spread across his torso. With my hips forward, and the way our bodies align, I feel every thick inch of him against my center.

Now, I'm shamelessly grinding my center over Rory's hard cock because I can't fucking help it when I'm near this man. *My husband.*

"Did I?" The innocence in my voice is in complete contrast to the sinful way I'm practically dry humping him.

"Yeah." He grins, his eyes dropping to the space between our chests.

The front of my overalls hangs open between us and I know he can see straight down them. Especially when he licks his lips, then slowly lifts his eyes back to my face.

Easing his hands out from behind his head, his warm palms encircle my waist before slowly moving upward until they dip inside my overalls. His fingertips wrap to the back of my ribcage, while his thumb teases inside the front. The anticipation of his thumb grazing the underside of my breast is torture. And when he does, it's a whisper of touch, nothing like the firm stroke I'm desperate for.

But then his hand is gone and I almost whimper at the loss.

"I like that you have no bra on. Does the material rub your nipples?"

I nod. "And if you could see the wet spot between my legs, you'd know I have no panties on, either."

"Fuck, Summer." He grips my hips, halting my movement before he lets out a pained groan. "I'm a minute away from coming in my shorts."

"Please don't. I want to make you come with my mouth."

"Not helping." He lets out a strained chuckle, but then he glances around and his lips curl up in a wicked grin.

"Do you have a new brush? One that hasn't been used before?"

"Are you going to paint me?" I ask. I'm hoping now isn't the time that he decides to explore his artistic side.

"No, I'm not an artist. I'm going to play with you, then make you come." He grins wickedly. "Now hand me that paintbrush."

thirty-nine

. . .

RORY

Summer grabs a new paintbrush from its package, then climbs back on my lap and hands it to me. I set it beside my hip on the futon so I can focus on the task at hand—stripping her out of these overalls.

My fingers lift to the metal clasp at the top of her overalls, and slip it free from the button with a soft click, my knuckles grazing against her skin as I lower the strap so it can fall behind her. With my fingertips slowly dancing across her collarbone, I move to the other side and repeat the process. But this time, I hold the bib up while I release the second strap. Finally, my hand releases the bib and it flops forward with a soft rustle, baring Summer completely.

I stare up at her. She's a fucking vision, overalls pooled around her waist. Hair in a messy bun with pieces falling loose and those adorable glasses.

"Distracted, Flipper?" She smirks.

"Distracted, destroyed—take your pick."

After coming in my pants last night, there's no point in playing it cool. Besides, I like telling Summer exactly how much she affects me. I want her to know how badly I want her. How desperate I am for her. She deserves to know.

I watch Summer's smirk fade into pure desire.

Her skin is smooth and golden. My fingers lift to trace the thin line of paler skin left from the ties of her bikini and Summer lets out a relieved sigh.

I'm dying to see her in her bikini, but my chest swells at the thought that seeing her like this is just for me. This version of Summer is all mine.

With paintbrush in hand, I stroke the bristles under her breast, then move to circle around her nipple. She gasps with pleasure, letting me know how good it feels to be teased.

I sit up, moving Summer to her back. The shift of our positions allows me to pull the material of her overalls past her hips, down her thighs and off her legs. Now she's naked and staring up at me.

I pick up the paintbrush again and twirl it between my fingers.

"You told me to behave, Wildflower, but when you're looking at me like that, it's impossible." I drag the wooden handle along the inside of her thigh and she gasps.

My eyes find hers to gauge her reaction. There's surprise there, but also desire. Hunger. Want.

"Do you trust me?" I ask, teasing the paintbrush handle closer to the center of her legs, to where she's wet for me.

"Yes." She nods, and knowing my intention, she parts her legs farther in invitation.

My lips drop to the skin above her knee. I can feel them

shaking from the tension coiled inside her. I kiss along her sensitive skin until I reach the apex of her thighs.

I can't resist a taste first, so I tease her open with the end of the paintbrush, then lick through her center.

"Fuck, you're so wet for me." I groan, knowing I'm already addicted to her taste.

Summer's hands push through my hair like she's looking for something to anchor her while her hips grind upwards, searching for more.

So, I give her more.

Slowly, I ease the paintbrush handle inside her, watching her face to gauge her reaction.

As the handle slips inside, Summer's head falls back, a low moan spilling from her lips. The sight of her sends a sizzle of heat to the top of my cock.

Keep it together, Rory.

I give her another inch and she exhales roughly. Hips shifting as she chases every press and drag of the smooth handle now deep inside her.

The sight of her has me spellbound.

"You should see yourself, Wildflower," my voice is thick with heat. "Spread out like this, flushed and shaking, dripping all over my brush like you were made for this."

"It's *my* brush." She sighs.

"Not anymore." Her breath hitches as I sink the handle back inside her. "This one's mine now."

Through her haze of lust, Summer arches a brow in challenge. She's panting as I fuck her with a paintbrush, yet still ready to argue with me. I love it.

I chuckle against her inner thigh before lowering my mouth to flick her clit with my tongue.

I love—

I don't finish that thought because if I do, I'll be in trouble.

From where her pussy is filled with the paintbrush, my gaze moves up Summer's body to where her breasts are bouncing softly with every thrust. Her chest is flush, making her skin glow, her nipples tight and aching. Instinctively, I cup her in my hand and brush my thumb over the sensitive peak.

I can't take my eyes off her. Her full, parted lips, her ravenous eyes and gorgeously messy hair.

Yeah, she looks perfect, but the fact that she's letting me have her like this?

You're already in so much fucking trouble.

"Look at you," I murmur, stroking her nipple with the same rhythm I'm using between her legs. "Falling apart in my hands."

She arches into my touch. I know she's close, so I drop my mouth to her clit and give her the pressure there that she needs.

I watch her brows furrow in concentration, before relaxing as the pleasure flows through her body.

"Ahh," she cries out. "*Rory. Yesss.*"

Hearing my name on her lips when she's coming has my chest swelling with pride.

She lies there, a satisfied grin on her face.

"I can't believe you just got me off with a paintbrush handle."

I ease the paintbrush out of her, letting it graze against her inner thigh, which has her squirming.

Staring at the paintbrush handle now covered in Summer's orgasm, I give it a lick.

"Oh my god. What are you doing?"

"What?" I chuckle. "It's the same as licking you."

"Yeah, but now I have the visual of you sucking on a paintbrush handle burned into my brain."

I like that she's just as affected as I am.

"I'll clean it...eventually. Or maybe I'll leave it just like this so you remember exactly what it did to you.

"Every time you pick it up," I whisper against her jaw, voice low, "you'll think about how good it felt when I fucked you with it."

Her arms wrap around my neck while her legs wrap around my waist. I press her into the futon, loving the feel of our bodies connected.

She sighs dramatically. "I'll never paint again. I'll be too distracted."

"Well at least the brushes won't go to waste."

My mouth drops to hers for a sweet kiss. Our kiss goes from slow and languid to burning hot in a matter of seconds.

Finally, I feel the push of her hands on my chest and I lean back, giving her some space. But she doesn't want space, she wants me on my back.

"My turn." Summer reaches between us to hook her fingers inside the waistband of my joggers, but then she looks up to find me watching her.

I see the moment her hands fumble with hesitation, like she wants to take control, but she's not sure she's allowed to.

Reaching up, I tuck a strand of loose hair behind her ear. "Hey. You don't have to be careful with me."

Her eyes search mine before they drop to my lips. I lean forward to cup her face in my hands, then kiss her.

"I want you." I lift her hand to press a kiss to her palm before placing it against my hammering heart. "So bad, Wildflower. I can't think straight when you look at me like that."

Something shifts in her. Like my words soothe away the uncertainty. Her shoulders visibly relax, while her fingers trail down my torso to find themselves at my waistband again.

Keeping my shit together while watching Summer come undone around a paintbrush handle was no small feat. But now, the look she's giving me as she crawls over me with renewed confidence, tells me I'm fucking done for.

She slides her hand inside my joggers and beneath my boxer briefs. Her hand, soft, yet firm, wraps around my cock.

"I want to make you feel as good as you make me feel."

My hips lift, chasing her hand, but she pulls back just enough to leave me wanting more.

"I need these off." She releases me to start pulling at the waistband of my joggers.

I need her hand back on my cock, so I lift my ass and help her tug my joggers and boxer briefs off in one quick motion.

From above me, Summer's lips curve into a smile, a smug little smile as her nails drag down my thighs.

She shifts, moving to slide between my legs, her mouth following the trail her fingertips have carved out.

The second her mouth is on me, I'm a goner.

I've thought about this moment countless times since I met Summer. Since I put a ring on her finger. None of my fantasies have done this moment justice.

She's so beautiful. All rosy cheeks and wild hair, with the look of fierce devotion in her eyes as her perfect, wet lips surround me so stunningly.

A needy sound, soft and strangled, tears out of me, and my cheeks flush. But I can't even care. I'm too far gone. Too wound tight from the way she's touching me, like I'm hers to enjoy. To study. To *keep*.

"Summer," I rasp, voice raw and barely tethered. "I—fuck—I'm close already."

She slows her strokes, but the way her thumb drags across the head of my cock makes my stomach clench. My breathing turns to shallow pants.

I'm hers.

There's no need to pretend otherwise.

"I thought Olympic swimmers would have more stamina."

Her hands wrap around my base, pumping me slow and steady.

"Relax," she coos, and I realize now I've married a fucking siren.

I blow out a breath to do what she says.

"Good boy," she whispers against my skin, her lips parting to suck me back into her mouth.

Those two words do something to me. They unlock a part of me I never knew existed—a part that craves something deeper than just praise for achievements. It's the desire to be recognized, not for what I've accomplished, but for who I am when I'm with her. The man I am when I'm with Summer isn't the swimmer, the competitor, or the guy everyone expects me to be. With her, I'm just me—vulnerable, exposed, and completely hers. It's a feeling that digs deeper into my chest, unraveling the walls I've built up. I didn't realize how much I needed this until she gave it to me.

I rock my hips faster, and Summer takes more of me down her throat.

I reach down, fingers threading through her hair, tugging her gently. She looks up at me, eyes heavy with a mix of mischief and something deeper, something tender.

That look alone sends me spiraling toward my orgasm.

"I going to come." It's a warning, but Summer doesn't

release me. She sucks me deeper until I explode against her tongue, my cock pulsing deep in her throat.

"Summer..." I murmur, my voice a rasp that barely forms the word. I want more than this, more than just the heat between us, more than what we've shared tonight. But I don't know how to say it. Not yet.

forty

. . .

Sucking Rory's cock, seeing how I affect him, and watching him come will forever be burned into my brain. That, as well as how devilishly handsome he looked peering up from between my legs while he fucked me with a paintbrush handle. That moment, and how turned on it made me, will never be forgotten.

But being intimate with Rory had brought up feelings from the past. When I'd reached to touch him, I'd had a moment of hesitation, old insecurities creeping in, but with his reassuring words and sweet kisses, Rory helped me push them aside.

With his arms wrapped around my midsection, he pulls me closer against him. That feels impossible since we're already sandwiched together on the futon. He's shirtless, having only pulled his joggers back on while I stole his hoodie.

"New marriage rule." He presses a kiss to my jaw, his

hands exploring beneath the hoodie I'm wearing. "Orgasms, every day."

"You really think you're going to find time for that with your schedule?" I tease, nuzzling against his bare shoulder.

But seriously, his schedule is insane.

"I always find time for the things that matter the most to me."

"Like orgasms?" My lips twitch with amusement.

"Sure, but really anything that has to do with you." His voice is low and tender. When I glance up to see his face, he's smiling softly at me. "*My wife.*"

My throat tightens, which instinctively makes me want to laugh it off. Say something snarky, but the look in his eyes makes it impossible.

Why does he do this to me?

Why is he making me start to feel things I promised myself I wouldn't?

I swallow, forcing a grin. "You're annoyingly good at this fake marriage thing."

Even as I try to remind us what this is, my heart pounds too fast against my ribs. It's beating to its own rhythm, completely ignoring my brain's warnings. To not let Rory's sweet words blur the lines.

"It's easy to pretend with you." He slides a finger along my jaw. "So easy, I don't have to fake it."

My fingers, still exploring his chest, unwilling to let go.

"What about you? I think you like being held more than you let on."

I bite my lip, remembering the night he proposed this marriage of convenience. How I'd shoved him away when he tried to sit beside me in the booth. A reflex I'd honed in my last relationship.

You're too needy, Summer. I can't give you attention all the time.

Holding hands? What are we, in middle school?

Maybe I'd want you to touch me more if you weren't so clingy.

"Remember when you asked what my love language is?"

"Yeah, and you told me it was personal space."

He slips a warm hand underneath my—his—sweatshirt.

"It's not personal space," I admit.

"Oh, really?" His brows, teasing, but knowing.

I trace his collarbone, his shoulder, the curve of his arm.

"It's physical touch." My throat bobs as I swallow.

He's quiet for a moment.

"I know, Wildflower."

He threads his fingers through mine, holding our hands against his chest where the mermaid and dolphin are painted.

"You do?" I ask, surprised. But I shouldn't be. Rory sees me.

"You lean into me, even when you act like I'm annoying you. You linger when we hug. And every night, you sleep with your foot touching mine."

"But I put up the pillow wall."

"Your foot found a workaround." He grins. "I'm not mad about it. I like you touching me."

His words almost undo me. All the moments that used to make me feel like too much—too clingy, too desperate—feel tender now. Safe. The shame I carried from my ex's words fades under Rory's hands. The way he draws lazy circles on my skin like it's the most natural thing in the world.

"I'm still trying to believe someone could want all of me," I whisper.

His hand stills. Then he pulls me in, kissing me softly. "I do."

It would be so easy to lose myself in him again, but I remember I have something to show him.

Reluctant to leave the safety of his arms, I sit up and tug on his hand. "Come with me. I want to show you something."

A lazy grin appears on his face. "I'll follow you anywhere."

"Stop being such a cheese ball."

We walk into the bedroom, and I motion toward the newly framed painting now hanging on the wall.

"I figured it deserved a proper frame. And a better resting place than the dresser."

"It's perfect." He smiles, wrapping his warms around me from behind and pressing a kiss to my cheek. "You know your stuff. Thank you for framing it."

"It was nothing. I saw the frame while I was walking the dogs." But I can't help the flutter of pride in my chest when I turn to see his expression. How he looks at the art like it matters. Then, when our eyes connect, like *I* matter.

"Did they have a second frame?" he asks.

"I don't think so. Why?"

"Just a sec."

He releases me and disappears, only to return a moment later with a package wrapped in brown paper. When he unwraps it, my breath catches.

It's the Covey that was auctioned off at The Golden Lane Project gala.

"How did you get that?" I ask, stepping closer. I know every brushstroke, but seeing it in Rory's hands, it feels different.

"I asked Vivi to call in an anonymous bid."

"Why?" I whisper.

"I wanted it." He gestures toward both paintings. "I'm starting a collection."

A collection?

I'm about to hyperventilate.

"I can't explain it, but at the gala, when I saw it, it stirred something inside me. The lone swimmer at golden hour. The colors. The way the paint dried in this 3D effect." His laugh comes out awestruck. "I guess I fell in love with it. I figured, being an artist, you'd understand it more than anyone."

Rory wanted the paintings without knowing their connection to me. It makes the flutter of pride surging behind my ribs mean even more. Because it was one thing to find the Covey painting of his beach house and keep it, but to spend twenty-two thousand dollars on the painting at the gala? That was insane.

The pride I'd felt a moment ago has given way to panic.

Rory loves my art, but what if he loves it less if he finds out I painted it? I don't want to disappoint him.

It may not be logical, but it's those kinds of thoughts that have kept me painting in the shadows. It's the remnants of hiding myself to please others. Doubting myself because all the outside voices were louder and quieted my confidence.

My chest tightens and I realize I'm not breathing.

When I finally attempt to suck in a breath, it's shallow and I end up coughing.

"Summer, what—" Rory starts.

As the wheezing starts, I rush into the bathroom and pull open the drawer to grab my inhaler. Rory's right behind me. A soothing presence as I take a deep inhale of my medication. With the inhaler piece between my lips, I glance up at him to find his eyes full of concern.

Once I've taken my medication, Rory lifts me up onto the counter. With his hands on either side of my thighs, he gives me enough space to breathe, but stays close enough to keep a watchful eye.

"That's it," he coaxes, his eyes scanning over my face and chest. "Deep breaths."

I focus on his chest, how calmly it rises and falls.

We stay in this position for a while, until my breathing has evened out.

His hands lift to cup my face, then he lowers his head down until our foreheads press together.

"Talk to me, Summer. Please."

"I forgot to take my medication earlier. I was busy and I guess I got too worked up. I'm sorry."

He pulls back to study me.

"You don't have to be sorry, but I do need you to be honest with me."

I nod my head.

"Did me buying the Covey painting upset you? I think your art is brilliant. The swimmer painting you're working on is priceless to me. Me liking the Covey paintings doesn't mean I'm not obsessed with your art as well."

But am I ready to reveal myself to Rory?

Haven't I already?

One more deep breath and I shift Rory backwards so I can get off the counter. Taking his hand in mine, I lead him back into my art studio.

He doesn't say anything as I move toward the closet.

Then, I open the door and pull him inside.

And for the first time in a long time, I don't hold my breath.

Behind me Rory is silent, taking it all in. Maybe he

doesn't know what I'm showing him. Or maybe he does and is too shocked for words.

"These are all mine." I swallow thickly. "I painted them."

I meet his eyes and see the surprise there. But there's tenderness and adoration, too.

"Summer," Rory's voice is soft. "You're Covey."

It's not a question but more him saying it out loud to process.

He moves closer to the paintings lining the floor of the closet and brushes his fingers along the edges.

"Of course you are."

My heart hammers in my chest. "What does that mean?"

A self-effacing laugh escapes from his lips. "I've been quietly obsessed with Covey ever since I found the painting of my house. Not because it was my house, but because of the way it made me feel. Raw and grounded. Like I could breathe a little deeper even when everything else was chaos." He turns to meet my gaze. "It's the way I feel when I'm with you.

"It's obvious now why I had such a strong connection with the painting at the gala. With the Covey artist's work." His lips curve into a wide smile. "It's you."

I'd thought revealing my secret identity to Rory would be the hardest part, but talking about my art feels even more challenging.

"Your house—this house—was the first one I connected with when I arrived in Coral Cove. I loved how it was charming but not perfect. Right on the beach but not ostentatious. It made me feel welcome."

Rory sees everything. The vulnerability in my eyes. The way I hold my breath waiting for judgment. And he's looking at me like my brushstrokes rearranged something in him he didn't even know was out of place.

"I hope you know this doesn't change how I see you. It just makes everything make sense.

"Your art is more than a souvenir from a coastal beach town. People love it because it's real. It's you in every brush-stroke," he says, his voice low, yet filled with so much sincerity that I feel my chest tighten.

He leans in, brushing his lips against my knuckles, before bringing our hands to his chest, right above his heart. "It's you. All of you. And I see that now."

For the first time, it feels good to be known. Not exposed or cornered. Just...seen.

I swallow, my throat tight with emotion. I've spent so long hiding parts of myself, letting the world think I was just the carefree girl who lived in a van and painted the world. But Rory doesn't just see the image I project. He sees the depth behind it. The fears, the longings, the hidden parts I've kept locked away. And he doesn't shy away from any of it.

"I never thought anyone would understand," I whisper, my voice barely a breath, as if speaking it out loud will make the weight of it all too real.

Rory's gaze softens, his thumb still gently caressing the tattoo on my wrist. "You don't have to hide from me, Summer. I've always seen more than what's on the surface." His smile is soft, almost vulnerable. "You've got layers, and I want to know every one of them."

I feel my breath catch, the weight of his words settling deep inside of me. I know I should say something, but for once, the words feel tangled in my throat. I'm not ready to let him in completely, not yet. But a part of me wants to. Wants him to see it all.

I pull him closer, the fingers of my free hand reaching to tangle in the short hair at the nape of his neck. My lips find his, slow and tentative at first, as though I'm testing the waters of this new, uncharted territory between us.

But he deepens the kiss, his hands tracing up my arms, grounding me, pulling me back into him. And in that moment, I'm not just the girl with the secret. I'm not just the artist or the traveler. I'm the woman who feels seen by the man who's always been right there, waiting for me to let him in.

When we pull apart, his forehead rests against mine, our breaths mingling. I can't help but smile, though there's a faint flutter of uncertainty in my chest. It feels so good to be known, but it also feels a little too big. A little too much.

His voice is soft, almost a whisper. "You're not just the artist of those paintings, Summer. You're the masterpiece."

I laugh quietly, a breathless sound. "You're laying it on pretty thick, Flipper."

His lips curl up in a teasing grin, but there's something deeper there. Something raw. "I mean it. You've always been more than just your art, Summer."

I bite my lip, the words threatening to spill, but I hold them back. I'm not ready to say it yet, not ready to name what's shifting inside me.

forty-one

. . .

The pool echoes with the slap of water as Coach Owens calls out the start of the next set.

Diving in, I pull hard through the first hundred meters, before my thoughts drift again to the look on Summer's face when she showed me the closet of Coveys.

Her paintings.

Her heart on canvas, layered in brushstrokes she'd hidden from the world.

From me.

It had hit me like a wave. Not just the fact that Summer was the Covey artist, but that she'd trusted me enough to reveal herself.

I surface at the end of the lane and pull my goggles up, blinking water away.

"Shields! You're missing the interval," Coach Owens barks.

Fuck.

There's no time to rest, so I adjust my goggles, then push hard off the wall to start the next interval, determined to catch up.

My head is all over the place. Summer's reveal isn't the only thing messing with my emotions.

With each stroke, images from last night flash through my head.

The way Summer had trusted me to play with her. How pretty she looked when she came around that paintbrush deep inside her.

The sight of her lips wrapped around my cock. And the way she'd called me a "good boy." My chest squeezes at the recollection.

Then, after she'd revealed her art to me, we talked over a late dinner before I carried her into the shower and washed her body. Scrubbing away flecks of paint on her arms and neck before I buried my face between her thighs again.

Waking up this morning with Summer's sleep warm body wrapped around mine made it nearly impossible to get out of bed. Beneath the covers in the early morning light, we'd teased and explored each other again. I'll never get enough of her.

With my fingers buried between Summer's legs and my mouth around her nipple, my eyes happened to catch the time on the alarm clock.

At that moment I had to choose. Either leave my wife unsatisfied or be late to practice.

So, I was late to practice.

And I'm never late.

It was only ten minutes, but it was noticeable. The rest of the team had already started their dry-land exercises when I made my appearance on the pool deck, and I've been struggling to catch up ever since.

The more concerning issue was the moment I woke up with Summer curled into my chest and I'd wondered what it would be like to skip my alarm. I'd let my mind explore a life that didn't involve early morning wakeups, three practices a day, and a schedule jam packed full of meetings, appointments, and appearances.

There were a few times during my injury rehab that I wondered if I'd get the privilege of keeping my rigorous schedule. The idea that I might not be able to have it is what kept me going. I'd fought my way back to it, determined to not let anyone tell me when I was done with my swimming career. Maybe that's the difference. Now, having Summer in my life, knowing she supports me, is making the idea of life after swimming not as terrifying.

It's with the thought of what Summer and I could be that surges me into the home stretch of the final set.

I glide into the wall and look up to find Logan and Eli hanging on the ropes on either side of my lane.

Logan's there grinning as he shakes water from his hair. "Whoa. Did Captain Consistency miss his send-off?"

"Or maybe he's just distracted." Eli smirks. "You okay, man? Blink twice if you're thinking about your fake wife again."

I'm busted, and I can't even be mad about it.

I wipe water from my face and try not to smile. "I'm fine."

"Yeah, you're fine. That was the slowest set of hundreds I've seen you do since...ever."

"Judging from that smile on your face, you're not taking it to heart."

"I'll get in some extra laps."

Coach Owens approaches and it's clear he wants to talk to me.

"We'll catch you later," Logan says, pushing off the rope to swim for the ladder. After a nod, Eli follows behind him.

I climb out of the pool, immediately noticing the difference in my body. Today wasn't about my body not being able to keep up, it was the fact that my head wasn't in it.

"You're off today. You good?" Owens asks, arms crossed while his firm gaze studies me.

"Yeah. Just thinking."

"You missed your interval. Twice. That's not like you."

"I know. I've got a lot on my mind."

Coach had instructed me to stay focused. To not let what happens outside of the pool affect me here, and I never thought it would. Nothing has before. But this thing developing between me and Summer is different. It feels bigger than swimming.

I let my fingers thread through the water. I never imagined anything could be more important than this.

"She get in your head?" His voice is quieter now.

I crack a small grin. "She's under my skin, Coach."

He nods. "Either jump in with both feet or shake it off before Nationals, because if you're trying to do both, you're gonna drown."

I consider what he's saying. It's not an ultimatum, but a reality check.

If I can't figure out my feelings for Summer and have that part of my life settled, then I'm going to keep struggling. And I don't have time to struggle. This is my last shot at gold and securing my legacy.

I want to finish on my own terms, but more than that, I want Summer beside me for all of it.

"Got it."

"Good. Now go ice that knee." Coach Owens walks off to leave me with my thoughts.

Normally after a disappointing practice, I'd force myself to swim extra laps or watch race footage, but even though I was off-pace today, I can't bring myself to enforce my old rules. Slogging through more laps isn't going to get my head straight. I need something else.

In the locker room, the air is warm and humid. Most of the guys have already showered and are walking around with towels slung low on their waists. A few feet away, a locker door bangs while loud voices echo off the cement walls.

When I enter my locker section, Logan is pulling a Pooh Bear with his t-shirt on and no pants, so I avert my eyes and grab my phone from my locker.

> How are the pups this morning?

SUMMER

Full of energy. And Cal caught a fish!

She sends me an image of Cal holding up a tiny fish and I like the photo.

> I want to take you somewhere later. Secret spot. Perfect view. Thought you might want to bring your paints.

SUMMER

Are you trying to seduce me with scenic views?

> Is it working?

SUMMER

Maybe. What's the catch?

> No catch. Just a pretty overlook, some snacks, and a guy who likes spending time with you.

SUMMER

I thought you said you wanted to take me.
Who's this guy you speak of?

I walked right into that one, didn't I?

SUMMER

It was the perfect set up.

To clear things up, your devoted husband
will be in attendance. Lots of snacks and a
cozy blanket…the necessities.

SUMMER

Okay. I'm in. See you soon!

I'm about to respond to Summer when Logan's voice cuts through my thoughts.

"No fucking way!" Logan shouts.

I look up to find Logan wearing shorts now while he glances at the phone Charlie's holding out to him.

"Cap, have you seen this?" Charlie asks, handing me his phone.

With my head focused on Summer, it takes me a moment to process what I'm looking at.

It's a candid photo of Whitney and Connor. He's got his arm wrapped around her shoulders, smiling down at her, while Whitney is looking up at him laughing. They're in their swimsuits, so there's a lot of skin touching. I remind myself that's not because they want it to be but because it's the nature of their wardrobe. There's another one where Connor has his arm wrapped around her waist while they pose at what appears to be a dinner with program directors and foundation chairs.

It's a business dinner. There's no reason for him to be touching her like that.

"These were posted to the Rising Tide Swim Foundation's social media," Charlie comments.

Beside me, Xio leans in. "Damn. They look cozy."

"Is something going on between Whitney and Connor?" Eli asks.

I open my mouth to deny it, but then I realize I don't know if it would be accurate. I haven't spoken to Whitney since she left for the tour. It had been a surprise to learn Connor was going with her, but I'd seen it as a break from Connor, and when Summer brought up the idea of Connor and Whitney spending a lot of time together, I'd brushed it off.

Whitney knows my history with Connor. She's also a smart woman who I don't believe would be charmed by Connor's flashy, smooth-talking persona. Outside of his swimming talent, he's a walking red flag.

My gaze drops to the photo of his arm around her waist again.

If Connor's trying to pull some bullshit by messing with my sister, I'll do more than dominate him in the pool.

"They look good together." Finn smirks, but then catches my hard gaze and grins sheepishly. "Sorry."

"They're working together, that's all." I push the words out, then make a mental note to call Whitney later.

I think about Summer's advice to fix things with Connor. To let the tension go but part of me is still struggling to put effort towards the guy when he's shown no sign of changing his ways.

There's nothing I can do about Whitney and Connor right now, so I grab my towel and head for the showers.

Under the spray, I roll my shoulders back and let the warm water slide over my tired muscles. It's this time that my mind usually fixates on the future. But the interesting thing is I'm not spiraling about the Olympics. Or obsessing over times or splits or whether Coach Owens thinks I'm slacking.

No, my thoughts are drawn to the woman who paints in overalls and bare feet. The one who kisses like she doesn't trust it but needs it anyway. The woman who framed her own damn work and was finally brave enough to show it to me. And one day, I hope she shows the world.

My wife.

Swimming has always come first. That was the entire reason for marrying Summer.

Maybe this is what it feels like when the grip on your old dreams loosens, not because you don't care anymore, but because something new is taking root.

Owens was right. I need to get my head on straight. To focus.

But that doesn't mean it's the end of everything.

It's only the beginning.

forty-two

. . .

SUMMER

Rory wasn't kidding. The overlook is high above Coral Cove, hidden off a narrow trail only known to locals. It's quiet except for the rustling of leaves and the distant crash of the waves against the shore. The view is stunning; rolling dunes, the endless stretch of ocean, with the sky open and wild above.

"Will this do?" he asks, a curious smile on his face as he takes in the awe on mine.

He pulls out the blanket he promised to bring, then sets my portable easel on one corner of it.

I smooth out my features, deciding to play it cool.

"It's okay." I shrug casually, before motioning to the picture-perfect scene.

"Just okay?" He presses his lips together and takes a step closer to me.

His proximity makes me crack. A huge smile pulls at my

lips. "I mean, if you're into breathtaking views and insane scenery." I turn to motion to our surroundings.

When I glance back, he's right there. His hands move to cup my face while his eyes study me intently.

"I didn't have to come all the way out here for that."

He kisses me and it's playful and teasing, with a ripple of that electric chemistry that has always been pulsing between us.

My belly does that swoopy thing again. It's become a familiar sensation. One that I associate with Rory. And happiness.

Rory makes me happy.

The thought has me dizzy.

So, I do what I do best, and focus on setting up my art supplies to paint.

I rummage through my paints to select a palette of colors that fit the scene. Soft blues and briny greens, streaks of golden tan for the dry grasses down below, and a deep rust for the pop of color a far-off umbrella provides.

As my brush strokes over the canvas, it occurs to me that for the first time in a while, I'm not painting something to leave behind for strangers.

I'm painting something for me.

I glance to where Rory has settled onto the blanket beside me with a book in his hand.

Because of *him*.

We're quiet for a while. Me painting while Rory reads. It's that contented silence I appreciate about us.

Us.

I'm starting to like the sound of it.

"Summer?" Rory whispers.

"Yeah?" I say distractedly while I work to blend where the ocean meets the sky.

"Don't move."

My brush freezes. "Why?"

"There's a squirrel. And it's looking at me."

"And?"

Rory, as stealthily as he can, crawls his way over to hide behind me.

"It has murder in its eyes."

I turn around to find a chunky gray squirrel standing a few feet away from the blanket eyeing the snack bag with predatory intensity.

I press my lips together, barely stifling a laugh. "He wants your nuts."

Beside me, Rory pales. "*What?*"

"Your trail mix, Rory." I bite back a laugh. "He's coming for your snacks."

"Oh, right."

"So, you weren't lying with that whole terrified of squirrels thing? I thought that was all a bit to sleep in my van."

"Maybe it was and now I have to keep up the ruse. I guess you'll never know."

"Oh, I *know*. This six-foot-four Olympic swimmer fears woodland critters."

Rory tilts his head back and empties the rest of the trail mix bag into this mouth. When he's done chewing, he crumples up the bag and puts it into his backpack. "There. No more snacks, so leave."

"Hey," I pout. "I didn't get any snacks."

"Oops. Sorry. Want me to run back to the car and get you something?"

"And leave me here alone with the killer squirrel?" I lift a brow in jest.

"You're hilarious."

"I've got great material to work with."

"Yeah, you do."

The squirrel loses interest, and Rory relaxes again. But instead of picking up his book, he moves to sit next to me, draping his arms over his bent knees.

"What are you doing?" I ask.

"I'm watching you paint. And it's fascinating."

I blow out a breath, trying to ignore the tingle of nerves his presence brings me. After a few minutes, my strokes smooth out again, and I'm able to refocus on my painting.

"What is your goal with your art? Is it for fun, just for you? Or do you want to share it with the world?"

I shrug. It's easy to act like I don't have a plan. That it's just for fun, but the reality is I do want more.

"Hey." He slides a fingertip along the top of my thigh to get my attention. "It can be anything. Dream big."

The way he's looking at me with soft interest makes it easy to tell him everything.

"Okay. I want a gallery show. To be able to display my art with confidence." I smile, Rory's questions opening ideas in my mind that hadn't been there before. "It would be impossible to track them down, but it would be cool to see all the Coveys together. To see them as a collection."

I turn back to the canvas to add a few more brushstrokes to the horizon where the water meets the sky. That's when I notice the clouds are darker than before.

Then, a fat drop of rain hits my canvas and slides down the length of it.

"Oh shit." I pop up in a panic.

"Let's pack up." Rory rushes to get the rest of the picnic back into the backpack while I hurry to get my paints into their case.

One raindrop soon becomes ten, then a hundred.

"My painting!" It's still wet but I'm hugging it as close to my chest as I can without causing further damage.

Rory tosses the blanket over me for protection. "Can you run? You've got your inhaler?" he asks with concern in his voice.

"Yeah." I nod.

With my hand in his, he guides me toward the narrow trail.

Even as we move through the dense trees, the rain pelts us hard.

By the time we reach his Jeep, we're soaked through, clothes clinging to our bodies. The blanket is drenched, but by some miracle, my painting is only moderately damp.

Rory opens the back of the vehicle, giving us a reprieve.

"Get in, get in," he instructs, so I rush over to the passenger side while he loads our stuff. Inside the car, my skin slides against the leather seat, but it feels good to be out of the chaos of the storm. A moment later, the trunk slams shut and Rory rushes to the driver's side.

Outside, the rain is coming down in sheets now. We can't even see out the windshield.

"That came on fast." I pant, my breath coming in puffs from running and the excitement of it all.

"You good?" he asks.

"Yeah, I just need a minute." I inhale deeply to slow my breathing.

"From the looks of it, we're going to be here for a while."

When our eyes lock across the console, we both start laughing at our appearance.

Rory runs a hand through his hair, the wet, tousled strands making him look sexy as ever.

"How do you look so good right now?" I attempt to push

away the wet hair that's plastered to my forehead. "I'm a mess."

Rory's hand slides along my jaw, pushing the rest of the unruly hair out of my face. "You're perfect."

I shiver. "I'm freezing."

"Come here." He gives my wet shirt a tug, indicating I should join him in the driver's seat.

"You're just as wet as I am."

He reaches for the hem of his soaked t-shirt and pulls it off, tossing it to the floor. "Problem solved."

"I swear, any excuse for you to take off your shirt," I tease, but seeing him there in nothing but his wet shorts is already elevating my temperature.

"Thank you for bringing me here."

"You're welcome." His eyes drop to my lips.

That adrenaline rush is back. So is the swoop of my belly and tell-tale ache between my thighs. I want him. No, I *need* him.

And now we're stuck at the base of the trail waiting out the storm with no one else in sight.

Slowly, I climb over the console to the driver's seat and with one knee on each side of his hips, I settle onto his lap.

His hands move to grip my hips, and I shiver again in my wet clothes.

Rory peels my wet tank top up and off, exposing my bra. I wish it was something sexier than beige but when I put it on this morning, I hadn't planned for it to be on display.

"Better?" he asks.

"A little." I smile, but a shudder gives me away.

Rory's large hands move up my arms, spreading warmth followed by gooseflesh as he makes his way to my shoulders.

"What about this?" he whispers before his mouth drops

to my collarbone, trailing featherlight kisses across my chest.

"I'm getting warmer." I sigh, letting my fingers dive into his wet strands to hold his head where I want it.

His fingers nimbly unhook my bra and peel the wet material away. With better access now, his mouth descends on my nipple. The contrast of his warm mouth and my cold, pebbled nipple has me arching into him.

With his mouth sucking and teasing, while his fingertips explore under the hem of my shorts, it doesn't take him long to have me wound tight with every nerve sparking at a fever pitch.

"Rory. Please. I need more."

He pulls back, then with a hand across my sternum, Rory angles me back against the steering wheel, big hands cupping and massaging my breasts before he makes his way to my waistband. A quick flick of a button and drop of a zipper, and his hand dips inside my underwear.

Our eyes lock as he slips a finger inside me.

"I love how slick and needy you get for me, Wildflower."

In the past, words like that might have made me feel vulnerable and self-conscious, but from Rory's mouth, they embolden me. I rock against his finger, showing him just how much I like his touch. That I want more.

"You do that to me. No one else ever has."

It's honest. Maybe too honest, but I want him to know how good he makes me feel. That it's not just this heated moment. It's *him*.

I'm rewarded with a second finger before his mouth captures mine in a blistering kiss.

Every kiss, every touch, every sensation builds until I shatter around his fingers. As my world tilts on its axis, my arms wrap around his shoulders to ground me.

He lines my center up with his erection and presses me against it. "This is what you do to me."

We're a mess. With the cool rain outside and the heat of our bodies inside, the windows are fogged up.

I rock against him, loving the feel of his hard cock pressed against my clit.

He grips my hips to slow me.

The rain outside is deafening. It drowns out logic and common sense. It continues to hammer against the roof of the car, matching the rhythm of my heartbeat.

"Keep doing that, Wildflower, and I'm going to end up fucking you right here."

Rory's been so patient with me, but I'm done waiting.

"Good." I grind down harder. "That's what I want."

He pushes my hair back, tucking the wet strands behind my ears.

"You don't have to prove anything to me. I want you, Summer. Not just this—*you*."

I lean forward to kiss him. It's soft but insistent.

"So have me," I whisper against his lips.

He groans his agreement into my mouth.

Rory's large frame isn't meant for car sex, but I can tell by the look of determination in his eyes, he's not going to let awkward angles and low ceilings stop him from being inside me. Thank god.

We could climb to the back seat, but the way his cock is rubbing against my clit at the perfect angle tells me this reclined seat is going to be the best option.

With the steering wheel against my ass, I manage to free one leg from my shorts, and then the other. For Rory, it's an easy lift of his hips, then yank on his shorts and boxer briefs to free his cock.

After my gymnastic routine, I settle back onto his lap,

and realize I didn't even think to remove my thong. But for Rory, it's no challenge. With a firm finger, he hooks the crotch and tugs it aside.

The tip of his cock nudges against my entrance, and my breathing ceases.

In all the excitement, I've forgotten how long it's been since I had sex. And how big Rory is.

"I want you inside me, but it's been a while. And you're not the size of a paintbrush handle."

"Thanks for noticing." He wiggles his brows playfully, then his teasing smile softens into a thoughtful grin. "Don't worry. We'll take it easy. One inch at a time. Stretching you slowly until you can take me all like the good little wife you are."

I suck in a breath, his words lighting me up from the inside. "That's a really good plan."

"I'm a good husband."

"Fake husband," I tease, but Rory shakes his head, his expression turning thoughtful.

"You're mine, Summer. Right here. Like this. No more pretending."

I study his face and finally acknowledge what I see there.

Safe. Electric. *Real.*

He presses inside me. Just like he said. An inch at a time until I relax around him.

"That's it, Summer," he coaxes. "Let me have you."

At the same moment he lifts his hips again, I sink down onto him.

Oh, god.

The feeling of him inside me, filling me up in more ways than I could have ever imagined leaves me breathless. And the intensity of the moment has my eyes falling closed.

I exhale on a sigh and try to relax around him.

Rory's hand cups my jaw, his thumb tracing along my bottom lip.

"Look at me, Summer. I want to see you."

My eyes open to find him staring at me.

He rocks his hips and his cock presses deeper inside me.

"Do you feel that?"

All I can do is nod.

Our bodies melt into each other, and it's a moment of breath-stealing relief.

Relief that the intimacy I thought might hurt or expose too much is suddenly safe and so much better than I let myself imagine.

Even though I'm on top, Rory's unobstructed positioning gives him more control. He picks up the pace and all I can do is hold on for the ride. My knee is banging against the door but it's worth the bruise that might appear later. My breasts bounce with every thrust. Rory cups one tenderly while his other hand dips between my legs to rub my clit.

The second I let go, it's like the universe rewires itself. Everything is louder and brighter, and Rory's name is stitched into every one of my nerve endings.

He follows quickly after, pumping into me again before pulsing deep inside me.

"Rory...that was..."

"I know." He pulls me close, then smiles against my cheek before pressing a kiss to my jaw. "Just imagine what it could be like when we have space to move."

A laugh bubbles out of me. It's relaxed and easygoing.

Just imagine what it could be like if I let myself fall for you.

I collapse onto his chest and let him hold me there until the rain dissipates and we're forced to pull on our wet clothes and leave.

forty-three

. . .

RORY

I can still feel her in my hands. The way she clung to me in the Jeep like I was something solid in a world she wasn't quite sure of. The way her voice cracked open for me, soft and sweet and a little bit brave. It wasn't just sex. It never is with her.

It's been a week, but I keep catching myself staring at the empty passenger seat like she might suddenly materialize, paint-stained hoodie and all, eating those spicy pickles she can't get enough of.

We've spent every moment we can together since then. Afternoons sprawled in the sand, evenings side by side on the bench near the boardwalk, and mornings tangled up in my sheets.

And it still doesn't feel like enough.

I stretch out on the couch with my phone, scrolling back through our messages—not because I'm checking for a reply, just because I like seeing her words. She always sounds like herself. Straightforward. Funny. A little stubborn.

It's such a contrast from the rest of my life lately, all business and strategy and pressure. I've got a campaign shoot in a week and a meet right after. I should be dialed in, laser focused. But every time I close my eyes; it's her I see.

Her smile. Her laugh. That soft, surprised little moan she made when I kissed her in the rain.

I'm in trouble.

And not the "missed your interval, hit the pool deck" kind of trouble. The real kind. The kind where you start thinking about things like home, and not just where you sleep, but who you want to come home to.

I'm not saying it out loud. Not yet.

But I think she knows.

forty-four

. . .

Watching Rory and Edgar play together on the beach is like seeing pure joy in action. The way Edgar chases him across the sand, tongue hanging from his mouth with the effort, is the cutest thing I've ever seen. Edgar's not a human child but it's easy to see how good Rory would be with one. His playfulness and patience. The way he picks Edgar up when a large wave threatens to knock the small dog down.

It's been a week since I revealed to Rory that I'm Covey.

A week of spending our free time together. Walking down to Main Street to grab ice cream. Rory picking me up after my late shifts at the café. Visits to the boardwalk so Rory can practice skateboarding on a board that's his size. Nights on the couch relaxing with Edgar snoozing at our feet before we tease each other into a frenzy.

"I wore him out." Rory places Edgar on a beach towel we've laid out under the umbrella.

Edgar immediately drops his head onto his paws and closes his eyes.

Rory makes his way over to where I'm packing up my paints. With a finger hooking into one of the belt loops on my denim cutoffs, he tugs me toward him. "Your turn."

"Sorry, Flipper. I don't play fetch."

He pulls me close enough that the momentum has my hands lifting to press against his bare chest.

"Come in the water with me."

I eye the waves. They're steady but not too powerful. Nothing like the afternoon I played mermaid at the Lancaster party.

"Fine."

Wrapping my legs around his waist, Rory lifts me into his arms and walks us out into the water.

"How'd you know you'd be a good swimmer?" I ask, clinging to his broad chest. "Did you come out of the womb swimming?"

His hands grip my ass, holding me to him as the water flows around us.

"I wasn't good. I was terrible. Afraid of the water, especially putting my face in."

"No way." I can't imagine Rory ever not moving through water like he was born to do it.

"True story. You can ask my parents."

"Speaking of, your mom texted me earlier. She asked if I had any insight into finding a Covey, you know, with my regular person job at the café and all the people I see there. Sounds like she's desperate."

"She asked me for your number. I hope you don't mind."

"The fact that she's acknowledging my existence is entertainment enough."

"Don't worry, she'll grow to love you just like I do." He presses a kiss to my mouth and I can't help but gasp.

Did he just say what I think he said?

He said it so casually. Maybe I heard him wrong. The waves are noisy.

By the time we reach our towels where Edgar is still snoozing loudly, I've convinced myself that Rory didn't say 'I love you' because technically he didn't. He didn't stare deep into my eyes and whisper those three words. He said his mom would grow to love me like he does. That's totally different. Maybe he's referring to the love between friends or fake spouses.

Besides, that would be a breach of our contract. Even though we didn't sign anything, it was a verbal agreement. No falling in love. He promised. And I promised him back.

Hmm. I wonder if we'll both turn out to be liars.

Rory pulls out the snack cake he's worked so hard for all week. One from the new box I bought when I was at the store last night. I'd stood there for longer than I want to admit, staring at the shelves filled with bright yellow boxes with the sunshine logo stamped across the front.

My childhood in plastic wrappers.

I haven't had a Little Sunshine Cake in years. Not since I walked away from everything; my parents, their perfect corporate life, the legacy they planned to pass down to me and Tripp. The cakes are more than just sugar and nostalgia, like Rory said. They're a reminder of who they wanted me to be.

But Rory loves them. And weirdly, that makes it easier. It softens the hard edges.

"So good." Rory moans around his choco swirl roll like it came from a Michelin-star restaurant.

"Lucky you."

I sit beside him and watch him chew, my chest tightening in a way I don't entirely understand. It's not about the snack cake. It's about what it represents—everything I left behind. Everything I haven't told him.

But he doesn't know that. To him, it's just something small and sweet. A comfort. And somehow that makes it easier. Or at least...bearable.

"You okay?" he asks, licking a crumb from his thumb.

"Yeah," I lie softly. "I'm good."

He leans in to nudge his shoulder against mine. "You sure? You've got that look. It's like you're painting something in your head."

I smile at that. "Maybe I am."

He's quiet for a beat. Then, casually, "I hope you know you can tell me anything."

I nod, but my throat's too tight to answer. I'm not ready. Not yet. But I will be.

Just not today.

Instead, I watch as he polishes off the cake, grinning like he's just won a prize, and I wonder how he'd look at me if he knew the truth. If he knew I grew up surrounded by those snack cakes. If he knew how many of them I threw away in silent protest.

But he doesn't ask again. He just leans back on the towel, sunglasses tipped down his nose, sun glowing across his bare chest. He looks like home. And for now, I'll let myself be happy here.

forty-five

. . .

RORY

I miss your face

SUMMER

I miss your cock

Fuck, Wildflower. I'm going to have a boner
for the press conference

SUMMER

Oops

Are you painting?

SUMMER

Yes! I'm working on my swimmer today. I
might be able to finish it.

I snap a selfie and send it to her.

In case you need it for inspiration.

SUMMER

Gee, thanks

I've got to get in there.

SUMMER

Good luck, Flipper!

It's four days.

It's temporary, I remind myself.

Not being with Summer, but leaving her to travel. The swim pro series national meet in Fort Lauderdale.

It's been a week since we ended up soaked and freezing in my Jeep. Since she climbed into my lap and completely ruined me.

The way she looked with rain dripping down her hair, shirt clinging to her like a second skin, and her cheeks flushed from the cold rain. It was nothing compared to the way she looked when she took me inside her.

We didn't talk about what it meant. But the way she looked at me afterward told me what I needed to know. Summer was trying not to fall, but the fact she was trying so hard meant she already was.

The urge to ask her to change shifts at the café and cancel her dog walking clients was strong. But then it occurred to me, she doesn't need to rearrange her life just because I want her with me.

"Retirement. It's inevitable and with the toll training takes on an athlete's body, it's unlikely we'll see you back in another four years. Are you thinking coaching? Broadcasting? More commercial work? What's the dream?"

The press room is too cold, too bright, and too far from the girl I can't stop thinking about.

I adjust the mic in front of me and force a smile. "Right now, the dream is a good night's sleep and a solid meet."

A few chuckles ripple through the room. I glance at the reporters, all waiting for the polished soundbite, the headline-worthy quote.

"But seriously..." I run a hand through my hair. "I've spent most of my life chasing hundredths of a second. I'm still proud to be here. Still love competing. But for the first time, I'm starting to wonder what life looks like beyond the pool."

The words are out before I can second guess them. I haven't said them aloud before. Not to my coach. Not to my teammates. Not even to Summer.

Another reporter chimes in. "Does that mean this could be your last meet?"

"I've got more in the tank. I'm not done." My thoughts drift to Summer. To the version of myself I see in her eyes. "But, if I stay in the sport, I want it to be on my terms."

They write that down, of course.

But the real story isn't something I'm ready to share in a press room.

The real story is a girl with paint under her fingernails and a dog that snores louder than a human. It's late-night grocery runs and beach days and the jars of pickles she keeps stocked in our fridge.

The real story is that, for the first time in my life, I'm not just swimming toward the wall.

I'm swimming toward someone.

I'm adjusting my goggles when the sharp whistle cuts through the chatter of the warm-up pool.

"Shields!" Coach Owens's voice carries across the deck. "Get over here."

I jog over to where Coach is standing and my eyes go wide when I find Charlie on the bench, grimacing and clutching his shoulder while Winnie kneels beside him.

"What happened?" I ask.

"I felt a snap on the catch," Charlie says, his face contorting in pain.

"Rotator cuff, maybe," Coach says. "He's out."

Fuck.

His words hit like a punch. Not because our medley relay final is in thirty minutes but because I'm devastated for Charlie.

I hate seeing my friend in pain and more than the physical discomfort, I know first-hand that an injury brings mental and emotional stress. While the extent of his injury is unknown, not having a healthy body is demoralizing for any athlete. It fucking sucks and I wish I could tell him it's going to be okay, but I can't promise that.

"Hey, Charlie."

He turns around; expression somber.

"We got you," I tell him firmly. "No matter what."

He nods, then I watch as Winnie leads him to the medical facility to get him checked out.

As a team, all we can do right now is finish the meet while Charlie gets evaluated.

After we fill them in, Eli and Logan emerge from the warmup pool and the three of us huddle around Coach Owens to see how he wants to handle Charlie's withdrawal. Who he wants to put on the freestyle leg of our world record medley relay team.

"Who are you thinking? Xio?" I ask, taking in Coach's cross-armed thinking stance.

"His split is fast, but he's recovering from his fifty-meter win a few hours ago."

Movement over Logan's shoulder catches my eye.

It's Connor.

"I can do it." He nods at Coach.

Logan chuckles. "Yeah, right. I'm not swimming my ass off just to get a DQ because you can't handle the exchange."

Connor doesn't even flinch at Logan's insult. "I've been practicing takeovers."

Realizing Connor is being serious, Logan shakes his head. "Not with any of us."

Coach shakes his head. "You've got the individual medley prelims in an hour. It's not enough time to recover."

"I'll be fine. It's important. Please."

Coach looks at me.

My instinct is to say no. To put Xio on the leg even if he fades out on the final stretch. At least I can trust the kid.

But then I remember what Summer said about giving Connor another chance. Letting his current actions speak louder than his words from the past. And, if I don't give him a chance to prove he's changed, then I'm not the captain I want to be.

Slowly, I nod my head. "Yeah. Let's do it."

Coach nods in approval before walking off to make the change with the meet organizers.

"You're kidding, right?" Logan scoffs, ignoring the fact that Connor is still standing there.

Eli claps Logan on the shoulder. "Come on, we've got to finish our warm up."

Maybe I think Connor can't do it or maybe I want him to prove me wrong. Either way, this meet, this relay, feels like a hinge. A chance to shift things back into place and start fresh.

Connor joins us in the warmup pool, but we've already used up most of the time we had when Charlie hurt his shoulder, so we get a few laps in, then throw on our parka jackets and move to the ready room to await our announcement.

Connor sitting next to me feels off, but I know I can't let it affect me so I pull on my headphones, start my pre-race playlist, then close my eyes to visualize every stroke of my race.

Ten minutes later, the meet official signals for our event to line up, and one by one, the teams are announced to be escorted out to the pool deck.

In the lane next to ours the team from the Savannah Sharks stops to gawk. "Connor Fisk is on a relay team. Damn, did we just enter an alternate timeline?"

"Hey, Connor," Dorian Wells from the Milwaukee Marlins calls. "Didn't think you played well with others."

"Forget about them," I say. "They're just trying to get to you."

His jaw clenches. "Yeah, I know."

"Hey, Dorian, you worried about our lineup, or just pissed that we're still going to beat you?" I flash him a cocky grin.

Dorian lifts his brows. "Didn't think he was relay material."

I shrug. "Maybe you should spend more time training and less time running your mouth."

I feel Connor's eyes on me but I don't look at him. I focus on unsnapping my parka and dropping my slides in the bin behind our lane.

Eli drops into the water and grabs the backstroke ledge to start us off.

Logan, Connor, and I watch from the block as Eli struggles to hold off the Savannah Sharks swimmer.

This isn't the World Championship or Olympic team trials, but it's still an important meet that will start to shape the national team roster.

We should be winning this race but there's no ignoring that Charlie's injury and the aftermath of changing up our roster has shaken up our team, myself included.

I feel it the moment I hit the water. Something's off but it has nothing to do with my knee. It's mental.

Pulling through the water, with each stroke, I lean into my physical training and let my body do the work. It's enough to keep pace with our lane neighbors, but barely. Both the Savannah Sharks and the Milwaukee Marlins teams are giving us a challenge.

As I make contact with the wall, I hear the splash of Logan diving in behind me to begin his leg. With shaky limbs, I climb out of the water, and brace my hands on my knees. Eli and I share a look. There's no point in saying anything out loud. We don't want to add more pressure onto Connor when the pressure is already palpable.

By the time Logan finishes, it's still a tight race between us, Savannah, and Milwaukee.

I hold my breath as Connor hits the water, then slowly exhale when I see that he's made a clean exchange. When he resurfaces, he's nearly a foot in front of the other teams. His expertly executed take-off has given us a slight advantage over the other swimmers.

Eli and I give Logan a hand to help him out of the water, before our eyes return to our lane to trail Connor.

At the far end of the pool, Connor's strokes are crisp and

efficient as he flips underwater to touch the wall just over a second ahead of the rest of the field.

My heart pounds in my chest, not just from the adrenaline of the race, but from watching Connor slice through that first fifty meters like a man possessed. No panic. No wasted motion. Just power and precision.

Something tugs in my chest, an ache I can't name at first.

But then, I realize while my relationship with Summer has me looking to the future, it has me recognizing there are things from the past I don't want to hold onto anymore, especially my feud with Connor.

I still remember how it felt when Connor took the deal behind my back. The sting of it. The disbelief. I'd trusted him, mentored him, and then was blindsided.

But watching him give everything to this relay when I know he's got individual events to make the finals for is softening my frustration with him. It's helping me see that the version of Connor that took that deal isn't the guy in front of me anymore. And while the betrayal still hurt, it doesn't have to define us.

Now, I look on as Connor approaches the finish line with the poise of a veteran swimmer. Sometimes I forget that's what he is now. He's no longer the lanky kid that I mentored. The quiet teenager with something to prove and nowhere to belong.

He's not reckless and desperate. He's confident and ready. And while I didn't see it in the beginning, Connor showing up to train with the Current was his first step in wanting to make things right.

The crowd is deafening as our team cheers Connor on to the finish.

He glides into the wall and the results board lights up with our time.

Not only did we win, but we managed to pull a team best for time.

Logan and Eli drag Connor out of the pool then wrap their arms around his shoulders to celebrate the win. Connor's out of breath but smiling while Logan grabs his face and kisses him on the cheek.

"Not going to happen." Eli laughs. "Sorry, Fisk, I draw the line at kissing."

Finally, Logan moves to grab his warmups out of the bin, giving Connor space to breathe. With his hands on his knees, he looks up to meet my eyes.

I clap a hand to his wet shoulder. "You did good, kid."

"Thanks, old man." He grins through a pant.

I smirk, but let it slide. There's more to say between us, but that will come later.

For now, we head over to the mix zone where the media is waiting to interview us, and celebrate our victory.

forty-six

. . .

SUMMER

Edgar sighs dramatically from his spot on the couch like he, too, is personally offended that Rory isn't here. He's been doing that every few hours. Staring at the door. Hopping up at any sound like maybe Rory's back to sneak him extra peanut butter. Honestly, I'm not far behind him.

I miss him.

The house feels different without him. Not quieter exactly—between Edgar's huffs and the constant clatter of paintbrushes I keep knocking off the table, there's still plenty of chaos. But there's an absence. Like something solid is missing. Like the eye of the storm packed a bag and flew to Fort Lauderdale for a swim meet.

Rory's duffel bag isn't blocking the hallway. His sneakers aren't tripping me outside the bathroom. And no one's around to lecture me about the scientific benefits of putting the lid back on the peanut butter.

I wander into the kitchen and spot the empty container

that used to hold my favorite granola clusters—the ones he pretends he doesn't like but somehow keeps "accidentally" inhaling when I'm not looking. The container has a passive-aggressive sticky note on it now.

My handwriting: Not a snack cake. Buy your own.

His handwriting underneath: Couldn't help it. So crunchy. So sweet. Like you.

My chest squeezes.

He's ridiculous. He's charming. And his absence is making me admit things I've been avoiding.

Like the fact that I'm completely, stupidly in love with him.

And that maybe it's time to tell him the rest. The part about my parents. About the snack cake empire and why I can't look at a shelf of them without wanting to scream into a pillow. I keep thinking he'll look at me differently once he knows. That he'll stop seeing me and only see them.

But maybe that's just fear talking. Rory never asked me to be perfect. He just asked me to be real.

So I will be.

As soon as he gets back.

Maybe after I replace the granola.

forty-seven

. . .

RORY

SUMMER

You were amazing today. That finish? I'm so
proud of you.

Thanks. It felt good. I wish you were here.

SUMMER

Me too. We need to talk though. When you
get home?

I stare at her last message. My fingers hover over the screen
to respond, but then drop.

We need to talk.

My stomach summersaults and I realize I've never hated
four words more. There's no accompanying smiley face
emoji or red heart to ease the panic. But Summer isn't really
a smiley face emoji kind of girl, so maybe it's not so
ominous.

So, I pocket my phone and glance around the team

lounge until I spot Connor sitting alone on a chair in the corner looking at his phone.

We'd finished up the meet three hours ago, and after a team dinner, and a visit to Charlie, I'd decided to skip a round of *American Gridiron* in Logan's hotel room to catch up with Whitney. After her week on the road and a stellar performance today, hitting a personal record and meet record for the women's four-hundred-meter individual medley, I'd been excited to talk with her.

But even with all the excitement today, I couldn't shake the image of Charlie's face in my mind.

The doctor had just given him the news—his shoulder wasn't going to recover. At first, I thought he was going to fight it. Charlie's always been the kind of guy who pushed through any obstacle, but today, there was no defiance in his eyes. Only resignation. He'd looked at me and with quiet acceptance, said, "It's over."

I didn't know what to say, so I sat with him until he said he was tired and wanted to rest. It was hard to leave him like that, but I knew he needed his space.

When I got back to the hotel, though, I wasn't prepared for what I saw outside Whitney's room.

There they were—Whitney and Connor—locked in an embrace.

It wasn't just the fact that they'd spent a week together with The Rising Tides Foundation, but it was the look in Connor's eyes that made something uneasy twist in my stomach. The tension between them was undeniable, and for a split second, I wondered if it was more than just a friendship developing.

I asked Whitney about it, but she brushed it off, so I backed off.

Even after everything today, there's still one thing hanging over me.

Upon my approach, Connor straightens up and drops his phone to the low table in front of him.

"We need to talk."

Internally, I laugh at the irony of my words. Maybe that's why Summer's text is scaring the hell out of me. There's weight to it that I'm terrified won't be in my favor.

Connor nods. "Yeah, we do."

"Let's not waste time pretending this is something it's not. You know you screwed up. Taking that deal behind my back didn't just mess with a contract, it blew up everything we had. Trust. Respect. All of it."

My gaze stays locked on Connor, steady and unflinching.

"And what came after? You didn't even try to make it right. No apology. Just years of silence...and then contempt, like I was the one who betrayed you."

Connor's jaw tightens. "I know I messed up. But I never meant to betray your trust. I was desperate. I needed the money for my mom's treatment."

My chest tightens. "Shit. I didn't know." I drop my gaze, anger cooling into something heavier. "You should've told me."

"I wanted to. But my agent said if I did, the deal would be dead. I was naïve and didn't see that the whole thing was a set up to start a narrative of a rivalry I didn't want. I didn't see it for what it was until it was too late."

That guts me. That this whole thing started with him scared for his mom, and he was taken advantage of by someone who only saw dollar signs instead of people.

"When I finally got out of the contract, I cleaned house. New agent. New coach. And after years of training alone, I knew I needed a team again."

That's why he came to the Current.

I study him, seeing him a little clearer now.

"I thought if I showed up, apologized, and worked my ass off, we could move on. But you looked at me like I'd broken something that couldn't be fixed."

"I did feel that way. It felt like another ambush. Like you were trying to stir shit up again."

"That wasn't my intention." His voice dips. "But I was hurt too, man. I know I was the one who broke it, but when you cut me off like that...it felt like I didn't matter. Like all those years meant nothing."

I swallow hard. He's right. I didn't ask questions. I just shut the door and walked away.

"I'm sorry for not being there when you needed me most."

"Thanks." He leans back, his shoulders relaxing a little. "I'm sorry too. And I want to fix this. If we can."

"Yeah, me, too."

Connor smiles. "So...we're good?"

"We're on our way." I pause. "But trust isn't something I just hand out. You've got to earn it back."

"That's fair. I will."

I stand, ready to head back and pack, the weight between us finally easing. But then I remember the way Connor and Whitney were together in the hallway earlier, and I turn back.

"One thing, though."

Connor looks up from his phone.

I cross my arms. "Whitney. She's off-limits."

Connor blinks. "Rory, it's not—"

"You don't have to explain," I cut in, my voice calm but firm. "I saw the hug. And maybe it was just that. But if it's more, or you're thinking it might be...don't go there."

Connor's jaw tightens. He doesn't argue, but I can see the flicker of hesitation. The conflict in his eyes.

"I believe you want to be better." I say quietly. "But if you're really serious, then make sure the next thing you go after isn't something that could burn everything down again."

Connor nods. Slowly. But he nods.

"Got it."

I nod back. "You did good today. The anchor leg—smooth as hell."

A faint smile tugs at his mouth. "Thanks."

With things settled between me and Connor, I just want to get home to Coral Cove, and to Summer.

forty-eight

. . .

I'm just putting the finishing touches on the table setting when I hear the door to the garage click shut. I turn to find Rory standing in the doorway, dressed in a Carolina Current t-shirt and gray joggers, the ends of his golden wavy hair peeking out from underneath his backwards hat.

He might as well be in a tuxedo for how devastatingly good he looks.

He's only been gone four days; I need to chill. But chill is the last thing I'm capable of.

We've been texting all weekend, but it hasn't eased the ache of missing him. Even knowing the Current won the meet and Rory medaled doesn't compare to having him here.

I hadn't wanted to bother him while he was focused on swimming, so I'd texted him after his events, hoping to plant a seed for the necessary but uncomfortable conversation we need to have.

Now that he's here, I'm struggling to remember everything I need to say.

With a weighted gaze that never leaves mine, he gently sets his duffel bag on the floor, then slowly moves toward me.

His familiar scent hits me first. Driftwood and eucalyptus with a tinge of chlorine. It clings to him no matter how hard he scrubs, and I secretly hope it never fades.

He stares down at me with an expression I can't read. His typically easygoing grin is replaced by a tense line.

"I missed you so much it hurts."

"Me, too. Every second you were gone it felt like something was missing."

The corner of his mouth lifts, and he closes the miniscule gap between us, his body brushing against mine.

"I heard about your PR. Congratulations." I throw my arms around his neck and pull him in tight.

"Thank you." He squeezes me back. "There was this woman I was hoping to impress."

His hand drops low to the curve of my ass, those long fingers teasing the skin below the hem of my skirt.

"Well, mission accomplished," I say, breathless in his ear as our bodies cling to one another. His warm lips skim along the shell of my ear, causing me to forget everything else. "I'm always in awe of you."

"It feels so good to hold you. And you smell fucking fantastic."

When his mouth finds mine, I lose myself in him. Rory's kiss is both comforting and achingly exhilarating. It takes my breath away while at the same time grounding me. It's the thrill of being swept away, wild and free, while also tethered so you know you're safe.

When I pull back, the look in Rory's eyes is pure heat.

My stomach flips deliciously at the sight of his intense gaze, and I press my fingers to my swollen lips.

"I made dinner." I nod toward the table set for two.

"Yeah, you did." Rory's eyes snag on the table behind me, but quickly return to me. His gaze is hungry. Ready to devour.

My tongue darts out to lick my bottom lip and his eyes trace every movement. "I figured you would be hungry." I can't help but smirk. "You always are."

"You're right." His thumb trails along the column of my neck, his other fingers closing in at the base to add the slightest pressure. "I'm fucking starving."

In the blink of an eye, his left arm clears the table. Plates, silverware, glasses. It all goes clattering to the floor. In the next instant, he lifts me onto the table.

"Those were our new dishes," I gasp, half-shocked, half-turned on. "Your parents sent them as a wedding gift."

"I'll replace them tomorrow," he says, voice low and unwavering, already tugging me toward the edge of the table like a man possessed.

The wicked gleam in his eyes makes it impossible to argue.

"I'd like my dinner now, sweet wife."

My breath catches. I guess the dishes aren't the only thing getting ruined tonight.

Reaching under my skirt, he hooks his fingers into my underwear, quickly yanking them down my legs. Then, he presses my knees apart and steps between them. My skirt has ridden up my hips, exposing me to him.

He swipes a finger down my center where I'm wet and needy for him, then brings it to his mouth for a taste.

"Mmm." He groans, licking his fingers clean. "My favorite."

He does it again, this time swiping his slick finger coated in my arousal against my mouth.

"You're my favorite meal, Summer," he murmurs against my lips. "I could eat you every day."

Then, Rory sinks to his knees, his breath warm against my skin. One slow stroke of his tongue and I'm undone. His mouth is reverent, his rhythm deliberate. Like he's memorizing every inch of me.

My hands find his hair, the wavy strands the perfect length to tug as he works me toward orgasm.

With the same determination he trains with he brings me to the brink.

"I want you messy, Summer. I want your pussy dripping all over this table so I can lick up every drop."

When he dips two fingers inside me, it's gentle, yet commanding, and exactly what I need to let go.

"Rory!" I cry out, my body arching as a wave of pleasure crashes over me. It rolls through me, sharp and shattering, leaving me trembling and breathless, clinging to him like he's the only solid thing left in the world.

I lie there, my skin slick with sweat and the shockwaves of my orgasm slowly dissipating.

Rory's tongue swirls against my inner thigh, one side then the other, cleaning me up like he said he would. His fingers still working inside me as I come down from the high.

His mouth and fingers are phenomenal, but I want more.

I want his cock.

Tugging gently on his hair, I pull him up to me. His lips immediately descend on mine, letting me taste myself and sending another rush of arousal between my legs. His fingers tease under my shirt, his mouth retreating for a moment to lift it up and over my head.

"I'm nowhere near done with you," he growls, voice thick with heat as he hovers above me. He nips at my lower lip, his fingers sliding inside the cup of my bra to tease an achy nipple.

"Good," I whisper, tugging his shirt upward. "I'm not done with you, either."

He lifts his arms so I can pull his shirt all the way off, then reaches around to unclasp my bra.

But just as heat begins to flood through me, he pauses. Pulling back instead of pressing in. His eyes lock on mine, steady and unreadable, and for a breathless second, I wonder if I've said too much. If my words revealed more than I'd intended to.

I sit there, bare from the waist up, legs dangling off the edge of the table, heart pounding.

"Good," he says at last, his voice low but firmer now. "It's settled. No one's done here. Not by a long shot."

He lifts me off the table, wrapping my legs around his waist and carries me toward our bedroom.

"You didn't want me on the table?" I ask, wrapping my arms around his neck.

"Another time. Right now, I'm going to enjoy you in our bed."

He crosses the threshold, then gently lays me on the bed, taking my skirt with him as he steps back.

I let my knees fall open, exposing myself to him. Rory's gaze drops between my legs. One hand dips inside his boxer briefs to stroke his erection while his other hand's palm skates up and down his jaw in an intense, contemplative motion.

I smile at how adorable he is when he's distracted, but

then his eyes lift to mine and all that intensity is focused on my face.

I watch him drop his boxer briefs, exposing his thick cock. Dying to taste him, I push myself forward and lick up the front of his shaft, my tongue tracing over the throbbing vein, then swirling around his head, tasting the saltiness of his precum.

I only get a few licks in before he's urging me backwards and against the bed.

He crawls over me, his erection pressing against my inner thigh.

"I haven't had you in four days, Wildflower. I'm fucking desperate for you."

Then, he kisses me, sweet and gentle, like he's my best friend.

It's his super power. Turning me on so explicitly, while also making me feel safe and taken care of.

A moment later, he presses inside me.

And just like that, it's not pretend anymore—not for me.

forty-nine

. . .

RORY

When I press inside Summer, I'm home.

Maybe that sounds cheesy, but it's exactly how I feel. Like no matter how long it took me to get here, it's where I've always belonged.

Seeing her again after these days apart, it's like every nerve in my body wakes up the second I touch her. The way she feels in my arms—soft, warm, perfect—isn't something I've ever let myself crave this badly before. But right now, it's undeniable.

While my pulse races, my hands are desperate to hold her tighter, to pull her closer.

I drown in the heat of her mouth, the fire that's been burning inside me since the first time she looked at me like I was the only thing she wanted. I can't hold back. I don't want to.

Everything I've tried to push down, everything I've been afraid to want, it's all crashing through me now.

The truth is, this is it.

She's it for me.

And for once, I'm not afraid to want more.

"You have no idea how much I've missed this. Missed you."

Her legs wrap around my waist, holding me to her as I fuck her with firm strokes. She meets my thrusts, just as ravenous as I am.

"God, you feel so fucking good."

Her breath hitches, and her hands fly to my shoulders, nails digging in as she arches beneath me.

"Rory," she whispers, like she's stunned I'm real, like I've been gone for longer than four days. Her eyes lock on mine, wide and glassy, and in them I see everything I've been too much of a coward to ask for.

"I missed you," she says, her voice catching. "More than I should've."

That's it. That's the moment I fall completely, irreversibly, fuck-it-all-in love with her.

I kiss her like I'm sealing something sacred between us. Our bodies move in sync, every thrust deep and deliberate, a promise I can't say out loud yet.

Her legs tighten around me. Her breaths come in short, sharp bursts.

"I'm close," she gasps, her back bowing off the bed. "Rory—don't stop—"

"I've got you, Wildflower," I grit, holding her tighter. "Come for me."

She shatters around me, her cry like a spark setting me off. I follow seconds later, spilling inside her with a groan against her neck. My body shakes with the force of it, with how fucking right this feels.

We stay like that for a long moment.

Tangled. Breathless. Completely undone.

My forehead rests against hers. Our chests rising and falling in sync while her fingers trace lazy circles on my back.

I don't want to move, but finally, I press a kiss to her cheek and pull back. "Don't move."

She blinks up at me, a little hazy. "Bossy."

"Just taking care of you."

I grab a clean towel from the bathroom and return, kneeling beside her. She's watching me with a soft, open look that makes my chest ache. I clean her up slowly. Trying not to make it weird, but also not pretending like this moment isn't something. Like she isn't everything.

"You good?" I ask, brushing my knuckles over her thigh.

"Yeah," she breathes. "I'm really good."

I toss the towel aside and pull her into my arms again.

For a while, we just breathe together.

The silence between us isn't awkward, it's full. Heavy with everything we're still not saying.

Then, in the middle of that charged quiet, my stomach releases a monstrous growl.

Summer dissolves into a fit of laughter, her body shaking against mine.

I pull back just enough to see her, breathless and flushed. Her smile hits me right in the chest.

"Really?" she says, eyebrows raised. "That's your afterglow?"

I give her a sheepish grin. "I wanted to get home, so I skipped eating with the guys."

"That's why I made dinner." She sits up slightly, her bra dangling off one arm. "And this is why you didn't get to eat it."

"Worth it."

"Orgasms are always fun," she says dryly, glancing around, "but now we have to clean up the mess."

I kiss her, slow and lingering. "Sorry I knocked everything on the floor."

Her eyes soften, a smile tugging at her lips. "I'm not. But you're going to be sad to know it was barbecue chicken. Your favorite."

"Damn it." I groan, tipping my head back dramatically. "Tragic loss."

Still, I can't bring myself to regret anything, especially not the way Summer looked on that table, legs spread and moaning my name like a prayer.

With a soft laugh, Summer climbs out from under me, reaching for a t-shirt and underwear. I grab my boxers and joggers and follow her. Together, we head into the dining room to assess the damage. My damage.

"My parents actually sent these?" I ask, crouching to pick up pieces of ceramic from the floor.

"Yeah, maybe a peace offering?"

I chuckle. "Or a way of inviting themselves over for dinner."

Summer laughs, her cheeks turning pink. "I'll never be able to have anyone over without thinking about what we just did on that table."

She's not wrong. The sight of her laid out for me is a core memory now.

"And just think," I murmur, grinning. "I didn't even bend you over it yet."

I shoot her a wicked smile. A promise.

She smirks. "Dinner first."

"Since you don't know my mom that well," I say, scooping up the rest of the mess, "she's not great at apologies. She sends gifts instead."

"Noted," Summer says, dropping the last shards into the trash can while I mop up the spilled barbecue chicken. The heavenly aroma taunts me with every swipe.

"You want dinner from Lucy's?" I ask. "I'll order."

"Sure." Summer answers before handing me the vacuum.

Once cleanup is finished, I reach for the yellow box of Little Sunshine Cakes and pull out a package of choco swirl rolls.

"Victory snack time."

I'm halfway to my first bite when Summer appears in front of me, face suddenly serious.

"Don't worry, this won't ruin my dinner," I say, motioning to the sugar-laden snack cake. "I'll still eat all of mine and probably half of yours."

"It's not that." She swallows. "We need to talk."

Shit. *The* talk.

For a moment, I'd forgotten about her text from earlier.

I lower the snack cake and set it on the counter.

Her gaze flicks to it before meeting mine.

"My parents own that company."

"What company?"

She nods to the snack cake beside me. "Little Sunshine Cakes."

I blink, trying to make sense of it. My eyes land on the yellow box with the sun logo. I think back to the little girl that used to be on it. Blonde hair. Blue eyes.

It clicks.

That was Summer.

I stare at her, stunned.

Her family owns the company I've been obsessed with since I was a kid. The same family who didn't support her art. Who tried to marry her off to some asshole for business gain. The same people who have money—but left her without health insurance, without the meds she needed—because she wouldn't play by their rules.

And I've been scarfing down their snack cakes this whole time, telling her how much I love them. That must've stung. Or at the very least, made her hesitate to tell me more about them.

Anger surges in my chest.

I walk to the pantry, pull out the rest of the boxes and toss them in the trash.

When I look up, Summer's staring at me, eyes wide. "You don't have to throw them out!"

"I'm not eating another damn thing that came from the people who made you feel like less." My jaw tightens. "You're worth more than that."

I'm not mad at her. I'm furious at them. I've never met her family, but anyone who made my wife question her worth doesn't deserve a place in our life.

She presses her lips together and nods. "Well at least recycle the boxes."

I know she's trying to create some levity, but I'm still too fired up to laugh.

"Why did you keep buying them for me?" I ask.

She shrugs. "Because you love them and they make you happy."

"I love *you*." I reach for her. "You make me happy."

"Rory," she exhales, emotion welling in her eyes.

It's the truth. One that's been sitting on my tongue for weeks. Maybe since the day I met her.

"You make me happier than any snack cake ever could. And that's saying a lot because those little guys are filled with like twelve kinds of chemically engineered joy."

She laughs, and I feel some of the tension dissolve between us.

I slide a hand into her hair, threading my fingers through the soft waves.

"Well, you can't eat me for your cheat day snack."

"That's what you think." I lift a brow, grinning.

She shakes her head at me, tears in her eyes and a small smile on her lips.

"About what you said? That I make you happy and that—"

"I love you." I say it again firmer this time.

"You promised you wouldn't fall in love with me."

"Yeah, well, you promised the same."

She exhales, not in frustration, but in surrender.

"Guess we're both liars then."

"Speak for yourself. I've never been more honest in my life."

I take her left hand, feeling the cool ridges of her diamond wedding band beneath my thumb.

"I didn't think I'd ever want more than swimming, but then you showed up, messy and brilliant and wild, and now I can't imagine my life without you in it."

Something cool and wet nudges my ankle.

I glance down at Edgar. "You too, buddy."

When I look back at Summer, she's giving me a look—part amused, part exasperated.

"Did you say messy?" she asks, narrowing her eyes.

I nod, pressing a kiss to her pout. "But in the best way."

There's so much to tell her but right now I want her to know what matters most. Our life together.

"I don't know what happens next with swimming. I've never been more uncertain about the future. But I do know is that I want you there. Whatever happens—win or lose, gold or nothing—I want you beside me."

She nods, eyes shining.

We stand there, quiet for a beat, just holding each other.

"Rory?" she says softly.

"Hmm?"

"I love you, too."

My chest squeezes at her words.

I pull back to look at her. My beautiful, talented wife.

"I love the way you look at me like I matter. I love that you don't let me hide, but you know when I need a safe place, too." Her fingers tease along my jaw. "I even love how you think squirrels are out to get you."

"They are out to get me," I mutter. "One of them threw an acorn at my head last week with sniper-like precision."

"You're ridiculous," she says softly.

"I'm yours."

"Good," she whispers. "Because I'm yours, too."

epilogue

. . .

SUMMER

"You know I don't like surprises."

Rory squeezes my thigh in a comforting gesture. "You're going to like this one. I promise."

"*Promises, promises,*" I sing from the passenger seat as Rory drives us toward an unknown destination. When I say unknown, I mean it. He not only refused to tell me; he asked me to wear a blindfold. It's technically an eye mask, but still.

We got back from his swim meet in Sacramento last night, and after a breakfast shift at the café this morning, I'm running on fumes.

"If you don't love it, I promise I'll never surprise you again."

My lips twitch. "Your confidence is admirable."

I wish I could see him right now. Watching him from the driver's seat is one of my favorite things. It's his profile, I think. That and the way he sings to himself or chuckles at prank calls on his favorite radio station before catching me staring and throwing me a wink.

My husband.

Still can't believe we got real married for a fake relationship.

Except now, we're in love.

And marriage isn't what it was when we thought we were doing each other a favor.

I told myself I'd never get married. That love was too fragile, too breakable. I'd seen what it did to my parents. How vows turned to silence, then to distance, and eventually to nothing. I didn't want to follow that same crumbling path.

But Rory makes it feel different. Solid. Like love could actually be a safe place, not a ticking clock.

The car slows and stops. I hear Rory climb out, then my door opens.

"Okay, careful." He helps me out and holds both my hands, guiding me forward.

We step inside a building, and he says, "All right. You can take it off."

I lift the eye mask and blink against the light.

After being in the dark, the first thing I notice is the bright white walls. They're blinding at first, but then I notice the paintings.

My paintings.

But not recent ones. They're Coveys.

The anonymous works I left around Coral Cove over the past few months are now hanging in perfect, deliberate arrangement across a warehouse gallery space.

"How?" I ask. My brain stutters, trying to piece it together.

"The social media page was a good start," Rory says, "but then I had some help."

A woman in a black blazer, cropped jeans, and heels walks over.

"Hadley Smith," she says. "I'm the art curator at Shoreline Gallery in Southampton, and I'm a huge fan of yours."

"Southampton?" My brows lift.

"New York," she confirms.

"I know," I smile, then glance sideways at Rory. "Why are you here?"

"She was one of the first people to find a Covey," he says. "When I contacted her about tracking them down so you could see them all together, she wanted to help."

Hadley beams. "I've been following the Covey artist since the beginning. It's an honor to meet you."

I glance around nervously, until I realize we're the only ones here.

"Don't worry," Hadley says. "The show's not open yet."

"The show?" I echo.

"The *Covey Collection*." She gestures to a wall near the entrance where big black lettering reads, *Covey: A Collection by* and a blank space where the artist's name would be.

My name.

"You told me once you'd love to see them all together," Rory says, "I wanted to make that happen."

"Rory..." I'm still absorbing it. The layout, the lighting, the precision. All my little soul-offerings, collected and honored. Rory's pieces are here too. His beach house and the golden hour swimmer in the distance.

I look again at the wall.

"I wanted it to be your choice," he says. "You can stay anonymous, or—" Hadley hands him a paintbrush and canister of black paint "—you can sign your name."

"Either way," she adds, "I have a list of clients who want commissions from you. Whether you're anonymous or not, the world wants your art."

My throat tightens. I glance at Rory, tears in my eyes.

"I'm overwhelmed," I whisper. "And speechless."

He sets down the brush and paint, then wraps me in his arms.

"I know I've said it before, but I'm going to keep saying it. The world needs your art. And if you're not ready to reveal yourself, then you don't have to."

I nod, wiping furiously at a tear.

I've always believed I was an artist. Why else would I have kept going when it was easier not to? But Rory has helped me believe that my art deserves to be seen. To be celebrated.

"I wasn't ready to retire," Rory says, "because I couldn't imagine my life without swimming. I didn't know what I wanted. That's changed."

"Oh, yeah?" I smile. "What do you want, Flipper?"

"You and me. Married. For real."

I swallow hard. "We are married."

"We have a certificate," he says, grinning. "But I want the kind that doesn't come with conditions or convenience. Just love."

I take a breath, and let it fill all the scared, uncertain spaces in me.

"Even if I come with baggage, and battery-powered backup?"

His grin widens. "Big Dill's solid. Reliable. I respect that in a teammate."

He brushes a hand into my hair, his huge grin softening with quiet sincerity.

"Let me keep you, Wildflower." He kisses my cheek, then

my temple. "We could give Edgar some siblings. I'm thinking a sister named Edwina."

I burst out laughing.

"You want to name our dog *Edwina*?"

Rory shrugs, only half serious. "It's dignified. Regal. She'll wear little bowties on her ears and glare at tourists from the porch."

"I don't know if Edgar could share the spotlight."

"He needs a sibling. Someone to keep him humble."

I laugh again, my heart thudding wildly. I glance back at the wall—the blank space below *Covey: A Collection by*—and feel something shift. The part of me that always feared commitment, feared names and labels and permanence... stills.

I turn to Hadley. "Do you have a thinner brush?"

Her eyes brighten like she's been waiting for this.

She pulls one from her tote, and hands it over. Rory passes me the paint.

The brush is light in my hand. Familiar.

Like something I was always meant to hold.

And then I sign it.

Summer Shields.

It's small. But it's mine.

Rory slides an arm around my waist and tugs me close, his lips brushing my temple. "You did it," he murmurs. "You let the world see what I've seen all along."

"I did," I whisper back. Then add, "But I'm still not letting Edgar and Edwina sleep in the bed."

"Fair," he says. "But she gets the fancy food. It's only right."

I stand there in the middle of a gallery filled with art I once gave away in secret, and a love I never thought I'd trust.

And just like that, I know.

We're just getting started.

THE END

thank you

Dear Reader,

Thank you for taking the time to read my book. I hope you enjoyed Summer and Rory! There are so many books to choose from, so thank you for spending your precious time reading mine. If you have a minute, please consider leaving a review for Beyond the Stroke. Reviews help indie authors so much!

XO, Erin

acknowledgments

Thank you to my family—Eric and our three amazing kids—for your unwavering support through this roller coaster of a career. Your love, patience, and encouragement mean everything to me, especially on the wildest of writing days.

To my copy editor, Chelly—thank you for your keen eye, thoughtful edits, and for always making the process such a pleasure. I'm so grateful we get to work together.

To my assistant, Taylor—thank you for being a constant sounding board, for keeping things running smoothly behind the scenes, and for always believing in the work (even when I second-guess everything).

And to Jenny at PenPal PR—thank you for your guidance, your enthusiasm, and for helping get my stories into readers' hands.

I'm lucky to have such an incredible team behind me.

about the author

Erin Hawkins is a spicy romcom author who lives in Colorado with her husband and three young children. She enjoys reading, working out, spending time in the mountains and with her family, watching reality TV, and brunch that lasts all day.

www.ingramcontent.com/pod-product-compliance
Lightning Source LLC
Chambersburg PA
CBHW010603310726
48969CB00010B/2549